FAR WORLD

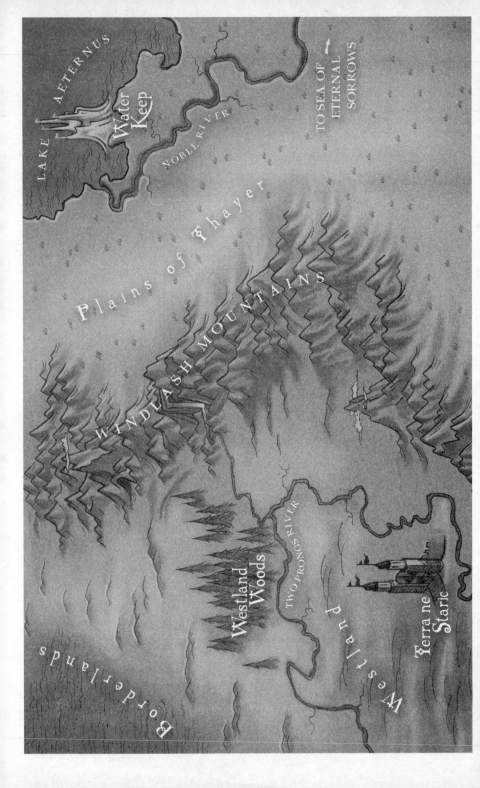

FAR WORLD
WATER KEEP

BOOK ONE

J. SCOTT SAVAGE

SHADOW
MOUNTAIN

Illustrations © 2008 Brandon Dorman

Text © 2008 J. Scott Savage

Visit us at ShadowMountain.com

First printing in hardbound 2008.
First printing in paperbound 2013.

Library of Congress Cataloging-in-Publication Data

Savage, J. Scott.
   Water Keep / J. Scott Savage.
      p. cm. — (Farworld ; bk. 1)
   Summary: Found in the desert as a baby by monks who named him, thirteen-year-old Marcus, who has been confined to a wheelchair ever since he can remember, knows nothing of his background and endures the difficulties of his daily life in various foster homes and schools by dreaming of Farworld, a magical place whose pull seems to be getting increasingly stronger.
    ISBN 978-1-59038-962-1 (hardcover : alk. paper)
    ISBN 978-1-60907-330-5 (paperbound)
    [1. Foundlings—Fiction.   2. People with disabilities—Fiction.   3. Magic—Fiction.
4. Fantasy.]   I. Title.
PZ7.S25897Wa 2008
[Fic]—dc22   2008010392

Printed in the United States of America
R. R. Donnelley, Harrisonburg, VA

10   9   8   7   6

To my kid brother, Mark Savage, who encouraged,
browbeat, and cheered me all the way to the finish of this book.
Thanks for all the years of solving Ultima games and
reading fantasy novels. You're the best.

See the Lords of Water—
Beyond the waves they leap

See the Lords of Land—
Beneath the ground they sleep

See the Lords of Air—
Above the clouds they creep

See the Lords of Fire—
Around the flames they reap

Water. Land. Air. Fire.
Together, the balance of Farworld they keep.

CONTENTS

PART 1: ESCAPE

PART 2: DISCOVERY

PART 3: JOURNEY

PART 4: NEGOTIATION

PART I

Escape

CHAPTER 1

BONESPLINTER

BUNDLED SAFE IN HER underground burrow with eight fuzzy babies snuggled against her warm body, the ishkabiddle woke to a curious rumbling. Her milky-white eyes—interested, but not yet frightened—slid open as she tilted her head, listening. For a moment the rumbling seemed to be fading away. Then, all at once, it grew much louder, and bits of dirt crumbled onto the ishkabiddle's dappled, gray fur. Alarmed, she clawed her way up through the dark, dusty tunnel she had dug out years earlier, and stopped at the edge of the opening.

Perched half-in, half-out of the burrow entrance, she paused. A pair of bald, pink feelers rose quivering from her fur-covered body. Cautiously, she slipped out of her hole and blinked. Somewhere far off a bird screeched, but that wasn't what was making the ground tremble so the tops of the grass shivered to and fro.

From the tips of her feelers, the ishkabiddle sent out a cloud of gray specks—each no bigger than a grain of sand. One by one, the specks floated out into the cold night air, buzzing and spinning as they bounced from one blade of grass to another. Had she found any sign of a predator, the ishkabiddle would have scurried back into her hole quick as two winks. But nothing she discovered was threatening.

For a moment everything was perfectly still, and the insects that had gone silent resumed making their nighttime music. Without any warning, the ground exploded into the air less than ten feet away, and the ishkabiddle found herself staring into a pair of deadly yellow eyes. The glistening diamond-shaped head of a huge black snake narrowed, and its eyes—each bigger than the entire ishkabiddle—fixed on the poor, shivering creature. The snake rose out of the ground, its scaled body—thick as the trunk of a mature tree—gliding skyward.

The ishkabiddle could not move. Her body paralyzed by fear, the poor creature could only watch as death slithered to her very doorstep. The nightmare snake opened its mouth, revealing wickedly shining fangs. Its tongue flicked out and touched the tip of the ishkabiddle's wilting, pink feelers.

"Boo!" the snake said, and the ishkabiddle's muscles turned to water. She dropped into her tunnel and rolled all the way to the bottom of her burrow where she hid, trembling, for the rest of the night.

The iskabiddle didn't see how the snake's armor-like scales began to slide and change. She didn't see how its long body twisted and shortened, or how its head filled out as its mouth and nose shrunk. Above the burrow, the snake disappeared and was replaced by a man in a flowing black cape and hood. The man raised his forked staff and slammed it on the ground with a wicked laugh.

"Lucky for you, I've already had dinner," he whispered with dark mirth. "Perhaps I'll come back for you later."

But the man had no time for such trivial things now. The three moons were almost directly overhead, one a full white face staring watchfully down from the inky black sky, another an orange three-quarter, and the last a tiny reddish sliver. It was nearly midnight.

Glancing about to be sure no one was watching, the figure stole quickly over a brush-covered hill and stopped at a tall outcropping of stone. Placing the tip of his staff into an all but invisible moss-lined crevice in the rock, he bowed his head and uttered a quick series of grunts and hisses. At once the outcropping slid aside, revealing a damp, downward-sloping tunnel.

The man entered the opening, and the rock slammed shut behind him, turning the tunnel pitch-black. He could have lit the way with his staff, but there was no need. He could see perfectly well in the dark. He followed the passage deep into the earth over slick, wet stone. He had only been summoned here once before, and a thrill of excitement ran up his spine as he licked his dry lips, wondering what might be asked of him—and how he might turn it to his advantage.

At last, the floor of the passageway leveled out, and the man's keen eyes spotted a closed door in the distance. He approached the door and rapped his staff, once, three times, and once again—the heavy black metal echoing in the close corridor. The door opened, and the stench of rotted meat drifted out. The man tried not to show his disgust at the foul smell of the figure that stood before him.

"Remove your hood," said the creature that looked as though it had only recently pulled itself out of the grave. Though the creature's head barely came to the man's waist, its twisted arms and legs appeared too long for its body. From the neck down it could have been human, but the feather-covered head had the sharp beak and wide probing eyes of an owl. Body and head were coated in wet, green mold.

The man pulled back the hood of his dark cloak, revealing a narrow face with thin, pale lips and glittering, silver eyes. A twisting scar, nearly as thick as a finger, ran from the base of his jaw to just below the hairline on his right temple.

"You have come alone?" the owl asked.

"Of course," the man hissed, anxious to get away from the stink.

"In a hurry to meet *him,* are you?"

All at once the man remembered who this shriveled little creature worked for, and his calculating eyes flicked from the owl to the dark corridor beyond as he fingered the scar on the side of his face. "I only wish to be . . . *prompt,* so I do not keep the master waiting."

"*Of course,*" the owl said, its dark eyes gleaming. "Keeping him waiting would be unwise."

The creature stepped aside, and the man walked through the doorway. As he began to climb the steep staircase, a pair of eight-legged, skin-and-bone dogs appeared out of the darkness, flanking him at either side. Foam dripped off the twin tongues that dangled from their hungry-looking jaws, and their red eyes studied him voraciously.

At the top of the stairs he paused before a long, damp-smelling hallway. The rough stone walls seemed to radiate a cold that sank deep into his bones. Beside him, the dogs snarled, urging him forward with their glowing eyes.

The sides of the hall were lined with hundreds of strange and obscure objects, many of which even *he* didn't recognize. As he passed a three-pronged spear with something like dried blood crusted on its tips, it swiveled as though waiting for a chance to strike. A few steps later, a pair of spiked balls hanging from a rusty chain rattled at his passing, and a tiny, stone statue with the face of a pig whispered, "Come closer, my pretty."

The robed man ignored them all, just as he ignored the many other doors behind which unknown creatures snarled and moaned. Only when he arrived at an ornate, blood-red door at the end of the hallway did he stop. As he reached for the gleaming brass latch, a pair of sharp talons mounted in the center of the door snapped closed onto his hand, and it was only with the strongest resolve that he managed not to cry out. But when the claws released their grip, the skin of his hand was unmarked.

Silently, the door swung open, and the man stepped through.

Inside, the icy cold of the hallway was replaced by an oppressive heat that brought beads of sweat to his forehead. Sulfur-smelling smoke swirled in the cathedral-like room, glowing orange from the light of the sputtering torches. Dimly-seen arches along the walls rose into the darkness far overhead. The man walked to the center of the room and dropped to one knee, laying his staff crosswise on the floor at his feet.

He bowed his head, and in a voice that trembled only slightly said, "Your obedient follower desires to serve."

"Approach," said a voice that sounded like the sizzle of hot steel plunged into icy water.

The man rose and moved forward. He could see only a short distance in front of him through the swirling smoke. It wasn't until he reached the curved steps where the smoke cleared away that he craned his neck to stare up at the two chained, red beasts watching him hungrily from either side of the stairway.

Summoners. Terrifying creatures of mythic power.

Even with bony wings folded against the sides of their red, serpent-like bodies and thick, magically-enhanced chains locked around their necks, they made the spit in his mouth dry up. From the razor-sharp talons—which were taller than the man—to the mouths filled with two rows of spear-like teeth, they towered almost to the ceiling of the room.

Even more fearsome than their physical weapons was their magic, the man knew. Stories were told of how they could drive a human insane with only a look, call tornadoes out of clear skies, command the ground itself to swallow armies of the living, and summon back the dead under the control of dark magic. No one knew for sure what twisted magic was used to create such terrifying monsters. But those who dared speak of them at all agreed that somewhere deep inside the Summoners remained the warped souls of those who had once been human, twisted and defiled until nothing could stand against their dark rage.

That the master had not one, but *two* Summoners under his control was a clear demonstration of the power he wielded. The thought of commanding such force made the man dizzy. And yet he had to be so very, very careful.

Turning his eyes from the Summoners' hypnotic gaze, he climbed the steps and approached the figure that he knew sat hidden in the shadows. The man gazed intently into the darkness, but not even his keen eyes could penetrate the gloom surrounding the jeweled throne.

"Master, what is it you desire of me?" he asked, dropping to his knees. He tried to hide the eagerness in his voice, but he could do nothing about the way his heart thumped like a trapped animal in his chest.

"Thirteen years I have searched," the voice spoke from the darkness. "Armies of creatures at my disposal scoured the mountains and forests. At times I nearly despaired. It wasn't until I ripped open the doorway that I finally knew the prize was within my grasp. And today . . . I found it."

The man desperately searched his memory. He knew he should understand what the Master was talking about. But he couldn't quite . . . Then it came to him, and his throat constricted.

"The child?" he blurted out, unable to hide his surprise. "But I thought . . ." Unconsciously, the fingers of his right hand reached toward the scar on his face, but he managed to pull them back.

"You thought the child was dead?" the voice questioned dryly. "Everyone assumed the child's wounds were mortal. But not I. I vowed to search until I touched the remains with my own hands. Now I discover the child lives and . . . there is not one, but two."

"*Two* children?" The man licked his lips, trying to decide what to make of the unexpected news. How would this play out? Was the Master giving him another chance to prove himself? To show he could be trusted with more responsibility?

"A boy and a girl." The voice in the darkness sounded hungry, and the man hungered as well for the rewards the Master could grant—if he succeeded in whatever task was placed before him.

"What do you wish me to do, Master?"

The voice was silent for a moment, as though considering the question. "You failed me once before," it said at last.

From his spot in front of the throne, the man couldn't keep from trembling—not in fear, but excitement. *One more chance,* he thought. *Only one more chance to prove I am worthy.* This time his fingers *did* go to the scar, where they traced the twisting line that disfigured his face. His thirst for power was so strong he could feel it thrumming in his veins like a beating drum. "I won't fail you again. Only tell me what I must do."

"You need not worry yourself with the girl," the voice said. "She will be taken care of shortly. You must go to the world called Earth and take the boy."

A withered hand extended out of the darkness, its skin gray and papery. At the base of its longest finger, a gold ring glittered. The man had never seen the symbol carved into the top of the ring, but he'd heard about it. It showed two creatures locked in mortal battle. One was clearly a Summoner. The other he didn't recognize.

Quickly, he leaned forward and pressed his lips to the ring. The skin beneath the gold ring burned his lips with a cold fire, but he did not pull back. Instead, he imagined what it would be like to wear that ring on his own finger. He kept his mouth pressed against the wrinkled hand until it retreated into the darkness.

"Once I have him?" the man asked.

"Bonesplinter," the voice said, and the man thought he heard the sound of a tongue rasp across paper-dry lips. "You have been my most faithful Thrathkin S'Bae for many years. Once you find the boy, do as you will with him. Just be sure he is dead when you are finished."

CHAPTER 2

THE FREAK

HURRY UP, YOU LOSERS. The freak's gonna be here any minute." Chet Hawkins hunched outside the entrance to the second floor dormitory of the Philo T. Justice Boys School in Cove Valley, Arizona. He peered through the doorway before turning his beefy red face back toward the small group of boys gathered around a mop bucket in the dimly-lit hallway.

At nearly sixteen—a year older than any of the other boys, and a full head taller—Chet was the meanest kid in the school and didn't mind proving it. He balled up his large, freckled fists, and the others immediately stepped away. "Finish up. And make sure it's slippery!"

Crowded together around the top of the narrow, wooden staircase, the boys had been mopping a puddle of soapy, gray water onto the splintered, oak boards of the hall floor.

"Gimme that." Pete Lampson, a gawky, twelve-year-old boy with greasy black hair and a neck like an underfed turkey, yanked the mop from Squint, the smaller boy standing next to him. He splashed the mop into the metal bucket, swirled it around and added a final coat to the floor in front of the top step.

Squint tested the boards with the tip of his sneaker. As he ran his shoe across the wet boards, his foot slipped out from under him, and he nearly fell over backwards.

"Clumsy idiot," Chet said. He sneaked a quick peek into the dormitory again, but there was no sign of the freak's wheelchair. Good thing, too. This was the third time he'd tried to get the kid alone. If the boys in the hallway messed it up this time, he'd pound them all.

"Get this stuff out of sight." Chet crossed to the boys in three quick steps, took the mop from Pete and tossed it in Squint's direction.

"Geez!" Squint howled as the wet mop splashed against the front of his pant legs. "You didn't have to get water all over me."

"Quit being a girl." Chet grinned, exposing a wide gap between his two front teeth.

Muttering, Squint picked up the mop and carried it across the hall. Beaver, a chubby boy with large front teeth and a blond crew cut, took the bucket.

"Don't forget," Chet whispered. "As soon as the kid comes through the door, Pete and I will grab him while you two throw his wheelchair down the stairs."

"Then, pow!" Squint said, punching his fist into his palm with a nasty giggle.

"Right." Chet nodded with a wicked grin. "Everybody gets a shot at him. Just make sure I get the first punch."

"It's him," Pete suddenly hissed.

Freezing in place, they all strained to hear. From the next room, came the *reek, reek, reek,* of a wheelchair badly in need of oil.

"Hide." Chet pushed Beaver and Squint to the right side of the door and joined Pete on the left.

Chet listened intently. As the sound of the squeaky wheelchair drew closer, he rubbed his right fist in the palm of his left hand, dark eyes glittering. Every kid who came to Philo T. Justice—or Pit Juice, as most of the boys called it—got beat up by Chet. It was his little way of welcoming the greenies into their new school.

Usually he got to them in the first few days after they arrived, but the new kid had managed to slip away from him twice already. That a greenie had escaped a beating was bad enough. But the fact that the greenie who escaped was stuck in a wheelchair made Chet furious.

It was like the kid knew just what they were planning for him. Even when they had him trapped, he somehow disappeared. Just two days earlier, Chet had sworn he'd seen the little freak wheel that clunky chair of his into the music room. But when Chet scanned the halls for teachers and followed him inside only a few seconds later, the room was empty. Chet had looked everywhere—even in the instrument closets, although there was no way a wheelchair would have fit in them—but the kid was gone. The whole thing was a little spooky.

Today would be different. The dormitory only had two doors. The one at the back led into the bathroom where Chet had seen the freak head a few minutes earlier. The second door was the one Chet and his gang were crowded around. To get downstairs, the freak would have to wheel out this door and take the small, old-fashioned elevator at the end of the hallway. There was no way to go past them without them seeing him.

The plan was to grab the kid as he came out of the dormitory. They'd push his chair down the stairs, give him a major beating, and tell everyone it had been an accident. They'd been mopping the floor when the wheels of the kid's chair slipped in the soapy water and he fell out of his chair. Oops.

See how the baby will get around with his wittle chair broken in a dozen pieces, Chet thought. *And if the freak gives us any trouble this time, he might go over the stairs right behind it.* Not that anyone would be able to tell. The kid was already a cripple. What difference would a few broken bones make?

Chet wanted to get in the first punch though. This kid had been way too lucky, and Chet was itching to get his hands on him.

Reek, reek, reek came the sound of the wheelchair.

Almost here, Chet thought. He and Pete leaned forward on the balls of their feet. On the opposite side of the doorway, Squint and Beaver did the same, their hands ready to grab the chair at the first sign of movement.

Reek, reek . . .

Just inside the door the squeaking stopped. Chet tilted his head. Had the kid somehow sensed what was waiting for him again? It didn't matter. One way or the other, he was going to get what was coming to him this time. Chet considered reaching into the room and just grabbing the kid. But as he was about to plunge through the doorway, the wheelchair started moving again.

Reek, reek, re—

"Now!" Chet shouted as a chipped silver frame and gray rubber wheels appeared through the door. Squint and Beaver grabbed the sides of the wheelchair, and with a great push, sent it sailing across the soapy hallway and into the stairwell.

For a split second the chair seemed to hang suspended in mid-air. Then gravity took hold, and it went crashing end-over-end down the rickety steps with a clanging of steel and the *thunk, thunk, thunk* of rubber against wood.

"Yes!" Squint shouted, swinging his arms and doing a little dance down the middle of the hallway until he slipped in the water, landed on his rear, and laughed like a lunatic.

"What's wrong?" Beaver asked Chet, realizing he and Pete were not celebrating.

"Isn't something *missing?*" Chet asked, his face turning red.

Beaver scratched his head for a moment; then his eyes lit up. "Hey, where's the kid?"

Chet shook his head in amazement, wondering why he hung around with these brainless wonders. "Obviously the freak hid in the dormitory and pushed his chair through the door."

The kid thought he was being tricky. But that just meant he was going to get it even worse. Chet leaped through the doorway, hands spread wide.

But the dorm was empty. He dropped to his knees and looked under the saggy-mattressed beds lined along both sides of the room. There was nothing but a lot of dust balls. Chet jumped to his feet and yanked Pete by his skinny arm. "Check the bathroom. He's gotta be hiding in there."

Pete sprinted across the dorm, his greasy black hair flopping against his forehead. A minute later he came running back, puffing and out of breath. "He ain't there."

"That's impossible," Chet said, cracking his big red knuckles. He returned to the top of the stairs, careful to keep from slipping in the mop water. At the bottom of the staircase, the wheelchair lay toppled on its side. One wheel slowly spun around and around. A bent spoke poked up from it like a broken antenna. But where was the kid?

"What the—" he began. Before he could complete his sentence, something hard cracked against the back of his head. He turned in time to see a mop handle rise high in the air and swing toward him again. This time the mop caught him squarely on the nose, creating a flash of purple and yellow light before his eyes.

CHAPTER 3

Now You See Him

MARCUS KANENAS, a thirteen-year-old boy with scruffy, reddish-brown hair, sat on the worn hallway floor in patched blue jeans and a school T-shirt that still looked new and stiff. The shirt hung like a sail on his skinny frame and narrow shoulders. His right arm, which held the mop tucked under it, was corded with wiry muscle from years of pushing himself around in his wheelchair.

By comparison, his left arm, withered and weak, looked like a broken chicken wing with the left three fingers tucked into a permanent fist. His right hand was fitted with a soft leather glove to protect it from the friction of wheeling his chair. His left leg jutted forward as he rested on his right leg, which was nearly as useless as his arm. But he faced the four boys standing in front of him with a fearless grin.

Marcus shook his hair out of his blue eyes. *"En garde!"* he shouted, copying a line he'd read in a book about the Three

Musketeers. He waved the mop in his leather-gloved right hand like a knight brandishing his sword.

"How'd the freak get over there?" Pete crowed. He gave a confused glance toward the dormitory door before starting toward Marcus with balled fists.

Marcus swung the mop handle in a lightning-quick slash that struck Pete on the back of the hand.

"Ouch!" Pete sucked on his quickly reddening welt. "That kid's crazy."

"Crazy is right," Marcus said, waving the mop in his direction. Pete rapidly backed away to a safe distance.

"Let's get him," Squint said. He and Beaver advanced on Marcus, but before they could take three steps, Marcus shifted the mop. Balancing the handle between the thumb and index finger of his weak left hand like a pool cue, he jabbed it forward with his right.

"Ugh," Squint grunted, doubling over as the tip of the handle hit him in the stomach, knocking the wind out of him. His face turned the color of overcooked broccoli, and he looked like he might throw up.

Beaver took a hesitant step toward Marcus, but a jab to the middle of his kneecap made the thunking sound of a bat connecting with a baseball. Beaver howled and hobbled away like an old man trying to catch a city bus.

"Had enough?" Marcus asked, lowering the end of the mop slightly.

Chet, who'd been standing at the top of the stairs with a faintly confused expression on his broad, sweaty face, shook his head as though coming out of a daze. Focusing his eyes on Marcus like a bull taking aim at a matador's cape, he rubbed the purple goose egg on his nose.

"You are dead," he grunted. "I was gonna let you off easy before. Now I'm gonna bust you up so bad you won't ever ride that chair of yours again unless somebody's pushing you."

Bending low, hands held loosely before him, he moved in, splashing soapy water with his big feet.

Marcus pivoted on the damp floor, swinging the wet mop left and right. He pulled it out of reach just as Chet swiped at the handle with one beefy paw.

Chet grinned, the tip of his tongue showing through the gap between his front teeth. "Looks like that mop's getting heavy. You ain't gonna be able to hold it up much longer."

"Long enough," Marcus replied. Sweat dripped down his forehead. "Why don't you leave me alone?"

"I could," Chet said. He fingered the back of his head where a lump matching the one on his face had risen. "Maybe we can call it even. First you'd have to put down the mop so I know you won't hit me from the back again like a coward."

"You're the one who needs three friends to take on one kid half his size." Marcus swallowed, his eyes measuring the distance between Chet and himself. Finally he nodded. "You four move away to the door, and I'll put down the mop."

"Fair enough." Sending Pete, Beaver, and Squint to the door, Chet held out his hands palms up and moved back a step. Marcus lowered the tip of the mop.

"See," Chet said, taking another, slightly smaller, step away. "We can all be friends here."

Marcus lowered the mop a little farther. Instantly, Chet raced forward and snatched at the wooden handle. Before Marcus could bring the mop up, Chet ripped it from his grasp.

"Now you're gonna get it, freak-a-zoid," Chet said. He lunged ahead, clearly expecting Marcus to try to escape. Instead, Marcus tucked his head against his chest in a tight ball and rolled directly at Chet.

Unprepared for the attack, Chet stumbled backward. The mop, still swinging in his grip, caught between his legs, and he lost his balance on the slick floor. He reached for something to hang onto, but his hands found only empty space. For a moment he balanced on the edge of the stairwell, a look of surprised indignation on his face. Then, with a loud cry, he tumbled down the steps and disappeared from view.

CHAPTER 4

CRIME AND PUNISHMENT

WHAT'S GOING ON HERE?" Principal Teagarden appeared at the bottom of the stairs as Chet was trying to untangle himself from Marcus's wheelchair. The principal was a tall, stork-like man with wintry gray eyes and rimless glasses that balanced on the end of his sharp nose. Thinning hair was combed in a complicated pattern on the top of his scalp to disguise the fact that he'd been mostly bald for the last five years.

Marcus gulped. For some reason, Principal Teagarden hadn't liked him since the day they met. Marcus didn't think the current situation was going to change that. Especially since Teagarden was Chet's uncle.

"Well?" the principal shouted, tugging on the knot of his tie. "Will someone tell me what is going on here?"

At the top of the staircase, Marcus, Pete, Squint, and Beaver glanced at one another nervously. As Marcus began to open his mouth, Chet pointed up the stairs and blurted out, "It was *his* fault.

We were just mopping the floor like you asked us to when he came wheeling out of nowhere and knocked me down the stairs."

Principal Teagarden eyed the wheelchair—now looking more battered than ever—with disgust, and glared up at Marcus. "Is that true?" he demanded, apparently overlooking the fact that while Marcus's chair was at the bottom of the stairs, *he* was still at the top.

Marcus licked his lips. He glanced at the three scowling boys next to him and down at Chet who was clenching and unclenching his fists. He knew he was going to get in trouble no matter what he said, and it was only a matter of time before Chet and his gang caught up with him again. Maybe taking the blame this time would make things easier next time—although he doubted it.

He nodded. "I . . . wasn't looking where I was going. My wheels hit the soapy water. It was an accident."

"An accident?" the principal bellowed. "An *accident?* There are no such things as accidents at Philo T. Justice. There are only rule-*keepers* and rule-*breakers*. And you Mr. . . . Mr. . . ."

"Kanenas," Marcus murmured, keeping his eyes lowered.

"You are a rule-*breaker*." The principal pulled out his handkerchief and blotted his red cheeks. "You race around on this contraption of yours," he said giving Marcus's wheelchair a distasteful nudge with the tip of his shoe, "and you endanger the lives of every other boy in this school. I've got a good mind to—"

"Principal Teagarden." Mr. Allen, the English teacher and track coach, appeared out of nowhere. Quickly taking in the situation, he placed a hand on the principal's shoulder. "Perhaps I can be of some assistance."

"I've got this under control," Principal Teagarden said, glaring at Marcus. He gave his cheeks a final pat with his damp handkerchief and tucked it inside his coat. "This young man has violated school rules, and I am going to see he is punished. Someone could have been seriously hurt here."

"Yes, they could," Mr. Allen said, his deep brown eyes giving a speculative glance to Chet and the wheelchair at the bottom of the stairs—and Marcus at the top. "But aren't you forgetting your five-thirty appointment?"

"What?" Principal Teagarden checked his watch, and his eyes widened. "I didn't realize it was that late already." He gave Marcus a last sharp look and leaned toward Mr. Allen. "See that the trouble-maker is punished."

Mr. Allen moved past the principal to stand beside Chet, who was busy shooting threatening looks at Marcus. "Oh, I will," he said.

When the principal was out of sight, Mr. Allen folded his arms across his chest and glanced down at Chet. "You seem to be involved in a lot of accidents, Mr. Hawkins. Only usually you're the one on the giving end, and the other boys are the ones who end up hurt."

Chet scowled and shrugged his shoulders.

Mr. Allen returned his attention to Marcus. "You understand running—or in your case wheeling through the halls at high speeds—is a violation of school policy. If you still want to stick to your version of what happened, I'll have no choice but to give you two hours in seclusion."

Marcus had no idea what *seclusion* was, but it couldn't be any worse than some of the punishments he'd suffered at his other schools, and he imagined it was *much* better than what Chet had in mind if he caught him alone again.

Averting his eyes from Chet's threatening glare, he gave a quick bob of his head. "That's the way it happened."

"Very well," Mr. Allen said, clearly not believing a word of the story, but unable to prove it. "Chet, you and your friends will take

Marcus's wheelchair to Mr. Finley in the boiler room. You will wait until Mr. Finley has finished repairing it, and you will wash it and return it to the dormitory. You seem to have a way with soapy water."

"But we'll miss dinner," Chet whined.

"I'm sure you'll survive." Mr. Allen placed a firm hand on Chet's shoulder. "And if I find a single bolt out of place on that chair, or if Mr. Kanenas turns up with any unexplained bruises or cuts in the next week, you will be mopping these floors until you turn twenty."

Chet grimaced, his eyes burning with anger. "I'll tell my uncle."

Mr. Allen's expression hardened, but his voice was just above a whisper. "I imagine Principal Teagarden would be interested in knowing who broke into his office last week and stole his silver dollar collection—the collection I found under your mattress this afternoon."

Chet's face paled, the freckles on his cheeks standing out like ink spots. He shot a final look at Marcus and mouthed *later* before yanking the wheelchair up off the floor. "Come on," he muttered.

As Chet and his friends carried the broken wheelchair out of sight, Mr. Allen turned to Marcus. "I'm afraid you'll have to come with me. Can you make it on your own, or shall I see if I can find another wheelchair?"

"I can make it on my own," Marcus said. And to demonstrate, he scooted down the stairs and across the hall faster than a boy with two good legs and arms.

CHAPTER 5

SECRETS

LYING IS NO WAY TO START off at a new school." Mr. Allen glanced down at Marcus.

"Yes, sir." Marcus shrugged. They were in front of a white metal door. Unlike the doors to the school's classrooms, which had large windows in the upper half, this one had only a tiny glass pane less than two inches square. Mr. Allen was standing. Marcus crouched on the floor, his bad leg tucked under him, his good leg sticking straight out. It was an angle which looked awkward but to which he had grown accustomed over the years.

"I suppose I understand why you did it. You're the first boy at this school who's stood up to Chet and his friends. They'll leave you alone for a few days. But eventually they'll come looking for you. I can't keep an eye on them all the time."

Marcus's face tightened, his deep blue eyes gleaming. He clenched his fist in his lap. "I can take care of myself."

Mr. Allen grinned, surprising Marcus. "I don't doubt that at all."

The teacher nodded toward the door. "This is seclusion. There is a chair inside, but no lights or diversions. You are not allowed to read or speak. The door locks behind you once you enter. It will unlock automatically if there is a fire or other emergency. Otherwise I will come to let you out at . . ." He checked his watch. "Seven-thirty sharp. Do you need to go to the bathroom first?"

Marcus shook his head. He didn't mind being by himself, and at least he'd be safe from Chet and his friends for the next two hours. As he reached for the doorknob, the sleeve of his shirt rode up, revealing a pink circular mark on the outside of his shoulder just above his bicep.

"What is that?" Mr. Allen asked, taking Marcus's arm in his hand.

Seeing what the teacher was looking at, Marcus tried to pull free, but the teacher's grip was too strong.

Mr. Allen tilted his head and leaned closer to get a better look. "Is it some kind of tattoo?"

"No," Marcus answered without bothering to look himself. He'd seen the mark so many times he had it memorized. Upon first glance it seemed to be a scar or birthmark. But on closer examination, an image had been burned into the skin of his shoulder—like a brand on a cow. Hard ridges of scar tissue formed a precise likeness of two creatures doing battle inside an elaborately designed circle.

On the right was what looked like a mixture of a snake and a dragon—with a long, scaled body, a mouthful of wicked teeth, great wings, and sharp talons. It was locked in combat with another make-believe creature that seemed to have the head of a boar, complete with long curved tusks, the tail of a fish, and a bird-like body with long, feathered wings. Two pairs of horns sprouted from the bird-boar-fish's head, and a pair of human arms held a flaming sword high in the air. The serpent had its talons locked on the front of the bird's throat, while the tusks of the boar were closed on the snake's writhing body.

Mr. Allen ran his fingers over the hardened skin. "Who did this to you?"

Marcus shrugged. He'd had it since he was a baby.

"Did you do that to yourself?" he asked, at last releasing his grip.

Marcus shook his head and pulled his shirt sleeve down over his shoulder. Most scars faded with time. But this one was every bit as vivid as the first time he'd been old enough to realize it was there. Having had it for as long as he could remember, he saw it almost as a birthmark of sorts. But the attention people paid to it embarrassed him, and he tried to keep it hidden.

"I'm sorry," the teacher said. "I didn't mean to make you uncomfortable."

"It's okay," Marcus said, shrugging again.

Mr. Allen rubbed the back of his neck. "Well, I guess I'll see you in two hours."

Marcus grabbed the door knob, this time being careful to keep his sleeve from sliding up. He pulled open the door and scooted into the room on the seat of his pants, pushing himself with his good arm and pulling with his good leg, and guiding himself with his crooked leg like the rudder of a ship.

Ignoring the chair in the center of the tile floor, Marcus slid to the far corner of the room and leaned his head against the wall. Chairs were made for people with two good legs and a straight back. For him they were a constant pain, causing him to squirm and wriggle until he could finally get out. The cushioned seat of his wheelchair was better, but he preferred to sit on the ground.

Some kids were afraid of the dark. That's why the schools he'd attended always kept nightlights on in the dormitories. But he liked the invisibility the dark provided. In the darkness no one made fun of his deformed body or asked the questions he'd heard a thousand times before. *What happened to you? Does it hurt? Were you born that way?* And many far worse.

Closing his eyes, he tried to relax. But it was hard to take his mind off the way other kids saw him. How they acted around him.

The truth was, he had no idea what had caused his deformities. Abandoned as a baby at the edge of a Greek Orthodox Monastery in the Sonoran Desert, he'd been taken for dead by the novice who found him while working in the citrus groves. His tiny body had been so badly crushed doctors gave him less than a five percent chance to live.

Elder Ephraim, the monastery's abbot, had taken a special interest in the baby. Visiting Marcus often in the hospital, and later as he was moved from one home to another, Elder Ephraim tried to keep his spirits up and give him hope. The abbot said it was only through the faith and prayers of the monks that he'd survived at all and that made him God's child—*whatever that means.* Marcus wasn't too sure of that, but he had come to love the old man and respect his advice. He'd been heartsick at the abbot's death three years earlier.

It was Elder Ephraim who'd given Marcus his name when the police were unable to discover his identity. *Marcus,* after Marcus Eugenicus, Bishop of Ephesus, and one of Elder Ephraim's favorite theologians. *Kanenas* because it was the Greek word for nobody. The little nobody who had come from nowhere.

Unfortunately, the monks had no way to care for an infant, and even if they did, the state would never have allowed it. So he was transferred from one foster family to another. None of them could take the constant stress of caring for a child with Marcus's disabilities for long, and eventually he was shuffled from one state-run boys' school to another.

These days it wasn't his disabilities that kept him on the move. He'd learned to cope as well as could be expected, and could do most things a normal boy could. Only he *wasn't* normal. Sometime around the age of six, he'd discovered he had certain . . . *abilities* . . . that other children didn't. Abilities like how he'd been able to sense Chet's trap, and how he'd slipped out of the dormitory without the boys seeing him.

He tried to hide the things he could do—the things he could see. But eventually a day like today would come, when he was forced into revealing his differences. From that point on, the others would watch him more closely, ganging up on him until he was labeled a trouble-maker and moved along to the next school.

How long would it be before Chet and his friends noticed Marcus's differences? Tonight? In a few days? Weeks? Or had they already? It didn't really matter, because eventually they'd force him to leave this school, just like all the others.

From outside in the hallway came the sound of boys' laughter, and Marcus jerked forward. Was it Chet and his gang coming for him after all? The door was locked from the inside, but was it locked from the outside, too? He looked for a place to hide, but there was nowhere to go. Even with his abilities, he was trapped. He didn't even have anything to protect himself with.

Pressing his back against the wall, he waited for the sound of the door opening. But the boys outside moved down the hall, their laughter fading with them.

Stretching out on the cold floor, he closed his eyes again. Sometimes he tried to imagine what could have happened to force his parents to abandon him. Maybe there'd been a car accident and his mother had wandered deliriously for help, leaving him near the orange trees before she disappeared into the desert. Maybe a vicious kidnapper had stolen him from his parents. If his father had fought to protect him, that might explain the injuries. Anything to keep from having to accept that his parents had left him for dead.

What did it matter anyway? Whatever the reason, he was alone, and nothing would change that. There was no point in worrying about things he couldn't control. That was another thing Elder Ephraim had told him.

As Marcus allowed his worries to slip away, a feeling of calmness came over him, and he let his mind wander. When he was depressed or scared, he liked to imagine a place far away where everything was green and alive, where fish could jump out of the water, sprout color-ful wings, and fly off into the sky. Where trees talked and animals told corny jokes. A place where people could do magic and nothing was impossible. He called this imaginary place Farworld. It was the perfect name for a world so far away from the hot, dry, lonely one he knew.

Sometimes he liked to imagine he had a friend there. A girl his age, with long, dark hair, emerald-green eyes, and skin that was a warm brown from spending so much time outdoors. She usually wore a green robe that matched her eyes, and some kind of necklace around her throat. He thought her name might be something like Kelly or Kristen.

He wasn't sure why he imagined his friend as a girl. He certainly hadn't spent much time around girls as he was shuffled from one boys' school to another. But a friend was a friend, and he didn't have many of those. At least not *real* friends.

Lying in the dark room, his breathing slow and relaxed, Marcus imagined he and his friend were on the balcony of a tall white building that twisted gracefully into the sky. From this spot, he could see for miles in any direction. It was early morning, and the sun cast a pink glow on the snowcapped mountains to the east—at least he thought it was east. At the edge of town, a crystal river lapped playfully against its banks.

On the far side of the river, fields of tiny purple flowers waved to and fro, although Marcus could feel no breeze from where he sat, and the grass around the flowers wasn't moving at all. He had the feeling the flowers were performing a dance of welcoming for the sun, and if he were only a little closer, he would hear them singing as well.

Past the meadow was a deep forest filled with trees like none he had ever seen. For one thing, they were at least as tall as the building he was standing on, and many were even taller. As tall as skyscrapers. Some of them actually disappeared into the thick, white clouds that seemed to remain in place above them. For another thing, their branches were constantly in motion, waving up and down like big, graceful fans. He had no idea why they would do such a thing, but it was lovely to watch.

He thought it would be the most wonderful thing in the world to sit below those slow-moving branches, breathing in the aroma of their needles and sap. He turned to ask the girl standing beside him if the trees smelled as good as he imagined, but she was gone. Swiveling his head left and right, he searched the balcony, but the girl was nowhere to be seen.

All at once, a feeling of icy dread wrapped itself around his heart like a steel glove. He turned back to the field and saw the flowers had all tucked their purple heads down to the ground. And beyond, the trees of the forest had wrapped their branches tightly around themselves. Their trunks seemed to strain away from the great building where Marcus stood, as though they yearned to rip their roots from the ground and flee, screaming in terror.

What could make something as strong and majestic as those trees afraid? he wondered.

Above the forest, the bank of clouds which had been white and puffy only moments earlier was roiling and thickening into a great, black fist. From his perch on the balcony, Marcus felt a cold wind whip across his face and heard a roar of thunder. Not like the thunder he was used to in Arizona. This sounded like the growl of an angry beast.

A cold rain slashed down from the sky, and Marcus realized he didn't want to be in Farworld any longer. This had never happened to him before. Farworld had always been a place of protection—a place for him to leave all his cares behind. But now it felt like one of those haunted houses they put up at Halloween. He had the feeling something terrible and grotesque might pop out at any time.

Brilliant green lightning flashed just above his head, tearing open the sky. He tried to scream, but the frigid wind ripped the sound away. Whatever was happening here was terribly wrong, and all at once he knew if he didn't run now he might never have the chance. He tried to free his mind from the dream, but he couldn't seem to break away.

He turned to escape down the stairs and found a black-cloaked figure blocking his path. As the figure stepped toward him, icy-blue flames raced up and down the cloak like living fire. Marcus pressed himself against the wall of the balcony, holding his hands out before him.

"Stay away!" he wanted to shout, only his jaws felt locked in place.

The figure took another step closer and raised its arms. An

unseen force lifted Marcus off the stone floor of the balcony. Looking down, he saw he was suspended in mid-air, the hard ground hundreds of feet below him.

He tried to convince himself this was only a dream, but his ice-cold body told him otherwise. "What do you want?" he cried, not sure if the words ever left his mouth.

Standing at the edge of the balcony, the dark figure slowly shook its head. A sudden gust of wind blew back the man's hood, and Marcus found himself staring into the most evil face he'd ever seen. Piercing, silvery eyes stared out from above a sharp nose with a bump at the top like a tree knot. Thin, nearly-white lips snarled over perfect teeth. A thick rope-like scar curled from the base of his jaw to his right temple.

Without a word, the man dropped his arms, and Marcus plummeted toward the ground.

Marcus felt his head slam against the floor, and his eyes flew open. He was back in the school. Before he could shake off the effects of the dream, the door opened and light flooded into the room. Squinting his eyes, he saw Principal Teagarden standing in the doorway.

"Asleep?" the principal asked with a scornful look on his pallid face.

Marcus rubbed his eyes, still trying to get over the fright of his dream.

"Come here," Principal Teagarden said, tugging the knot of his tie. "I want you to meet someone." Teagarden glanced to his left, and Marcus realized the principal was nervous. He decided to stay where he was for the moment, pressed into the back corner of the room.

"Very well," said the principal, coughing into his fist. "Then I guess he can come in and meet *you*."

As the principal moved away from the door, someone else eased past him and peered into the room. For a moment, Marcus thought he must be imagining things—then his heart squeezed in his chest, and his throat tightened to the size of a soda straw.

Although the man was smiling, his lips still looked bloodless. His nose had the same bump at the top. But it was his eyes Marcus recognized best.

It was the man from his nightmare.

CHAPTER 6

GETTING DOWN FROM A TREE

KYJA WOKE TO THE FEEL of a rough tongue tickling the sole of her left foot.

"Wake up, sleepy head," an exasperated voice called.

"What time is it?" She rolled over on her straw mattress, saw it was barely light out, and pulled her pillow over her face.

"You have to get up early today." Something tugged at a strand of her long, dark hair.

"Stop that," she groaned, waving a hand in the air above her head.

"Okay," the voice called. "You asked for it." All at once, a sharp beak closed on the tip of her big toe.

"Ouch!" Kyja shouted. She sat up to find a teal-blue, reptilian face staring at her from the foot of her bed. Pointed leathery ears wagged back and forth as a pair of bulbous, yellow eyes blinked owlishly.

"Let go, Riph Raph!" she shouted, trying to pull her foot away.

"'Ot until you 'remise 'o gee' up," the skyte said around a mouthful of foot. It wrapped its scaly tail about its glistening blue body and flapped its small wings.

"I can't understand a word you're saying." Kyja pulled her foot again.

Riph Raph released her toe. "I said, not until you promise to get up."

"Well, I'm up now." Kyja wiped her foot on the edge of her blanket. "Skyte spit. Disgusting."

"Not as disgusting as that toe," Riph Raff said, belching out a fist-sized ball of blue fire. "What did you do, wade through pig manure yesterday? I've eaten dead rats that tasted better."

"*You* should talk," Kyja said, climbing out of bed and pulling a worn, dark green robe over her head, covering an ivory amulet that hung from a chain around her neck. "Have you gotten a whiff of your own breath lately?"

The small, dragon-like creature blinked and licked its foreleg. "I'm just saying you could afford to take a bath more than once a week."

"I bathe every day." Kyja looked at her reflection in the square metal mirror hanging from a plank on the wall, wrinkled her nose, and began running a brush through her tangled hair. Below her, in the main level of the barn that she called home, she heard the Goodnuffs' cows and horses beginning to stir. They would be nice and warm with their thick coats of hair, but in the loft, *she* was freezing.

"I don't know why you had to get me up so early," she groused to the skyte, who was happily sharpening his talons on the wooden floor. Mr. and Mrs. Goodnuff, the owners of the farm and the family that had taken her in, would still be in bed in their cozy little house across the dirt path, as would their son Timton.

35

Not that she held that against them. They'd been kind enough to take her in when she'd been found abandoned as a baby. They'd provided her with a place to live, food, and clothing for the last thirteen years. And they'd never once looked down on her or treated her badly because of her . . . *differences.*

Riph Raph flapped his stubby little wings and flew up onto the dresser. "If you want to miss your appointment with Master Therapass, that's up to you. I just thought—"

"My appointment!" Kyja cried, dropping her brush. "I forgot all about seeing the wizard today. How could you let me forget?"

Skytes hate being interrupted above all else, and Riph Raph was no exception. Wiggling his pointed ears he let out a disgusted *harrumph.* "What do you think I've been trying to tell you about all morning? If you'd ever pay attention to a word I said, these kinds of things wouldn't happen."

"If you ever said anything worth listening to, I might pay attention," Kyja said. She put on her slippers and raced across the room to the ladder that led down to the barn.

Reaching the barn floor, she hurried to where the oats were stored and began feeding the horses. Chance, a gray and white stallion, stomped his hoof to get her attention and shook his long mane.

"I've got a new one for you," he said, in a deep voice.

"I don't have time for jokes this morning," Kyja said as she filled his feed bucket. "I'm supposed to meet Master Therapass for a magic lesson."

"What did the veterinarian say to the shrinking cow?" the horse asked, over her protest.

When Kyja ignored his question and moved on to the next stall, Pepper, a black filly with a white patch on her forehead neighed, "What did he say?"

"I guess you'll just have to be a little patient," the stallion answered. "A *little* patient." All across the barn, the horses whinnied laughter and stomped their hooves.

Kyja rolled her eyes. She'd only heard that joke about a hundred times. Farm animals were nearly as dumb as a head of cabbage, but somehow they could remember the same jokes for years.

"I heard that cow joke," a plump cow mooed at the stallion as Kyja crossed the barn and began forking hay.

At the water trough, Kyja pistoned the pump handle up and down until a stream of clear, icy-cold water poured from the spout. "I'm sorry," she said, trying to catch her breath. "I can't milk you right now. I'm supposed to meet with a wizard in twenty minutes. But I'll leave a note for Mr. Goodnuff."

"That's okay, dear," mooed Sassy. "I won't pop. But I'd keep an eye on Marla if I were you. She's been going a little heavy on the alfalfa."

As Sassy was speaking, a roan bull sidled up to Kyja and said, "What has four legs, a tail, a long nose, and flies?"

"No idea." Kyja hung up the pitchfork and started toward the door. The bull gave her a sly wink and whispered out of the side of his mouth, "A smelly horse."

"Oh, Brutus," Sassy giggled, giving her long tail an extra big swish, "you are so-o-o funny."

In the farmyard things were no better. As Kyja carried her bag of corn to the edge of the pond, a gaggle of geese hurried up onto the bank. "How do you get down from a tree?" the biggest of the geese honked.

"You don't," another one shouted. "You get down from a goose! Get it? *Goose* down." At that, all of the geese rolled about on the ground, bursting into gales of laughter until several fell into the pond, where they nearly choked because they were laughing so hard.

Not to be outdone, one of the chickens called out, "Why do pigs have pink skin?"

"To keep their insides from falling out!" the rest of them said in unison.

In their pen, the pigs stopped wallowing in the mud for a minute and gave the chickens a dirty glare.

"Lowbrows," one of them said in a snooty voice.

"Heathens," agreed another.

The pigs were the only farm animals that had absolutely no sense of humor. As far as they were concerned, the other animals only showed their ignorance by repeating the silly little jokes. Normally Kyja found the animals at least mildly entertaining, but this morning she had to agree with the pigs.

"Hurry up," Riph Raph called from the top of the henhouse as Kyja gathered the eggs. "You'll be late."

"I'm going as fast as I can," she said. It seemed like every day there were fewer eggs to collect than the day before. Today was no exception, but she had no time to worry about it this morning. Lifting the last of the hens from its roost with an unceremonious shove, Kyja grabbed the final egg and darted outside.

MASTER THERAPASS

B Y THE TIME SHE REACHED the path that led from the western gates of Terra ne Staric to the tower, the sun was fully above the tops of the mountains. Kyja was completely out of breath. Normally she paused on her way into the city to admire the stone sculpture of Tankum Heartstrong that stood just outside the gates. She often wondered what it would have been like to see the great warrior in battle—mythic blades swinging, lips pulled back into a snarl. But today she barely gave it a glance.

"Get a move on," Riph Raph said, flying just above her shoulder. "I've seen slow-worms move faster than you."

"If you wanted to be helpful," she answered in an irritated tone, "you could carry this basket of eggs to the kitchen for me."

Riph Raph flipped his ears. "You know perfectly well I can't. A skyte's wings are for transportation only. We are *not* beasts of burden."

"You certainly seem like a burden to me." Kyja raced onto a footbridge and over a burbling creek, ignoring the tiny golden fish

39

that leaped from the water and buzzed about her head before splashing back again.

Past the bridge, the flagstone path wound in a spiral up a steep hill to the base of the tower. Every hundred yards or so, a golden fountain sprayed colorful patterns of water—one in the shape of a fish, another, a giant eye that stared balefully at anyone who passed. Between the fountains, statues of Westland's most famous wizards and warriors guarded the grounds with stern expressions.

Visitors to the tower were to stop at each fountain and wash their hands—purifying themselves before meeting with a member of the council or the High Lord himself. But Kyja had no time for such niceties. She cut directly up the side of the hill, ignoring the blades of royal grass that shouted, "Keep off! Keep off!" and, "No trespassing!" in their tiny, high-pitched voices.

From their spots along the path, the statues turned and gave her dark scowls. But she ignored them, too. As frightening as the statues looked, they couldn't actually tattle on her. And by the time the groundskeepers got up in another hour, the grass would have forgotten all about her transgression.

At the top of the hill, she leaned against the cold, smooth wall of the tower, panting. After catching her breath, she hurried up the white marble steps and through the entryway, while Riph Raph broke off and soared up into the sky. Just inside the massive gate, she stopped and curtsied to a stern-looking guard. "Eggs for the kitchen."

The burly man eyed her threadbare robe through the grate of his plumed helmet, his steel-gloved hand resting on the hilt of his sword. "Very well," he granted at last. "You may proceed."

After curtseying again, she scurried toward the kitchen, waiting until she was out of the guard's sight before pulling her robe up to her knees and breaking into a full run.

This time of the morning, the tower kitchen was bustling with activity. Men and women pulled loaves of bread from blistering ovens, rotated whole pigs on metal spits, and stirred huge pots with large, wooden spoons. Here and there one person or another waved a length of branch or a piece of carved horn, and hunks of meat magically dropped into neat, thin slices, or ladles flew through the air, spooning broth into pewter bowls.

Ordinarily Kyja would have stopped to admire their spells, but today she barely gave them a glance. At the far end of the kitchen, a sweaty woman with arms like fire logs was overseeing the staff.

"Your eggs," Kyja said, dropping a quick curtsey.

Bella took the basket with a hearty laugh. "I've told you a hundred times child, you *don't* need to curtsy to me. I'm just the kitchen help."

"You're the High Lord's personal chef," Kyja said with a grin. "And I've told you *two hundred* times it's my duty to show you the respect you deserve."

Bella shook her head and armed big beads of sweat from her forehead. "Can you stay for a bowl of pudding?"

"No time. I'm late for my lesson with Master Therapass."

"Well then, move along, child." The cook waved a heat-reddened palm toward a dim hallway. "Take the back passage. You'll get there quicker."

Bobbing her head, Kyja disappeared into the dark hallway. Every few feet, the shadows were broken by magical torches that never burned out. Occasionally she passed a heavy wooden door. On one of the doors a thick, metal lock cried out, "Who goes there?" through its keyhole. But she was past it before she had a chance to answer.

At the end of the hall, a narrow staircase spiraled up out of sight. Climbing higher and higher into the tower, Kyja carefully counted her steps as she always did. At exactly every fortieth step a doorway opened into a hall lined with brightly-colored tapestries. At the seventh such door, she turned into the hall. Riph Raph soared through the window and landed on her shoulder.

"How late am I?" Kyja asked.

Riph Raph cocked his head. "Fifteen minutes, give or take."

Kyja passed a tapestry showing two wizards on horseback bringing down a swarm of giant, bloodthirsty cave bats, and turned left into the next hallway. A woman's face painted on a large vase watched her suspiciously as she walked by, and a stone dragon gave a great roar that nearly frightened Riph Raph off his perch.

"Ouch!" Kyja said as the skyte's talons dug into her skin.

"Sorry," he said, glancing nervously over his shoulder. "That thing gives me the shivers every time."

They stopped before a large, oaken door that was standing halfway open.

"Master Therapass?" Kyja called. When there was no answer, she glanced at Riph Raph and stuck her head partway through the doorway.

"Hello? Is anyone here?"

"Maybe we should come back later," Riph Raph whispered. "I've got a bad feeling about this."

"No." Kyja shook her head firmly. "It's been months since my last lesson."

Taking a deep breath, she walked through the door. The wizard's study was a large, oval-shaped room with a domed ceiling. The only light came from a small, circular, stained-glass window set high in the wall and various candles that sputtered and flickered throughout the room.

Kyja's slippers sunk silently into the thick rugs that covered the marble floor. She passed shelves that rose nearly to the ceiling, filled with thick dusty books and various odds and ends—glass spheres, bottles of white powder, the skulls of small animals.

"This place always appears so homey," Riph Raph whispered, grimacing at what looked like a human finger.

"Shush," Kyja hissed.

As they rounded a dark, wooden table inlaid with various ivory symbols, Kyja caught a movement near the door out of the corner of her eye.

A huge, grizzled wolf rose from the rug in front of an empty fireplace. Muscles rippled as it gained its full height—its shoulders nearly as tall as Kyja. Brown eyes, as deep as wells, glittered, and its jaws crackled in a large yawn.

It grinned, showing a mouthful of razor sharp teeth. "You're late."

CHAPTER 8

MAGIC LESSONS

SORRY, MASTER THERAPASS," Kyja said, anxiously brushing the wrinkles from the front of her robe. "I overslept."

"It was my fault," Riph Raph said from his perch high on a bookshelf where he'd flown at the wolf's appearance.

"I see. We have two sleepyheads, hmm?" The big gray wolf turned toward the empty fireplace, and instantly, bright orange flames sprang to life. "Not to worry, little ones. I seem to have overslept a bit myself." He tilted his shaggy head, and the flames changed from orange to green and blue.

"I like that better. Don't you?" he asked, stretching his front legs out before the warmth of the fire. "There was a time when the chill in the morning air didn't bother me. Now, alas, my old bones don't move quite so easily as they once did."

As he turned from the fire and padded across the room, Kyja noticed the limp in his back right leg was worse than ever. "Can't you use your magic to make that any better?" Kyja asked.

The great wolf paused, and Kyja wondered if she had over-stepped her bounds. Without any warning, the creature disappeared. In its place stood a stooped man in a powder-blue robe.

Kyja couldn't help admiring the transformation. Other wizards could change briefly into animal form, but Master Therapass was the only wizard she'd ever met who could actually *become* another creature and stay that way for days at a time if necessary. Transmorphism was one of the most difficult of all the forms of magic, but the wizard made it look easy.

"There are some things magic can't cure." He shook his head ruefully, making his unruly gray beard waggle back and forth. "Old age is one of them."

"I'm sorry," Kyja stammered. "I didn't mean to suggest that . . ."

"Not at all, child. Not at all." The wizard rubbed his hip and walked to the table. "They who are too afraid to ask questions will remain forever ignorant."

"Now then," he said, spreading his long, slender fingers flat on the table. "I assume you've come to offer me a rematch at trill stones? Because I certainly can't allow a thirteen-year-old girl to beat me eleven straight times. I believe I am overdue for a victory."

He waved his right hand, and two dozen shiny red and green stones flew down from a shelf and arranged themselves in a perfect circle on the surface of the table.

"Master," Kyja wailed, twisting her hands in front of her robe.

"Not trill stones then?" With a wave of his hand, the stones stacked themselves neatly on top of one another and whisked back up to their spot on the shelf. At the same time a pair of cane-backed chairs walked nimbly across the room and took their places behind Kyja and the wizard.

Master Therapass lowered himself into his chair, but Kyja was

WATER KEEP

too anxious to sit. The old man clasped his hands before him, rested his chin on his steepled fingers, and gave a deep sigh. "You're here about the magic again."

"Yes," Kyja cried, so excited her feet couldn't help but tattoo a little happy dance of footprints on the floor. "I think I've figured out my problem. I'm not concentrating hard enough. All this month I've been practicing my *focus*. I stared and stared at one of my hair clips until my eyes were watering so badly I could hardly see. Then, all at once, I could swear one of them actually moved. Not much—only a jiggle, really. But it *did* move. Isn't that wonderful?"

Master Therapass glanced suspiciously up at Riph Raph, and the skyte quickly averted its big, yellow eyes. "Come, little one, and sit." The wizard pointed a finger at Kyja's chair, and she reluctantly took a seat.

The old man stroked his long, gray beard, his face crinkled in thought. "Kyja," he said softly. "A horse may wish to fly. And it may briefly be able to launch itself into the air. But shortly it must return to land again. A duck may wish to carry a melody like a song bird. A goat may wish to swim beneath the waters. But ultimately, every animal, plant, even the rock in the field, must accept what it is, and in doing so, achieve its potential."

Kyja could feel her lips trembling as her eyes began to fill with tears. "You're saying I should quit trying? Just give up?"

"Is casting spells really so important?" he asked, his deep brown eyes mirroring the pain in her glistening green ones.

"Yes!" Kyja cried, leaping from her chair. "Everyone has *some* magic. Cooks, farmers, blacksmiths. Babies turn their rattles into sweets. Mothers command scrub brushes to wash their children. Even plants and animals have magic."

"Everyone but you."

"Exactly!" Kyja began pacing about the room. "I'm an outcast. It's bad enough I can't do magic. But I can't even take part in the magic the other kids do. Charms don't work on me, spells bounce off, potions might as well be water for all the good they do me. I can't play in any of their games."

Master Therapass traced his bony fingers across the surface of the table. "Don't you see, little one? The very fact that magic does *not* affect you makes you special."

"Not special—*strange,*" Kyja said, unable to stop the tears from dripping down her cheeks. "Do you have any idea how I feel when the other kids make fun because I can't do spells? They laugh behind my back and call me *half-wit*. They say I have to live in a barn because I'm as dumb as a cow. I don't want to be *different*. I want to fit in."

She waved her hand up at Riph Raph. "Even *he* has . . ." Sudden understanding dawned on her as she stared up at the little skyte. "It was *you*, wasn't it? You were the one who made my hair clip move."

Riph Raph tucked his head under his wing in shame. "I'm sorry," he said, his voice muffled. "I just wanted to help. I was watching you try so hard. And I was concentrating with you. And suddenly . . ."

"Ohhhh," Kyja cried. She dropped into her chair, burying her face in her arms. "I'll never be able to do magic. Never!"

"There, there." The old wizard hobbled around the table and laid his hand gently upon the back of Kyja's head. When her sobs changed to sniffles, he took her chin in his knobby fingers and raised it so she was looking into his eyes.

"Listen to me," he said, his face dark and serious. "You are right. Everything does have magic in it. From the smallest insect to the mighty trees of Before Time."

Kyja looked up at him miserably. "But not me."

Master Therapass smiled. "Even you, little one. But magic is not just spells. The magic you see on the outside—making pots and pans fly or brewing potions to make boys swoon before you—is but a tiny fraction of the power of *true* magic. The real power of magic lies *within* you. Who you are, what you do, and most importantly of all, what you may become."

Kyja wiped her eyes with the back of her hand. "You really think I might have some magic inside me then?"

The wizard nodded. "I *know* you do."

CHAPTER 9

LOST AND FOUND

MARCUS STUDIED THE BUSINESS card in his hand.

Ben Linstrope
Child Welfare Attorney
State of Arizona

"Well, speak up, son. You don't seem very grateful, considering this man has spent the last six months trying to find you." For the first time Marcus had ever seen, Principal Teagarden had his tie pulled all the way up to his skinny neck. And he seemed to be wearing a fresh white shirt. Marcus supposed he was trying to make a good impression on the man from the state.

"Um, thanks." Marcus turned the card over in his fingers before slipping it into his pants pocket. It was all too amazing to believe.

From where he stood in the corner of Principal Teagarden's office, Mr. Linstrope gave Marcus a toothy grin. "My pleasure, young Mr. Kanenas." The grin disappeared as Linstrope moved toward Marcus and ran a long, thin finger down the wheel of his chair. "I only wish we could have identified you sooner. Your parents never gave up hope. But I'm afraid the authorities feared the worst when they caught up with the people who'd abducted you and learned of the atrocities they had committed upon such a tiny baby."

Marcus felt a lump rise in his throat. *Parents.* The man in the expensive black suit was telling him his parents had been looking for him all this time. They *hadn't* abandoned him after all. "Where . . . are my parents?"

The attorney opened his black portfolio and handed Marcus a 5x7 photograph. It showed a man and woman, in their early twenties Marcus guessed, holding a baby. Even though the baby couldn't have been more than a few months old, Marcus recognized his own features on the infant's face. His eyes lingered on the chubby little perfect arms and legs. *Will my parents still love me when they learn I'm in a wheelchair?* he wondered.

" . . . living in Boston for the last three years."

Marcus hadn't been paying attention to the man's words, but now he set the picture aside. "Boston?" he asked, leaning forward in his freshly-washed and repaired wheelchair. "Is that where I'm from? Boston?"

"Actually, a small town a few miles south of there. For a long time after you were kidnapped, your parents were afraid to move from the house they were living in, just in case someone tried to contact them. It was only when everyone else had given up hope that they relented and moved into the city."

"Why aren't they here?" Marcus asked.

"They *wanted* to be, believe me," Mr. Linstrope said, closing his portfolio. "They would like nothing more than to take their son in their arms for the first time since he was a baby. Only, we have to be sure you *are* their son."

He folded his arms across his chest, a pained expression on his face. "There have been some . . . *mistakes* . . . in the past. Boys they thought were their son, only to have their hopes dashed."

Marcus felt his insides go cold. "You mean they might *not* be my parents?" He picked up the photograph again and studied the faces. The baby in the picture had to be him. It *had* to.

Principal Teagarden glared at him from across his paper-strewn desk as though he suspected Marcus of trying to pull off some elaborate hoax.

Mr. Linstrope tapped a manicured nail on the spine of his portfolio. "We can match fingerprints and such, of course. But that could take several days. And your mother and father are so eager to have you returned home—*if* you are the right boy."

"What about the picture?" Marcus asked, holding it up beside his face. "I look just like them. And you said yourself, the people who took me admitted doing this to my arm and leg."

"The similarities are uncanny," agreed the attorney. "But there is one way we could find out for sure right now."

"What is it?" Marcus asked, leaning forward. "Whatever you need, just tell me. Anything."

Mr. Linstrope opened his portfolio again and flipped through the pages. He pulled a single sheet of paper from the stack. "The boy we are looking for has a unique mark of sorts."

Marcus felt the skin on his arms break out into tiny goose bumps. "What kind of mark?"

"The police believe the band of thugs who abducted the child burned a rather unique mark upon the child." Mr. Linstrope grimaced as if the thought pained him. "Who knows why people do such horrible things? But if you had such a brand on you, it would provide all the proof I need."

Mr. Linstrope held out the page, revealing an image Marcus had seen all his life—an image he could draw with his eyes closed. "Does this look familiar?" he asked, his eyes gleaming.

Marcus sucked in his breath. Part of him wanted to admit he had the mark. After all the years of being alone, how would it feel to have a family to go home to? To have someone tuck you into bed at night and be there for you in the morning? To have someone tell you they loved you?

But another part of him was thinking about his dream. Looking back on it, he tried to remember if it had been this man's face after all. Sitting in the darkened room, he'd been sure. But now—under the bright lights of Principal Teagarden's office—he wasn't quite so confident.

The features *were* similar to the face he'd imagined. But they were also different. And the scar was missing. He wasn't even sure the figure in his dream had been human. Still, something about the attorney's eyes made him very uncomfortable—they made him feel like he was being picked apart and put back together with some pieces missing.

"Well?" Principal Teagarden spouted. "Do you have the mark or not? Speak up, boy."

Marcus barely heard him. He was studying Mr. Linstrope's eyes, and something in them was setting off huge warning bells inside his head. The mark on his arm itched almost uncontrollably, and it was all he could do to keep from reaching up and putting his hand over it.

Marcus shook his head. "I guess I'm not the right one."

Mr. Linstrope's expression narrowed, and the corners of his lips rose ever so slightly, as if he knew Marcus was lying. "No? You're sure there's nothing on, say, one of your *shoulders?*"

Looking into Mr. Linstrope's eyes, Marcus suddenly found himself wanting to admit he had the mark. *Tell him,* whispered a voice inside his head. *You can trust him. He'll take you to your family.* Marcus tried to shut the voice off, but it wouldn't go away. He tried to pull his eyes from Mr. Linstrope's dark gaze, but he couldn't seem to turn.

Show him. Show him. SHOW HIM! The voice drummed over and over in his mind. His hand was trying to reach up toward his shoulder, but he wouldn't let it. It took every bit of his control to keep his fingers locked on the arm of his wheelchair. If only he could manage to look away, even for a second.

"There!" Principal Teagarden shouted, and Marcus felt the grip on his mind release at once. Turning, Marcus realized that while his eyes had been locked on the attorney's, the principal had come around from behind his desk. He was holding up Marcus's right shirt sleeve.

"The mark," Principal Teagarden said. "It's right here, just like the man said. It matches the drawing perfectly."

Marcus reached for his shirt to pull it back down, but it was too late. Mr. Linstrope was leering like a large, predatory beast.

"It looks like we have our boy."

CHAPTER 10

THE ALL-SEEING EYE

KYJA STOOD AT THE CENTER of a whirling vortex of blue flame that danced and crackled about her entire body. Around her feet the white marble floor turned black and began to crack, while the air between herself and Master Therapass shimmered from the heat.

"Do you feel *anything?*" the wizard asked, his ivory and silver wand held out before him.

Kyja sighed and shook her head. Nothing at all. Not so much as a single bead of sweat.

"Dragon droppings," he said, lowering his wand. Immediately the flames disappeared. "I really thought we had something that time." He waved his hand, and the floor returned to its former sparkling white beauty as the rug unrolled itself from the wall.

Clinging to his perch on the bookshelf, Riph Raph's big yellow eyes peeked out from behind his wings. "Is all that fire really necessary? It seems so . . . dangerous."

Lowering her head, Kyja dropped back into her chair. "Not to me. I could have ten tons of magic cow manure dropped on my head and I'd still walk away smelling like a rose. But I'm sure I'd be the one who'd have to scoop it up."

"Speaking of which, you need to get back home, or Mr. Goodnuff's going to be very unhappy." Master Therapass returned his wand to his robe pocket and sat across the table from Kyja.

"Please," she begged. "Just one more try. You said there was magic somewhere inside me. We just have to find it."

Master Therapass rubbed the top of his head. "Perhaps there is one more thing we could try today. But only for a minute. You have chores to do, and I have a meeting with High Lord Dinslith to attend to."

He glanced around the room as though searching for something. "Have I ever shown you my *aptura discerna?*"

Kyja shook her head. "Your *what?*"

"Ah, there you are," he said, looking up toward the ceiling. "Come down here at once, you little imp."

To Kyja's surprise, the small, stained-glass window near the top of the room slid down the wall, zoomed across the floor, and climbed up onto the table, where it lay flat, still reflecting sunlight up through its multicolored surface. Where it had been, the wall looked as solid as if no opening ever existed.

"Aptura discerna," the wizard said. "The all-seeing eye." He tapped the center of the window with his wand, and the colors began to swirl and spin. Finally, the swirling subsided, and the window took on a pinkish hue—although light continued to glow up out of it.

"Is it like a crystal ball?" Kyja asked, looking down into the window's milky depths. She wondered if she was supposed to see something in it.

"Not exactly." Master Therapass placed his hands on either side of the window, his wrinkled face illuminated by its pink glow. "Most windows look out on the world. This window looks in. I sense that much of your unhappiness, little one, comes from your confusion about who you are and where you fit in. And I am to blame for most of that confusion. One day, I hope to be able to clear that up. In the meantime, if you could just gain a glimpse of what's really inside you . . ."

Kyja looked up into the wizard's face uncertainly. She had no idea what he meant about taking the blame for her unhappiness. "If I can't be affected by magic, how can this help me?"

"Perhaps it won't." The old man blew into the window, and some of the haze seemed to clear away. "But unlike magic spells, potions, charms, and so forth, aptura discerna does not seek to change the person who looks into it. It merely explores the depths of whoever gazes into its surface and displays what it finds. Would you like to give it a try?"

"Yes," Kyja said at once, bending over the aptura discerna so her dark hair pooled to either side of the window. "How does it work?"

Master Therapass leaned back in his chair. "First, you must give yourself over to the window."

"I don't understand," Kyja started.

"Look into the window and remove the barriers between your inner self and your outer self. Break down the walls you have built up to protect you from hurt and disappointment. In order for aptura discerna to see clearly, you must abandon fear, anger, and resentment. You must set aside your jealousies and disappointments. And perhaps most difficult of all, you must discard all past hurts, whether real or perceived."

Kyja's mind whirled at the wizard's words. Her thoughts filled with the years of taunting and cruelty she'd been forced to endure—not only from the other children, but from adults as well. The nights she'd cried herself to sleep, knowing she was, and always would be, an outcast. Under her gaze, the mist in the window thickened and grew dark, going from pink to magenta, and finally turning a scarlet, blood red.

Kyja felt her emotions grow darker with the colors in the window. How could she forget her hurts? How could she set aside the cruelties as if they were just an old pair of shoes? The wizard was asking too much of her.

"I can't," she cried.

"Try remembering the people who've been kind to you," Master Therapass said, his words gentle and soothing.

"People who've been kind," Kyja repeated softly. She thought of the wizard himself. He'd found a home for her when she'd been discovered abandoned as a baby. He'd seen to it that she always had food and warm clothing. And even when she'd despaired of ever being normal, he'd provided a shoulder to cry on. Then there was Bella the cook, who always had a slice of buttered toast or a piece of cake for her when she came into the tower kitchen.

Little by little, the aptura discerna began to clear. But then—like an uninvited guest—another memory rose in Kyja's mind. She'd been no more than five or six at the time, playing with another girl about her age near the vendors' carts while Mrs. Goodnuff shopped for vegetables. Kyja was offering her new friend one of her carved wooden dolls when the girl's mother came running down the cobblestone street, screaming at her daughter.

"Tessa! Stay away from that girl. Don't you know she's diseased?"

Skidding to a stop in front of a shocked Kyja, the woman had yanked at her daughter's hand as if saving her from a rabid animal.

"Don't come anywhere near my daughter!" the woman shrieked, causing all the people nearby to turn and see what the commotion was about. "I've heard about you. It's bad enough *you* have no magic. Don't you dare infect my Tessa!"

As one, the crowd edged away from Kyja, giving her hard glares, leaving her standing alone and terrified in the middle of the street, hot tears running down her cheeks.

"Kindnesses," Master Therapass urged, as the window began to darken again. Concentrating fiercely, Kyja managed to push the bad memory away.

Instead, she thought of Farmer Hendrick Goodnuff and his wife, Altha, who were stern taskmasters, but who had provided her with a room and a way to earn a living. And their little boy Timton who called out, "Ky-Ky," and wrapped his chubby arms around her waist whenever he saw her.

She remembered Anthor, the weapons master, who always had a sweet word and a fresh pear for her. And how he fashioned a tiny, wooden sword for her to practice with when she came by his shop.

Slowly the window began to clear again.

Quickly she searched her mind for memories, cutting off the bad experiences before they could take hold. There was Lady Jintette, the tower prophetess, who always foretold the most unlikely but well-intentioned futures. And Jade, the seamstress, who showed her how to patch her robes so they looked almost new.

"Now, remember the kindnesses *you* have done to *others*," said the wizard, his voice soft and distant.

Kindnesses she had done to others? *Had* she been kind to others, or had she been too caught up in her own misery to consider that others might have their own problems?

For a moment the mist in the window started to thicken and

turn red once more. Then she remembered Riph Raph. She'd found him injured by a catamount when she was seven or eight, and he only a few weeks old. She'd felt almost guided to the crevice in the rocks where the tiny skyte was hidden. She'd nursed him back to health, even though he pecked her and burned her fingers with his little fireballs at first.

And Singale, the man who'd lost his right arm battling Rock Giants. She'd discovered him penniless outside the city gates one day. She'd given him some of her hard earned money and found him a job working in the kitchen.

Then there was Char Everwood, the mother of two small children, whose husband Rhaidnan had gone off hunting and never returned. Kyja had knocked on their door and offered them leftovers from the Goodnuff's garden. She'd tended the children until Char could get work spinning and sewing.

Looking into the window, Kyja was startled to see that the images of the people weren't just in her head. There were Char and her children fishing for golden-eyes in the Two Prong River, Char's little girl giggling as she pulled in an especially big fish. And there was Singale, stealing a kiss from Bella when they thought no one was looking. Who knew that tough old Bella had a romantic streak?

But what did any of this have to do with *her?* Kyja wondered. She thought the window was supposed to give her some insight into her soul—a glimpse of what kind of magic she might possess. But all she was seeing were people she'd known. She stared intently into the aptura discerna, hoping for some clue of spells or abilities.

Suddenly the image in the window changed, from people she knew to a boy she'd never seen before—except his features were vaguely familiar, as if she'd glimpsed his face long ago, in a forgotten dream. He was sitting in a silvery cart of some kind with big, gray wheels, his eyes fixed on something out of sight. His clothing was odd, and what little of the room she could make out was strange and unfamiliar.

As she watched, a skinny man with a length of cloth wrapped about his neck like a narrow scarf walked into view and pulled up the sleeve of the boy's shirt. What Kyja saw there made her gasp in surprise. Standing out clearly on the boy's arm was an image Kyja knew well. That exact same image was engraved on the amulet she wore about her neck—the amulet Master Therapass had given her for her eighth birthday.

All at once, the boy seemed to wake from his trance. The view in the window shifted to show another man. Although he was dressed in the same type of clothing as the man with the scarf around his neck, Kyja knew at once he was not like the man or the boy. He was a monster in disguise.

She knew something else as well. The man wanted the boy, and unless something happened soon, the boy didn't have long to live.

Without any warning the window went black, and Kyja looked up to find Master Therapass shaking her. His face had turned a deathly gray, and she realized with shock that his hands were trembling. He was saying something. But it took her a moment to comprehend his words.

"Terrible danger," he gasped, his eyes wide with fear. "They've found him. You could be next. You must go. Now!"

CHAPTER 11

RHYMES AND REVELATIONS

MARCUS HAD TO ESCAPE. Is was either that or go with Mr. Linstrope—if that was really his name. And he didn't like his chances with the so-called attorney once they left the school.

"Hurry up, boy," Principal Teagarden said, folding his bony arms across his chest.

Marcus looked up from the well-used suitcase that he was packing with his few belongings and wished it was Mr. Allen standing behind him in the dormitory. Not that he thought the English teacher would have helped him escape the school, but at least Mr. Allen would have listened. Marcus could just imagine telling Principal Teagarden, "I saw a monster in my dream that had Mr. Linstrope's eyes." They'd cart him off to the home for hopelessly insane boys before the last word left his mouth. Instead, he shrugged his shoulders and muttered, "Just a few more things."

"Well, snap to it," the principal said, tapping his watch. "Mr. Linstrope is a busy man. He has a tight schedule to keep."

"Yes, sir." Marcus nodded, shifting in his wheelchair. His stomach was in knots. He was nearly positive the man who claimed to be a state lawyer had no intention of taking him to his family. But if not, what was the point of going to all the trouble of making up such an elaborate hoax?

What did Marcus have that the man could possibly want? It couldn't be money. There was only about thirteen dollars hidden under the lining of his suitcase—money he'd saved up over the years doing odd jobs. It was a lot of money to Marcus, but not enough to interest a man like Mr. Linstrope.

What if Linstrope was the man who'd kidnapped Marcus in the first place? Maybe he'd come back to erase the evidence of his crime. But Marcus was a baby when he'd been found. He couldn't even remember his real name, and he certainly couldn't remember any kidnapper. If Linstrope was involved in the abduction, Marcus wouldn't be a threat to him.

None of it made any sense, but Marcus had only two choices—he could go with Mr. Linstrope and hope for the best, or he could try to escape before the attorney got his hands on him. It wasn't a very hard decision.

Leaning protectively over his suitcase to block the principal's view, Marcus removed his cash and the only other important possession he owned—a creased picture of Elder Ephraim. After a moment's hesitation, he also grabbed an extra pair of underpants and stuffed them into his pocket. If he somehow managed to escape, at least he'd have a change of underwear.

Snapping his suitcase shut, he glanced toward Principal Teagarden and past him at the open door that led to the stairs. Somewhere below was the man who claimed to be from the state. But he'd worry about getting past Linstrope if and when he got that far.

"Finally," Principal Teagarden said, snatching the suitcase off the bed. "Let's go."

Marcus searched desperately around the room. He needed some kind of distraction. His eyes landed on the doorway at the back of the dormitory.

"I have to go to the bathroom," he lied.

"What?" Teagarden growled, his cheeks turning purple. "There's no time. You have a plane to catch."

"I have to go bad." Marcus leaned forward in his wheelchair, faking a pained look. "I think it's the pork and beans we had for lunch today." In truth, lunch had been peanut butter and jelly sandwiches, but he knew the principal never went near the cafeteria, much less ate anything served there.

"Well . . ." Teagarden's eyes darted toward the door, and Marcus realized the principal was as scared of Mr. Linstrope as he was.

"If I can't go to the toilet right now, I'm gonna . . ." Marcus leaned forward in his wheelchair, clenched his arms over his stomach, and gave a loud moan.

Principal Teagarden jumped backward as if he'd just stepped on a scorpion. "Hurry up then," he said, wrinkling his nose in disgust. "Anything to get you out of here."

Checking to be sure the principal wasn't following him, Marcus wheeled his chair into the bathroom at the end of the dormitory. Once he was out of sight, he climbed up on his knees, pushed open the window and peeked outside. Under the full, silver moon, the field behind the school was empty. He wished he could climb out the window and scale the wall. But even if he'd had a rope—which he didn't—he wouldn't be able to climb down with only one good hand.

Glancing toward the door, he slid onto the cold tile, released the locks on his wheelchair and folded it closed. It had survived one fall today already; he hoped it would survive a second. Marcus leaned the chair against the wall and tried to push it up to the window. Beads of sweat popped out on his forehead as he strained against the heavy, old-fashioned chair with his good arm. It rose an inch or two, but then one of the handles caught on the ledge of the window, and it dropped back to the floor with a thud.

"What's going on in there?" Principal Teagarden called from the other room.

"Cramps!" Marcus shouted back, giving out a deep groan. Panic-stricken, he looked around the small bathroom. The wheelchair was too heavy. The bulky contraption would ruin any chance he might have of escape, but he wouldn't get far without it once he left the school. He spotted the wooden ramp Mr. Finley, the school custodian, had built so Marcus could reach the sink.

Quickly he scooted across the bathroom, put his back against the ramp, and pushed off the wall with his good leg. For a moment nothing happened, and he worried the ramp might be attached to the floor somehow. Then, all it once, it slid across the tiles with a loud *screeee*.

"What was *that?*" the Principal shouted.

"Sorry. Guess I had a little gas," Marcus called back, blushing furiously.

Careful to keep from making any more noise, he finished pushing the plywood ramp until it rested against the wall, just beneath the window. Silently he wheeled his chair up the ramp and got out. Holding his breath, he tipped the chair and pushed until he could feel it begin to slide forward on its own. "Bombs away," he whispered, and let go.

A dull thump came from outside the window as the chair landed on the grass. He waited a moment to be sure Principal Teagarden hadn't heard the fall, then tugged the window shut. There was no time to do anything about the ramp, but hopefully he'd be gone by the time anyone discovered it.

Now came the hard part, when his plan either succeeded or failed. He was counting on one of the abilities that had gotten him in the most trouble at other schools. It had worked for him this morning against Chet and his friends, but the problem was, it didn't *always* work. And unfortunately, he wouldn't know for sure whether it had worked or not until he was actually in the dormitory.

Closing his eyes, he pictured himself sitting on the bathroom floor, and began to whisper.

"Nobody came to see me today. Nobody saw him arrive." It was a silly little rhyme he'd made up years before. He felt stupid saying it, but it seemed to help him gain the concentration necessary to make his trick work.

"Nobody saw him walk away. Nobody knows he's alive."

Concentrating on the image of himself in his mind, he imagined himself beginning to fade.

"Nobody knows when he comes and goes. Nobody seems to care."

With his eyes still closed, he pictured his body getting dimmer and dimmer, until it was really nothing more than a shadow.

"Nobody, take me away with you. Take me into your care."

Marcus *Nobody* was now Marcus *Nowhere*. And as long as he was silent, no one would notice him passing by. At least he hoped so.

Praying his trick had worked, he opened his eyes and leaned around the edge of the door jamb. Principal Teagarden was pacing the floor, alternating looks between his watch and the hallway. Marcus couldn't help smiling as he imagined how long it would take the principal to finally work up the courage to come anywhere near the boys' toilets.

Ready or not, here I come, he said to himself, and scooted out of the bathroom into the dormitory. Trying not to make a sound, Marcus scooted to the side of the room as far away from Principal Teagarden as possible. Using his good hand and foot as leverage, he slid under the first bed and peeked out. Principal Teagarden wasn't even looking in his direction.

The second bed was Chet's. Its unmade blankets smelled like mashed peas and old sweat socks. The next two—Pete's and Beaver's—were only a little more tolerable. He was almost halfway down the room, and Principal Teagarden hadn't looked in his direction once. Marcus allowed himself to hope he was going to make it out after all.

With his eyes fixed on the principal, Marcus didn't see the baseball until he bumped it with his elbow, sending it rolling across the dormitory floor.

"What's that?" Principal Teagarden said, spinning around. Marcus froze in place. From experience, Marcus knew his trick only worked about half the time, and only then when people weren't looking directly at him. It didn't seem to be invisibility exactly—which would have been far more useful—but more like camouflage. When people glanced in his general direction their vision seemed to deflect off him.

But now Principal Teagarden was walking directly toward the bed he was hiding under. Marcus pressed himself against the wall, as far beneath the bed as he could get. What would he do if the principal saw him? He couldn't let himself be caught, and yet, how could he manage to escape? Three feet from the bed, Principal Teagarden bent and picked up the baseball. Turning it over in his hands, he glanced curiously toward the line of beds and then at the bathroom door.

"Marcus!" he shouted. "Are you playing some kind of game?

Without waiting to see if the principal would turn back in his direction, Marcus shimmied under the last of the six beds and slipped out the door. Skipping the elevator, he slid down the stairs on the seat of his pants. Three-fourths of the way down, he paused and peeked into the lobby. He was sure Mr. Linstrope would be waiting for him. But the hallway was empty.

After another quick look in both directions, he crossed the cold, tile floor and pushed open the front door. Just like that he was outside, breathing in the cool night air. Up to this point, he hadn't given a thought to what he'd do once he actually managed to escape. Now he realized that getting out of the school was only his first step. A boy rolling a wheelchair down the side of the road wouldn't exactly be difficult to spot.

Where would he go? How would he get there? What would he do for money?

The difficulties were almost overwhelming. He was only thirteen. He shouldn't have to be worrying about those kinds of things. He pulled the photograph of Elder Ephraim out of his pocket. If only the abbot was here to help him now. Elder Ephraim never seemed anxious or afraid.

Don't worry about what you can't control, the old man's gentle voice seemed to whisper into Marcus's ear. *The longest journey is but a series of small steps.* Marcus nodded his head and took a deep breath. Okay, he would take it one step at a time. The next step was getting his wheelchair. After that, he'd deal with where he was going.

As Marcus was putting the picture back into his pocket, he heard a familiar voice from inside the school doors.

"Gimme one of them cigarettes, fungus breath." It was Chet, probably with his friends. No doubt they were coming outside to smoke. Smoking was against the school rules, but Chet and his friends did it anyway. Usually behind the school—right where Marcus had left his wheelchair.

With no time to waste, Marcus dropped to his hands and knees and scrambled around the bushes that ran along the side of the school to the corner of the building. Behind him, he could hear the sound of the school doors opening and closing, accompanied by the squawk of harsh laughter. Bits of rock and sticks bit through the soft leather gloves Marcus wore and into his palms as he scooted along the side of the school, but he took no notice.

Although it was night, the moon was bright, and it would be easy for the boys to spot Marcus if he didn't manage to get himself and his wheelchair around the building before they arrived. Rounding the back corner of the building, he started toward the spot where he'd dropped the wheelchair, then froze.

His chair was gone. At first he thought he must have come to the wrong spot. But he could see the imprint in the mostly dead grass where he'd dropped it, and a little farther back, the square of light shining down through the glass of the bathroom window. But the silver gleam of metal which should have been there was gone.

Something moved to Marcus's left. He turned in time to see a dark figure slip from the shadows.

A hand clamped around his wrist, and a voice whispered, "Now you're mine."

CHAPTER 12

THE BOY IN THE WINDOW

MASTER THERAPASS LOOKED LIKE a madman. Muttering to himself, he paced back and forth across the room, his fingers combing grooves through his long beard. "They can't be there . . . Yet clearly . . . If anything happens to him . . . All my fault . . ."

"Master Therapass, what is it?" Kyja rose from her chair and tugged the old man's sleeve.

He looked down as though he'd completely forgotten she was there. Then his eyes seemed to clear. "The boy in the window. Have you ever seen him before?"

Kyja shook her head. "No. Never. That is, I thought for a minute . . . But, no."

Bending down, he took her by the shoulders and stared into her eyes. "Are you sure? This is important. The image of the boy came as a direct result of your looking into the window. Are you absolutely certain you've never seen him?"

Kyja shut her eyes tightly, trying to replay the scene in her mind. She'd certainly never been in a room that looked anything like the one in the window. The people had been dressed so strangely, and she was sure she'd recall the silvery cart if she'd seen it before.

Yet there was something about the boy's face—the way his jaw was set and the way his eyes burned with intensity when he'd been so focused. "I don't think I've ever . . . *met* him. But it feels as if I might have dreamed about him. Does that make any sense? Could I have imagined him?"

"You didn't imagine him. He's very real." Master Therapass released Kyja's shoulders and gazed up at the bookcase where Riph Raph was watching them both intently. "I should have predicted that," he muttered, his eyes far away. "Of course he'd try to find a way, whether he knew it or not. And she would be the most logical one to reach out to."

All at once, Master Therapass took Kyja by the arm and began pulling her toward the door. "If they've found *him,* they're bound to come looking for *you* as well. Of course they'll check the city first. But once they find you've left, they'll spread out. They could even be here now."

Kyja set her feet, pulling her wrist from the wizard's grip. "What are you talking about?"

The old man gave her a measuring look before taking her hand. "There's no time to explain now. You must leave immediately. Do not tell anyone where you are going, except for Bella. She will give you food enough to last several days. Take one of Farmer Goodnuff's horses—you'd be questioned if I provided you with a mount from the tower—and ride out of town as far and fast as you can. I'll catch up with you when I'm able."

Master Therapass rubbed the top of his head. "The necklace I gave you. Do you still have it?"

"Of course." She slid the gold chain from inside her robe, revealing the ivory amulet.

"Continue to wear it, but keep it out of sight," the wizard whispered, glancing toward the open door. "Take the back passage through the kitchen. And don't talk to anyone you don't recognize."

"What about the boy?" Kyja asked, fingering her amulet and remembering the mark she'd seen on the boy's shoulder in her dream.

"He'll have to fend for himself." The wizard shook his head, and his eyes told Kyja how little chance he gave the boy. "There's nothing we can do for him."

Before Kyja could ask anything else, Master Therapass was pressing her through the doorway. He turned to Riph Raph. "Fly high above the city and look for anything out of the ordinary. If you see any sign of danger, warn Kyja immediately. She must be outside the gates before they arrive."

Kyja wanted to ask who *they* were, but Master Therapass would allow no further questions. The next thing she knew, Riph Raph had flown out the window he'd originally come in through, and she was racing down the staircase with no clear idea of what she was running from or where she was going. What would the Goodnuffs think when they discovered she had not only neglected to milk the cows but had taken one of their horses as well?

For a moment she considered asking Bella to let her hide in the kitchen. Nothing could threaten her in the tower of Terra ne Staric. The capital city had over two hundred guards and over ten thousand citizens capable of taking up arms. But then she thought about the look she'd seen on the wizard's face.

Master Therapass was old, but no one would ever accuse him of being a coward. Mr. Goodnuff once told Kyja that, in his prime, Master Therapass had been the most feared and respected wizard in all of Westland. Kyja didn't doubt it. She'd seen the way even the Captain of the Guard showed him deference. If Master Therapass believed there was something to be afraid of, she believed it too.

Reaching the bottom of the stairs, Kyja raced through the dimly lit hallway. Somewhere outside the tower she could hear the ringing sound of trumpets and wondered what they announced. At the kitchen doorway, she found Bella waiting.

"Take this," Bella said, handing her a bulging grain sack.

"But when—"

"Hush, child." The stout cook placed a finger to her lips. "Too many big ears and even bigger mouths in this kitchen."

Bella clutched Kyja against her ample waist and pushed open a scarred wooden door. Quickly they hustled down a hallway Kyja had never used before. The downward sloping passage was much narrower than most of the tower hallways and covered with bits of straw. Kyja's feet skidded on the slick stone floor. As they made their way along the passage, the air began to fill with the smell of cows and pigs.

"This leads to the livestock pen," Bella said in a low voice. "Shouldn't be anyone using it this time of day."

"How did you know I was coming?" Kyja asked when they were safely out of the kitchen.

"Never you mind. Master Therapass has his ways." Bella looked down at Kyja with worried eyes. "What are you running from child? I've never seen the wizard so worked up."

"That's just it," Kyja said, trying to keep her footing. "I don't know. I don't even know how long I'll be gone. Did he tell you anything?"

"Only that I was to get you out of the tower as quickly and quietly as possible."

All at once, the passage leveled out and opened into a fenced yard. On one side, a dozen fat sows rolled and snorted in the mud. On the other side, a flock of turkeys huddled together as Bella lifted the metal latch and opened the long, wooden gate.

"Hush your beak," Bella warned as the largest of the turkeys gave his waddle a shake and spread his tail feathers, "or you'll be on the dinner menu tonight."

"Come on," she said, taking Kyja's hand. They crossed the mucky livestock yard and passed through a second gate. A narrow dirt path, rutted by years of hoof prints, bordered a stone wall and led past the edge of an apple orchard. Although Kyja had never been this way, she understood roughly where they were.

"Here," Bella said, pulling a dark, gray scarf from her apron pocket. "Tie this around your head and keep it on until you get out of town. Master Therapass wanted me to remind you not to talk to anyone, and to stay out of sight as much as possible."

As they left the orchard, the path wound through a maze of tall hedges and ended before a rusted metal gate. Bella produced a key and unlocked the gate as Kyja tied the scarf beneath her chin.

"If you run into trouble, send that skyte of yours with a message and I'll—" Bella's words died in her mouth as she and Kyja rounded the corner. Not more than twenty yards away, where the path met the road, two dozen of the royal guards marched in formation. In the center of the formation was the High Lord himself, riding on a tall black stallion side-by-side with a man Kyja had never seen.

Before Bella could push Kyja behind her thick body, the stranger

CHAPTER 13

PROBLEM SOLVER

THE BIRD HAS FLOWN THE COOP." Mr. Linstrope grinned darkly. "Such a naughty little bird."

Marcus squirmed and tried to twist out of the man's grasp, but Linstrope's fingers dug into the skin of his arm like a steel trap, twisting until it felt like the bone was going to break.

"Don't scream, or I'll kill you here and now," the man hissed.

"What do you want?" Marcus asked, trying not to cry from the pain.

"I thought that was quite clear." Linstrope eased the pressure on Marcus's arm a fraction and leaned down until they were face to face. "I want *you*."

Marcus searched the dark schoolyard for anyone who might be able to see what was happening. At this point, even Chet and his friends would be a welcome relief.

Linstrope must have had the same idea, because he too glanced quickly about. With no effort, he swung Marcus into the air and dropped him into the wheelchair he'd hidden in the shadows. "Personally, I wouldn't mind disposing of those four little trolls from the school," he said, pushing Marcus and the wheelchair across the sandy grass toward a small grove of trees several hundred yards away. "But I think more privacy is called for."

"Who are you?" Marcus asked as they bumped and rattled across the field.

Linstrope laughed again. It was a dangerous sound—papery and dry like a scorpion stalking its prey along an empty river bed. "I suppose formal introductions *are* called for. Though, I rather enjoyed being Mr. Linstrope. I'm fascinated by the concept of lawyers—people whose entire reason for being is to twist the rules to suit their own purposes. Quite a noble profession, don't you think? It's a pity they don't exist where I come from."

He pointed a long finger to the ground, and Marcus jerked backward as the grass near his feet burst into flame. A moment later, he realized the flames spelled out the same words he'd seen earlier on the man's business card.

His face highlighted by the moon's silvery light, Linstrope raised an eyebrow as one side of his mouth lifted in an amused grin. "Watch closely now, little bird. I'd hate to have you blink and miss it."

Pursing his lips, the man blew toward the words. Like magic, the burning letters reading *Ben Linstrope* rearranged themselves into a new name: *Bonesplinter*. Below them, *Child Welfare Attorney* and *State of Arizona* faded away, replaced by *Problem Solver* and *State of No Return*. Then the entire thing flared brightly before disappearing into ashes.

Marcus looked up and realized the man's face had changed as well. His mouth was bigger, the nose flatter and wider. His eyes were farther apart, and his cheekbones had disappeared entirely, giving him a sunk-in look. And the scar from Marcus's dream had reappeared—a jagged line running up the side of his face.

"Quite a clever little trick, don't you think?" Linstrope said. "I imagine I could turn a pretty penny here, doing birthday parties and magic shows. Although it's not nearly as useful as your tricks, is it, little bird?"

Marcus's stomach went cold. "I don't know what you're talking about."

"Oh, I think you do." Bonesplinter tightened his grip, and Marcus felt as if spikes were being driven into the muscles of his arm. "Your disappearing act is quite impressive—especially considering your current . . . circumstances. But not nearly as impressive as what you might have learned to do over time. It's a shame you'll never have that time."

They had reached the edge of the field. Looking over his shoulder, Marcus thought he could see figures walking around the back of the school. Before he could be sure, Bonesplinter pushed him into the grove of trees.

"What are you going to do to me?" Marcus asked through gritted teeth.

Bonesplinter stopped deep in the shadows. "*I'd* like to spend a little time getting to know you," he said. "I'd like to study you like a fine watch and see what makes you tick."

In the darkness the man's face was still changing. His eyes looked even farther apart and his nose flattened until it was almost gone. His whole head appeared to compress and shift, while his mouth grew huge. His voice was changing too, growing deeper and raspier.

"Unfortunately," Bonesplinter whispered, "it's not up to me. It won't be long before the others come looking for you, and my orders are quite clear. I'm afraid, little bird, that you won't be returning to your nest."

As Bonesplinter leaned forward, his head emerged from the shadows into a shaft of moonlight. His yellow eyes gleamed hungrily. Teeth like sharpened daggers filled his mouth. But worst of all, Bonesplinter's skin had turned black and scaly.

Marcus screamed. He was looking into the face of a huge, deadly snake. Mouth wide open, it darted toward him.

CHAPTER 14

TAKING A CHANCE

"**B**ELLA, WHAT A SURPRISE. I expected you would be in the kitchen, preparing breakfast."

Cowering behind Bella's wide backside, Kyja recognized the voice of High Lord Dinslith. But who was the man with him? Kyja had never seen him before, which was not so unusual by itself. Visitors came from all parts of the world to consult with the wizards of Westland. Master Therapass had specifically warned her against speaking to any strangers, but surely he didn't mean anyone accompanied by the High Lord.

"Breakfast is awaiting your return, High Lord. I'm on my way to fetch more chickens for lunch." Bella's voice sounded calm and worry-free, as if she were just out running a perfectly ordinary errand. But with her hands hidden behind her back she gave Kyja a hard push. "I know how you and the council like fresh poultry."

What was Bella doing? Did she want Kyja to leave—by herself?

What was safer than being near the High Lord and his personal guards?

"Your culinary expertise is renowned far and wide. I am truly as honored to sample your cooking as I am to meet with the council," said a silky voice Kyja didn't recognize. She felt sure it must belong to the High Lord's visitor.

Bella chuckled. "You are too kind. I'd best get to those chickens then, or risk ruining my hard-won reputation." She gave another shove backward. "I'm sure you men have things to attend to as well, so I won't keep you any longer."

"And who is your little friend?" the silky voice inquired.

This time Bella's meaning was unmistakable as she practically knocked Kyja down with her strong hands. Kyja stepped backward, still blocked from view by Bella's body.

"Friend?" Bella asked. Kyja turned and ducked around the hedges. The gate was locked, but she thought the bars were just wide enough to squeeze through.

"The girl. The one standing beside you just a moment ago." Kyja could still hear the stranger's voice—sounding slightly irritated—as she pushed her head between the bars. At first they seemed too tight, but with a little more effort she managed to make it through. Turning her shoulders, she climbed between the rusted bars to the other side of the gate.

"I didn't see any girl. It must have been one of the . . ." Bella's voice faded as Kyja raced past the hedges and into the orchard. Did Bella really think the man with High Lord Dinslith was dangerous? That was crazy. What would a respected visitor of the council's want with a girl who fed chickens and milked cows?

As Kyja ran through the orchard, the trees began to shake their branches in her direction, rattling their leaves and offering fresh fruit.

"Apples! Try my apples; they're quite juicy."

"Over here. Ripest fruit you've ever seen. I'd eat them myself if I could. Come and pick a few before the birds get them."

"Call those shriveled little things apples?" said a third tree. It waved a gnarled branch at the other trees' fruits, which were a little smaller than normal. "If you want rosy cheeks and white teeth, I've got just the thing for you."

"Be quiet," Kyja whispered, hoping their voices wouldn't carry back to the High Lord's entourage. If the stranger really was the one Master Therapass had warned her about, then he might have recognized her. And that meant she had to get out of town now. She checked the sky for Riph Raph, but the skyte was nowhere in sight.

At the edge of the trees, Kyja scaled a crumbling stone wall and stopped before another row of hedges. She'd come this way as a little girl, sneaking apples from the orchard. The hedges surrounding the orchard *looked* ordinary enough, but they were actually cursed to keep out trespassers. Anyone who tried to get past them suffered the embarrassment of having his or her head swell up and turn bright red, until they looked just like the apples they were trying to steal.

But because Kyja wasn't affected by curses, her so-called friends recruited her to sneak inside and bring back fruit. That lasted right up until Mrs. Goodnuff found out what was going on. Kyja and the other apple thieves had been forced to spend a week weeding and raking the grounds to pay for their theft. Those had been the most expensive apples Kyja had ever eaten.

She'd never taken any since. But she still recalled the way out of the orchard. Lying on her belly, she wormed into the base of the hedges. Prickly branches tugged at her robe and caught at the bag of food she dragged behind her. At least there weren't any thorns. Kyja was much bigger than the last time she'd come this way, and crawling through was more difficult than she remembered.

At last she pushed aside a branch of the waxy leaves and emerged into bright sunlight on the other side. Like the tower, the orchard was set up on a hill. Lying on her stomach with her head just protruding from the foliage, Kyja could see all the way to the Goodnuffs' farm. The sun was now well into the sky, and all about Terra ne Staric the cobblestone streets were filling with horse-drawn carts and people going about their day's business. Kyja couldn't see anything out of the ordinary. But then again, she didn't know what she was looking for.

"Are you going to hide in those bushes forever? You look like a worm trying to decide if it will come out of the apple."

Kyja jumped at the unexpected voice, a nearby branch sharply poking the back of her head.

"Riph Raph! Don't sneak up on me like that," she grumped as she climbed out of the bushes and brushed herself off.

"Maybe you just weren't being observant." The skyte flapped up onto her shoulder and plucked a stray leaf from her hair.

"I was being as observant as I could. I just didn't expect a nosy skyte to land next to my head," Kyja said, straightening her scarf.

"Nosy!" Riph Raph huffed, and a ball of flame nearly singed Kyja's eyebrow. "Then I suppose you don't want to hear about what I saw flying all over the city while you were hiding under bushes."

"I'm sorry." Kyja ran a knuckle down the bumpy ridge of skin on the back of Riph Raph's head. "I'm just worried. *Did* you see anything on your flight?"

Riph Raph made a noise that was half purr, half growl, and arched his back as Kyja petted him. "Nothing except the High Lord and his guards. I wonder where they were coming back from so early in the morning. I didn't like the looks of the stranger with him. He had suspicious eyes."

"That's just your imagination. The High Lord would never consort with untrustworthy people," Kyja said. But she was still glad the orchard and hedges were between her and the High Lord's visitor. "What about the farm? Did you see anything there?"

Riph Raph gave a little sigh as Kyja stopped rubbing his back. He shook his head, making his floppy ears waggle. "Nothing except a bunch of dumb animals. The Goodnuffs are still eating breakfast. But I'd hurry if you're going to get a horse. It won't be long before Mr. Goodnuff heads out to the barn."

"Right." Kyja trotted down the hill, with Riph Raph flying just above and behind her. At the base of the hill, she cut across a field and ducked through the back of the tannery. Wrinkling her nose as she passed large, round vats of lye and stacks of cured hides, she slipped quietly past the building and hurried up the alleyway.

It felt silly to be sneaking around like a thief in the town she'd known all her life. But at the same time, something *did* feel wrong. It was probably just her imagination at work. With nothing specific to be on the lookout for, she found herself seeing menacing shadows in every doorway and watchful eyes in every window.

Maybe it was because of the boy she'd seen in the aptura discerna. Thinking back on it, she couldn't remember why she had been so sure the boy was in danger, but she *was* sure. And it seemed unthinkable that she could see his danger and not be able to do something. What was the point of seeing someone in need if you couldn't help him?

Keeping her head tucked low to her chest and her scarf pulled far down on her forehead, she hurried past the rows of shops and turned toward the western gate. Convinced that someone would stop her before she could get out of the city, she hunched her shoulders as she passed through the gate. But the guards who lounged casually to either side of the entrance barely glanced in her direction.

Once through the gate, Kyja raced along the side of the dirt road, her feet kicking up tiny plumes of dust behind her. Half a mile down the road, she turned and cut through the Broomheads' farm. Mrs. Broomhead, who was outside hanging clothing on the line, peered curiously in her direction, but Kyja didn't stop to wave. The feeling of unease was growing stronger inside her. And along with it came a sense of urgency, of something dark coming.

At the edge of the Broomheads' yard, Kyja vaulted the split-rail fence and raced through the rows of the Goodnuffs' strawberries. She was sure there would be something waiting for her inside the barn. But only the cows and horses looked up from eating their oats and hay when she entered the dark interior.

"It's about time you got here," said Sassy.

"Sorry," Kyja said, looking quickly around the shadowy building. "Has anyone other than the Goodnuffs been here since I left?"

Sassy rolled her big brown eyes, shook her head, and went back to eating her hay. Other than remembering jokes, farm animals weren't known for having long memories. But as far as Kyja could see, nothing appeared to be out of the ordinary. Still, she hurried up to the loft, gathered her few belongings and added them to her food sack.

She considered leaving a note for the Goodnuffs, but what could she tell them that would make any sense? And if someone did come along looking for her, it might be better if they didn't find a message. Instead, she climbed down the ladder and took a saddle and tack from the wall. Normally she chose Pepper when she went horseback riding, but today she needed speed. Chance, a retired war horse, was the oldest in the Goodnuffs' stable, but he was also the biggest and fastest.

Kyja carried the saddle to Chance's stall and leaned close to the big, gray-and-white stallion's ear. "Listen carefully," she whispered. "You and I are going on a trip. But I need you to be very quiet until we get outside of town. Do you understand?"

Chance studied her for a moment before nodding his big head.

"Good boy," Kyja said, and lifted the heavy saddle onto his broad back.

She was just sliding the bit into Chance's mouth when Riph Raph flew into the barn. He landed on the edge of the stall with a flurry of his little leather wings, overcorrected, and nearly fell into the hay.

"Coming!" the skyte said, panting. "Fast."

Kyja spun around, holding Chance's reins in her hand. "What's coming?" she asked, an icicle of fear forming inside her chest.

"Don't know," Riph Raph said, still trying to catch his breath. "Never seen . . . anything . . . like it before. But it's coming fast. We need to leave now."

"How do you know it's coming *here?*" Kyja asked. She was trying to stay calm, but Riph Raph's anxiety was contagious.

"Followed it." The skyte waved its wings, nearly taking flight again. "Some kind of dust cloud making a beeline for the farm. No time to talk." He flapped his wings so hard that he actually did take flight. "Come on!" he shouted so loudly the rest of the farm animals looked up to see what the commotion was.

Kyja pushed open the stall door with shaking fingers and put her foot in Chance's stirrup. Lifting her leg over the food sack she'd tied on, she climbed into the saddle. Now Chance seemed to sense something as well. He shook his head, snorted and pranced backward in the stall.

"Come on," Kyja said, urging the big horse forward with her heels. "Let's go."

Chance didn't need any further persuasion. In three quick strides, he left the stall and raced out of the barn. Kyja started to ride toward the road, but Riph Raph flew in front of her, cutting her off. "Not that way," he shouted. "Across the field, to the creek."

Kyja glanced toward the road and her heart jumped up into her throat. Less than a mile away, something was raising huge plumes of dust in the road. Whatever was making the dust was too fast to be on foot, or even on horseback. In the few seconds she watched, the cloud closed a third of the distance to the Goodnuffs' farm. And now Kyja thought she could actually feel the very ground shaking.

"I need to warn the Goodnuffs," she called. She looked toward the little house with smoke curling from its chimney.

"No time!" Riph Raph shouted, nearly hitting her with his wings as he flew about her head. "It's almost here. Besides, Master Therapass said it's *you* who's in danger."

Kyja gave one last glance toward the house before yanking at Chance's reins. Turning him toward the field, she jabbed his flanks with her heels. "Be off!" she shouted, and the big stallion sprang to life so quickly it was all Kyja could do to hang on.

Green stalks of corn passed in a blur as Kyja and Chance raced toward the creek. Over the clatter of the horse's hooves, Kyja heard the sound of the farm animals mooing, crowing, honking, and squawking. Then the animal noises were drowned out by a roar that threatened to burst her eardrums.

Clinging tightly to the reins, she glanced over her shoulder. What she saw there was so incredible she couldn't look away. Despite her fear, she yanked back on Chance's reins, and the big horse skidded to a halt, kicking up clods of dirt. The billowing cloud of dust had reached the entrance to the Goodnuffs' farm. Floating just above the road, like a giant hand poised to smash an insect, the dust cloud turned and raced up the gravel drive that led to the Goodnuffs' house.

In a patch of clover-filled meadow, midway between the barn and the house, the roaring stopped as quickly as it had started. Clenching her fists, Kyja watched as the cloud drifted slowly to the ground. She squinted her eyes, expecting something truly awful to appear. But when the dust cleared away, there was nothing to see. The ground where the cloud had been had a slightly bumpy look to it, but it was empty.

Relief flooded through her body. Maybe it was a false alarm. Maybe whatever had caused the cloud realized she was gone and changed its mind. If she returned to the farm she might be able to—

Without any warning, the meadow exploded. The ground jumped and swayed beneath Chance's hooves as dirt, rocks, and wood flew into the air. As the debris fell back to the ground Kyja felt sure her eyes must be playing some kind of trick on her. The meadow, the barn, the house; all of it was gone—reduced to a pile of splintered boards and broken stone.

"No," she gasped. At this time of the morning Mr. Goodnuff would have returned to the house from his morning chores. Mrs. Goodnuff would be in the kitchen serving breakfast to her husband and little . . . "Timton," she whispered, feeling her head begin to grow light.

As Kyja watched, three black snakes as big around as tree trunks and nearly twenty feet long slithered out of the ground and wrapped themselves into tight coils. In the blink of an eye, where the three snakes had been, three men appeared, their heads covered in dark cowls.

Before Kyja could see anything more, Chance turned and galloped into a grove of trees. With a burst of speed, the old warhorse leapt up and over the creek. Hot tears dripping down her cheeks, Kyja pressed her face against the horse's mane and held tight.

CHAPTER 15

THE GOLDEN ROPE

MAYBE THEY WEREN'T in the house at all. Maybe . . ." Kyja's words dried up as her throat tightened. She stood trembling beside Chance, whose heaving flanks were covered in sweat.

In the small willow tree where he perched, Riph Raph looked away, his bright yellow eyes damp.

"Why would they kill the Goodnuffs?" Kyja cried, rubbing her cheeks furiously with the palms of her hands. "They weren't even looking for them. They were looking for *me.*"

Riph Raph anxiously twitched his tail back and forth. "They were . . . that is . . . I don't know."

Kyja felt her legs wobble and had to grab Chance's saddle for support. She'd been riding all-out for the last half hour, sure that any minute the black snakes would rise up from the ground and swallow her whole. Even now, she fearfully scanned the open terrain around her for any sign of a dust cloud.

"Do you think they're following us?"

"I don't see any sign of them." Riph Raph shivered. "If they were, I don't think we'd be here."

Kyja walked to a nearby stream and bathed her face with handfuls of cold water. Had Master Therapass known about the huge snake things? Why hadn't he given her more warning? Maybe he thought the very idea would have frightened her so badly she wouldn't be able to leave the tower.

If so, he was right. After thirty minutes of hard riding, the town of Terra ne Staric had shrunk in the distance. But the tower rose clearly above the horizon like a giant sewing needle. Looking at it, she desperately wished she was high within its protection.

Riph Raph flapped down from the tree branch and landed beside the stream. A handful of tiny green and red flickets, drawn by the ripples from Kyja's fingertips had leapt from the water and were circling Kyja's head, flittering about on nearly transparent wings. Riph Raph snatched two of them out of the air with his beak as the rest dove back into the cover of the water.

"How can you eat at a time like this?" Kyja demanded.

"Sorry," the skyte said, crunching them between his teeth. "I was hungry."

"Why do you think Master Therapass didn't have us stay in the tower?" Kyja asked, trying to ignore the disgusting bits of fish stuck between the skyte's teeth.

Riph Raph scratched his tail with his right talon. "Maybe he didn't know what form the danger would take."

Kyja hadn't thought of that. She'd just assumed if the wizard knew Kyja was being pursued, he'd also know *what* was pursuing her. And if he didn't know about the snakes, what else might he not know about? All at once she felt incredibly alone and vulnerable. Why not head back into town? If the snakes had learned she was no

longer in Terra ne Staric, they'd go looking for her elsewhere. Master
Therapass had said so himself.

But he'd also said to keep riding until he caught up with her. She
wasn't sure how long that would be, or even how he'd know where
to look. But the wizard had been right about the danger, so she supposed she'd trust his advice on this as well.

Looking at her reflection in the rippling brook made her think
about the aptura discerna again. What did the boy she'd seen in the
window have to do with her? And why did his danger mean she was
in danger also? The only link she could see between the two of them
was the mark on the boy's shoulder and the necklace Master Therapass had given her when she was a little girl.

She slipped the amulet out from her robe and studied the image
carved into it. She'd always found it both repulsive and compelling
at the same time. What were the beasts supposed to be, and why
were they fighting with one another? She'd been grateful that Master
Therapass thought enough of her to give her such an expensive-
looking heirloom. But until today she'd never questioned why he
gave her this specific piece of jewelry.

"Those snake-men were looking for me," she said. "Do you
think the man who came after the boy in the aptura discerna was one
of them too?"

Riph Raph cocked his head. "Master Therapass said there was nothing you could do for the boy, so there's no point in worrying about it."

"I know." She rubbed the tip of her thumb across the amulet. But
she couldn't stop thinking about him. If the man she'd seen was one
of the snake creatures, the boy didn't stand a chance. So why show
her something she could do nothing about? Master Therapass had
said that the aptura discerna might help her discover the magic inside
her. Did that mean the boy had something to do with her magic?

Staring into the water, she tried to recall the boy's face. His hair had been reddish-brown and messy, as if he hadn't had it cut in months. His body looked thin and weak, but his eyes seemed filled with an inner strength. Master Therapass said that the aptura discerna was only an eye that could see into Kyja's soul. Was it possible she could find the boy on her own?

Closing her eyes, she tried to pull up the images she'd seen in the window just before the boy had appeared: Riph Raph young and helpless. Char and her children catching fish. Bella kissing Singale. They were all people she had helped. Had she somehow helped the boy, too? Or was she *supposed* to help him?

Without warning, she suddenly saw the boy again in her mind. He was still in his silver cart, only he was no longer inside the strange room. He was outside, and it was night. Something was wrong. The boy looked terrified. His mouth was open as if he were screaming.

The view shifted, and Kyja's skin went cold. Glittering in the moonlight was the black-scaled head of a snake. Its teeth gleamed wickedly. *No!* Kyja screamed in her head. The boy turned in her direction for a second as if he'd heard her. Then he reached for something in his pocket. Whatever it was, Kyja knew it wouldn't be enough. The boy was going to die unless someone helped him. The only one who *could* help him was Kyja, but she didn't know how.

I won't let you die, she screamed silently. *I won't!*

Concentrating with all her might, she tried to reach out to the boy. In her hand, the amulet burned as an image appeared in her head. It was a long, golden rope hanging just above the boy's head. She had no idea what the rope meant or how to use it, but there was no time to worry about that now. As the snake struck, she mentally pulled on the rope as hard as she could.

CHAPTER 16

AN ELASTIC ESCAPE

A MILLION DIFFERENT THOUGHTS raced through Marcus's head as the giant black snake lunged toward him, but none of them would help him escape. There was no time to run. No time to try his disappearing trick. He heard his voice screaming as though he were outside his head, but no one was close enough to help.

Then, impossible as it seemed, someone *was* there. A girl was standing beside him—a girl with long, dark hair and a green robe. As the snake's head came forward, the girl cried out, "No!"

Marcus dodged to the side, and the girl's sudden appearance seemed to throw off the snake's aim just enough that its scaly head missed Marcus's neck by inches. He could feel the snake's hot breath. Something dripped from its mouth onto the back of his arm. Instantly his skin began to burn as drops of clear liquid bubbled and hissed. He wiped his arm against the front of his shirt, watching with horror as the liquid ate through the fabric.

He looked for the girl, but she was gone. It must have been his imagination.

And yet the snake seemed to be looking for the girl as well. Its yellow eyes darted left and right as its head weaved through the night air. "A very good illusion. A much better trick than I would have thought you capable of. You are full of surprises," the snake hissed, venom dripping from its fangs in tiny, sizzling drops. "But they won't save you."

Marcus had no idea what the snake was talking about. He'd had nothing to do with the girl. But if the snake thought he did . . . ?

"I can do it again," he said. "But this time it won't just be a girl. It'll be a . . . a *monster.*"

For a moment the snake seemed to take his threat seriously. Then its eyes narrowed as it shook its diamond-shaped head. "You're bluffing. Enough of these games. It's time for you to die."

Marcus searched the wooded ground for some kind of weapon—a stick or anything he could use to defend himself.

Opening its mouth wide, the snake coiled itself and prepared to launch again.

Marcus's right hand went to his pants pocket and he felt something there. Without the time to even think about what it was, he pulled the item from his pocket and held it up before him as the snake struck.

This time the snake didn't miss.

The item Marcus held in his hands was ripped from his fingers as the snake's head connected solidly with his chest. The strike was so hard Marcus was knocked against the seat of his wheelchair and rolled backward five or six feet. And yet the snake's fangs didn't pierce him.

As the snake recoiled, Marcus looked up. Only a few feet away, the snake was swinging its broad, flat head wildly back and forth and struggling to snap its jaws. It was close enough to kill Marcus with one bite, only it couldn't see what it was doing because its head was trapped inside Marcus's extra pair of underwear.

For a moment, Marcus could only sit frozen in place, transfixed by the sight of the frustrated snake. It was so ridiculous he would have burst out laughing if he hadn't been so terrified. The beast shook its head and gnashed its teeth, but the elastic of his Fruit of the Looms stretched out and back with every movement of the snake's head.

Realizing he only had seconds until the snake managed to free itself, Marcus grabbed the wheels of his chair and raced toward the school. Behind him, he heard a ripping sound, and a moment later a hiss of rage and the slithering of scales on dirt.

As Marcus reached the edge of the trees and broke out onto open grass, he glanced backward. The snake was less than ten feet behind and gaining. Its long, black body slithered through the trees in blindingly quick undulations. At the edge of the grass, it coiled and launched itself into the air toward him.

Marcus ducked his head. Wheeling his chair with every ounce of strength he had, he squeezed his eyes shut against the strike that he knew would not miss this time. Suddenly his shoulder burned white hot, and an overpowering force rocked him forward. He tried to hang on to the arms of his chair, but his body was spinning. His stomach felt as if it were being turned inside out.

He braced himself to hit the ground. Instead, he landed in something wet and very cold. His eyes flew open, and everything was wrong. Instead of night, the sun was up. Instead of lying on the sandy grass of an Arizona ball field, he was lying half in lush, green grass, and half in an icy creek.

He turned around, looking for the snake that was about to kill him, and found himself staring into the face of a big-eyed, blue lizard. The lizard shook its scaly head, wiggling a pair of pointy ears and spoke. "Who are you?"

Scrambling deeper into the water, Marcus saw the girl he'd dreamed about. Her eyes were wide, green circles against her pale skin, and her mouth hung open with a look of terrified surprise that must have matched his. Behind the girl, a large, gray horse winked and said, "What's the difference between a duck and a boy?"

Marcus fainted.

PART 2

Discovery

CHAPTER 17

POISON POLLY

THE FIRST THING MARCUS NOTICED when he awoke was the smell. The air was a perfume of new grass, fertile soil, fresh water, and incredibly fragrant blossoms. He'd never smelled anything like it before, and he sucked it greedily into his lungs. The second thing was the quiet—no cars, airplanes, or shouting boys, just the burbling of running water and the chirping of birds somewhere nearby.

His eyes fluttered open, and he blinked against the bright sun overhead. For a moment his vision refused to adjust to the brilliant light. He sat up, and his stomach leaped as he took in his surroundings. The memories came rushing back.

"He's awake," the lizard-like thing whispered to the dark-haired girl. She nodded, watching Marcus warily from a few feet away.

Marcus lurched backwards, reached for his wheelchair, and nearly fell into a small brook.

"I waded into the water to pull you out once," the girl said. "If you fall in again, you're on your own."

Marcus looked around anxiously. Where was he? This was definitely not Arizona. He was lying in the middle of a field of tall, green grass that danced to and fro in the breeze. A few feet away, a strange-looking tree dropped fuzzy pink leaves to the ground. His wheelchair was nowhere in sight. Where was the snake that had been chasing him?

His first thought was that the snake had killed him. "I'm dead, aren't I?" he asked, rubbing his hand across his face.

"What kind of a question is that?" The lizard snorted, and a ball of what looked like blue fire came out of its nostrils. "And why are his clothes so strange?"

"Don't be rude," the girl told the lizard. She smiled hesitantly at Marcus. "You're not dead. But I think you would have been if I hadn't rescued you."

Marcus checked himself for bruises or broken bones. He didn't *feel* dead.

"I don't trust him," the lizard said. "I think he might be crazy."

"Riph Raph!" The girl swatted the lizard on the back of the head, and it rose up into the air. Shocked, Marcus realized the lizard had tiny little wings. It flew a few feet away and, with an offended glare, landed on the branch of the pink-leafed tree.

Everything looked so strange and yet so familiar at the same time. "Where am I?" he asked the girl.

She gave him an odd look. "A little north of Terra ne Staric."

"Terra ne-what?" He rubbed his head and wondered if he had passed out.

"In Westland."

"Westland?" Suddenly he realized why everything looked so familiar. "Farworld," he whispered, not even aware he was speaking.

"Of course." She nodded with an odd smile.

"That's impossible." He shook his head, trying to clear his thoughts. "I'm dreaming. This is Farworld, and you're the girl I imagine sometimes." Of course it was a dream, but his dreams had never been this real before.

"I don't know what you've imagined," the girl said, her cheeks coloring. "But you're not dreaming. I think I brought you here somehow."

As if to confirm this was indeed a dream, Marcus looked down at his legs and realized that both of them were pointing straight out before him. That was impossible. His right leg had been permanently twisted since he was a baby. Now he tried bending it, and it actually moved a little—not much, but enough that he managed to kick a small rock. And something felt different about his arm, too. It was still twisted, but he could actually open and close his fingers.

Of course, this wasn't the first time he'd dreamed of being able to move his arms and legs, but it was definitely the most vivid. In most of his *healed* dreams, his arms and legs were as perfect as those of anyone else. Better, even. But for some reason in this dream, he could only move them a little. Still, that didn't make it any less impossible.

"Maybe the snake *did* get me, and I'm dying. Or maybe the whole snake thing was a dream, too." Yes, that made sense. Men didn't turn into snakes, and burning words didn't magically change. Maybe Chet had knocked him down the stairs or hit him over the head with the mop, and he was in the hospital.

The girl shook her head, but he ignored her.

"I've never dreamed of a flying lizard before," he said.

"Lizard!" the creature yelped from his spot in the tree. He flapped his wings and puffed out another ball of fire. "I am *not* a lizard."

The girl put a hand to her mouth, only partially hiding a grin. "He's a skyte. His name is Riph Raph. Skytes hate to be called lizards. It's kind of an insult."

Marcus shook his head. "This is the strangest dream I've ever had." He tried getting to his feet and nearly toppled over. The girl hurried to his side and took his arm. His right leg didn't seem to want to hold his weight, but he was standing—at least for the moment.

Turning slowly, he looked around him. The sky was such an amazingly deep shade of blue it was like looking into the ocean. And the field looked so inviting he wished he'd dreamed of having two completely healthy legs so he could run through it. To his left, he saw what he first took to be tiny green and red insects. But no, they were *fish* flying above the surface of the brook catching even tinier insects.

On the bank, he saw a beautiful, bright yellow flower with jagged petals that looked like miniature saw blades. Putting most of his weight on his good leg, he knelt beside the flower.

"Don't!" the girl warned as he reached toward the blossom. But it was too late. Marcus touched the flower and it spit a stream of dark liquid on his finger.

"Ouch," he cried. Instantly, his finger swelled up to twice its normal size and burned like a bee sting.

He stuck his wounded finger in his mouth just as the girl warned, "Don't put it in your . . . mouth."

Now his tongue was burning too. "My mouth!" he tried to

scream, but his tongue had swollen so much that it came out as, "om mob."

"Yep. He's definitely loony," the lizard said.

The girl knelt by Marcus's side. "Put your finger in the water," she said. Taking him by the wrist, she plunged his hand into the ice-cold brook. Instantly the burning lessened, and the swelling went down. She cupped her hands into the stream and filled them with water.

"Rinse your mouth out and spit," she said, holding her cupped hands to him. "But don't swallow unless you want a really bad stomach ache."

He sipped the water from her hands, swished it around in his mouth, and spit.

"Better?" she asked.

He nodded. The pain had lessened to a dull tingling and the swelling in his tongue was beginning to go down. "Wha' ith tha'?" he asked, studying the yellow flower from a safe distance.

"A Poison Polly," the girl answered. "It's not really poisonous, but it hurts like it is, doesn't it?"

Marcus gently squeezed his throbbing finger. In dreams you were supposed to wake up when you were about to get hurt. But then he'd *never* had a dream like this. He studied the girl. She was a few inches taller than he'd imagined her, with long arms and legs and a determined, yet friendly face. Her dark hair was draped over her shoulders instead of in the ponytail she wore in his dreams. But there was no question—she was the girl he'd seen.

"Ith your name Kristen or Kelly?" His mouth felt as if he'd received a shot of Novocain.

She shook her head and laughed. "*Kris*-ten? What a strange name! I'm Kyja."

"Kyja." He carefully tried the name on his tongue. And she thought *Kristen* was a strange name? But *Kyja* seemed to fit her. "This really isn't a dream, Kyja?"

"After what I've seen today, I wish it were. But unless I'm dreaming too, I'm pretty sure it's real." She tucked a strand of hair behind her right ear. "What's your name?"

"Marcus."

"Marcus," she pronounced the name slowly and carefully as if it were difficult for her lips and tongue to form. "Where are you from?"

"Does Arizona mean anything to you?"

She shook her head with a puzzled smile.

"America?" he tried again.

"Sorry."

"How about Earth?"

This time it was the skyte that answered. "He's lying. Whoever heard of names like *Amrica* or *Ert?*"

Marcus felt a surge of anger at the skyte's mocking tone. "Until today, I'd never heard of a skyte. Does that mean *you* aren't real?"

"Never heard of a skyte? That's nonsense." The skyte flipped its little blue tail and soared off into the air.

"Ignore Riph Raph," Kyja said, waving a hand after the skyte. "He's just suspicious of people he doesn't know."

"That's all right," Marcus said, watching the odd little creature glide through the sky. "But if I'm not dreaming, how . . ." He tried standing again. This time he was able to get up by himself. But as soon as he tried to take a step, his right leg collapsed beneath him, and he fell to the ground. Still, he could move it. He could actually stand on his own. He tried unbending his left arm. It wouldn't move at all, but he found he could almost completely straighten his fingers.

"How is this possible?" he asked. "How can my arm and leg suddenly begin working?"

Kyja only shrugged her shoulders.

Leaning back on the cool grass, Marcus studied the geography of the land. The brook behind him seemed to flow from a ridge of rocky foothills far off to his left. A few yards to his right, the brook met a wide dirt road and disappeared briefly beneath a wooden bridge. Gazing in the direction the skyte had flown, he saw a glittering, white fingertip poking up from the horizon.

He remembered his dream. "That's a tower, isn't it? With a white stone balcony at the top?"

Kyja followed his gaze. "You've been here before?"

"No. But I dreamed about it. You and I were standing on the balcony, looking down at a field of purple flowers. And there were strange trees with waving branches. Then everything changed, and when I looked for you, you were gone. In your place was a man in a black robe."

"The snake man?" Kyja asked, shivering despite the warm afternoon air.

Riph Raph glided to the ground. "We need to leave. I saw something in the distance. I couldn't tell for sure, but I think it might have been the snakes we saw back at the farm."

CHAPTER 18

MAGIC AND MACHINES

ANY MORE SIGN OF THE SNAKES?" Kyja asked as Riph Raph swooped down from the sky to perch on her shoulder. She and Marcus had been riding Chance for nearly five hours while the skyte kept an eye out from the air above them. The sun, which had been directly overhead when they started, was nearly touching the woods far to the west.

"Not that I could see," Riph Raph said. "I think we lost them." He faced straight ahead, ignoring Marcus, who was seated behind Kyja—the two of them fitting easily in Chance's large saddle. At first Marcus had clung tightly to Kyja's waist, but as he became more comfortable with the horse's easy gait, he began to relax.

"You didn't fly too high, did you?" Kyja asked. They had left the road and were sticking to the rough hills and valleys, riding through the lengthening shadows of the approaching evening. But if the snakes were on the lookout for her, they might be on the lookout for Riph Raph as well.

"Of course not. I'm not crazy like *some* people." Riph Raph snorted and glared at Marcus.

Marcus grimaced. "It's a good thing there are no skytes on Earth. They would have been caught and put into cages a long time ago just so people wouldn't have to listen to them blab on and on. *Soundproof* cages."

Riph Raph stuck out his tongue and shook his head back and forth. "See what I mean? Crazy as a door beetle."

"Riph Raph, that's enough," Kyja said in a scolding tone. "If you can't be nice, then you can just go back to scouting."

"Fine." Riph Raph sunk his talons a little too tightly into Kyja's shoulder before flapping into the air. "But I wouldn't sit too close to him if I were you. It might be catching."

"Sorry," she said, glancing over her shoulder at Marcus. "I think he's still a little upset about you calling him a lizard."

"How was I supposed to know?" Marcus said. "I've never seen anything like him."

Kyja twisted around in the saddle, holding the reins loosely. "There are really no skytes on Ert?"

"Earth," Marcus corrected. "The closest thing we have are bats. But they don't blow fire or speak. *No* animals speak. Except for parrots. And they only copy what you say to them."

"Pa-rots," Kyja repeated. For the last few hours she and Marcus had been comparing notes on their two worlds.

In some ways, they'd discovered, things were very similar. When she described the Goodnuffs' farm—trying not to think about what had happened to them—he seemed to know exactly what she meant. He said he'd lived with a farm family for almost two years. But other things he told her seemed so incredible it was all she could do to keep from calling him an out-and-out liar.

"People really fly through the sky like birds on Ert?" she asked, twisting almost completely around so she could study Marcus's eyes.

"Well the *people* don't actually fly. They ride in big metal machines called *airplanes* that have long wings and sometimes leave white cloud trails behind them."

Machines. Although Marcus had used the word before, Kyja still didn't understand exactly what it meant. "These machines are some kind of magic then?"

"Magic?" Marcus laughed. "There's no such thing as magic. That's just in books and movies."

Now it was Kyja's turn to laugh. She had no idea what a *moovy* was, but even babies knew about magic. "That's ridiculous. Next thing you'll tell me you don't believe in water or air."

Marcus tilted his head as though waiting for the punchline of a joke. "You're talking about *real* magic? Not just pretend tricks?"

"Of course," Kyja answered.

"Spells and potions and things? Abracadabra, hocus-pocus, bibbidi-bobbidi-boo?"

"I don't know about hocus-pocus or bibbidi-whatever. But everyone knows about spells and potions. You act like . . ." All at once it dawned on her. "You don't have magic in your world?"

"No." Marcus began to shake his head, then seemed to reconsider. Finally he shook his head. "You're talking about making things move around by themselves and creating fire out of nothing?"

"Yes," she said, delighted by how excited he was over something as ordinary as magic.

"That is *so* cool," he said, his eyes all agog. "Can I see your wand? Do you fly on brooms and send letters with owls like Harry Potter?"

"A hairy what?" She was finding it hard to keep up.

"Never mind." He closed his eyes. "Okay, cast a spell on me. Turn me into a frog or make my nose really long."

Kyja bit her lip.

After a moment, Marcus opened his eyes. "Did you cast it already?" He felt his nose.

She shook her head. She knew she should tell him she couldn't do magic. But after making such a big deal about how common magic was in this world—and especially after all the amazing things he'd told her about *his* world—she didn't want to admit she couldn't cast even the simplest spell.

Marcus's eyes narrowed. "You were making it up, weren't you? It was all a big story to see how dumb you could make me look."

"No! I didn't make any of it up."

"Well then, prove it," he said, still looking suspicious. "Make a rock float up in the air. Or turn my hair green. Cast any spell you want . . . unless you *can't.*"

Marcus's words cut into Kyja like a knife. How dare he accuse her of lying? Especially when his world didn't even *have* magic. Of course, she knew she should tell him the truth about herself—it was only a matter of time before he found out anyway. But she couldn't bear to admit it while he was looking at her that way.

"Maybe I just don't want to," she snapped. "If I can't do magic, then explain how I brought you here. Maybe I should have left you back with the snake!" With that she turned around, not wanting him to see her hot cheeks or her trembling lips.

For the next hour, they rode silently over the small, rock-strewn rises and down through grassy valleys. Chance kept a steady mile-eating pace while Riph Raph ranged ahead and behind.

As the sun turned the distant horizon a dozen brilliant shades of red and orange, Marcus shifted in the saddle. "I'm sorry I didn't believe you could do magic," he said. "And I *am* glad you brought me here—even if I'm not really sure where *here* is."

Kyja turned back to see if he was really serious. When she saw he was, she felt even worse for letting him think she could do magic. Tomorrow she'd tell him the truth. "I'm glad you're here too. I'm still scared, but I'd be terrified if I were by myself."

Marcus looked about the landscape that contained so many things he'd never seen before. "Me too."

As he finished speaking, his stomach gave a growl loud enough that even Chance turned his head. Marcus eyed the bag tied to the back of the saddle. "That wouldn't have any food in it, would it?"

"You've never eaten Bella's cooking. You're in for a treat," Kyja said. She studied the horizon behind them and sighed. "I'd hoped Master Therapass would have caught up with us before now, but we'd probably better stop for the night."

"Good thing," Marcus said, rubbing his backside. "I think my rear end is now permanently shaped like this saddle."

CHAPTER 19

THE VISITOR

MARCUS CHEWED THE LAST BIT of meat off a chicken leg and tossed the bone up to Riph Raph, who was perched in a crooked pine tree. Riph Raph caught the bone in one talon and crunched into its marrow with his beak. Either the skyte had called a temporary truce for the night, or he just wanted Marcus's leftovers.

"That was by far the best meal I've ever had," Marcus said, wiping up the last of his beans with a corner of biscuit.

"I should hope so," Kyja said. She'd watched him polish off two chicken breasts, a pair of legs, almost half a pot of baked beans, and four biscuits. "If you keep eating like that, our food won't last two days."

"Sorry. I didn't have dinner last night—or this morning, or whenever it was." But that was only part of it. The food here, like the air, was incredible—filled with flavors and spices he didn't know existed. If restaurants on Earth served chicken like this, they'd never be able to close their doors.

He leaned back against a mossy boulder and accidentally let out a large belch. "Excuse me," he said, covering his mouth.

Not to be outdone, Kyja burped even louder. "You're excused," she said with a mischievous grin.

They both burst into gales of laughter. Marcus had no idea where he was, how he'd gotten here, or how he was going to get back home, but for the moment he felt more content than he'd ever felt in his life.

"I don't understand how the food stays warm and doesn't go bad," he said, brushing the crumbs off his metal plate into the fire. Before Kyja could answer, he held up one hand, palm out, in a stopping gesture. "Let me guess. Magic?"

Kyja only smiled.

Marcus stretched out his bad leg on the grassy meadow. His stomach was in seventh heaven, but his leg ached, and his rear felt like someone had beaten it with a baseball bat.

"Do you think your wizard friend will come tonight?" he asked. On the horse and over dinner, Kyja had told Marcus about how Master Therapass had looked out for her her whole life and about the wizard's powerful magic.

"I'm not sure," Kyja said, tugging at the chain of her necklace. "I thought he'd be here before now. I hope nothing's happened to him."

"Like what?" Marcus was fascinated by the idea of meeting a great wizard—especially one who could turn into a wolf.

She stood and tossed another stick into the fire. "Until today I would have said there was nothing that could stop Master Therapass from doing anything he wanted. But until today I'd never seen him scared. And after seeing those snakes come up out of the ground like that . . ." She shook her head, the worry clear on her face.

"Maybe he just wants to make sure no one follows him," Marcus suggested.

"I hope you're right. Maybe he waited until night so he could sneak out of the city without being noticed. He's probably on his way here now."

Marcus yawned widely. He tried to count how many hours he'd been up, but kept getting confused. He picked up his plate and fork, scooted around to the other side of the fire, and reached for Kyja's plate. "I'll take these down to the stream and wash them."

"You'd fall asleep halfway there," Kyja said with a grin. "I'll wash the plates tonight, and you can do them in the morning."

She nodded toward a spot of flattened grass near the blazing logs. "I'm sorry I didn't think to bring any blankets. But if you curl up near the fire, you should be warm enough. Riph Raph and I will keep it burning all night while we take turns on watch."

"I want to take a turn too," Marcus said.

"I don't think so." Kyja glanced out into the night that hung like a dark curtain just beyond the fire's glow and then at Marcus's twisted arm. "There are things out there you might not have in your world. The fire should keep them away. But if it doesn't, you wouldn't know what to do."

"How hard can it be? If anything comes close, I'll wake you." He stared back at her defiantly. "As long as I'm with you two, I'm doing my part. I'm a lot stronger than I look."

Kyja looked up at Riph Raph, who swallowed the last of his dinner and shrugged his wings. "The worst he can do is get us all killed."

"You're not being very nice," Kyja said, with a roll of her eyes. She studied Marcus intently. He was right. Eventually he would need to take part.

"Okay," she finally agreed. "You go to sleep, and I'll wake you when it's your turn."

"Don't forget," Marcus said. He stretched out on the ground, rested his head on his arm, and fell asleep almost instantly.

———— ◆ ————

What seemed like only minutes later, Kyja was shaking him. Marcus sat up and rubbed his eyes. Stretching, he felt as if every muscle in his body had been viciously twisted and pulled completely out of shape.

"Ugh," he grunted.

"Still sure you want to take a watch?" Kyja asked softly.

He nodded.

Kyja handed him a thick shawl that felt dewy to the touch. "It's a little damp from the night air," she said, "but it should keep you warm."

She kicked another piece of wood into the flames and helped Marcus stand up and move to a nearby fallen log.

"Any sign of the wizard?" Marcus asked.

Kyja shook her head with a worried frown.

"Get some sleep," he said. "I'm sure he'll be here by morning."

"I hope so." Kyja started toward the fire and hesitated. "Don't wander out into the darkness. Keep the fire burning at all times. And wake me up if you see or hear anything. Most of the really dangerous creatures live in the woods or the mountains, but there are plenty of things that can hurt you even here if you're not careful."

Marcus waved her back to the camp. "They can't be any worse than Chet and his friends."

She gave him an uncertain look before curling up on the spot of grass he'd just left.

Marcus pulled the shawl over his head and folded his arms beneath it. The night air was cold, but after a few minutes he began to warm up. Looking out into the darkness, he saw a white mist had risen from the ground while he was sleeping. It spun and twirled at the slightest breeze, as if it had a life of its own.

The night sky, however, was perfectly clear. As he looked up, the reality of where he was hit him like a lead fist. His stomach lurched and goose bumps rose on the backs of his arms. The stars, twinkling like gems on a bed of velvet, formed none of the constellations he was familiar with—no Big Dipper, Orion's Belt, or North Star. Even stranger, three different moons were visible in the night sky.

He wasn't just visiting a friend in another state or in some foreign country. He was on a different planet. A different solar system. Maybe even a different galaxy. The thought made him feel light-headed.

He thought about what Kyja had said about magic. She'd asked him earlier if there was magic on Earth. For a moment he'd remembered his ability to grow dim and to know things in advance. It almost seemed like magic at times. But it couldn't be. It was more of a talent. Like people who could multiply huge numbers in their head or wiggle their ears.

He turned his eyes toward Kyja, who seemed to be resting fitfully. He hadn't spent much time around girls in his life, and the few he'd met were always giggling or fussing with their hair. But this one was different. For one thing, she hadn't shied away from him because of his crippled leg and arm. Over dinner, she'd asked him about his injuries—but not in a cruel way. She'd allowed him to tell her as much as he was comfortable with and hadn't pushed any further. And she hadn't recoiled when he needed help climbing onto Chase's saddle.

He hadn't known her long—certainly not long enough to feel he could trust her. Still, she'd been brave under circumstances that would have driven most kids to tears—and probably most adults, too.

A few feet away from her, Chance was asleep in the grass, and above them both, Riph Raph perched on his tree branch with his head tucked under one wing. Marcus liked the horse. On the ride that afternoon, they had swapped jokes until Kyja told them they were driving her crazy.

He still wasn't sure about the skyte. He thought that with time, Riph Raph and he might come to be—

Something snapped behind him, and Marcus spun around. He stared out into the night, but saw nothing. Carefully, he slipped off the log and peered over it, wishing he'd thought to bring over one of the big sticks from the fire. Trying to force his eyes to adjust to the darkness, he gazed through the mist for some sign of movement. He should probably wake Kyja, but what if it was nothing?

He thought he saw a shape looming out of the night and leaned forward a little. A gust of wind parted the mist for a moment, and a pair of eyes gleamed in the silvery moonlight. Marcus jerked backward as the white curtain closed again. He glanced toward Kyja— knowing he should wake her—then back toward the spot where he'd seen the eyes.

Maybe it was the wizard.

As if it had heard Marcus's thoughts, a large black wolf emerged from the mist several yards away. Its eyes glimmered in the night.

"Master Therapass?" Marcus stammered, shrinking backward.

Instantly the figure transformed from a wolf into a stooped, old man. Marcus couldn't make out any of the man's features, but he could see the long, gray beard Kyja had described.

"Put out the fire," the man commanded without coming any closer.

"What?" Marcus looked over his shoulder, hoping Kyja would wake up.

"The fire," the man said more urgently. His voice sounded gravelly and out of breath. "Put it out now. They're only a few minutes behind me. Extinguish the light before they see it. You haven't any time to waste."

"Right." Marcus scurried as fast as he could, picked up a pot Kyja had left to soak overnight, and dumped water onto the fire. The flames diminished as steam rose into the air.

"More," the man called out.

Marcus began throwing handfuls of dirt onto the fire.

"What's going on?" Kyja sat up, rubbing her eyes.

"The wizard is here," Marcus said, continuing to put out the fire.

"Master Therapass?" Kyja looked up as the man moved forward out of the shadows.

"No!" she screamed.

Marcus turned from the smoldering fire and froze. In the shadows, at a distance, the figure had looked like an old man. But now he was much closer, and Marcus could see something was horribly wrong. The beard was not a beard at all, but merely a waggling piece of gray flesh shaped like a beard. And above it, the man's face was a blank white surface with just a hint of where eyes and mouth should be.

Marcus reached for a stick, but before he could move, the figure disappeared from sight—replaced by a large, menacing shape. Something shot out of the darkness, and a hot and sticky substance wrapped around Marcus, pinning him in place.

CHAPTER 20

THE MIMICKER

WRAPPED INSIDE A NET of thick, sticky cords, Kyja watched the massive creature make its way toward them. A few feet away, she could hear Marcus panting as he tried to fight his way loose.

"Stop struggling," she whispered. "The more you fight, the tighter it gets."

She was afraid he would keep fighting anyway. Many people did, trying to break free until they could no longer breathe. "If you relax, the web won't be so tight."

Finally he stopped moving, although she could still hear his rough breathing. She couldn't blame him. It took everything she had to keep from clawing at the sticky ropes herself.

"What is that thing?" Marcus gasped.

"A mimicker. It reads your thoughts and creates an image of what you're thinking about."

"I thought it was Master Therapass. It told me to put out the fire." Marcus sounded as if he was trying not to panic. Kyja couldn't blame him. The creature was almost to their campsite now. From the pincers of its armored legs to the top of its multi-eyed head, it was taller than Chance and nearly twice as long.

A segmented tail was tucked against its back, and a pair of thick, wicked-looking claws waved back and forth before it, testing the air.

"It wanted the fire out because it can't stand the light." Kyja tried to keep her voice composed, but her heart was racing. Because of their sensitivity to light, mimickers stayed in their underground nests during the day and normally avoided any type of illumination at night. That this one had approached their camp meant it was either sick or very, very hungry. And as far as she knew, mimickers only ate live food.

Kyja slipped her fingers through an opening in the web, trying to reach a piece of wood she could throw onto the embers, but she was too far away. She glanced up at the empty tree branch above her. Riph Raph was gone.

Avoiding the fire pit, the mimicker lifted Kyja's food bag with one of its thick claws and examined the sack with its many eyes before tossing it aside.

"Cast a spell," Marcus cried out. The creature turned and trundled toward him. Its armored plates rubbed against each other, making a soft clicking sound. "Please!"

Kyja licked her lips, desperately trying to think of some way out of this.

The mimicker stopped just above where Marcus lay pinned to the ground. It tilted its massive head and leaned down, studying him. Kyja could hear Marcus gasping for breath. It wouldn't be long before he lost all control and the net shut so tightly around his chest he wouldn't be able to breathe. The mimicker closed its claw on Marcus's leg and lifted him into the air.

"Do something!" he screamed to Kyja. "Use your magic."

Kyja pushed at the webbing; instantly it tightened around her. She ripped at the thick strands with her teeth even though she knew it was hopeless. "I can't!" she wailed, tears burning in her eyes.

The mimicker swung Marcus back and forth like a toy on the end of a string. "What do . . . you mean . . . you *can't?*" Marcus's voice was hoarse with pain and terror.

"I can't do magic." Kyja sobbed. She should have admitted it from the start. She never should have let Marcus take a watch by himself. This was all her fault.

The mimicker opened its giant mandibles. A soft keening sound came from deep within its throat. Marcus screamed as the creature raised him to its mouth. Kyja clamped her eyes shut.

All at once a high-pitched screech filled the air, and a bright light flashed through Kyja's closed eyelids. She forced her eyes open just in time to see a blue ball of flame explode on top of the mimicker's head.

The mimicker raised its claws to protect its eyes. Still holding Marcus, it began to back away. Another fireball shot out of the darkness. This one struck the creature on its exposed tail. It spun around, searching for its attacker.

A flurry of wings and a long blue tail appeared out of the night sky as three more fireballs hit the mimicker in rapid succession.

"Riph Raph!" Kyja shouted.

The skyte wheeled about in mid-air, let out a terrific roar for such a small creature, and dove directly at the mimicker's head. At the last minute, he coughed out a ball of flame that struck the mimicker directly in its sensitive eyes, and rose back into the air.

With a wail of pain, the mimicker flung Marcus aside.

Riph Raph turned to make another run, and the mimicker suddenly rose up on its back legs.

"Look out!" Kyja screamed. But it was too late. As Riph Raph banked away, the mimicker lifted one of its huge black claws and knocked the skyte out of the air. Riph Raph crashed to the ground in a crumpled heap near Marcus.

At once, the mimicker was after the skyte, snapping its claws with vicious fury. Riph Raph tried to take flight, but his left wing flapped uselessly.

Kyja struggled, helpless in her webbing. But the net which trapped Marcus had been cut slightly by the mimicker's claw.

As the mimicker descended on Riph Raph, Marcus managed to get his left leg free and shove it in front of the beast. The mimicker stumbled over Marcus's raised foot. Roaring with rage, it opened its mouth and plunged toward Marcus.

At that moment, an explosion rocked the air, and a whirlwind of blue and green flames shot up from the fire pit. The mimicker squealed and swung its head away from the light. Into the fire's glow leapt a huge, gray wolf. Swiftly rotating its backside toward the wolf, the mimicker shot a string of sticky web.

As if it knew what was coming, the wolf ducked under the web and charged.

Instantaneously, the mimicker was replaced by a slasher, a creature Kyja had heard of but never actually seen. Nearly twice as tall as the mimicker, the slasher had two snarling heads—one at each end of its body—and six claw-like legs. Covering its muscular body, dozens of ropey, bristled limbs swung wildly about in the air. As Kyja watched, one of the limbs snapped like a whip at the wolf.

With a sharp bark, the wolf leapt aside, narrowly avoiding the whip which dug a deep groove in the ground at its feet. A second later, another whip barely missed the wolf's head.

Before the slasher could strike a third time, the wolf snapped its teeth closed on the creature's limb, tearing off its tip. Black fluid gushed from the open wound.

The slasher gave a horrible shriek. Again it changed, this time into an ugly, toad-shaped monster with four large, watery eyes and a squat body covered with heavily-armored plates. One of its legs had a deep red gash in it.

With a wet-sounding, "Grok, grok," the monster opened its mouth and spat a stream of vile liquid onto the wolf. Immediately the wolf's fur began to smoke. Wailing, the wolf rolled about on the grass until its fur stopped smoking.

The monster opened its mouth again, but the wolf leaped forward and ripped at the monster's eyes with sharp claws.

The mimicker assumed another shape before it could be damaged further. Covered with a thick pelt of coarse fur, the new beast stood eight-feet tall or more. Long, muscular arms hung nearly to its knees. Its head looked as if someone had jammed a pebbly-skinned melon onto its neck and gouged out the eyes and a mouth using only their fingers.

Although the mimicker had changed forms, the damage from the wolf still carried over. Its right leg was bleeding quite badly and one of its eyes was closed in a small, dark slit.

Dropping onto all fours, the beast leapt up the side of the hill and wrapped its long arms around the log where Marcus and Kyja had sat keeping guard. Kyja was sure the log must weigh twice as much as the creature, and yet it lifted it into the air effortlessly.

Growling deep in its throat, the wolf crouched low and approached the mimicker with great care. The beast swung the log. Again the wolf leapt, narrowly avoiding the blow. But as it landed, its left rear leg gave out.

At once the hairy creature was upon it. Kyja watched, terrified, as the mimicker knocked the wolf to the ground. With a howl, the wolf rolled back to its feet. The creature swung the log again, hitting the wolf in the side of its ribs with a terrible crunch and sending it sprawling toward the fire.

"No!" Kyja shouted.

The mimicker bounded down the hill toward the wolf and raised the log above its head for a killing blow.

With a roar of rage, the wolf sprang away from the crashing log. A silver blur in the darkness, it darted between the creature's legs and snapped at its ankle. Screaming, the creature spun around, trying to reach its attacker. But the wolf slipped behind it. Another flash of teeth, and the beast dropped its log as its leg collapsed.

The wolf attacked. The mimicker began to change so rapidly it was impossible to keep up. Big creatures and small. Some with wings. Some with horns. One that seemed to be nothing but smoke.

But each time it changed, the wolf was on top of it, biting, snarling, and scratching. Furiously darting in and out, the wolf seemed to be everywhere—in front of the mimicker, behind it, ripping at its head and body.

At last, badly injured and barely able to see, the mimicker returned to its original shape. The beast raised its claws to attack, but the wolf was too quick. Plunging between the creature's deadly pincers, the wolf launched itself into the air, and clamped its sharp fangs on the unprotected flesh directly beneath the mimicker's jaw.

As the mimicker collapsed to the ground, the wolf shook its furry head, staring at the fallen beast with deadly eyes. Sitting back on its haunches, it raised its grizzled muzzle to the three moons and howled.

Master Therapass had arrived.

CHAPTER 21

THE BLAME GAME

I WOULDN'T BELIEVE IT if I wasn't seeing it with my own eyes," Master Therapass said, studying Marcus as though half convinced he were some kind of illusion.

Marcus felt himself blush under Master Therapass's scrutiny.

The old man looked from Marcus to Kyja and back again, shaking his head. "The two of you. Here. Together."

"How about paying some attention to me?" Riph Raph piped up from where he lay on the wizard's lap.

Marcus watched closely as Master Therapass ran his gnarled fingers over Riph Raph's injured wing.

"Hasn't anyone ever told you that skyte fire is more appropriately used for lighting tinder than attacking beasts one hundred times your size?" the wizard asked as he probed and prodded.

"Hmphh," Riph Raph grunted. "I would've had that thing if it hadn't broken my wing. A lucky hit."

"Indeed." Master Therapass nodded, his beard waggling to and fro. "I have seldom seen man or beast acquit himself more bravely than you did with that mimicker. I believe you would have subdued the creature even if I hadn't arrived when I did."

The wizard took an intricately-carved silver ball from the pocket of his robe and rolled it gently over Riph Raph's wing, mumbling words Marcus couldn't understand. A moment later, the skyte's wing briefly glowed red.

"Better?" Master Therapass asked, returning the ball to his robe.

Riph Raph hesitantly extended his wing, then gave it a more confident flap. "Wahoo!" he cried, launching himself into the air. "It's good as new. Better than new!"

Marcus watched with wide-eyed wonder as the skyte soared up into the sky, flying like its wing had never been damaged. Glancing down at his bent arm, he started to speak, then pressed his lips together and looked away.

Master Therapass rubbed his beard and studied Marcus with a perceptive—and somehow sad—look in his eyes. "I believe I know what you wish to ask," he said, his voice soft. "And I fear the answer is not what you might hope for. But please ask anyway, as I am perhaps the only one capable of providing you with the answer. I am certainly culpable for my actions."

"Culpable?" Marcus asked.

"It means guilty. And I am afraid I have much to answer for, to both you and Kyja."

From her spot on a log several yards away, Kyja looked up briefly before returning to fingering the folds of her robe.

"You don't have anything to answer for to *me*," Marcus said. "You've never even met me before."

Instead of responding, Master Therapass looked to the east, where the sun was just beginning to cast a golden halo over the highest peaks of the snow-capped mountains. "Have you ever heard the dawn chimes greet the morning?"

Marcus looked out over the meadow he and Kyja had ridden across the previous evening. Barely illuminated by a sky which was still the gray of fading night, purple flowers with blossoms shaped like tiny bells were rising up out of the grass. "Just like in my dream," he whispered.

"Listen carefully," the wizard said, with a wistful smile.

Looking from the wizard to the flowers that were now beginning to appear all over, Marcus strained to hear, wondering what he was listening for. At first there was nothing. And then—like a single silver bell so far away its ring barely carried to where he was sitting—he thought he heard a note of perfect clarity.

A moment later, another note joined in—slightly different, but so close the two notes immediately joined together, forming a completely new chord. Just as it seemed the chord was about to fade away, another flower joined in, then a fourth. At first the music was so pure, Marcus thought he was listening to some sort of instruments but as it began to rise and swell, he realized they were actually voices singing.

"I once knew a man who told me dawn chimes are fairies who put down roots so they could be the first to welcome every new day," Master Therapass said. "He claimed to be able to understand their song. Perhaps if you focus hard enough, you'll be able to understand some of it as well."

Closing his eyes, Marcus concentrated on the melody. One minute it swirled and broke like a stream dashing itself against rocks and boulders. The next minute it was a baby bird being pushed from the nest for the first time.

Images began to form and combine in his mind. A breath of

morning mist turned into a white cloud sailing across an azure sky. A falling leaf changed into a red-eyed frog that leaped and became a running child who raised her hands and was swept into a flock of the most glitteringly colorful birds Marcus had never seen.

As the music swirled about him, he thought he could almost make out words. They were right there—so close he could nearly touch them. And yet the harder he tried to make them out, the more they eluded him. Opening his eyes, he saw the blossoms nodding back and forth in a dance that didn't seem in time with the music at all. It was almost as if—

Suddenly he had it. They weren't dancing *to* the music, they were dancing *with* the music. Motion and sound together formed an elaborate arrangement. Letting it wash over him, he discovered that he was getting snippets of the song—words and phrases that overlapped rather than proceeded one after the other.

A new creation . . . glory to all . . . noble . . . made clean . . . again . . . hope renewed . . . everlasting . . . cherish the light . . .

Suddenly he could swear he heard the voices say his name. But that was crazy.

He glanced toward the wizard and saw he was beaming.

"Did you get any of it?" Master Therapass asked.

Marcus nodded. "Yes. I think so. At least a part." He felt as if he had just been bathed in warm sunlight even though the sun was barely peeking above the mountain tops.

"I believe the man who told me about the dawn chimes would be glad to hear that," the wizard said, wiping the back of his hand across his eyes. "He sacrificed his life so *you* could hear their song."

"I don't understand," Marcus said. The dawn chimes had finished their singing—the blossoms bowing down out of sight until the next morning—but he could still hear their voices in his head. It made him feel wonderful but a little woozy.

"All in due time," the wizard said. "First, I could use a good meal." He removed a gray traveling cloak from his shoulders and swirled it over the ground. Three chairs and a table—complete with place settings, crystal goblets, and covered silver chafing dishes—appeared out of nowhere. There was even a small plate with three whole fish on it for Riph Raph.

"Wow!" Marcus gawked. "Do you think *I* could ever learn to make food appear?"

Master Therapass chuckled as he took his seat at the table. "We'll have to see about that. But I've yet to meet a boy your age who couldn't make a plateful of food *dis*appear. Especially when it comes courtesy of the lovely and talented Bella. By the way, Kyja, Bella asked me to tell you . . ."

The wizard turned toward Kyja, his expression clouding when he realized she was still seated on the log on the other side of the clearing—her eyes locked on the ground at her feet.

"Aren't you going to join us?" he asked.

"I'm not hungry," she said.

Master Therapass got up from the table and walked to where she sat. "You're not blaming yourself for what happened with the mimicker, are you?"

Marcus blinked. He wouldn't dream of saying it out loud, but a part of him *did* blame Kyja—at least a little. Why hadn't she told him she couldn't do magic in the first place? And why hadn't she warned him about things like the mimicker?

"I'm useless," Kyja said, without looking up. "We all could have died, and it was my fault."

"Useless?" Master Therapass furrowed his brow as he raised himself up to his full height. In the wizard's dark eyes, Marcus saw the same fire he'd seen in the wolf's eyes.

"Do you have any idea what would have happened to this boy if it wasn't for you?" the wizard thundered. "I've been trying in vain for the last thirteen years to find a way to bring him here. Frankly, I'd just about given up hope, and I don't have the faintest clue how you managed to achieve it. But I can tell you without the slightest doubt that by bringing him here, you saved his life, and I suspect you may have saved it again last night."

Marcus gulped as Master Therapass turned his stony gaze in his direction. "How did you know not to struggle inside the mimicker's web?"

"Kyja w-warned me," Marcus stammered.

"And did she not tell you to keep the fire lit?"

Marcus wilted under the wizard's scrutiny. He felt like a jerk. After all, Kyja *had* warned him to keep the fire burning. She'd also told him to wake her at the first sign of trouble. But he'd assumed he could handle anything that came up. And he hadn't even thought to thank her for saving his life from Bonesplinter. He hung his head.

As the wizard looked from Marcus to Kyja—both of whom wore abashed expressions—a trace of a smile crossed the old man's face. "I'm not sure I've ever seen two sorrier looking travelers in my life. Come sit at the table, and I'll tell you a story that is long overdue."

CHAPTER 22

SIGNS

NEARLY THIRTEEN YEARS AGO to the day," Master Therapass said, popping a forkful of sausage into his mouth, "a wizard and a warrior of some small renown set out together for a town called Windshold in the far northern reaches of Valdemeer."

Kyja started. Though she couldn't remember exactly where she'd heard of Windshold, the name gave her a cold feeling in the pit of her stomach.

Noting her uneasiness, Master Therapass nodded. "I imagine the stories have carried even this far. Dark tales seem to have a much farther reach than light."

All at once she had it. "The city of the dead where everyone was—"

"Yes," Master Therapass cut in with a warning look in her direction. "But back then, Windshold was a town not so much different from Terra ne Staric. Smaller, to be sure, and with a higher ratio of soldiers to citizens, as is the case with most border outposts, but other than that, perfectly ordinary.

"In the normal course of events, the wizard and the warrior might never have visited the town except in passing. But an occurrence of possible interest to the tower reached the High Lord of Terra ne Staric, and he thought it worthwhile to perform at least a minimal investigation."

Master Therapass laid down his fork and pushed his mostly uneaten food aside with a sigh. "I must tell you that at the time, the incident was viewed as a misunderstanding at best, and more than likely a complete hoax. This in no way excuses the behavior of the wizard or the warrior. But you must understand. If they'd had even an inkling that the story might be true, armies would have been sent instead of only two men."

"I don't understand," Kyja said, pushing away her food as well. "What was the event and why would the tower send armies?"

Master Therapass spread his hands wide. "Not just the tower. Every town and city within a hundred days' ride would have sent representatives. You see, a story—a myth, most people believe—has been passed down from parents to children from so long ago that no one knows where it started.

"According to the story, when Farworld was created, each living thing was granted its own part and parcel. Winged creatures were given the sky. Swimming creatures the water. The land was divided equally between the plants, the beasts of the field, and man. Some were granted the forests, some the plains, some the deserts, and some to burrow in the ground."

"Sounds fair to me," Marcus said, piling more eggs, bacon, and toasted bread onto his plate. He and Riph Raph were the only ones who seemed to still have plenty of appetite.

"It does," Master Therapass continued, giving Marcus a level look. "But according to the story, a day would come when the inhabitants of the world were no longer satisfied with what they had. When they would make war upon each other in an attempt to take more than their fair share. And when that day came, their strife would open the door to a terrible power. A darkness would fall upon the world that would threaten to destroy everything."

"What kind of power?" Kyja asked leaning closer. "There isn't any darkness here."

"We tend to judge the world by what we see closest to home," the wizard said. "Terra ne Staric has been affected only minimally so far—a slightly longer winter, crops and animals producing a little less. But the darkness *has* taken hold far from here, and like a disease, it spreads quickly. You helped Singale find a job in the kitchen when he lost an arm. But did you ever think to wonder why he was battling Rock Giants in the first place? They are generally a peaceful race."

Kyja shook her head, wondering what else she had failed to notice.

"It's an easy mistake to make—assuming all is well because the danger isn't under our nose. I, along with the other wizards in Terra ne Staric, believed the same thing thirteen years ago. So when word of a sign came from a small town in the middle of nowhere, no one really believed it."

"What sort of sign?" Marcus asked, shoving food into his mouth.

The wizard tugged at his beard. "As I said, there are many different variations of the story. But all of the versions seem clear that when the time of darkness comes, a special child would be born."

The wizard bowed his neck, rubbing his forehead. "The wizard and the warrior—thinking they were on a fool's errand—took their time getting to the city. But another group did not. And by the time the wizard and the warrior reached Windshold, the gates that had held for hundreds of years were thrown down and . . ."

"Everyone was dead," Kyja whispered, her face a sickly gray.

"*Nearly* everyone," the wizard said. Kyja thought his normally gentle eyes looked like bottomless pits. "The wizard and the warrior searched the city from top to bottom, hoping someone had survived to tell them what had happened—what could have destroyed an entire city so quickly and efficiently. Unfortunately the only survivor could tell them nothing. Buried beneath the dead body of the Captain of the Guard, they found a baby—the only living person in Windshold. The child from the legend."

"How could you know it was the right baby?" Marcus asked.

"A fair question," the wizard said. "There is only one way. The story speaks of a symbol—signifying the battle had begun."

"A symbol?" Kyja suddenly leapt from her chair and pulled the amulet from inside her robe. "The battle for the world between the creatures of air, land, and sea. This is it, isn't it? The sign. See? All the different creatures fighting with each other."

Marcus choked on a piece of bacon when he saw what was on Kyja's necklace. "Where did you get that?" he said.

Master Therapass nodded. "The symbol you both carry is the sign of the great battle. A symbol found on only the most ancient of documents. Until that day, I had never actually seen it for myself. When the High Lord heard that such a sign was rumored to have been found in the city of Windshold, he sent the wizard and the warrior to investigate. Everyone assumed, of course, that nothing would come of it. After all, where was the proof? Where was the *dark power?*"

"Who was the baby?" Marcus gasped.

"I thought you would have guessed." Master Therapass looked from one of them to the other. "It was you, Marcus."

CHAPTER 23

BALANCED SCALES

HAT'S CRAZY," MARCUS SAID, bursting into laughter. "I've never even been to Farworld before yesterday. I was found by the monks in Sonora, Arizona."

Master Therapass tugged at his beard, his expression unreadable. "I am the one who sent you there."

Marcus felt like someone had just hit him on the side of the head with a brick. "You . . . you what?" The world seemed to be spinning, and he clutched the edge of the table to keep from falling.

"I was the wizard sent by the tower. And Tankum, my best friend and survivor of battles too numerous to count, was the warrior."

"*Tankum Heartstrong?*" Kyja asked. "The one whose statue is just outside the west gate?"

Master Therapass nodded. "The same."

"But he's been dead for . . ."

"Thirteen years. When Tankum and I discovered Marcus, we thought at first he was dead. Seeing the brand on his arm, we understood he could be the child spoken of in the legend and despaired that we were not in time. Then the baby gave a cry, and we realized he was still alive. I tried to heal him but, like the rest of the inhabitants of that poor, doomed city, he had been attacked by a power which I quickly discovered my magic could not touch.

"As soon as I realized dark magic was at work, Tankum and I tried to take the child and flee. It was too late. We had wondered what kind of army could destroy an entire city without leaving behind any of its own dead. We quickly learned the answer.

"Out of the ground rose hundreds—thousands—of Fallen Ones. Men and beasts whose bodies had died, but whose spirits had been brought back by a wizard more powerful and terrible than anyone could imagine—venomous spiders, mutated hounds, things which were nothing but teeth. Leading them all were three dark wizards known as Thrathkin S'Bae. Literally translated as *masters of the dead who walk,* they are servants of the Dark Circle. It was as if we had suddenly been surrounded by a blanket of thick, black smoke which attacked us from all sides with teeth, claws, and blades.

"Tankum fought ferociously. Whirling and slashing—ancient swords gripped tightly in both hands—he actually managed to force the dark legion back for a moment. Holding the child in my arms, I protected Tankum with my magic as best as I could, clearing our path with lightning bolts. But before we were halfway to the south wall, we realized our efforts were in vain. For every creature we cut down, three more rose up from the ground to take its place. The only way to save Marcus was to send him somewhere the dark wizard couldn't follow."

"Ert," Kyja said.

"Yes." Master Therapass looked to the sky, and Marcus saw tears were dripping down the old wizard's wrinkled cheeks. "Opening a door to another world is a risky proposition at best. Less than a handful of wizards possessed the knowledge at the time, and until yesterday, I'd have sworn I was the only one left alive who retained the ability. Tankum knew I would not be able to protect him while attempting the spell, yet without a moment's hesitation, he pushed the child and me against the wall of a ruined tavern and stepped between us and the horde to make his final stand.

"As I knelt before the wall—shielding the child from the dark creatures while I prepared the spell—I could hear the furious battle raging behind me. Once I glanced over my shoulder and saw Tankum wielding his swords while three pitch-black creatures hung from his body by needle-sharp teeth. Blood dripped from more wounds than I could count, and the tip of the sword in his right hand had been shattered.

"I started to drop the doorway spell and began to transform into a wolf. Tankum sensed what I was doing and gave a shake of his massive head. Then he winked, ripped two of the creatures from his body, and dove back into the fray.

"When I realized he had no intention of coming out of the battle alive, I committed myself to completing the spell as well as I could, so his death—and mine—would not be futile. I thought my spell had failed. But all at once the air around my head began to waver and sparkle. The clouds overhead went black and filled with electricity.

"At the time I was not sure the doorway opened to the world I was attempting to reach. But as the air ripped open before me, Tankum finally went down, and the creatures swarmed over him. With no time to see where I was sending him, I pushed the baby through the portal and released the spell.

"The doorway slammed shut with a clap of thunder, and I

turned to save Tankum or lose my life trying. But as one, the creatures sank back into the ground—apparently realizing their prey was out of reach. Tankum lay stretched upon the blood-soaked street, sword hilts still clasped in both hands. Unable to stand, I crawled to where he had collapsed. At first I thought he was dead; no man could take the kind of injuries he had and live.

"But then his right hand released its sword and found my arm. 'Is the child safe?' he asked with the last of his strength.

"When I nodded, he squeezed my arm one final time as the life slipped out of him."

Marcus sat stunned, trying to absorb everything he had just heard. "He died saving me," he whispered.

The wizard nodded.

Marcus swallowed. It was too much. "I . . . That is . . ." He wiped his hand across his lips, trying to collect his thoughts. "Do you know my name? My *real* name?"

Master Therapass shook his head. "The tower wasn't provided a name. Only that a child had been born. I returned to the city to search for information about you, but if any records existed before the Dark Circle arrived, they were stolen or destroyed."

"And my . . . parents?"

"I'm sorry."

"Then they really are dead," Marcus said, feeling numb all over. Over the last few years he'd pretty much come to that conclusion himself, but to hear it stated as cold fact . . . He rubbed his hands on his pants.

"Why did you leave him on Ert?" Kyja asked. "Why not bring him back once you were safely at the tower?"

"It's a mistake I've regretted ever since." Master Therapass grimaced. "I can blame it on the speed with which I had to create the door or the limited amount of knowledge we have of such passage-ways. But the truth of the matter is, I miscalculated. You see, in order to move a person from one world to another, you must balance the scales."

"What scales?" Kyja asked, shaking her head.

"The Scales of Order. From what little I had been able to dis-cover about creating portals, I understood that to send Marcus to Earth, I would have to take a person back. A person of equal value to what I sent. In simple terms, I performed a trade—a person destined to change the future of this world for a person destined to change the future of the world I sent him to."

Master Therapass rubbed his palms together as though trying to wash them with thin air. "I assumed the trade would only be for a brief time. No more than a matter of minutes, if I survived. Days, if another wizard needed to perform the return spell. My mistake was in assuming I could send the other person back to Earth, and thus return our child to this world. But you see, the person I summoned here could not be returned."

"Why not?" Kyja asked.

Master Therapass studied her carefully before answering. "I could not send her back because she was immune to magic. The per-son I traded Marcus for was you, Kyja."

———◇———

Now it was Kyja's turn to feel as if she'd just been slapped. *She was from Ert? A world of flying machines and strange clothing? A place where magic was only for little children?* The idea terrified her and angered her all at the same time.

"Why didn't you tell me?" she demanded, feeling her face grow hot.

"I wanted to." Master Therapass reached for Kyja's hand, but she pulled it away.

"You let me think I was a *mutant*. You pretended to be my friend." She felt betrayed by the person she trusted most in the world. "How could you do that to me?"

The wizard let her take her anger out on him before saying, "It was the only way to protect you."

She blinked. "I don't understand. How could lying protect me?"

Confused, she now allowed Master Therapass to take her hand. "As soon as I brought you to this world, I knew I must keep your identity a secret. If word got out of what I'd done, your life would be in great danger. As long as you were alive, there was the possibility I might discover a way to bring Marcus back. If you were dead, it would be impossible to balance the Scales of Order. Marcus would never be able to return. The forces of darkness would prevail.

"I never even told the High Lord or the other members of the council. I let them think that Tankum and I had discovered nothing. Kyja was simply an orphan, a child who survived the attack."

"But what about my family?" Kyja asked, her head spinning. "Do my parents even know what happened to me?"

"I'm sorry. If I'd only known." The wizard shook his head, his face looking older than Kyja could ever remember. "It's no excuse. The worst thing a wizard can do is practice magic he does not understand. If there was any way to undo what I've done . . ."

Master Therapass buried his face in his hands.

For a moment the three of them sat in quiet thought. Then Kyja reached out to the wizard, gently pulling his hands away from his face until she could look into his tired eyes. "It's all right. I forgive you."

Master Therapass squeezed her small hands with his long, wrinkled fingers. "If there is any way. *Any* way to get you home again."

Kyja gave an understanding nod.

"There's one thing I don't get," Marcus said. "What was so important about the child? If I really am the child from the legend, what am I supposed to do that would make the Dark Circle want to kill me?"

Master Therapass sighed. "Every version of the story has two different endings. In one version the child turns back the dark evil and restores order to his world." The wizard closed his eyes and spoke as if repeating memorized lines. *"He shall make whole that which was torn asunder. Restore that which was lost. And all shall be as one."*

"And in the other?"

The old man studied Marcus with sadness in his eyes. "In the other ending—the ending spoken of only in the quietest of whispers around fires late at night—the child joins the forces of darkness, and Farworld is destroyed."

CHAPTER 24

QUESTIONS AND ANSWERS

SOMETHING DOESN'T MAKE SENSE," Kyja blurted out. Marcus and Master Therapass turned in her direction. "If the only way to bring Marcus back was to send me to Ert—"

"Earth," Marcus corrected, but Kyja just waved her hand.

"If the only way to bring Marcus back was to send me to . . . Er-at," she tried to pronounce it the way Marcus had, but it still came out sounding like *Ert*. "Then how are Marcus and I both here?"

As Master Therapass stood, the food and place settings disappeared from the table. "That is one of the things I need to discover," he said. "I have a hunch. If I am right, Marcus's time here may be shorter than you think, and he still has much to do. I must return to the tower at once and search every scrap of information on the subject."

"You're leaving?" Kyja and Marcus said together.

"What are *we* supposed to do?" Kyja asked.

"What do you mean, my time here may be shorter than you think?" Marcus demanded, slapping his hand on the table.

Master Therapass held both hands in front of him, palms out. "Your questions will have to wait. I must go back to the tower at once. It would not be wise for my absence to be noticed right now. And it would be extremely dangerous for either of you to come with me. As far as I can tell, the Thrathkin S'Bae have lost your trail. But if they find out about Marcus's presence here, that will change quickly.

"Just over a day's ride north is the Westland Woods. You will be safe there until I return. If my suspicions prove correct, you will need answers I cannot provide. But there is one who may be able to help you. When you reach the forest, seek out Olden. I will send word ahead to expect you."

"Who is this Olden person?" Marcus asked.

The wizard chuckled. "Olden is not a person. Olden is a tree— the most ancient in Westland and the first of the Weather Guardians. Olden has watched generations of man come and go. If there are answers to be found, that is the first place you should look."

As Master Therapass turned to leave, Kyja stepped in front of him, arms folded across her chest, jaw set. "You can't just tell us a story like that and then leave," she said. "I've got a million questions."

The wizard rubbed his chin and smiled down at her. "Very well, little one. I don't have time for a million. But I'll try and answer one question for each of you before I go."

Kyja didn't have to consider which question she wanted answered most. She'd been thinking about it ever since Master Therapass told her she was really from Ert. "In the tower, you promised me I had magic. But now you tell me I am from a planet that doesn't have magic. Why did you lie?"

The wizard scratched at something in his beard, and a small, glittering orange and gold insect buzzed angrily before crawling out from between the long whiskers and flying away. "I've been known to trim my beard less often than I should. I have been accused more than once—and rightfully so—of acting before thinking things through. But I never lie."

His eyes darkened as his face grew stern. "You *do* have magic, Kyja. Every person on every world has magic. Some just forget how to use it, or neglect it for so long that it withers away and dies. Do not think for a minute that because your magic is less obvious it does not exist. If you won't take my word for it, consider this:

"When I opened the doorway that sent Marcus to Earth, I knew another person would be brought to this world—it was demanded by the Scales of Order. But it wasn't until I returned to the tower that I discovered who had taken his place here. You were drawn to this world precisely because of the strength of the magic you possess and your importance to the future of Earth."

"But then, why—"

Master Therapass raised a hand, cutting her off mid-sentence. "It is not wise to examine your own magic too closely. Let it show itself when it will." He turned to Marcus, who sat quietly at the table. "Your question?"

Marcus swallowed and rubbed his bad leg as though trying to muster up his courage. "When I was on Earth, I couldn't move my leg or arm almost at all. But here . . ." Marcus opened and closed the fingers of his left hand and, pulling himself up on the edge of the table, took a hesitant, limping step forward.

"Most intriguing," the wizard said. "One thing that has always troubled me is how you managed to survive the Dark Circle's first attack when you were an infant. The injuries you sustained should have killed you. The Fallen Ones destroyed every living thing except the one person they came in search of."

Marcus's face paled, and Kyja noticed how his hand unconsciously went to his bad leg.

"At the time, I assumed it was simply an almost unbelievable oversight," Master Therapass continued. "The creatures which attacked the child assumed he was dead and left without making completely sure. It never set quite right with me, but what other explanation was there?"

Marcus shrugged. "But now you don't think so?"

"I've always known there was a connection between the future of the child in the legend and the future of Farworld. What I didn't realize was how strong that connection might be. What if the Fallen Ones *did* kill you—or at least injured you severely enough that you should have died?"

"But then how did I survive?" Marcus asked.

"Precisely." The old wizard tapped his fingers against his robe-covered knee. "That your injuries seem less severe here on Farworld brings to memory a version of the legend I once came across recorded in a small village far to the northwest, near the border of the Trees of Before Time. According to the story handed down through generations of the farmers there, the child who was destined to save or destroy our world was linked to Farworld not only by his future, but by a mysterious connection much stronger.

"Marcus, I think it's possible you survived the Dark Circle's attack because your health is somehow linked inseparably to the health of this world. Perhaps the Dark Circle attacked you not just because you might one day lead a battle against them, but because your death might in and of itself bring about the fall of the world you are destined to save or destroy."

Marcus rubbed at his leg even more fiercely. "So I didn't die because . . . ?"

"Because Farworld—while weakened by the Dark Circle's strength—was not yet ready to fall. Your near-death was a blow to Farworld, but you were saved by the magic of the world itself. When I transported you to Earth, you were robbed of this world's sustaining magic. But by returning here you have reestablished hope for our world, and your injuries are lessened."

"But if that's true, then why haven't I been healed completely?"

Master Therapass nodded slowly. "Because Farworld is still in danger."

Marcus's face lit up with sudden understanding. "You're saying that if I save Farworld, Farworld will heal me?"

"I think that is entirely possible."

"But what happens if the Dark Circle succeeds?" Kyja asked.

The wizard's eye's darkened. "If Farworld falls, I believe Marcus will die, and likewise, if Marcus falls, it spells the inevitable demise of this world."

"If my health is tied to Farworld's health," Marcus said quickly, "couldn't we just find a way to cure me and save Farworld at the same time? You said your magic couldn't heal my injuries when I was a baby. But does that mean you still can't . . . that magic can't . . ." He let his words fade away.

Master Therapass knelt by Marcus's side, wincing a little as he bent, and gently touched Marcus's leg. "Magic is a strange thing," he said with a measured look. "Who is to say what magic can or cannot do? Just because *I* can't cure the wounds inflicted upon you—

or upon myself, for that matter—by the Dark Circle, does not mean the wounds are not curable.

"But just because a thing can be done with magic does not mean it *should* be done." As he got to his feet, the wizard took in both Marcus and Kyja with his deep, dark eyes. "Sometimes the things we view as our biggest weaknesses turn out to be our greatest strengths. Don't be too eager to rid yourself of your burdens. Your burdens are what shape you."

He began to turn away, then stopped and looked back at Marcus. "How are you feeling? Are you well?"

"A little confused," Marcus said. "But other than that, all right, I guess."

"Good." A troubled look seemed to pass over the wizard's face for a brief moment, but then he smiled. "Travel safely, keep your fire burning at night, and keep that skyte from terrorizing the local wildlife. I should join you shortly after you reach the forest." With that, he changed into his wolf form and loped off across the meadow.

———◆———

The rest of the day passed uneventfully, and the night held only the ordinary sounds of nocturnal animals, which stayed away from the fire Kyja, Riph Raph, and Marcus kept blazing much higher than necessary. The next morning, Marcus awoke with a queasy feeling in his stomach and a slight pressure behind his eyes.

"Are you all right?" Kyja asked when he barely touched his breakfast.

"Sure," Marcus said. He tried to eat another bite of egg. The flavor was every bit as fantastic as it had been the day before, but his stomach jolted in a way that made him quickly push his plate away. "I think I might be coming down with a cold."

"What's a *cold?*" Kyja asked.

Marcus grunted. "Believe me, if you don't have those here, you don't want to know. Let's get packed up and moving. Maybe I'll feel better by lunch."

But by lunchtime, only a few miles from the Westland Woods, he was feeling worse. His head was aching, and sweat dripped down his face. Sitting beside him on a log by the brook where they'd stopped to rest, Kyja reached out and touched his forehead. "You're hot," she said, frowning.

"I don't feel so good," he admitted. The headache had turned to a pounding behind his eyes, and everything had taken on a slightly fuzzy look. He was starving, but just the thought of food made him gag. He wondered if he might be coming down with the flu. Did they have the flu here? Or maybe some worse Farworld illness to which his body hadn't built up resistance?

Kyja dipped a handkerchief in the cold water and pressed it to his forehead. "Is there anything else I can do for you?"

"Not unless you have penicillin or aspirin."

"Are those cures?" she asked with a worried look.

He nodded, but even that slight movement of his head made the pain in his temples roar.

"We have cures here. But I didn't bring any," she said. "Most of them are magic, so they don't affect me."

"I'll bet you'd love Extra-Strength Tylenol," he said and tried to grin.

"Maybe you'd better rest for a while before we ride any farther," Kyja suggested.

"I think you're right." He slid off the log and lay down on the cool grass. He hated to stop with the edge of the forest in sight, but he wasn't sure he could handle riding on Chance's back without throwing up. The wet cloth over his head helped a little—if only he could make the ground stop spinning beneath him.

He had hardly closed his eyes when something jerked him awake. His heart was racing, and his mouth had gone dry. Sitting up, he looked quickly around. Everything seemed fine, but a feeling of terrible danger roared through his body.

"What is it?" Kyja asked, sensing his alarm.

"I don't . . . I don't know," he stammered. He couldn't seem to breathe. The feeling of imminent peril was so strong he could practically taste it. "We have to get out of—"

Riph Raph dropped from the sky, cutting off Marcus mid-sentence. The skyte's yellow eyes bulged with fear.

"Thrathkin S'Bae!"

CHAPTER 25

THRATHKIN S'BAE

RIPH RAPH HOPPED ABOUT the ground, flapping his leathery wings wildly.

"Where did they come from?" Kyja asked. "How did they get here?"

"I don't know!" Riph Raph squawked. "One minute there was nothing—no dust clouds, no movement—and the next they were here."

Kyja patted the skyte's wing, trying to calm him. "All right, then. Which direction are they?"

"Every direction!" Riph Raph flew three feet into the air and swiveled his head right and left. "Only two of the Thrathkin S'Bae, but lots of horrible looking dog things sniffing around searching for you."

Marcus sat up and moaned, shading his eyes against the sun.

"Can we reach the forest?" Kyja asked. "Master Therapass said we'd be safe there."

"No. I don't think they've seen us yet, but they will soon. They're all over." In his panic, Riph Raph coughed out a ball of flame that barely missed burning off Marcus's left eyebrow.

Kyja grabbed Chance's reins, searching for the approach of the dark creatures. There was no sign of them yet, but if Riph Raph said they were out there, she believed him. "We'll have to run for it," she said, trying not to think about how fast the snakes had reached the Goodnuff's farm.

"You'll never make it," Riph Raph almost shrieked. "The dogs have us surrounded."

Kyja grimaced, wishing for the millionth time that she had some kind of magic she could use. "We don't have any choice."

"Maybe I can . . . help."

Kyja turned to see Marcus pull himself onto the log. Sweat bathed his face and matted his hair, but his eyes held the same determination she'd seen when he was facing down the man in Master Therapass's aptura discerna.

"Boost me onto Chance," he said.

Kyja helped him up until he could get his left foot in the stirrup and his right hand on the saddle. Heat radiated from Marcus's body in sick waves. He was burning up.

Pulling himself with his right arm, Marcus swung his weak leg over the pommel. "Now you . . . behind me." Marcus swayed in the saddle and Kyja had to steady him as she climbed onto Chance's back.

"This may not work on you, so duck down behind me," Marcus said, his voice raw. "And I don't even know if I can use it with a horse. But there's only one way to find out."

Kyja had no idea what he was talking about, but she thought she could hear the Fallen Ones moving about nearby. "Whatever you're going to try, do it now," she whispered. Turning to Riph Raph, she pointed in the opposite direction of the forest. "Fly that way. Maybe some of them will follow you."

As the skyte launched himself into the air, Kyja wrapped her arms around Marcus's waist and picked up Chance's reins.

"Nobody came to see me today," Marcus muttered under his breath.

"What?" Kyja asked. But Marcus shook his head. Whoever he was talking to, it wasn't her. A cough wracked his body as he started again.

"Nobody came to see *us* today, nobody saw *us* arrive."

"Quiet," Kyja whispered. "They'll hear you." What was he doing? Was he delirious? She was sure she could hear movement now, and not very far away, a low-pitched growling carried on the still air.

"Nobody saw us walk away. Nobody knows we're alive." Marcus had dropped his voice, but his words still made no sense.

Chance whinnied softly as a dark shape appeared out of the tall grass less than thirty yards away before slipping out of sight again. Kyja tightened her hands on the reins, trying to decide which way to ride, but Marcus put his hand over hers in a not-yet gesture.

"Nobody knows when we come and go. Nobody seems to care."

Something was coming. The grass to their left rustled back and forth.

"Nobody take us away with you. Take us into your care." What was he talking about? It had to be the fever talking.

On the other side of the brook, a pitch-black head emerged from the grass. Something that looked like an eight-legged dog—so skinny its ribs poked out from its matted fur—stood panting on a small rise less than twenty feet away. Its red eyes glittered as a pair of long, pink tongues curled and uncurled from its mouth filled with needle-sharp teeth. The creature raised its snout to the air and looked directly at them.

Kyja turned from the foul creature and her breath caught in her throat. Marcus and Chance were gone. She blinked and they were back again. Deciding she'd been seeing things, she lifted the reins and started to dig her heels into Chance's flanks. Before she could, Marcus caught her hand. "Don't move," he whispered so softly she could barely make out what he was saying.

Marcus stared over his shoulder at Kyja with a grim urgency. His face seemed to swim before her, blurry and indistinct. She rubbed her eyes furiously—wondering if she was getting sick too—and again tightened her fingers on Chance's reins. But Marcus shook his head and put a finger to his lips.

Kyja turned toward the eight-legged dog. Clearly in sight, it should have charged them, but it continued to sniff the air, searching the meadow as saliva dripped from its tongues. What was it doing? Chance rolled his big, gray eyes but remained steady as Kyja ran her fingertips along his neck.

After a moment, the dog-thing leaped over the brook and disappeared into the grass on the other side. Leaning forward in the saddle, Marcus pointed a shaking finger toward the edge of the woods. "Go forward," he whispered. "Quietly."

Kyja nudged Chance with her heels, keeping the reins tight, and the horse started at a gentle walk. Was the dog blind? Is that why it hadn't seen them? A hundred feet to the left, another dog appeared. Its skull-like head swiveled toward Kyja and Marcus.

Kyja pulled back on the reins, but again Marcus gestured forward. As if they were being protected by some kind of magic, the dog's eyes passed over them, and the creature skulked away.

All at once she understood. "Magic," she whispered. "You can do magic, can't you?"

Marcus shrugged his shoulders, wiped the sweat from his face, and whispered, "Not . . . magic. Just a . . . gift."

The dogs were everywhere now, growling and whining, snapping at each other. They clearly could smell Marcus and Kyja, but were unable to find them.

"But how can your magic work on *me?*" Kyja asked. "Magic doesn't affect me."

"Not sure," Marcus said, the strain evident in his voice. "I don't . . . think I'm actually . . . making us invisible as much I'm bending the light. Stay close. And hope no one comes from behind. Don't think it would work on you from that direction."

"How long can you keep this up?" Kyja asked, sliding closer.

"Normally . . . not this hard," Marcus panted. "Feels like something's fighting against me—trying to pull off whatever makes us hard to see."

Kyja looked forward and sucked in a sharp breath. Standing between them and the forest were two figures with black cloaks pulled over their heads—the Thrathkin S'Bae. Both held black staffs forked at the top. Tongues of flame danced over the cloaks and arched across the tops of the staffs.

Marcus muttered something that sounded like "dream" and slumped a little in the saddle.

A scream sounded from overhead, and Kyja looked up to see Riph Raph flying low in the air, drawing at least a dozen of the black dogs howling and snarling behind him. Staying just out of their reach, the Skyte turned his head and shot a ball of blue flame at the pack of dogs. The fire sent them scattering for a moment, but quickly they rejoined the chase.

One of the Thrathkin S'Bae raised his staff, and a bolt of green lightning split the sky, narrowly missing Riph Raph. As the skyte reached the edge of the woods, another of the lightning bolts clipped his left wing. He wheeled into the trees and disappeared from view.

"Can't . . . hold on," Marcus murmured. "Too strong."

"You have to," Kyja whispered. It was a hundred yards to the figures and another quarter mile beyond them to the first trees. They'd never make it to the forest if they were spotted.

Marcus moaned and slumped forward. Wrapping her arms around Marcus's chest to hold him up, she urged Chance to go a little faster. Would her hands be visible if anyone or anything looked in their direction? It didn't matter, because she could feel Marcus swaying more and more in the saddle. She was sure if she didn't hold onto him, he would fall right off the horse.

The two cloaked figures stood about a hundred feet apart. Each held his staff in both hands, waving them before their bodies in a circular fashion. Although Kyja couldn't feel anything, Marcus began to tremble as they drew near the two men.

Marcus's labored breathing was so loud Kyja was sure he would be heard. "Hang on," she said under her breath. She clasped the reins tightly—her heart thudding—and tried to look in both directions at once, expecting to see one or both of the hooded heads turn. Then they were past, with no other creatures visible between them and the woods.

As she released a noiseless sigh of relief, Marcus jerked in her arms and gave a rasping cough. Both of the figures spun around.

"*Nhet tei gar,*" one of the men cried out.

Kyja had no idea what that meant, but she kicked Chance with the heels of her slippers and shouted, "Fly!"

Chance was old, but it seemed he still understood danger.

Almost before the word was out of Kyja's mouth, the old warhorse broke into a gallop that nearly tore Marcus's limp body from her grasp.

Still, the woods seemed impossibly far away. Peeking over her shoulder, Kyja watched as both figures raised their staffs. Bolts of bright green energy sizzled through the air toward her. The one on the right missed, but the one on the left hit her directly between the shoulder blades. She grimaced, bracing herself for the pain, but the bolt bounced harmlessly away. Her immunity to magic had protected her, and for once she was glad to be different.

Realizing their prey was escaping, both men raised their arms and transformed into the huge snakes Kyja had seen before. Leaning as far forward in the saddle as she could while still holding onto Marcus, Kyja shouted encouragement to Chance. The old gray and white stallion snorted and pumped his legs furiously.

Kyja risked a quick glance over her shoulder. Grass and rocks flew past, but the snakes were coming even faster. They would never make it to the forest before the snakes reached them.

Clutching Marcus's body, she shouted for Chance to give everything he had. Foam flew from the stallion's mouth as he charged toward the trees. Kyja heard a sharp hiss behind her and turned to see one of the snakes launch itself through the air. She yanked the reins hard to the left, and Chance turned sharply, churning up clumps of dirt and grass with his hooves as the snake flew harmlessly by.

With effortless speed, the other snake slithered up next to her. Looking into its golden eyes, Kyja felt her heart stop beating. The snake's pupils grew and spun, and Kyja began to lose her balance. The snake opened its mouth, which was big enough to swallow her whole. Its forked tongue flicked toward her, and Kyja's robe sizzled and smoked where it touched.

Kyja tried to tear her gaze from the snake's entrancing golden eyes. They were almost to the woods, but it was too late. She felt herself slipping from the saddle as the world spun around her. The snake opened its mouth, and Kyja was falling onto glistening razor-sharp fangs.

But then a long, brown limb reached out from the woods and crashed down across the glittering, black scales. The snake's eyes blazed with fury as its body twisted and writhed. A second limb slapped down on the coils, and Kyja thought she heard something snap. Then she dropped from Chance's back, and the world went black.

CHAPTER 26

THE WEATHER GUARDIANS

MARCUS AWOKE TO THE TOUCH of something cool and slippery on his cheek.

"Open your mouth," said a deep voice that sounded as if it were coming from inside a drum.

His lips parted, and a warm liquid flowed over his tongue. It tasted sweet but burned as it touched the back of his throat. Gasping, he opened his eyes and tried to sit up, but the slippery limbs held him pinned to the ground. He jerked and twisted, unable to see in the dim light what he was fighting against.

"It's all right," a familiar voice said. "They're trying to help you."

"Kyja," he murmured, as a face appeared in the shadows above him.

He allowed his body to sink back to the ground. He had no choice. What little energy he possessed was used up quickly in his struggles. His head felt like it weighed a thousand pounds.

"Where am I?" he tried to ask, but his tongue wouldn't form the words.

"Relax," the deep voice said. "You are safe."

Marcus fell asleep.

—◆—

He'd been having a dream in which he was playing a game with Elder Ephraim. The game involved moving colored rocks. Elder Ephraim explained the only way to win was by patiently waiting for your adversary to reveal his or her strategy. The first person to make the wrong move almost always lost. He tried to remember exactly what the rules of the game were, but the dream faded too quickly.

An orchestra of cheeps, chirps, and croaks filled the cool, damp air. Lifting his head, Marcus opened his eyes and saw that he was glowing. As he started to sit up, a cloud of shimmering, red sparks rose from his skin and clothing. They held the shape of his body in the air for a moment before breaking up and humming away into the darkness.

Looking to his left, he saw a frog no bigger than the tip of his finger. The frog's eyes glowed an eerie green. Marcus watched the frog open its mouth and begin to swell—first to the size of an apricot, then a baseball, and finally a balloon. Its skin stretched so thin Marcus could see its heart pumping inside its body, illuminated by the light from its eyes. Just when he was sure it was going to pop, the frog released all the air inside it with a rapid, *tee-tee-tee-tee tee-tee-tee-tee,* and hopped out of sight.

Where was he? He vaguely remembered running from some danger he couldn't quite recall, and then . . . nothing.

Now sitting up, he realized two things. The first was that he was lying in the branch or branches of a tree—resting on a bed of what felt like pine needles, only they were as soft as feathers. The second was that the ground was more than a hundred feet below him. Gasping, he rolled over and wrapped his arm around the nearest branch.

Somewhere nearby, a voice chuckled. "The child is afraid of tumbling from its nest? Perhaps the child should stay out of high places." Marcus's first thought was of Bonesplinter. But the voice wasn't the same. The needles rustled beneath him as if a strong breeze had blown through the branches.

Marcus searched for the voice, but there was no one in sight. Looking up, he couldn't see the sun. Was it night then? If it was, how could he see at all?

Still clinging to the branch, he noticed that the millions of the tiny red lights which had covered his body flickered from the tree branches around him. Looking closer, he saw there were other colors as well—orange, purple, gold, pink.

The branches trembled beneath him again and Marcus remembered the song about the baby sleeping in the treetops.

"Rock-ee by, rock-ee by," the voice sang as though reading his mind. This time the branch actually dropped a foot or two, and Marcus felt his hold on the branch begin to slip.

"Stop it," scolded a second voice. "You're scaring him." Neither of the voices sounded human. For one thing, they sang more than spoke. And for another, they had a deep echoing quality to them. But Marcus thought the first voice sounded male, while the second had a more feminine tone.

"What's wrong with scaring him a little?" the first voice said. "He brought the Dark Circle with him."

"He didn't do it on purpose," the second voice said. "Let the boy down."

A groan shook the branches of the tree he was in, and Marcus could feel the wood vibrating beneath his fingers. "Fine. But I still say it would save us a lot of trouble if I let him fall."

The branch Marcus was holding drooped, and he felt himself beginning to slip. Holding as tight as he could with his good hand, he tried to find some purchase with his left foot.

"It's all right," the second voice said. "Let go. Ithspin won't drop you."

Ithspin? Closing his eyes, Marcus released his grip on the branch. He felt himself falling and reached out. Before he could grab anything, he dropped onto another bed of needles. That branch lowered and he slid from it onto another branch. Before he knew it, he landed with a gentle plop on the moss-covered ground.

Someone approached, and Marcus tensed as he peered into the darkness.

"How are you feeling?" Kyja emerged from the shadows, a halo of miniscule pink lights circling her head.

All at once, Marcus remembered how sick he'd been. How *did* he feel? "Better," he said. His stomach still felt a little queasy, but the pounding in his head had disappeared. "I think my fever's gone."

Kyja gave a sigh of relief. "I was worried about you."

"You were?" Marcus felt a strange warmth in the center of his chest. They were silent for a moment, listening to the sounds of the forest. It was impossible to separate all the different hums, chirps, and clicks. There were hundreds of them blending together from all around the forest like a natural orchestra.

"Here," Kyja said, holding out a length of tree branch to him. It was a little thicker than his wrist at the top and narrowed to half that size at the tip.

"What's this?" he asked, running his fingers along the polished smoothness of the wood.

Kyja blushed. "I found it over there a bit," she said, pointing off into the trees. "I thought it could be a kind of walking staff. That maybe it would help you . . . get around."

"Like a cane," Marcus said, grinning. "Kyja, that's a great idea!"

Kyja smiled—obviously pleased—as Marcus used the staff to push himself carefully to his feet. Leaning his weight on the staff, he found he could walk. Slow and limping it might be, but still, it was walking.

"This is awesome!" he said, shuffling around the forest floor.

Kyja beamed. "It even sort of looks like you."

"Huh?" Marcus turned the staff in his hands and discovered a gnarled knot about six inches below the top that actually did resemble a face if you squinted a little.

"Wrinkled old thing looks more like Master Therapass." He tried to scowl, but couldn't help grinning.

Kyja clapped both hands to her mouth, not doing a very good job of hiding her giggles.

"Where are we?" Marcus asked, as something that sounded like a squirrel chattered above him.

"The Westland Woods," Kyja said. "Don't you remember coming here? You cast a spell that made it so the Fallen Ones couldn't see us."

"I can't cast spells," Marcus said, shaking his head. "The last thing I remember clearly is breakfast this morning. The rest of it is all fuzzy."

Kyja giggled, her laughter blending in with the other sounds. Somewhere in the distance came three distinct hoots. "Breakfast was two days ago. You've been sleeping since then."

Marcus could only stare, dumbfounded. He'd been asleep for two whole days?

"The trees have been caring for you," Kyja said. "I think their sap is what made you better—along with the wood sprites' magic."

"Wood sprites?" Marcus asked looking around.

Kyja held out her hand, and several of the tiny pink specks rose briefly from her palm before fluttering slowly back. Marcus leaned closer. They looked like tiny sparks, but if he squinted his eyes, he could almost make out thin bodies and transparent wings.

"Why didn't you tell me you could do magic?" Kyja asked. In the darkness it was hard to make out her expression.

"I . . . didn't. That is I . . ." he stammered. He'd never told anyone about his abilities before—never trusted anyone enough to share his secret. "It's not really magic. It's just sometimes I can make people look away from me. And now and then I seem to know things before they happen."

Before Kyja could respond, a golden toad hopped across the forest floor and said in a clear voice, "Olden will see you now."

CHAPTER 27

OLDEN

"WHERE IS IT TAKING US?" Marcus asked.

Kyja raised her hands in a *who-knows* gesture. Over the two days Marcus had slept, the trees had stopped her from wandering very far. They said it was to keep her from getting lost, but Kyja suspected it was to keep her from snooping around. They told her Riph Raph was being kept somewhere else—apparently the trees had a problem with animals that could blow fire—and Chance was safely eating grass in a meadow nearby.

For the last twenty minutes, she and Marcus had been following the golden toad down one dark, tree-lined passageway after another, far from anywhere Kyja had explored. Despite the toad's constant urging to go faster, Kyja walked slowly so that Marcus could keep up with her and let him stop as often as he needed. With the only illumination coming from the clouds of multicolored wood sprites above their heads and spread among the tree branches, the toad could be leading them in circles, for all she knew.

At one point Marcus refused to go any farther. Rubbing his bad leg, he demanded the toad tell them where they were headed and how long it would take to get there. But the toad only admonished them that they were going to be late if they didn't hurry, and hopped off into the darkness. Marcus tried to keep up with it, muttering something that sounded like *Mad Hatter*.

"Why do the tree branches wave around like that?" Marcus asked.

Again Kyja shrugged. Of course she'd noticed how the trees flapped their long limbs slowly up and down, creating their own fragrant breezes, but they were as much of a mystery to her as they were to him.

As they headed down into a gully, the path grew wet and spongy. Marcus grimaced when the tip of his staff sank deep into the muck and he was forced to drop to the seat of his pants. "I envy you," he said, trying to scoot along the dank forest floor and brush the wet pine needles from his hands at the same time.

"Me?" Kyja asked, carrying his staff. She couldn't remember anyone ever envying her before. It was always the other way around. "Why would you envy *me?*"

"You have two good arms and legs. You don't have to look up at everyone. You never have to ask anyone to help you reach something on a tall shelf. You don't have to crawl across the ground like a . . . a bug."

"I never thought of that," Kyja said watching Marcus scuttle along the path beside her. "You make it seem so easy. Actually I envy *you.*"

Marcus cocked his head and narrowed his eyes as though he suspected she was joking. "Me?"

Kyja nodded. "All my life I've wanted to do magic. Even something as simple as making a pot boil. Then you come along and make an entire horse disappear without giving it a second thought."

They both followed the toad silently, contemplating the other's words. As she walked, Kyja studied their surroundings. Although the forest was full of animal life, except for an occasional waist-high fern the trees were the only plant life in the forest. They were so tall and their branches so thick it was impossible to see their tops. Now and then, she caught an occasional glimpse of something dark gray high up through the interlacing green, but not a trace of sunlight.

Pausing for a moment, Kyja touched the side of a nearby tree. The bark was a deep, almost brown, red—rough but fragrant. As she ran her hand over its bumpy surface, one of her fingers touched a fuzzy spot about the size of her knuckle. When she pressed against it, her fingertip sank into the bark.

"What are you doing?" thrummed a deep voice. "Stop that."

"Oh!" Kyja jumped backward, pulling her hand from the tree. "I was just . . . um . . ."

"Humph," the tree grunted. "Keep your hands to yourself."

"Sorry," Kyja said. She wondered what the soft spot was. She'd seen the same thing on other trees while exploring—fuzzy gray splotches on the otherwise perfect bark.

"Look at that," Marcus said, interrupting her thoughts.

Kyja followed Marcus's gaze to see the toad hop onto a spiral staircase. As she and Marcus approached the stairs, they discovered the staircase was actually composed of tree branches—spread out and down to form steps circling up the trunk. Marcus crawled onto the first branch. Seeing that it held his weight just fine, Kyja followed him, still carrying his staff. Climbing the steps, Kyja realized she'd been hearing the growing roar of rushing water for some time now.

Several feet ahead of them, the toad stopped and looked back. "Step lively now," it croaked.

Kyja and Marcus hurried behind it to discover they were perched forty or more feet above the bank of a fast-moving river. White water crashed and cascaded against glistening boulders. Kyja tried to picture a map of the land they'd traveled—wondering if this was the same Two Prong River that ran beside Terra ne Staric—but she'd never been this far from the city before.

Down below, the forest had blocked much of the sound, but up here, with an unobstructed view of the river, the roar was thunderous. The branch steps seemed to end at the platform they were standing on.

"What now?" Marcus asked, trying to make his voice heard over the river.

In answer, the toad hopped to the edge of the branch and leaped into midair.

Kyja gasped. Then something amazing happened. All along the bank of the river, the trees waved their branches like giant umbrellas. Instead of falling, the toad spread out its long legs and seemed to fly. Like a bird or a skimmer, it glided across the river and landed softly on the far bank.

"Hurry up!" it croaked, shouting above the din of the river.

Marcus and Kyja looked at each other with wide eyes, then at the toad. "How do we get across?" Kyja yelled.

"Jump!" the toad said impatiently.

With an impish grin, Marcus shrugged his shoulders. He took his staff from Kyja and crawled out on the branch until it bent beneath his weight. Holding the staff in both hands he said, "Here goes nothing."

"No," Kyja said, reaching for him. Before she could grab him, he launched himself from the branch. For a moment he plummeted toward the river, and Kyja's heart lodged firmly in her throat. Then, as the trees again beat their branches against the air, he, too, appeared to fly.

"Ya-hooo!" he whooped, waving at Kyja with his staff. Reaching the far bank, he hit the ground softly and executed a perfect somersault. "Try it," he shouted with a huge grin. "It's great!"

Kyja looked down at the raging white water and clutched a branch above her head. What if it didn't work for her? What if it was some kind of magic? She turned to go back down the way she'd come, but the steps had disappeared.

"Come on!" Marcus yelled as the toad began hopping into the woods on the other side of the river.

Kyja gazed at the rocks so far below. Blood pounded in her ears.

"Don't be afraid," said a deep but gentle voice. "We won't let you fall."

"P-promise?" she stammered.

"Of course," said the voice. "Weather Guardian's oath."

Gritting her teeth, she slid her feet a few inches away from the trunk of the tree. One at a time, she pried her fingers from the branch. Squeezing her eyes shut, she mustered all of her courage and jumped.

She was falling! Opening her eyes, she saw the river rushing up toward her. It hadn't worked after all. Just as she felt sure she was going to crash into the fast-moving water, something like a warm hand cupped her body and raised her into the air. Wind lifted her long hair off her neck and blew it away from her face.

"You're doing great!" a voice called.

She turned to see Marcus waving at her, grinning like an idiot. Gently as a feather, the wind set her on the bank.

"Great job!" Marcus patted her shoulder before turning to follow the toad.

Still trying to catch her breath, Kyja looked across the river at the tree from which she'd jumped. The enormous pine tipped a branch in her direction. Kyja waved back, then hurried after Marcus.

"This way," Marcus said, limping up the side of a steep hill. Kyja trotted up next to him.

At the top of the hill, the toad waited. When it saw them, it hopped down the path and into a large clearing.

As she followed the toad into the opening, Kyja blinked her eyes. It wasn't exactly sunny, but for the first time she could see all the way to the sky. A tiny circle of blue was cut out of the thick, gray clouds.

"Your majesty," the toad said, stopping at the edge of the path, "I present Kyja and Marcus."

Across the clearing—past a scrubby little tree that looked more like a bush—were three of the most magnificent trees Kyja had ever seen. Each of their trunks was thicker across than she could stretch her arms. They rose up into the sky—disappearing into the clouds and then emerging through the round, blue opening of sky.

Kyja glanced at Marcus, and his eyes silently asked the same question she was wondering. *Which of the three is Olden?* Kyja gave a tiny shrug of her shoulders. In front of them, the toad tilted its head, the meaning on its warty little face obvious: step up and say something.

Kyja waved Marcus forward with a jerk of her hand, and together the two of them approached the three trees.

"It's an honor to meet you . . . your majesty." Kyja hesitated a moment before curtseying in the direction of the middle tree. Putting most of his weight on his staff, Marcus performed an awkward bow.

The trees remained silent.

Marcus shot her a nervous glance before turning to the tree on the right. "It's a pleasure to meet you. Thank you for helping us."

Again the trees said nothing.

Together they turned to the tree on the left and Kyja said, "Is there anything we can do to repay you?"

Still the trees towered mutely above them.

Just when they were beginning to wonder if they'd done something wrong, a voice spoke.

"The first thing you can do is turn around and stop looking at my sons, you foolish children," said a high-pitched, waspish voice that sounded like an old woman. "If I must speak with you, I would prefer *not* to look at your backsides."

Marcus and Kyja spun around to face the scraggly little tree they had passed by.

CHAPTER 28

THE DARK CIRCLE

NOT WHAT YOU IMAGINED?" the gnarled tree snipped.

Marcus and Kyja glanced uncomfortably toward each other.

"Bah! See how *you* look when you're a thousand years old."

"I'm sorry," Marcus said, scratching his shoulder. "I was just expecting . . ." He let his voice trail away, unsure how to complete the thought.

"Something *taller?*" Olden asked, her voice dripping with sarcasm.

"I guess so." Marcus shifted his feet. "The rest of the trees in the forest are so big."

"For your information, there *was* no forest here when I was a sapling. It was all dry, empty plain. If it wasn't for the Weather Guardians, it still would be. Westland can thank me and my children for guiding the clouds to send the rain it receives. But do you think they ever show any gratitude?"

"I had no idea," Kyja said.

"Hummph," Olden grunted.

"Is that why you all do that thing with your arms . . . er branches?" Marcus asked, hoping to change the subject to something more agreeable.

"Weather channeling," the tree said. "It was my idea. We send the clouds to where moisture is needed."

"Neat," Marcus said. He was not exactly sure how to have a conversation with a tree. Where were you supposed to look when speaking to something that didn't seem to have a mouth or face? He scuffed his tennis shoe in the dirt, wondering if all trees were this grumpy.

"Well?" the tree said impatiently. "What do you want? Speak up. I don't have all day."

"I . . . er . . ." Marcus glanced at Kyja, hoping she'd help him out, but she didn't seem to have any more clue about what to say than he did.

"Is that all you came here for? To show me your backsides, insult me, and inquire about the weather? I don't know why the wizard bothered asking me to talk to you at all. Neither of you seem very intelligent, and I've got a million things to do today."

Marcus wondered exactly what kinds of things trees did all day, but thought it better not to ask. He held his tongue. Kyja curtsied and said in a humble tone, "We appreciate you seeing us, Your Highness. Master Therapass said you are the wisest tree in all of Westland, and if we wanted to learn about the past, you were the only one to speak with."

"He did, did he?"

Marcus wasn't sure, but he thought Olden might have been smiling a little—if trees could smile. She certainly sounded pleased.

"Oh, yes," Kyja said. "He told us the trees of Westland Woods were the smartest living things in all of Westland, and you were the smartest of them all."

Marcus certainly hadn't heard the wizard say *that*, but a sharp glance from Kyja kept his lips sealed.

"Well." Olden fluffed her mostly-bare branches and rustled her needles. "I suppose I do know quite a bit. You can't live as long as I have without hearing things."

"What have you heard about the snake-men?" Marcus blurted out. Kyja shot him an irritated look.

"Thrathkin S'Bae," Olden said, drawing her branches close to her trunk. "Wizards of the Dark Circle. No one has seen them in these parts for hundreds of years. That you brought them here is a bad omen for all of us. We do not wish to draw the attention of the Fallen Ones. If not for Master Therapass, we would have left you to them."

Kyja shuddered visibly. "Master Therapass said the Thrathkin S'Bae are chasing us because of a legend." She pulled the amulet from her robe. "Show them your shoulder, Marcus."

Marcus hesitated. After all the years of hiding the brand on his arm, he wasn't any more comfortable showing it to others than he was talking about his abilities. Finally, he relented and lifted his shirt sleeve.

Olden bent forward, and Marcus could almost see eyes staring out of the tree's bark.

"Does it mean anything to you?" Kyja asked.

"No," Olden snapped suddenly—her tone even colder than when they'd first met. She pulled her bent trunk to its full height. "I've never seen it before."

"What about the legend?" Marcus tried. "Master Therapass said you might be able to tell us about the legend of the living things of the world fighting with each other."

"Humans invent stories all the time. It makes them feel better for living such pitifully short lives. Now, if you'll excuse me, I have to get my morning sunlight. Anura, please see them out of the woods."

At the tree's command, the golden toad hopped toward the trail and looked expectantly back at Marcus and Kyja with its bulging eyes.

"Wait," Marcus said. "You can't just send us away. The Thrathkin S'Bae might still be out there."

"Better out there than in here. We have no quarrel with the Dark Circle, and I intend to keep it that way."

A murmur of approval came from the nearby trees.

"So you're just going to let them kill us?" Marcus swiped his hand across his brow. His head felt hot again, and his stomach was roiling.

Olden waved her branches in a shooing gesture. "We saved you once. If the legend *is* true, you should have no fear of the Fallen Ones. After all, you're the one who's prophesied to banish them."

"Then you *do* know about the legend," Marcus said.

Olden's trunk stiffened, and all of her branches seemed to shake at once. "Both of you children leave now, before I have you thrown out."

Marcus turned to Kyja, who had a strangely thoughtful look on her face. She stepped toward one of the three trees they'd mistaken for Olden at first and placed her fingertips on its trunk.

"What are you doing?" a gruff voice said.

Kyja looked up with an expression of wonderment. "You're sick."

"What?" the tree thundered. "That's nonsense."

Ignoring it, Kyja moved to the next tree and placed her hand against what looked like a piece of gray fuzz on its rough bark. "You're sick, too."

She hurried to the next huge tree. "You too. All of you are sick." She spun around to stare at Olden. "The entire forest is slowly dying. And you know all about it, don't you?"

Marcus had no idea what she was talking about. Olden looked like she was about to wither into sawdust, but as far as the rest of the forest, he'd never seen healthier trees in his life.

"Get these two out of here now!" Olden screeched. At once, the trees started to wave their broad branches, and the same wind that had carried Marcus and Kyja over the river began pushing them from the clearing.

Clinging to his staff, Marcus was blown to the ground. His fingers clawed and slipped in the loose soil, but Kyja leaned into the wind—the thoughtful look still locked on her face.

"It's just like the prophecy warned," she said, her words whipped away by the wind that slapped her hair across her face. "You're taking too much. You changed the weather to meet your needs. You took all the moisture you wanted, but you didn't consider the other plants."

Marcus grasped at a nearby root with his good hand, but it flicked him off like a bug, and he found himself rolling down the pathway.

"It may not be in my lifetime," Kyja shouted above the gale. "But eventually, this entire forest will be gone if you don't do something."

A burst of wind actually lifted her off the ground, and, looking back, Marcus was afraid she would be crushed against one of the immense trunks.

"I can help you!" she screamed.

All at once the wind stopped, dropping her to the dirt, and a deep voice rumbled, "How?"

CHAPTER 29

A DARK FATE

Y OU'RE ONLY A GIRL," SAID the middle of the three trees. "What makes you think you know what's wrong with us?"

Kyja got slowly to her feet, brushing the dirt from the front of her robe as Marcus pulled himself up with his staff and limped back into the clearing.

"I don't know *how* I know, but I do," Kyja said. She let a handful of dirt trickle through her fingers. Marcus saw that it was composed almost completely of dead needles. "Don't you see? You created the perfect condition for your own kind. But you forgot one thing. You're taking all the nutrients from the soil. You need other plants to absorb the food you leave and to create the food you need."

Kyja walked to the closest of the large trees and rested her hands on its coarse trunk, like a doctor examining a patient. "I can feel it in you. On the outside it's just a few spots. But on the inside you're . . . weak. If you are attacked by bugs or disease or . . . whatever, you won't have the resistance to fight back. Can't you feel it too?"

"Frog squattle," Olden said. "We've lived just fine for a thousand years. We'll live a thousand more." But Marcus noticed the other trees weren't so quick to ignore Kyja's words. He could hear them whispering quietly among themselves. Finally the middle tree spoke up.

"Perhaps there *is* something in what you say. We have sensed a certain . . . *strangeness*. But even if it is true, what can you do about it?"

Kyja folded her arms across her chest and lowered her head as though in deep thought. After a moment, she looked up. "The tower groundskeepers at Terra ne Staric. They know all about keeping plants healthy. I'm sure they could help you restore the balance in the woods."

"And you can convince them to help us?" the tree asked.

"If not, *I* can," a voice said from behind them.

Kyja and Marcus turned to see Master Therapass stride swiftly through the trees, his dark cloak flowing out behind him. He entered the clearing, winked at Kyja and Marcus, and dipped low in an elaborate bow before Olden.

"Your majesty, it is a pleasure to see you again. As always, you look magnificent." He turned to the three large trees and performed the same bow, holding his cloak behind him with his left hand while clutching his right fist before his chest. "Council of Weather Guardians, if I may be of assistance, only say the word."

The trees seemed to confer together, their branches rustling gently.

"How did you know all that?" Marcus whispered to Kyja. "About the trees dying?"

She frowned. "I'm not sure. I just . . . knew." But *how* did she know? It felt a little like when she'd looked into the aptura discerna, or when she'd pulled Marcus from Ert. First there was a feeling in the pit of her stomach—she knew there was something wrong with the trees, and she wanted to help. Then it was just there . . . in her head.

As Master Therapass glanced down at Marcus and her, Kyja noticed his beard was freshly trimmed and less tangled than usual. She wondered if that was because of the business he'd been attending to in Terra ne Staric. "You two seem to have things in control here," he said.

"Thanks to Kyja," Marcus said. "I thought we were goners for a minute."

"*Goners?*" Master Therapass raised an eyebrow.

"You know. Dead ducks. Something about the symbol on my arm and Kyja's amulet really set them off. They would have sent us out to face the Fallen Ones if it weren't for Kyja."

"Really?" Master Therapass gazed down thoughtfully at Kyja.

"I just wanted to help," she said.

The trees stopped their rustling, and Marcus, Kyja, and the wizard all turned in their direction.

"We have reached a decision," the middle tree said in a booming voice. "It's possible the girl's words are true. We have noticed some changes over the last hundred years. Perhaps we miscalculated."

Olden coughed, and Marcus wondered again how a tree with no visible mouth could do such a thing. "We will accept your help," she said, "*if* it is offered freely. We will not be forced into making any alliances with you or taking sides in something that is not our concern."

Master Therapass fingered the tip of his beard. "My help is offered freely, but it won't be of much value if the Dark Circle overruns Terra ne Staric."

Kyja started. Was it really possible the Dark Circle might attack the capital of Westland? If Terra ne Staric wasn't safe, what was?

"The Dark Circle is not our concern," Olden said with a trace of contempt in her voice. "Their quarrel is with humans, not us."

Master Therapass threw back his cloak. Kyja could almost feel the wizard's stature grow as he stared at the wasted tree.

"Do not underestimate the evil intent of the Dark Circle." Master Therapass's voice was every bit as impressive as the largest of the trees.

Kyja had never heard the wizard speak so forcefully before. He held his hands out, palms raised to the sky, and a clear globe appeared above his fingertips. As he spread his hands, the globe grew and rose.

"Disease and soil are the least of your concerns if the Dark Circle has its way," Master Therapass thundered. "Behold your fate."

An image appeared inside the globe. It was fuzzy at first, but soon the picture cleared, revealing a forest that might have been the Westland Woods. Birds chirped. Animals played. Everything looked just as it should, and Kyja wondered if Master Therapass had made a mistake.

"I don't see what—" Olden began to speak, but Master Therapass cut her off with a single word.

"Look."

The dark-cloaked figures Kyja had seen in the meadow appeared in the globe. Only this time, instead of two, there were dozens, hundreds—their dark mass blocked nearly everything else from sight. Each held a forked staff, and Kyja watched in horror as the figures raised their staffs and a wall of flame engulfed the trees.

"No!" Olden gasped, clutching her frail branches to her trunk. All around the clearing, the other trees were also covering their trunks and leaning as far away from the scene as they could. The entire forest seemed to tremble.

Popping sounds came from inside the globe as one tree after another turned into a pillar of flames. Kyja thought she could hear the sound of screaming, too—hundreds of voices crying out together. Birds and animals fled the burning mess as the cloaked figures swept deeper into the woods.

"Take it away," Olden pleaded.

Master Therapass clapped his hands and the image disappeared at once.

"It's a lie," one of the trees said from the edge of the clearing. "The wizard is trying to frighten us."

"I only wish I were," said Master Therapass, his voice soft again. "But Olden knows the truth, don't you?"

In front of him, the old tree seemed to wilt. "Where did you find that?" she asked.

"It was in the tower archives—stored away for centuries. The entire forest was burned to the ground in less than three days. The only plants that survived were the seedlings, buried deep enough in the soil to survive the heat." Master Therapass ran a finger gently across Olden's nearest branch. "You were one of those seedlings, weren't you?"

The answer was a barely audible, "Yes."

"It's why you sought to control the weather. You thought if you remade the forest bigger than before, if you could force the clouds to obey you, this would never happen again. But the fire that burned your forest a thousand years ago—that killed your mother and father, your brothers and sisters—cannot be put out with rain. When the Dark Circle returns, they will burn this woods to the ground, just like they did back then. Only this time, they'll see that nothing will ever grow here again."

"No," Olden said—her voice fierce with determination. "Last time we got involved. This time we won't. The Dark Circle will have no reason to harm us if we stay out of their fight."

"That's where you're wrong. The Dark Circle is determined to destroy everything praiseworthy. You only have two choices. Stand against them and fight, or join them and look forward to this."

Again Master Therapass held out his hands. This time the globe showed a forest of warped, black trees. Bare, twisted branches hung limply beneath a steel-gray, cloudless sky. The ground under the trees was an oily-looking swamp empty of any other life. The wizard turned to eye each of the trees around him, letting them see the carnage.

For once Olden was silent.

"What do you want of us?" she finally asked.

The wizard placed a hand on Marcus's shoulder. "I firmly believe Marcus is the key to the future of Farworld. If we are to have any chance of holding off the Dark Circle, we must find a way to return him to our world."

Marcus jerked under Master Therapass's grip. "What do you mean, return me? I'm already here."

"No," the wizard said, an odd look on his face. "You are not."

NOWHERE

MARCUS TRIED TO SPEAK but couldn't. His vocal cords seemed to have dried up, and the best he could manage was a sandy croak that would have embarrassed a frog.

Master Therapass touched Marcus's forehead. "How do you feel?"

Marcus pulled away from the wizard's touch. How did he *feel?* Confused, tired, and sick to his stomach. A few days ago, his biggest worry had been what Chet and his friends were up to. Now everything kept changing. How was he supposed to feel after learning he was from this strange world where magic was real and plants and animals could talk? He didn't want nightmare creatures trying to kill him, and he definitely didn't want a world full of people he didn't know thinking he was going to save them.

"How do you think he feels?" Kyja said from Marcus's side, as though reading his mind. She jutted out her chin and shook back her long, dark hair as she stared at Master Therapass. "He's confused. And I'm confused too. Why can't you stop talking in riddles?"

"Sometimes riddles are the only answers we have," Master Therapass said. "By the time you're my age, you'll learn the clearest answers are often the most misleading, and the best answers are almost always the most difficult to understand at first. But this time I'm being as plain as I possibly can." He raised his weathered face to the circle of blue sky high above them, where a beam of sunlight glowed down.

"Hold out your hand," he said to Marcus. "Like this." The wizard pulled the sleeve of his robe up to his elbow and held out his hand, palm down.

Marcus had no idea what the point was, but he held his hand beside the wizard's wrinkled one. "Now what am I supposed to—"

His words were cut off by Kyja's gasped, "Oh!"

Following her gaze, Marcus looked at his hand and felt his stomach turn over. Illuminated by the sun's golden light, Master Therapass's weathered hand wavered slightly, casting a dark shadow on the heavily needled ground. Beside it, Marcus's hand was also lit by the sun. But somehow most of the light appeared to pass *through* his skin. He could see rays of sunlight glowing pinkly beneath the palm of his hand. And his shadow on the ground was a dim, barely visible, gray—the kind of shadow you might see under a full moon.

"As I expected," the wizard said.

Marcus jerked his arm back as if afraid of being burned. Sweat trickled down the sides of his face, and his head throbbed. "What is it?" he whispered, suddenly aware of how quiet the forest had become. "What's wrong with me?"

"Perhaps it would be better if we spoke of this somewhere else," the wizard said, taking Marcus's arm.

"No." Marcus pulled away. "Tell me now."

Master Therapass glanced around the clearing, then nodded slowly. "Very well. It might be better if we face it together at that. There's still much I don't understand." He glanced toward the three large trees. "Do you mind? I've come a long way, and I'd like to sit for a while."

"Not at all," the tree on the right answered. At once, the ground began to rumble, and three roots thicker than Marcus's waist rose out of the ground. Master Therapass lowered himself onto one of the roots with a sigh. "Go ahead," he told Marcus and Kyja. "We may be here awhile."

Kyja glanced at Marcus, shrugged, and sat on one of the roots. Marcus joined her.

"There is nothing wrong with you," Master Therapass said, resting his chin in his hands. "As I told you, I realized I'd made a mistake after sending you to Earth. True, it may have been the only chance to save your life, but I quickly discovered there was no way to bring you back."

"You were wrong," Marcus said. "Kyja brought me here."

"That's what confused me at first." The wizard rummaged inside his robe, and his hand emerged, holding a roll of fragile-looking parchment. He traced his finger down the page, shaking his head and mumbling under his breath. At last he looked up from the document.

"It's impossible. According to everything I can find on the subject, there is a balance that must be maintained between worlds." He set the parchment beside him on the Weather Guardian's root and held out both his hands. "When I opened the doorway that sent Marcus to Earth, I unbalanced the Scales." He raised his left hand while lowering his right.

"To rebalance the Scales, Kyja was sent here." He moved his hands so they were even again. "You see? There is no way to bring Marcus back without sending Kyja to Earth. And since she is not there, you are not here."

Marcus ran his fingers through his hair. As far as he could tell, this balance business was all a bunch of nonsense. "If I'm not here, than where am I?"

"Ah, that's the question," Master Therapass said. He tapped the parchment with one finger. "There is no record of anything like this before. But I think I might understand."

The wizard began rummaging around inside his robe again. "Now where did I put that?" he muttered. He stuck his hands into his pockets and pulled out a ball of glittery, red string, something pink and slimy that began to ooze away when he set it on the root next to the parchment, and a jawbone filled with enormous-looking teeth.

"Don't tell me I left it back at the tower," he said, looking around the grove as though whatever he was searching for might be somewhere among the trees. "Wait." He turned around and reached into the hood of his cloak.

"There you are," he said, pulling out what looked to Marcus like a big, multicolored pancake.

As Master Therapass flattened the pancake on the ground in front of him, Marcus saw light shine up from it in multi-colored rays.

"The aptura discerna," Kyja said, leaving her root and leaning over it. "This is how I saw you the first time, Marcus, in the room with the Thrathkin S'Bae."

"Bonesplinter," Marcus said, trying not to shudder. He leaned over the window too. "How does it work?"

Master Therapass tapped the aptura discerna with a white and silver rod, and the colors began to spin together.

"Is that a real wand?" Marcus asked. The spinning colors made him feel a little queasy, but he watched closely anyway. In most of the books he'd read back on earth, magic spells always required some kind of secrets words like "hocus-pocus" or "eye of newt, wing of bat, turn this frog into a hat." But he hadn't heard Master Therapass say anything.

The wand disappeared from the wizard's hand too quickly for Marcus to follow, and he glanced up Master Therapass's sleeve, wondering if that's where it had gone.

"Kyja," Master Therapass said as the aptura discerna turned a cloudy pink, "remember carefully. Do you recall what you were thinking when you summoned Marcus here?"

Kyja nodded her head immediately. "I saw the snake trying to bite him, and I knew I was the only one who could help. I didn't want him to die. I thought I would do anything to save him."

A hint of a smile played at the corner of the wizard's mouth as he nodded. Marcus thought he heard him mutter something that sounded like, "No magic indeed."

"As you look into the aptura discerna," the wizard said to Kyja, "try to recall those same feelings in your mind—even more importantly recall them in your heart."

Kyja leaned over the swirling circle as Marcus watched from over her shoulder. At first there was nothing but the pink clouds. Then slowly, an image appeared. Marcus caught his breath as he recognized himself. It was just after he'd come to Farworld. He was sitting half in, half out of the brook, looking around with wide, scared eyes, like someone had just jabbed him with a cattle prod.

"That's it," Master Therapass said softly.

The image changed, and Marcus saw himself wrapped in the mimicker's web, struggling and trying to fight his way out. Although no sound came from inside the window, he thought Kyja must have called to him, because he looked up from the dark and stopped struggling.

Again the image shifted. This time Marcus and Kyja were on Chance's back as the horse raced toward the Westland Woods. Marcus's body bounced limply in the saddle—held in place only by Kyja's firm grip. As the image of Kyja in the aptura discerna turned to see a bolt of green light shoot toward them, the real Kyja staring down on the image whispered, "Help him."

"That's right," Master Therapass said. "You wanted to help him."

All at once the image disappeared and was replaced by a silver nothingness that Marcus at first thought was empty.

"No," Kyja said, shaking her head. And again louder, "No!"

Marcus leaned closer to the aptura discerna and realized the window wasn't quite empty. In the middle of the nothingness, something small and white hung suspended. He leaned closer still, and a cold bead of sweat rolled down the middle of his back.

Floating like a ship in an endless sea of silvery clouds was a figure. It hung, unmoving, its arms and legs bent, and its hands clenched as though gripping a chair that wasn't there. Its eyes were closed, and its features were so small as to be impossible to make out. But he had no question who it was.

Himself.

CHAPTER 31

THE BEST OF INTENTIONS

KYJA PULLED BACK FROM the aptura discerna, her face bathed in sweat. The swirling silver clouds gave her a sick feeling in the pit of her stomach, even after she looked up from the window. Watching the other images was slightly disorienting, but none of them made her feel the way the nothingness had—as if human eyes weren't meant to see that shapeless mist.

"Where is that place?" she asked Master Therapass. "And how can Marcus be here and there at the same time?"

The wizard brushed his hand over the aptura discerna, and the window returned to its previous stained-glass appearance. "Part of Marcus *is* here. Your desire to save him from almost certain death appears to have forged a link between the two of you. You summoned him here using that link. But you couldn't bring him all the way across—the Scales of Order wouldn't allow it. Another part of him is trapped between our two worlds."

He looked at Kyja and chuckled. "You asked me back in the

tower if I thought you had magic, little one. That you were able to summon even a part of Marcus shows magic greater than any I have ever seen. Magic I don't even pretend to understand."

"Is that why he's sick?" she asked. "Because part of him is stuck between worlds?" They both turned to Marcus, whose face looked pale and drawn. His eyes—underscored by dark circles which hadn't been there an hour earlier—roved wearily between the wizard and Kyja.

Master Therapass nodded. "I believe it is. I returned to Terra ne Staric for two reasons. One I won't discuss with you at this time. The other was to uncover everything I could find on portals."

The wizard picked up the fragile-looking scroll and unrolled it again, tugging at the end of his beard as he studied it. Kyja leaned over his shoulder, but the words on the parchment were written in a language she couldn't read.

"It appears that being in two places at once is draining you," The wizard said. "Only half of your body is eating. Only half of your body is breathing. The nourishment from the Weather Guardians seems to have helped, but I can only surmise that ultimately your body will fail if this goes on much longer."

"We have to bring the rest of him here," Kyja said, her eyes shining. She reached for the aptura discerna, but Master Therapass touched her hand.

She looked up at his grave face. "What are we waiting for? Just tell me what to do."

"It's not that simple," he said, running his fingers down the tip of his beard.

"Of course it is. You said he can't stay in two places, so I need to bring him all the way here." She clutched her amulet in her hands and stared into the aptura discerna, focusing her concentration on the memory of Marcus as she'd seen him floating in the silver mist. She didn't care how sick looking at the nothingness made her feel, the idea of a part of Marcus trapped there made her feel even worse. She *would* get him out. She could feel the power to do it burning inside her.

"Go ahead," she said. "Use your wand to make the colors go away. I can bring him here. I know I can."

"This is not the way," Master Therapass said. He took her chin in his fingertips and tilted her head until her eager, green eyes were looking into his solemn, brown ones. "There are certain laws that all elements must obey. When we use magic, we ask the elements to voluntarily aid us. To ignore those laws is to *force* the elements to obey us. That is the way of black magic. It is the way of the Dark Circle, and it will corrupt, even if you use it with the best of intentions."

"What are we supposed to do? Just leave him there?" Kyja pulled away from the wizard.

But Marcus was nodding, understanding clear in his eyes. "You have to send me back, don't you?"

"No." Kyja glared at him. "You can't go back. What about the snake man—Bonesplinter? What if he's still looking for you? Who will protect you?"

"I'll protect myself," Marcus said. "I've done it before."

Master Therapass placed his hand on Marcus's shoulder. "The part of you that is trapped between worlds will go with you once you return to Earth, and you should recover quickly."

"And then what?" Kyja asked, seething. "You said yourself he can't save Farworld if he's not here."

"I'll do everything I can to find a way to return you to Earth, Kyja, and to bring Marcus here," the wizard said. "That you came so close gives me hope it can be done. But for now . . ."

"No." She folded her arms across her chest and scowled. "I won't do it. Do we even know where he'll end up if I send him back? What if I return him to Bonesplinter? What if I drop him off a cliff?"

Master Therapass opened his mouth, but it was Marcus who answered.

"I know you don't want to send me back to Earth. And I don't want to go. You're the first real friend I've ever had. But part of me is dying. I can feel it." He touched his hand to his chest.

He turned to Master Therapass. "If I go back to Earth, will my arm and leg still work?"

The wizard frowned. "I think not."

"That's it, then," said Kyja. "He can't go. It wouldn't be safe."

Marcus touched her shoulder, his eyes meeting hers. "We have to."

Kyja glared at Marcus and Master Therapass, her chin quivering. This wasn't right. What was the point of bringing Marcus here, only to turn around and send him back? But what choice did she have? If she were a wizard, she'd find a different way. If only she could do *real* magic. *If only.* It was the story of her life.

"Fine," she snapped, feeling Master Therapass had let her down. "I'll do it."

Kyja refused to meet the wizard's eyes as he touched his wand to the aptura discerna. Instead, she focused on the swirl of colors— trying to keep the tears that burned in her eyes from sliding down her cheeks.

"Just like before," Master Therapass said. "Remember, you're doing this for Marcus. To help him."

Kyja blinked her eyes as a warm tear dripped past her nose. It wasn't fair. Marcus shouldn't have to go, and she shouldn't have to send him.

A hand closed around hers. Surprised, she looked up to see tears in Marcus's eyes as well as he knelt beside her. "Take care of Riph Raph," he said, forcing a grin. "I think he's going to miss me the most."

"He'll miss calling you names." Kyja reached up to brush away her tears and suddenly hiccupped, giving both of them an unexpected case of the giggles.

"Concentrate," Master Therapass warned. "Sending him back may not be as easy as summoning him."

Marcus gave her hand a final squeeze before letting go. "Try not to drop me in a stream this time," he said with a trace of a smile, and Kyja bit her lip, torn between laughing and crying.

Focusing on the aptura discerna, she reminded herself she was doing this for Marcus's good. For a moment, the window remained clouded.

"Search your heart," Master Therapass whispered.

Kyja remembered how she'd felt when she saw the snake trying to kill Marcus. How desperately she wanted to help when he was trapped in the mimicker's net. How awful she felt when she thought the Fallen Ones were going to get him.

The aptura discerna cleared, and she saw the silver sea again, with Marcus floating in the middle. Staring at his limp figure trapped in the center of the nothingness, she knew she had to get him out of there.

Summon him, a voice said. She tried to look away from the aptura discerna to see who had spoken, but the swirling silver mist held her eyes locked on it.

Rescue him. The voice spoke again, and this time she wondered if it was actually coming from inside her own head. *Master Therapass doesn't know everything. He said so himself. Bring Marcus to you and protect him.*

Protect him? How could she protect him? It was only luck that had brought them to the Westland Woods without being killed by the creatures of night or eaten by the mimicker.

You have magic. Magic greater than Marcus's. Greater than the wizard's. But you're afraid to use it. The silver mist spun and swirled before her like a great, unfocused eye, and Kyja felt something move inside her. Something she'd never experienced before. Something that felt almost like . . . *magic?*

That's it, the voice urged. *Feel your magic. Feel its power within you. Bring him to you and protect him.*

Far off, she thought she could hear another voice calling to her. But it was so distant, she couldn't make out the words. Out of the mist dropped the golden rope she'd used to pull Marcus across the first time. She imagined her hand reaching forward and grasping it. All it would take was one tug.

Pull, the voice cried with an insistence that was irresistible. *Pull now.* In her hands, the amulet burned.

As Kyja began to pull on the rope, she thought she felt the ground tremble beneath her. In the aptura discerna, Marcus opened his eyes. But it wasn't gratitude she saw on his face, it was terror. All at once, she remembered Master Therapass's words. *To ignore those laws is to force the elements to obey us . . . it will corrupt, even if you use it with the best of intentions . . . that is the way of the Dark Circle.*

"No!" she screamed, and instead of pulling, she gritted her teeth and pushed at Marcus as hard as she could.

The aptura discerna flashed red, and Kyja was thrown backward onto the ground. There was a roaring in her ears, and she tasted blood in her mouth. Opening her eyes, she saw Master Therapass leaning over her, worry painted across his face.

"Did I . . ." She tried to sit up and everything started to spin. "Did I send him?"

"No," said a voice that she recognized immediately as Marcus's. "I'm still here."

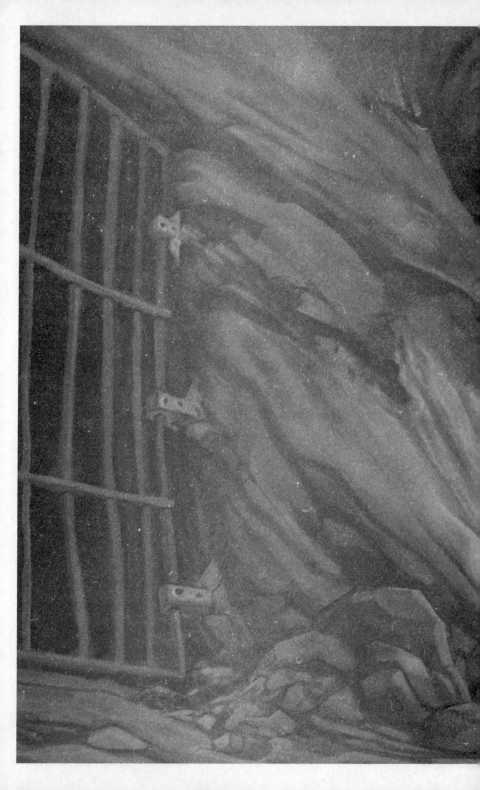

PART 3

Journey

CHAPTER 32

Y'SDINE'S FEINT

LET ME TRY AGAIN." Kyja was sitting on a root, rubbing her forehead. Her tongue throbbed where she'd bitten it, but the bloody taste was gone from her mouth.

"Absolutely not. It's too dangerous." Master Therapass looked pale and worried. The aptura discerna had disappeared back into his robe.

"I wasn't expecting anything to be in there," she said, getting up and pacing across the clearing. "This time I'll be prepared."

"It's not that," the wizard said, raising a stern finger. "Whatever you heard was waiting for you. It knew where Marcus was, and it knew you would come for him. If you had given in and succeeded in summoning Marcus completely to Farworld, both of you would have been corrupted; your presence would be welcomed only by the Dark Circle. The Fallen Ones tried to trick you and failed. Who knows what they might try next time."

Marcus had been leaning his head against one of the Weather

Guardian's roots, drinking the sap through a small, straw-like tube. He sat up, looking a little better. "What choice do we have?" he asked.

Master Therapass turned a small, colored stone in his hand. "For the moment, we wait."

"Wait?" Kyja asked, feeling her frustration boiling over. "First you tell me I have no choice but to send Marcus to Ert at once. Now you want to wait. What's the point?"

Master Therapass shook the sleeve of his robe, and more of the colored stones fell into his palm. Ignoring Kyja's angry stare, he spread the stones onto the root in a circle, alternating green and red. "Have you ever played Trill Stones, Marcus?"

Kyja snorted. She couldn't believe Master Therapass wanted to play games while Marcus might be dying. But Marcus moved beside the wizard to take a closer look.

"Kyja beats me as this game regularly," the wizard said. "But perhaps I'd have a better chance with someone a little less experienced."

Marcus rubbed his cheek absently. "It almost seems like I've seen this before."

"Really?" Master Therapass tilted his head. "The rules are actually quite simple. There are twenty-four playing pieces—twelve red and twelve green. The board consists of twelve concentric circles." As he waved his hand over the stones, twelve circles glowed just above the root in the same colors as the stones. "The goal is to get two of your stones into the center circle."

"Make him go first," Kyja said, taking an interest in spite of herself. Trill Stones was her favorite game. "The key to winning is waiting for him to—"

"—reveal his strategy," Marcus finished.

Kyja and Master Therapass both blinked in surprise. "You *have* played before then?" the wizard asked.

"Not that I remember, exactly," Marcus scratched the side of his head. "But I think maybe Elder Ephraim might have taught it to me when I was little."

"The man who rescued you on Ert?" Kyja asked.

Marcus nodded. "But that isn't possible, is it?" he asked Master Therapass.

Instead of answering, the wizard moved one of his stones two circles in.

"That's called Tanjin's Guard," Kyja said, edging closer. "You can take his spot with your marker or move into the space behind him. But if you move next to him, he can take your stone."

For the next thirty minutes, Kyja guided Marcus through the game step by step. At first he made simple mistakes, but before long, he was attempting moves even Kyja hadn't anticipated.

"Perhaps I underestimated you," Master Therapass said as he narrowly avoided a trap Marcus had set.

"I think you did," Marcus said. In a series of quick jumps, he took three of the wizard's stones and landed his first stone into the middle circle.

"Look out," Kyja warned when she saw what Marcus was doing. But it was too late. On the wizard's move, he jumped Marcus's stone and set himself up to win on his next turn.

Marcus stared at the board, dumbstruck. "I was so close," he said, moving a stone that had no impact on the final outcome.

"It's Y'sdine's feint," Kyja said as Master Therapass moved his second stone into the center circle, winning the game. "I used it against him all the time until he figured it out."

"You waited for me to spring my trap, then used it against me." Marcus shook his hair out of his eyes.

Kyja sat up straight. "That's why we're waiting, isn't it?" she blurted.

Master Therapass took out his wand, and the stones neatly stacked themselves and dropped into a small leather bag which appeared in his other hand.

Kyja tugged on the wizard's sleeve. "It's just like the game. You're waiting to see what the Dark Circle's going to do." Once she realized what Master Therapass was up to, her impatience disappeared. But why couldn't he have just told her?

Master Therapass handed the bag to Marcus. "Take these to practice with. When you can beat Kyja, you'll be good indeed." The wizard's eyes narrowed. "They may come in useful in other ways as well."

Marcus jiggled the bag of stones in his hands, making them clink softly together. "You think the Dark Circle was waiting for Kyja to send me back to Earth?"

Kyja realized how late in the afternoon it was getting. The patch of sky overhead had gone from bright blue to purple.

Master Therapass knuckled the small of his back and stood up to stretch. "It would explain why they haven't attempted to pursue you into the forest."

Kyja rubbed her sore tongue against the inside of her cheek, remembering how she'd been thrown backward by whatever was in the aptura discerna. "What does it matter?" she asked, her earlier excitement disappearing. "As long as they're waiting outside the forest and blocking me from sending Marcus back, we're trapped."

"I wonder," Marcus said, using a twig to doodle shapes in the dirt. "Can the Dark Circle create their own doorways like the one that sent me to Earth?"

"No," Master Therapass said, studying Marcus. "The portal I created for you uses white magic. The Dark Circle can only use black magic."

Marcus brushed away the shape he'd been drawing and started again. "Then where did Bonesplinter come from? I'm pretty sure he wasn't born on Earth."

Master Therapass listened intently as Marcus told him about Bonesplinter and what he'd seen him do behind the school.

"Of course," the wizard said, when Marcus had finished. "Once they discovered where I'd sent you, they came up with a plan to destroy you. They must have created a drift."

"What's a drift?" Kyja asked.

Olden and the rest of the Weather Guardians had been so silent Kyja had almost forgotten they were there. But apparently they had been listening all along, because Olden unexpectedly piped up.

"A drift is a passageway," she said in her high, scratchy voice. "A passageway between worlds. Don't they teach you children anything?"

"A passageway between here and Earth?" Marcus asked, spinning around on the seat of his pants to face the tree.

"No, silly boy," Olden chirped. "Between here and your dusty britches." The old tree cackled as if she'd told the funniest joke in the world.

"That's it then," Kyja said. She broke into a wide grin. "All we need to do is find the drift. Marcus can come through it to Farworld, and . . ." She paused, her eyes lit with wonder. "And I could go back to Ert. Maybe I could even find my parents."

But Master Therapass was shaking his head before she even

finished. "If the Dark Circle has created a drift, they did it by force. Before you could get halfway through, you'd be as foul as they are."

Kyja slumped back onto her root, dejected.

"I don't imagine there's a way we could build a drift of our own, is there?" Marcus asked.

Beside him, Olden cackled even louder than before. "By all means, children. Build a drift. You should get started right a-a-a-way." Her last word disappeared into a gale of rough laughter.

Kyja turned to Master Therapass, who was looking down in apparent disgust. "What's that crazy tree talking about?" she asked, shooting Olden a dirty look. Master Therapass turned to Kyja. "It's impossible to create a drift without using dark magic."

"Impossible?" Marcus asked. "But Olden . . ."

"Ignore her," Master Therapass said. "Trees have an odd sense of humor. I think the sap goes to their heads sometimes. The only way to create a drift without using dark magic would be if the four elements voluntarily worked in unison."

"What are *elements?*" Marcus asked.

Master Therapass knelt down and used Marcus's twig to draw four squares in the dirt. In each he drew a symbol. All of the symbols had a loop at one end, but the other ends were all different. The first looked a little like a crab claw, the second like a snapping whip, the third like the curl of a pig's tail, and the last like a small square within the larger square.

"The symbols of magic," Kyja said.

"Correct," he answered, examining his work. "Fire, Water, Air, and Land. The basis for all magic and—some say—all life. The four elements make up nearly everything around us. According to some of the most ancient and sacred writings, each of the elements is controlled by its own group of beings known as elementals."

"Just like the song," Kyja said. Clapping her hands, she repeated the words she'd learned as a child.

> *See the Lords of Water—*
> *Beyond the waves they leap*
>
> *See the Lords of Land—*
> *Beneath the ground they sleep*
>
> *See the Lords of Air—*
> *Above the clouds they creep*
>
> *See the Lords of Fire—*
> *Around the flames they reap*
>
> *Water. Land. Air. Fire.*
> *Together, the balance of Farworld they keep.*

"Where did you learn that?" Marcus asked.

Kyja grinned. "Lady Mangum taught it to all the children in magic school." But then her smile faded. "Before they told me I had to leave." She turned to Master Therapass. "But I thought elementals were make-believe creatures."

Master Therapass shrugged. "Some say yes. Some say no. Personally, I believe they exist."

"These elementals," Marcus said. "Are they living beings?"

"No one knows for sure what they are," Master Therapass said.

"People claim to have seen them on rare occasion, but no human has ever spoken to one."

"And the elementals could open a drift?" Kyja asked, warming to the subject.

"*Could* and *would* are two very different things." The wizard clapped his hands together, making a small, blue bowl of water and a flickering candle appear in the air before him. "The same writings that speak of elementals claim that by cooperating with one another they could indeed open a drift between worlds."

Kyja opened her mouth, but before she could say a word, the wizard nudged the bowl with his left hand. It approached the flame, then pulled suddenly back as though on a string. When the wizard pushed the candle toward the water, the same thing happened. "Combining elements in a spell is hard enough. But according to the scrolls, the elementals that control the elements are a thousand times more difficult. They are complete opposites of one another. You could no more ask a fire elemental to work with a water elemental than you could ask a fish to live on dry land."

"But don't they stand to lose as much as everyone else if the Dark Circle wins?" Marcus asked.

"No one knows how the elementals think." Master Therapass scratched out his pictures and laid the twig aside. "The elements don't talk to each other, and they absolutely don't talk to humans."

"When was the last time anyone tried?" Kyja asked, and the wizard gave her a strange look. "Doesn't it make sense that the elements would be against anyone who uses dark magic? Anyone who forces the elements to obey their will? The Dark Circle is corrupt. You said so yourself."

"What are you suggesting?" Master Therapass asked.

"Why don't we at least try talking to them and see if they'll listen? The Weather Guardians didn't want to help us at first, did they?"

For once Olden didn't laugh at one of Kyja's suggestions.

"It would be extremely difficult to locate them," Master Therapass said. "Everything I've read claims the elementals are impossible to find unless you know exactly where to look. I wouldn't have the faintest idea where to begin." But he seemed intrigued anyway.

"I do," Olden said, and this time she didn't sound like she was joking. "At least the water elementals. They live in a place called Water Keep. And I might even be willing to tell its location . . . for a price."

CHAPTER 33

GALESPINNER

I T WAS EARLY MORNING, and the damp, gray mist that hung in the cold air like wet cotton balls made Marcus feel as if he were standing in a cloudbank. Behind him, the movement of the trees' branches broke up the fog and sent its moisture skyward. But here at the edge of the forest, he could barely see more than ten feet ahead, and tiny drops of water clung to his face and arms.

Master Therapass had provided him with a traveling cloak—cut down so it wouldn't drag too badly when he was on his hands and knees—and a pair of pants with magical properties to keep out the moisture and cold. He had also replaced Marcus's worn gloves with a magic pair specially fitted to his hands. But somehow the water had made it inside his clothing anyway.

"I feel like someone dunked me in the river," he said, his teeth chattering.

"At least you can't blame it on me this time," Kyja said, wrapping her cloak more tightly around her.

Riph Raph, still crabby over being separated from the rest of the group by the Weather Guardians, cocked his head and said, "A little water couldn't hurt either of you. You were both starting to smell rather ripe, if you want my opinion."

"We don't," Kyja and Marcus said in unison.

"Humph," he snorted, flapping his wings. But Marcus noted the skyte didn't blow out a ball of blue flame as he normally did when he was upset. The Weather Guardians had been very clear about what they did to anyone who brought an open flame within a hundred feet of the trees, and it wasn't pretty.

Chance looked up from munching stalks of grass a few feet away and turned to Marcus. "Knock, knock."

"Who's there?" Marcus answered.

"Don't get him started," Kyja said with a shake of her head, that pulled her long ponytail free from the hood of her cloak.

"Dishes," Chance said, ignoring her.

"Dishes who?" Marcus asked. He'd missed the big horse and his silly jokes.

"Dishes the coldest it's been in weeks."

Marcus couldn't help laughing as the stallion whinnied at his own joke. Even Riph Raph seemed slightly amused. But Kyja only rolled her eyes in disgust as she tucked her hair back into her cloak.

"Where *is* Master Therapass?" she grumped. "He said he wanted to go first thing in the morning. I don't like the looks of this weather, and I'm tired of standing around listening to dumb jokes. "

Marcus shrugged. He knew that Kyja was really upset about the wizard's plan to leave the safety of the Westland Woods. But he, for one, was happy to be getting out of the forest. Having lived his whole life under wide-open skies with plenty of space around, the huge trees made him feel a little claustrophobic. He'd worry about the Dark Circle if and when he had to.

"You don't remember what it was like being chased by the Thrathkin S'Bae and those horrible dogs of theirs," Kyja said. "If you did, you wouldn't be so anxious to leave."

Marcus started. He knew Kyja couldn't actually listen in on his thoughts—at least he was pretty sure she couldn't. But it was still strange to be around someone who could read him so well. "Wasn't it your idea to go looking for the four elementals in the first place?" he said, rubbing his arms to try to get warm.

"Not if I'd known how long it would take. Water Keep is at least three weeks of travel away—if we can trust that nasty old tree. Personally, I think demanding Master Therapass's promise of protection for a stupid map is completely unacceptable. But even if she *is* telling the truth, you said yourself you can't last here that long. And that's just to reach the first of the elementals. What is Master Therapass thinking?"

Marcus cast his gaze on the thick fog, remembering that part of him was trapped in a place which looked very similar. Did that part of him know it was trapped? Could it feel cold or loneliness? The thought made him shudder. He fingered the leather bag Master Therapass had given him. Along with the colored stones, he'd also tucked his picture of Elder Ephraim and the thirteen dollars he'd taken from his suitcase into the bag.

"Elder Ephraim used to say the first step of any journey takes place in the mind. You wouldn't have suggested the trip if you didn't think we could find a way to accomplish it."

Before Kyja could respond, Master Therapass walked out of the mist, shaking the dew from his cloak. He wrung his beard, and a stream of water dripped from the tip. "You are ready then. Very good." He turned to Marcus. "How are you feeling?"

"Cold," Marcus said, rubbing his hands together.

"A little cold weather won't kill you," the wizard said. He removed a leather parchment from inside his robes and unrolled it for Marcus and Kyja to see. It was the map Olden had given them the night before.

Marcus pointed to a drawing of a city on the far right side of the map. It was located on the south edge of a huge lake. "Is that Water Keep?"

"If Olden's information is correct—and I have no reason to think it isn't—we should be able to reach Lake Aeternus before the snow starts to fall." The wizard traced his finger along a route that took them north out of the Westland Woods, up past the northern-most ridges of the Windlash Mountains, and then east, across the Plains of Theyer.

"Why not just go straight across the Windlash Mountains?" Marcus asked. It looked like it would cut the trip almost in half.

"No," Master Therapass said. "The Windlash Mountains are no place for children. Besides, the passes are closed by now. It would be impossible to get through."

"Are you sure we should go at all?" Kyja asked before he could say another word. "What if more of those Thrathkin S'Bae are out there?"

"The Dark Circle is, undoubtedly, waiting for us to leave the forest," Master Therapass said.

"Then why leave? Let's just stay until we come up with another plan," Kyja pleaded, edging closer into the trees.

Master Therapass slid his wand between his fingers. "If the Dark Circle wanted to flush us out, they could have burned the forest to the ground. They have waited not because they are unable to enter the forest, but because it is the perfect trap. They are hoping that as long as you feel secure, you won't leave. That suits them perfectly, while their focus is on other fronts."

"What other fronts?" Marcus asked.

The wizard's eyes narrowed. "Brute force is not the Dark Circle's only tool. Even as they search for you, they seek other means to insert their influence into the highest seats of power."

Kyja jumped as if someone had just pinched her. "The man I saw with the High Lord back in Terra ne Staric. Is he part of the Dark Circle? Is that one of the reasons you went back?"

Instantly Master Therapass placed a finger to her lips. "Some things are better not spoken of."

"Now then," he said straightening, "I think it's time for us to make our departure. The Fallen Ones can appear at any time, but early morning is when they are the least active. I've scouted far to the north, and for the moment, it's clear. I suspect they have placed most of their forces to the south, expecting us to return to Terra ne Staric. We should be able to gain a good head start. They may not even discover we've left."

"As for you." The wizard held out his arm to Riph Raph, and the skyte flew up onto the sleeve of his robe. "I want you to fly ahead of us. If you see anything out of place, return at once and report to me."

For once Riph Raph didn't have a snide comment. He flapped his ears and launched himself into the fog-shrouded sky.

"But what about Marcus?" Kyja asked. "You said yourself he can't stay in this world. He'll never make it on a trip this long."

The wizard nodded thoughtfully. "Yes. The Weather Guardians' sap will help him for a few days, but we'll need to find a way to return him to Earth before long. Perhaps the Dark Circle's guard will be down when they discover we've left the woods."

Still Kyja didn't seem convinced. "What if they find us?"

Master Therapass turned to stare out into the foggy morning. "They *will* find us eventually. The Dark Circle has too many spies to believe otherwise. We will deal with that eventuality when it comes."

"Will you stay with us this time?" Marcus asked.

A shadow crossed the wizard's face. "Yes. I believe my usefulness in the tower may be at an end. If we're going to have any hope, though, you'll need a faster mount."

"We're not taking Chance?" Marcus limped over to where the stallion was grazing. Chance raised his head, and Marcus petted the horse's nose.

"He brought you this far, but he'll be safer back in Terra ne Staric." He walked over and patted Chance's mane. "The Dark Circle shouldn't bother him on his own. Do you think you can find your way home, boy?"

Chance pawed the ground with his hoof and started into the woods. Just before he disappeared from sight, he stopped and turned back. "Knock, knock."

Master Therapass smiled. "Who's there?"

"Lass."

"Lass who?"

"Lass one home's a rotten egg."

Kyja snorted. "I've never heard that one before."

Marcus smirked. "I taught it to him."

With Chance gone, Marcus glanced around. "What are we supposed to ride now?"

Master Therapass put his fingers to his lips and gave two piercing whistles. Marcus turned to Kyja, but she only shrugged her shoulders, looking around curiously.

A moment later, Marcus caught a movement out of the corner of his eye. He turned in time to see something appear silently out of the fog. Although it stood on four legs, it wasn't any kind of horse *he* had ever seen. At least a foot taller than Chance and nearly twice as broad through the chest, its body was an almost blinding white.

But it was the head he couldn't take his eyes from. It was narrow and like a bird's, but covered with pale golden scales. And inside its beak-like mouth were sharp, white teeth. Growing from the top of its head and down the back of its neck was a mane of gauzy, golden tendrils that looked like fairy wings.

As he watched, the creature glared down at him with blazing, orange eyes, reared up on its hind legs, and snorted. Plumes of white steam shot from the creature's nostrils. Marcus backed away from it, scared to death. He was *not* going to get on the back of *that*.

But Kyja stepped slowly toward it, a look of awe on her face. She turned to Master Therapass. "A mist steed?"

The wizard nodded. "Her name's Galespinner. There's no need to be afraid, Marcus. She won't hurt you."

Marcus stared up at the huge beast. He couldn't even imagine riding her. "How would I ever get on?" he asked.

As if she had heard his question, the mist steed stepped toward him and lowered her head.

"Go on," said Master Therapass. "Take hold of her mane."

Positive he was about to be eaten, Marcus walked toward the creature and closed his fingers around the nearly invisible hairs. They looked insubstantial, but felt much stronger than they appeared—like holding onto a silken net. As soon as Marcus and Kyja had a firm grip on her mane, Galespinner raised her head and set them on her back in one swift motion.

It happened so quickly, Marcus didn't have time to be scared. And once he was on the mist steed's back, he found she fit his legs so perfectly there was no need for a saddle. "Is she magic?" he whispered to Kyja.

"Yes," she whispered back. "I've heard of them, but I've never actually seen one before. They're supposed to be as fast as the wind."

Master Therapass rubbed the mist steed's nose. "As a creature of pure white magic, she is immune to any harm the Dark Circle might try to cause her."

Marcus ran his hand along the animal's back. He could feel the strong muscles, but her skin was soft as silk. "I guess she doesn't tell jokes," he whispered.

Galespinner shook back her mane and snorted. Kyja shot him a dirty look. "Of course not."

Marcus turned to Master Therapass, who had been watching the two of them with an amused look on his face. "If we ride, how will you be able to keep up?"

Without a word, the wizard tucked his hands into his robes. In a blur of movement, he transformed into the great, gray wolf that had attacked the mimicker. Throwing back his head, the wolf gave a deafening howl that made Marcus jump. The wolf's pink tongue lolled out of his mouth, and Marcus thought he might be grinning.

"Don't worry," the wolf said in the wizard's voice. "I'll manage."

CHAPTER 34

STICKS AND AIR

B Y LATE THAT DAY, the fog had turned into a steady rain and Marcus and Kyja were soaked to the skin, despite their supposedly waterproof cloaks.

"I think the Weather Guardians did this on purpose," Kyja said.

Marcus grunted, too cold and tired to say more. At least his tailbone didn't ache like it had after riding Chance all day. He wanted to think it was because he'd become used to riding, but he suspected it was because Galespinner's gait was so smooth and silent he could barely tell she was moving if he closed his eyes.

For his part, Master Therapass seemed impervious to the rain. Marcus guessed a thick pelt of fur had its benefits. And if Galespinner was bothered by the water, she didn't show it in the least. In fact she didn't show much of anything, and Marcus found himself missing Chance's silliness. He considered trying a knock-knock joke on the mist steed, but was afraid he might offend her.

"Is it time to stop for the night yet?' he asked Master Therapass, who'd trotted along beside them all day without any rest. The only chance they'd had to stop was for bathroom breaks. Master Therapass insisted they even eat on the move.

The wolf glanced up at him with its dark, gleaming eyes, and Marcus had to remind himself it was actually the wizard inside. At least four feet tall at the shoulders, and with a mouth full of wickedly sharp teeth, he was an intimidating sight. Marcus was glad he was on their side.

"I thought you wanted to learn magic," Master Therapass said. "Or are you too tired for that?"

"I do," Marcus stammered. "I mean I'm not." Early that morning he'd asked Master Therapass how to do magic, hoping the wizard would teach him some special words or ingredients for a potion. He thought Master Therapass had forgotten his request. Apparently he'd been wrong.

The wolf stopped and sniffed the air. "I do not scent any trace of the Dark Circle. Perhaps we can spare a few minutes."

Kyja watched Master Therapass anxiously as Galespinner pawed the ground.

"When do we start?" Marcus asked. His mind filled with images of wands and glittering powders.

Instead, the wolf picked up a small branch in his jaws and, without a word, threw it at Marcus with a twist of his neck.

Marcus ducked, but not in time to keep the stick from beaning him squarely between the eyes.

"Ouch," he cried, rubbing his head and trying to ignore the mist steed's whinny that sounded suspiciously like laughter. "What was that for?"

"Your first magic lesson," the wolf answered. "Take the branch and throw it back at me."

What branch? he thought to himself, before realizing the stick which hit him in the head was floating a few inches from his left ear.

"How'd you do that?" he asked, snatching the stick out of the air.

"Throw it at me," the wolf said.

Marcus wound up and let go. Although his left arm could barely move, his right arm was strong, and he knew the throw was on target as soon as the stick left his hand. But at the last minute, it swerved and missed the wolf's head by a good two feet.

"Hey," he gasped. That would have come in handy playing dodge ball.

"It's all about land and air," the wizard said. "The branch moves easily because solid matter is heavier than air. To shield yourself from an object, you must ask the air in front of you to grow heavier than the object. Understand?"

"No." Marcus shook his head confused. "I mean, I understand what you're saying, but not how to do it. Maybe if I had a wand or something?"

The wolf barked. "Wands, staffs, and talismans are merely tools to focus your thoughts. Until you develop your magic more fully, they are of no use to you. Trust me, once you understand the magic behind it, your wand will find you.

"Now then, imagine the air as bread dough spread so thin you can't even see it. Then imagine kneading the air together until it becomes a solid mass. At the same time imagine rolling the wood out so flat it could fly away at the slightest breeze."

"But how do I make it do what I want?' Marcus asked. "What words do I say?"

"You don't *make* the elements do anything. You *ask* them. And you don't use words. What kind of words would air or a stick under-stand? Use your mind. Let's try again."

As the wolf picked up another branch, Marcus concentrated on the air in front of his face. *Thicken,* he said inside his head. If any-thing was happening, he couldn't tell. Master Therapass let the stick fly, but this time Marcus was ready. He ducked aside at the last minute, and the piece of wood flew harmlessly past.

"Hah!" he shouted. But his joy was short-lived as something thumped him on the back of the head, and he turned to see the stick floating in the air.

Marcus wanted to reach out and slap the branch away, but he knew if he did, Master Therapass would do something equally annoying, like make it drum him across the backs of his fingers.

Galespinner raised her head and whinnied, but this time it didn't sound like laughter. The wolf lifted his gray muzzle and scented the air. "It's time to leave."

For the next hour or so, the four of them continued at a steady clip. Every so often Master Therapass snatched up another stick without breaking stride and tossed it at Marcus until Marcus's head was a mass of scratches and bruises. By the time the sun reached the far edge of the horizon, it was almost too dim to make out the sticks at all. Kyja watched with surprising silence.

"One more try," Master Therapass said. "Then we'll stop for the night."

Marcus grimaced as the wizard snatched up another piece of wood, sure that he was about to get hit again. "Remember," the wolf said around the stick held between its teeth. "Don't *tell* the air what to do. *Ask* it."

Ask it, Marcus thought. But how was he supposed to ask air any-thing? When he wanted to hide, he imagined himself growing dim.

If what Master Therapass said was true, he was asking the air to deflect what others saw when they looked in his direction. How did he ask it to do that?

All he did was say a silly little rhyme. Could that be it? Was his rhyme, like a wand, just another tool to help him concentrate? What if he came up with a rhyme to make a shield? The wolf turned its head to throw and Marcus thought quickly.

Air like bread dough, thicken please
Stick fly off into the breeze

It was stupid and couldn't possibly work. Yet as Marcus watched the stick fly toward him, he thought he saw the air warp in front of his eyes. It was like he was looking through a pair of glasses with bent lenses.

At the last second he closed his eyes and . . . nothing. When he opened his eyes, the wolf was grinning.

"Perfect!" Master Therapass called.

"I did it?" Marcus asked, still trying to convince himself that the branch hadn't hit him.

"You did it," the wizard agreed.

"I did it!" Marcus shouted. He grabbed Kyja by the shoulders and shook her. "Did you see me? I did magic!"

"Congratulations," Kyja said, sounding less than thrilled.

All at once Marcus realized how she must be feeling. She'd wanted to do magic all her life and couldn't cast a spell. His success had to make her feel terrible. "I'm sorry," he said at once. "I wasn't thinking."

"No." She shook her head, forcing a smile. "It's fine. Really. I'm glad for you. I'm just tired."

"Sure," he agreed. Although he really wanted to keep practicing the trick now that he'd figured it out, he pretended to yawn. "I'm tired too. Master Therapass, you said we could stop after the next try."

They'd been climbing a small hill. At the top, the wolf halted, and the mist steed stopped beside it. Master Therapass raised his nose, scenting the air in all four directions.

Riph Raph, who'd been flying overhead all day, landed on Kyja's shoulder.

"Have you seen any sign of the Dark Circle?" Master Therapass asked, transforming back into his wizard self.

"No," the skyte said, shaking the water from his wings in a wide spray. "But unless they looked like clouds, I wouldn't have spotted them even if they were under my nose."

"Very well." Master Therapass pointed his finger to a spot near a waist-high boulder and a small fire appeared. "This will have to do until I've scouted the area. Marcus, Kyja, go ahead and get dinner started."

Marcus gripped Galespinner's gossamer mane, knowing from experience it would take awhile before the feeling completely came back into his legs.

"I'm starving," Kyja said as the mist steed set them on the ground.

"Me too," Marcus said. "I hope we get something hot." Lunch had been damp bread, cold cheese, and, for Marcus, more of the tree sap. The Weather Guardians said the sap would go bad after two or three days, but until then it should help him fight off the weakness.

"We'll eat quickly and extinguish the fire," Master Therapass said, looking out into the rain. "I've haven't seen or smelled anything, but I've had a feeling all day that something's out there."

Kyja dug into her bag and took out a small pan. "Put this on the fire. I think I still have some sausage left, and potatoes."

"Sounds great," Marcus said. Using a couple of rocks, he managed to prop the pan up over the flames. "You know. The thing about making that shield was—" He looked up from the fire to see Master Therapass watching the mist steed intently.

"What is it, Galespinner?" the wizard asked.

The mist steed pawed the ground and shook her head, blowing plumes of steam from her nostrils.

Master Therapass searched the misty valley. He reached into his robe and pulled out the ball of red, glittery string Marcus had seen the day before.

"What's wrong?" Kyja asked, her hand still on the food bag.

The wizard played out a length of string and held it tight between his fingers. Nothing happened, and the wizard released a low sigh.

Marcus gasped for air, unaware he'd stopped breathing for a moment.

"I was afraid they might have approached us from below ground," the wizard said.

Just as he began to wind the string back around the ball, it let out a loud twang. Vibrating in his hands, the entire ball began to glow. In an instant, the ball was gone from Master Therapass's hand and was replaced by his wand. He pointed a finger at the fire and it disappeared.

"Get back on the mist steed!" he shouted. The ground began shaking so hard Marcus was thrown onto his back.

"What's happening?" Kyja cried, pulling Marcus toward Galespinner.

Master Therapass set his feet and raised both hands into the air. Blue and green fire crackled from the tip of his wand and quickly spread over his entire body. A bolt of lightning split the bruised, purple sky, and Marcus saw the wizard's face set in grim determination.

"They are here!" the wizard shouted, and the night exploded around them.

CHAPTER 35

BACK FROM THE DEAD

THE BATTLE STARTED before Kyja and Marcus were even on Galespinner's back. Gripping the mist steed's mane, Kyja heard a deafening *thum, thum, thum* fill the air. Her first thought was thousands of drums, but what she saw when she turned her head made her skin go cold.

All across the field at the base of the hill, insect-like creatures burrowed out of the ground. Each creature was the size of a large dog with thick, short-snouted heads and bristly legs. Their bodies were covered with shiny, black shells, and their long pincers snapped open and closed as they converged on the top of the hill. There were at least a hundred of them, and more coming out of the ground every second.

Above them, the night sky filled with dozens of long-winged, bird-like creatures. It was their flapping wings that filled the air with the thrumming.

As the mist steed dropped Kyja and Marcus onto her back, the first of the insect creatures reached the top of the hill. Its yellow eyes glowed when it spotted Marcus. It raced toward him with a high-pitched squeal.

Before it could reach him, Master Therapass pointed his wand, and the creature exploded, its shell bursting into a million pieces. Two of the flying monsters dove out of the sky, their long teeth gleaming like sword blades as their jaws snapped. The wizard waved his hand, and a sheet of white flame engulfed them.

"Look out!" Marcus cried, as at least a dozen more insects came at Master Therapass from both sides. The wizard raised his hands, and again white flame jetted from his fingertips, frying the creatures in their shells.

By now the entire hillside was swarming with more of the creatures than Kyja could count, and the sky was filled with flapping wings and harsh screams. There was no way one person could stop them all. "Get back!" she shouted to Master Therapass.

If the wizard heard her, he gave no sign. Instead, still crackling with the green and blue fire, he raised his wand to the sky and shouted, "Firmaments open!"

At once, the night was filled with bright, orange light. Thousands of fireballs streaked down from the sky, seeking out the Fallen Ones with deadly accuracy. As each fireball struck its target, the insects exploded. The winged creatures fell from the air, and bits of smoking black shell covered the hillside.

Looking around, Kyja realized every one of the creatures had been destroyed.

"You did it!" Marcus shouted. "That was awesome. Can you show me how to—"

His words cut off as three Thrathkin S'Bae appeared at the bottom of the hill, their forked staffs burning brightly in the darkness. The first stepped forward, his face hidden by the cowl of his cloak.

"Give us the children, and none of you need die," the figure roared. His voice pierced Kyja's ears like the talon of a wild animal, and she clapped her hands to the sides of her head.

"There is nothing here for you," Master Therapass answered. His words were soft but filled with power.

The other two Thrathkin S'Bae stepped up beside the first, and the three of them raised their staffs. *"Ruet tei din,"* the three incanted simultaneously. A huge ball of bright green fire raced up the hill, leaving a trail of smoking grass in its wake.

Kyja squinted against the glare, but long before the ball reached the top of the hill, Master Therapass raised his hand, and the fire snuffed out of sight.

Again the three raised their staffs. *"Nhet an ter."*

The earth shook, ripping chunks of soil and rock from the side of the hill. Galespinner swung her head and pawed the ground nervously, snorting plumes of steam from her nostrils, but Master Therapass remained steady. He held out his hand palm down.

"Return to the grave!" he shouted. A rush of wind battered the Thrathkin S'Bae. The one on the right suddenly crumpled to the ground, his empty cloak blowing across the field.

"Turn back," the wizard said. Again he raised his hand, and a wave of dirt rose up in front of the two remaining cloaked figures, pausing for just a moment like a great, closed fist before crashing down on them.

The two remaining Thrathkin S'Bae disappeared beneath the pile of rocks and dust.

Kyja couldn't believe it. She knew Master Therapass was powerful, but she'd never seen anything like this before.

"Yes!" Marcus pumped his fist in the air. "That was so cool. Did you see the way—"

"Hush," Master Therapass warned without turning his head.

"What's wrong?" Kyja asked.

Marcus tried to dismount from the mist steed, but the wizard held a hand toward him. "Stay where you are. There's still something out there."

Kyja's mouth went dry. What else could there be? The Thrathkin S'Bae were gone, along with their foul creatures. The night was silent, yet Master Therapass continued to stare into the darkness, and Galespinner still seemed anxious, pawing the ground and raising her nose to the damp air.

"What is it?" Kyja whispered.

"I don't know." Still holding his wand out before him, Master Therapass knelt and placed his empty hand flat on the ground.

The air—which had been still only a moment before—began to dance and swirl in strange, cold drafts, kicking up bits of dirt and grass. Distant thunder boomed, although Kyja couldn't see any flashes of lightning. The clouds turned an angry, greenish color, extending nearly to the ground.

As the wizard rose to his feet, the wind increased, creating dozens of miniature cyclones—spinning funnels of dust and rock.

"Look out!" Marcus shouted, and Kyja turned to see something emerge from one of the funnels.

It was one of the insect things Master Therapass had destroyed. But at the same time, it wasn't. Its body seemed strangely twisted. The smooth, black shell was pitted and broken, as though it had been poorly glued together by a small child. One of its eyes blazed while the other remained dark and empty. It was dead—he'd seen

Master Therapass destroy it—and yet it lumbered toward them with slow, lurching steps.

Something squirmed and jerked near the spot where Marcus had set down the frying pan what seemed like ages ago. Kyja pressed her hands to her mouth to keep from screaming as a single burned wing slithered across the ground to join a dark lump of feathers. As the wing reached it, the lump moved, and a skeletal bird rose awkwardly into the air—one of its wings burned black, the other ripped in several places.

"What's happening?" Marcus shouted.

"You must leave," the wizard gasped to Kyja, his face pale.

At the base of the hill where the three Thrathkin S'Bae had fallen, the ground began to rise and fall. A bony hand flung itself from the dirt, and Kyja watched with horror as an arm rose stiffly from the ground, clawing at rocks and rubble until a deformed head appeared—clods of dirt in its hair and a patina of dust covering its face.

In fits and jerks, the figure pulled itself up out of its grave, its shredded, black cloak flapping in the wind. All across the hillside things were rising from the ground. And not just the beetles and birds. Dark shapes took form everywhere, rotted creatures crawling to life from the dust, bits of bone and tufts of fur clinging to their long-dead bodies.

A horrible screaming filled the air, tearing at Kyja's eardrums. Overhead the clouds began to spin like an upside-down whirlpool. Multiple bolts of lightning crashed to the ground, starting several patches of grass on fire. A huge, dark shape swooped out of the clouds and landed on the ground just behind the Thrathkin S'Bae, towering over them. At its appearance, the cloaked figures dropped to their knees.

Moonlight glimmered against its blood-red scales. Bony, red wings flapped from its serpent-like body. Talons the size of the mist steed ripped up the ground. It opened its mouth, revealing double rows of glittering teeth, and gave another mind-numbing scream. It was the creature from Kyja's amulet—from Marcus's brand.

"It's a Summoner," Master Therapass shouted. "Run!"

For a moment Kyja sat frozen, staring at the Summoner as it swayed gently back and forth. The creature raised its claw, and the sky above Master Therapass opened. A funnel of twisting fire shot down from the sky, knocking the wizard to the ground.

When Master Therapass looked up at her, Kyja saw a trickle of blood dripping from his cheek. She tried to leap from the mist steed's back, but the wizard held out his hand.

"Leave," he gasped, "while you still have time."

"No." Kyja tried to climb off Galespinner's back, but the mist steed reared up on its back legs.

"We can help you," Marcus cried.

The wizard shook his head and waved both hands toward them. "Galespinner, go now!"

Instantly the mist steed turned and raced down the hill.

"We have to do something," Marcus shouted in Kyja's ear.

But what could they do? The Fallen Ones were everywhere now. Not a few dozen like there had been back at the Westland Woods, but hundreds, filling the night air with their grunts and cries.

"He can protect himself," she said, hoping it was true.

"Over here," Riph Raph called from overhead. The skyte shot out a ball of flame to show them which way to go, and Galespinner changed direction.

A two-headed snake with rotting green scales rose up from the grass, and the mist steed leapt over it, just clearing its dirt-crusted fangs.

"Look out," Riph Raph shouted down at them, and Kyja watched a humpbacked figure with a skull-like face launch a deadly sharp spear. His throw was on target, but just before the spear hit them, Kyja heard Marcus mutter something that sounded like *breeze,* and the spear sailed off to the left.

Creatures appeared all around, and the mist steed was forced to constantly cut left and right to avoid them. Kyja had no idea where they were, or how far they'd gone. She looked back toward the hill but couldn't see Master Therapass anywhere.

"Thrathkin S'Bae!" Marcus shouted.

Kyja turned to see one of the dark-cloaked figures raise his staff. A second later a ball of green fire crackled through the air. Kyja leaned forward, putting herself between Marcus and the Thrathkin S'Bae. Amazingly the fire bounced off her, directly back at the dark wizard, and Kyja caught a glimpse of surprise on his shadowed face before he was knocked off his feet.

"Nice one," Marcus said.

Riph Raph flew just above Kyja's shoulder. "I think we're safe now, we—"

Suddenly, Galespinner stumbled, and Kyja and Marcus were nearly thrown off her back. Before the mist steed could regain her footing, there was a loud *twang,* and something dropped over them.

"A trap!" Marcus shouted as a net descended.

The mist steed reared into the air, pawing at the net, but the ropes pulled tight, jerking them all to the ground. Kyja had the wind knocked out of her. Gasping for breath, she turned her head to see Riph Raph clawing at the ropes from inside. Past him, one

Thrathkin S'Bae approached the net cautiously, its staff held up before it.

"Return to the grave," Marcus screamed holding out his hand.

Kyja knew he was trying to duplicate the spell he'd seen Master Therapass cast, but he lacked either the strength or the knowledge, or both. The Thrathkin S'Bae had paused at his words, but now it surged forward, confident of success.

Kyja knew what she had to do. She might not be able to save herself, but she wouldn't let them get Marcus. Closing her eyes, she gripped her amulet and focused on her memory of Marcus floating in the mist. The image came instantly.

"Kyja, no!" she heard Marcus shout distantly.

Just as it had before, the golden rope appeared before her eyes, and along with it the voice. *Bring him to you. Use your magic. Your powerful magic.*

But this time Kyja was ready. *No!* she cried out inside her head. Steeling herself against the pull of whatever waited in the mist for Marcus, Kyja forced herself to shake off its power. The rope winked out of sight, and Kyja thought she felt a sense of surprise and anger. Before the presence could try any other tricks, she reached out to the floating Marcus. Using all her strength, she pushed him as hard as she could.

It worked. One second he was drifting in front of her, and the next second, he was gone. She opened her eyes, and Marcus was no longer in the net.

"Good-bye," she whispered. "Be safe on Ert."

She braced herself as the Thrathkin S'Bae closed in. One of them leaned over her, and something strange happened. She felt a tug on her middle as if someone had grabbed her robe. She looked down, but nothing was there. Sudden terror flared inside her head. The thing in the mist. Had it managed to capture her after all?

"Ghet tei nak," one of the figures grunted. "Where is the boy?"

"Gone," Kyja said.

The tug came again. Kyja tried to shake it off.

The Thrathkin S'Bae reached toward Kyja, but before its black-gloved hand could touch her, she felt herself jerked so hard it seemed as if she would turn inside out.

All at once everything disappeared, and she was falling.

CHAPTER 36

HOME

KYJA CAME TO WITH A START. She raised her arm, trying to shield herself from the Thrathkin S'Bae. But something was wrong. The tall grass she'd been lying in was gone, replaced by fine sand that burned her skin. And it was daytime. The sun beat down with a fierce heat she didn't recognize. She rolled over and felt a stab in the side of the leg.

"Ouch," she cried. She reached for her leg, and needle-sharp teeth bit her hand.

"Oh!" She pulled her hand back to find three sharp spines sticking out of her finger.

"Careful. That's a prickly pear cactus. There're lots of them around here."

"Marcus?" She shielded her eyes from the sun, sure she must be hallucinating. "How did you get here?"

Marcus scratched the back of his head. "I'm pretty sure you sent me. Let me get those cactus spines."

As Marcus scooted across the sand to her, Kyja saw the way his right leg twisted beneath him. "Your leg?"

He shrugged. "Guess I'll need to get used to crawling everywhere again. Unless someone's conveniently left an unused wheelchair nearby." He tried to play it off as nothing, but Kyja could see the way his disability embarrassed him, and she quickly changed the subject.

"Where are we?" she asked as Marcus pulled the quills from her hand and leg. She'd never seen anything like the landscape that surrounded them. Unending waves of the same dun-colored sand without a tree in sight, and in the distance, high, red cliffs.

Marcus tossed the needles aside and pointed to a small, dusty-green plant with purple flowers. "Careful, that's another prickly pear." He scanned the area. "I don't think we're in Arizona. Maybe Nevada. Or possibly Utah."

"Arizona? Utah?" Understanding dawned on her, and Kyja's heart leapt in her throat. "Are we on . . ."

"Earth?" Marcus chuckled. "Yeah, I'm pretty sure."

Standing up unsteadily, she looked around. Heat baked up from the sand through the soles of her slippers. This was *her* world—her home. "It's . . . ugly."

Marcus laughed out loud. "Well it's not *all* this bad," he said with a smile. "I think you set us down in the middle of a desert."

"What's a desert?" Kyja asked.

"*This* is a desert," he said, sitting on the hot ground. He kicked at the sand and something almost the same color as the ground moved.

"What's that?" Kyja squawked, dancing backward.

Marcus studied the long-tailed creature crawling sluggishly across the sand. "Looks like some kind of lizard."

"Who's calling me a lizard?" the lizard growled, cocking its head. One eye turned right and the other looked left.

"Riph Raph?" Kyja gasped.

"Why does your voice sound so strange?" The lizard asked. It waggled its front legs and jumped a few inches into the air before falling back to the sand. "Where are we? And what's wrong with my wings?"

Kyja gawked down at the lizard, unable to believe it was actually Riph Raph. "You don't *have* any wings."

"What!" The lizard twisted its head around to look back at its body, and its already bulgy eyes bulged even more. "What happened to me?"

Kyja pressed her hands to her mouth, trying to keep from giggling. "You're a . . . lizard."

"I'm a *what?*" The lizard danced angrily around on the sand, shaking its front legs. It opened its mouth, and a long pink tongue unfurled.

"Awk," he cried, sticking out his tongue. "What's this in my mouth and why can't I breathe fire?"

Unable to stop herself, Kyja giggled helplessly, and Marcus soon joined in.

"I told you," Marcus said. "There are no such things as skytes on Earth. I guess a lizard is the closest thing we have. I think you're a chameleon. They don't have any middle ears, so they can only hear vibrations through the ground and things. That's probably why we sound funny to you."

"I don't want to be a lizard," Riph Raph cried. "I won't be a lizard! Change me back now."

"Actually, chameleons are pretty cool," Marcus said. "They can change colors, and I think if their tails fall off, they grow new ones. A family I used to live with had one as a pet."

"I . . . am . . . not . . . a . . . pet!" Riph Raph screamed. Puffing up his cheeks in anger, he accidentally uncurled his tongue onto the ground, covering the sticky pink tip with sand. "Ack. Ack." He coughed and spat, trying to wipe off the grains of sand.

"It could be worse," Kyja said. "You could still be trapped in the Thrathkin S'Bae's net." All at once, understanding dawned on her, and she turned to Marcus, her face blanching. *She* could still have been trapped with the Thrathkin S'Bae too—*should* have been trapped.

"You brought me here, didn't you?"

Marcus shrugged, averting his gaze. "I guess. I'm not really sure."

"But how did you?"

Finally he looked up at her, his expression both firm and embarrassed. "I told you not to send me, but you did anyway. For just a minute I found myself in the between place. I knew you were trying to send me back to Earth. I didn't want to leave you and Riph Raph alone with the Fallen Ones. I tried to hold on to you. When you pushed, I must have pulled you with me. Riph Raph, too."

"You *held on?*" Kyja stared at him, feelings at war with each other inside her. He'd saved her life, and Riph Raph's. But he'd taken a huge chance. "What if instead of pulling us with you, you'd stayed on Farworld? You risked your life."

Marcus stared back. "So did you."

Kyja swallowed. "That's . . . different."

"It isn't. But that doesn't matter, because we're here, whether we like it or not. The question is, what are we going to do about it?"

Kyja studied the forbidding landscape. She'd never seen anything like it in her world. Not even in pictures. It was terribly hot, and neither of them had any water. Their food bag apparently hadn't come across with them. "I could try to send you back," she said hesitantly.

"No." Marcus shook his head at once. "The Thrathkin S'Bae are still there. Probably the Summoner, too." They were both silent at the thought of the great, winged creature that had brought fire crashing down from the sky.

"What about Master Therapass?" Kyja said. "What if he's hurt or captured?"

Marcus sighed. "Like you said, he can protect himself without having to worry about us. That's probably why he stayed up on the hill—to keep the Dark Circle focused on him so we'd have a chance of escaping."

Kyja knelt on the hot sand and ran her finger along Riph Raph's new, pebbly skin. "Did you see Master Therapass?" she asked the brown lizard. "While you were flying?"

Riph Raph shook his ridged head. "I wouldn't worry. He was probably just waiting for the three of us to get safely away before he fried that overgrown snake with a fireball."

"I hope so," Kyja said. She looked from Marcus to the miles of empty desert. "This is your world. What do you think we should do?"

Marcus wiped the sweat from his forehead and shifted his weight from one side of his body to the other. "We've got to get out of the sun soon, or we'll die of heat or thirst or both."

The two of them searched the barren landscape. Other than the cliffs, which were much too far to reach on foot, there was no sign of shade anywhere.

Cupping her palm above her eyes, Kyja pointed toward a dark smudge far to the west. "Does that look like something to you?"

"Where?" Marcus asked, looking in the direction she pointed.

"Over there. Way off to the left of the little hill in the distance. If you squint your eyes, it almost looks like a building."

Marcus studied the horizon. "I guess it *could* be," he said with a dubious frown. "But even if it is, it's a lot farther than it looks. The desert plays tricks on your eyes. The sun would cook us before we got halfway there."

"What other choice do we have?" Kyja asked, fanning her face with her hands. Her robe, which had been so comfortable on Farworld, felt like a hot blanket, cooking her inside. "Come on." She picked up Marcus's staff and started to leave, but Marcus caught the edge of her cloak.

"Wait." Marcus glanced up at the bright desert sky, absently running his fingers through his hair. "I wonder . . ."

"What?" Kyja asked, flapping the front of her robe. Whatever they were going to do, it had to be soon.

Marcus stared hard at the ground.

"The sun's gone to his head," Riph Raph said. "It's baked his brain." Of the three of them, the now-lizard seemed the least bothered by the heat.

Ignoring Riph Raph, Marcus picked up a bone-dry sagebrush branch and began tossing it in the air with a faraway look.

"I think it might work," he said. He let the stick drop to the ground, pinched his eyes shut with an expression of deep concentration, and began mumbling something Kyja couldn't understand. Immediately the air just above their heads began to waver.

"What—" Riph Raph started to speak. But Kyja shushed him, pressing her finger to her lips. Something strange was happening. A silver-tinted circle was slowly growing a few feet above and behind Marcus. Looking through it was like looking at the desert through a lens of flowing water. The sand behind him shifted and danced beneath the circle's quivering surface.

As Marcus continued to mumble something that sounded like *thicken,* the circle grew until it was nearly six feet across, almost like a giant—

With a gasp, Kyja realized the sun no longer burned against her skin quite so intently. Looking down, she could see a clear shadow on the desert floor that continued to grow darker as the circle above them grew more and more solid. It was an umbrella—an umbrella made entirely of air.

When the circle had grown so dark that gazing up through it was like looking at the night sky, Marcus finally opened his eyes. Beads of sweat rolled off his forehead and cheeks, but he was smiling widely.

"I thought you said there was no magic on Ert," Kyja said, marveling at how much cooler it felt in the shade of Marcus's circle.

"I guess I was wrong." As Marcus wiped a hand across his face, Kyja noticed the way his fingers trembled. It was clear the magic he'd used to make the umbrella had taken more out of him than the shield Master Therapass had taught him on Farworld.

CHAPTER 37

SPIES EVERYWHERE

DO YOU WANT TO STOP AND REST?" Kyja asked.

"Just for . . . a . . . minute." Marcus tried not to show how exhausted his muscles were, but he couldn't help the way his watery arm and leg collapsed him to the sand as soon as he stopped moving, or the way every breath seemed harder to draw than the last.

Heat was no longer a problem. As the sun began to disappear on the western horizon, the blisteringly hot air was getting a chilly edge to it. But they were still far from the building—if that's even what it was—and he wasn't sure how much farther he could go on. He'd been okay at first, but now he couldn't seem to go more than a few hundred feet without stopping. Even his good arm and leg were nearly played out.

"Maybe I could carry you or something?" Kyja suggested.

"No!" he said, his eyes blazing. "I just need a minute, okay?"

"Fine." Kyja leaned against the side of a wind-smoothed rock

and emptied sand out of her slippers for the fourth time that afternoon. "Are you sure we're going the right way?"

"No. But I'm sure I don't want to go back the way we came."
Marcus stared longingly at the object that had grown from a smudge
to a blob, hoping it didn't turn out to be nothing but a bunch of
rocks. He flexed his arms and stretched out his leg, wincing at the
pain. He had to go on somehow.

Maintaining the air umbrella had kept the sun from burning
their skin, but it had also drained him much more than he'd
expected. He didn't know if doing magic on Earth was harder than
on Farworld or if it was the type of spell he had performed. Either
way, his head ached almost as badly as his body from the effort, and
he'd been hugely relived to release the umbrella once the sun had
dropped low enough in the sky.

Kyja pointed toward a shimmer in the distance. "Is *that* one
water?"

"No. Just another mirage."

The first time Kyja had seen what appeared to be a pool of water
in the distance, Marcus had been unable to convince her it was an
optical illusion. It was only after she chased the heat mirage for
almost twenty minutes that she finally admitted he was telling her
the truth.

"I'm s-o-o-o thirsty," she said, putting her slipper back on. "I'd
give anything for a cup of water."

"Don't talk about it. It just makes it worse." Marcus pulled off
his gloves and studied his right palm. His fingers throbbed and the
pad of flesh just below his thumb was red and swollen where he'd
accidentally brought his hand down on a prickly pear. He hoped it
wasn't infected.

The only one who seemed to be doing all right was Riph Raph.

Once he'd adjusted to the fact that he was a lizard, he'd been trying out his new abilities. Changing colors, looking in two different directions at once, catching things with his tongue.

As Marcus and Kyja rested, he was perched silently above a small hole in the sand, with his head cocked.

"What are you doing?" Kyja asked.

"Quiet," said Riph Raph. "There's something in there. I can hear it scurrying around."

At that moment, a small, black spider popped its head out of the hole. In an instant, the chameleon flicked its tongue, and the spider disappeared into its mouth.

"Delicious," Riph Raph said, munching the spider between his teeth. He smacked his lips. "Spider guts, yum."

Kyja wrinkled her nose in disgust. "Maybe I'm not quite so thirsty."

Riph Raph grinned a strange little lizard grin and searched for another spider. "You're just jealous."

"How are *you* feeling?" Marcus asked Kyja. "I mean other than hungry and thirsty."

"Hot. I hope I never see another desert again as long as I live."

"Me too." Marcus grimaced. "But that's not what I meant. I was just thinking that if *I* wasn't completely in Farworld, maybe *you* aren't completely on Earth. I feel better now—whole. But if . . ."

Kyja stopped and looked at him. "You think part of me is stuck between worlds?"

"It makes sense. Do you feel tired or weak?"

"Of course I do. But that doesn't have anything to do with being caught between worlds. It's just this stupid heat."

"I don't think you'll be able to stay here on Earth any longer than I could stay on Farworld," Marcus said. "We'll have to get you back once it's safe."

"Only if you come with—"

Kyja's words were interrupted by a strange *chk-chk-chk* sound— like a handful of beads being shaken.

"What's that?" she asked, looking toward the sound.

"Get back," Marcus shouted.

Kyja turned to him with a puzzled expression.

"It's a rattler," Marcus cried, and suddenly he had the strength to move again.

"What's a rattler?" She stared out into the dusk.

"A rattlesnake," he said, still trying to yank her away. "It's poisonous."

"A snake!" At once Kyja's expression changed from confusion to fear, and she nearly tumbled over Marcus as she scrambled away from the coiled serpent. Riph Raph arched his back and bared his teeth.

"Let it be," Marcus said "It's scared of us. That's why it's rattling. If we leave it alone, it'll leave us alone."

But as they backed carefully away from the snake, it uncoiled and began slithering toward them.

"What's it doing?" Kyja asked in a trembling voice.

"I don't know."

Marcus slid backward on the seat of his pants across the still-warm sand, not daring to take his eyes off the snake. Its diamond-shaped head swayed back and forth—its glittering, black eyes watching him as its tongue flicked in and out. Stopping a few feet away, it opened its pink mouth, revealing a pair of curved fangs, and hissed, "Marcus-s-s."

Marcus's mouth dropped open. "Did you hear that?" he asked Kyja.

Dipping to the ground, Kyja scooped up a handful of rocks. The first one she fired missed off to the left, but the second missile hit its target, striking one of the snake's fat coils. As she cocked back to throw another rock, the snake glared darkly at her with its shiny black eyes before slithering off into the desert.

Somewhere in the distance, a coyote howled. Its mournful cry had a distinctly human quality to it, and Marcus remembered Master Therapass saying the Dark Circle had spies everywhere. Did that include Earth?

"Come on," he said. "I think we'd better get far away from here as fast as we can."

CHAPTER 38

THE HOUSE

"CAN'T . . . GO . . . ON." Marcus dropped his head to the sand. He couldn't move. His arms and legs were knotted and screaming out in pain. The ground seemed to spin beneath him, and it was all he could do to keep from passing out.

"Just rest for a minute," Kyja said, kneeling beside him. "We have to be getting close."

After hours of scooting across the desert, Marcus's muscles had gone from aching to so numb he could barely feel them anymore. He tried to sit up and couldn't even do that. He turned his head and squinted, but the white sliver of moon barely gave any light, and beneath the twinkling stars, the wide, empty desert all looked the same.

"Think we're . . . lost," he said, finally admitting he had no idea where they were.

Riph Raph, who had been riding on Kyja's shoulder for the last hour, was much more forthcoming with his opinion. "Of course we're lost. Totally lost in the ugliest place I've ever seen. And it's all his fault."

"It is not," Kyja said. "Marcus is doing the best he can."

"I'd rather have taken my chances with the snake," Riph Raph said. "At least *it* seemed to know where it was going."

Marcus stared into the wide, empty desert, licking his parched lips with a tongue that felt swollen to twice its normal size. Riph Raph was right. They were going to die out here, and it would be his fault. For a moment he thought he saw something out of the corner of his eye. He turned his head, but there was only more black night and empty sand.

"Look," Kyja said, pointing. "What's that?"

"Where?" Marcus tried to follow the direction she was looking, but he could barely turn his head.

"Over there. Just on the other side of those rocks."

He looked to the right, and what he saw made his heart leap. It was the building. So close they'd almost gone right past it.

"Come on," Kyja said. Putting her arm under his, she pulled him to his feet and half-supported, half-dragged him toward the building.

But as they drew closer, they slowed to a halt. Even in the dim light of the moon, Marcus could see the small house or shack was long-since abandoned. The wooden boards of its walls were broken and scattered about. The windows were empty of glass; a few swatches of broken screen flapped from their black openings. He could just make out a slight depression where a road might once have been. If it *had* been a road, the sand of the desert had reclaimed it many years before.

Kyja looked from Marcus to the house.

"Is that what you've been leading us to all this time?" Riph Raph asked, rolling his eyes.

Marcus was too tired to even try to come up with a smart reply. Instead he loosened his arm from around Kyja's neck and collapsed to the ground.

"Even if this one is empty, there must be other houses nearby," said Kyja, kneeling at his side. "If we go just a little farther, we're bound to find a road."

"No use," Marcus said without looking up. "I can't go any farther. I can't." He knew he would eventually die if he stayed out in the desert, but he didn't have the strength to move.

A few minutes later, he heard Kyja walking away. She whispered something to Riph Raph that he couldn't make out. Good. Let her go on without him. On their own they might stand a chance. With him slowing them down, they never would.

He wasn't sure how long he lay out on the sand, but he must have dozed off, because some time later he felt Kyja shaking his shoulder. He tried to sit up, but his muscles were too stiff and locked with pain to move. "I can't," he said, dropping back to the ground.

But Kyja wouldn't give up. She was tugging at his arm and leg, rolling him over. "Go without me," Marcus rasped. He tried to pull away, but was too exhausted to manage even that.

"Maybe you should listen to him," Riph Raph said. "He hasn't been much help so far."

"And you *have?*" Kyja asked sharply. She continued to pull at Marcus, and he felt himself roll onto something soft but a little scratchy.

Opening his eyes, he found himself lying on an old wool blanket. The blanket was ragged and filled with holes. It smelled musty. "What are you doing?" he asked, trying to sit up.

Instead of answering, Kyja walked around to the front of the blanket and picked up a pair of splintery boards. As she lifted the boards, the blanket rose up too, settling Marcus into a kind of blanket-and-board hammock.

"See?" she said, taking a couple of steps forward. "I can pull you this way."

When Marcus realized what she intended, he tried to push himself off the blanket with his exhausted arms and legs.

"Stop that," Kyja said, dropping the boards. Marcus had managed to get himself halfway off the blanket, but Kyja lifted his legs and pushed him back on.

"I won't let you carry me," he said, scowling. "It's not right."

"Why?" she said, planting her hands on her hips. "Because I'm a girl?"

Before Marcus could sputter out an answer, she was standing over him with a scowl of her own. "You think you're better than me, because you're a boy? That you always have to be the hero? That you're stronger? Well, it doesn't work that way. You probably saved my life back by the woods with your magic, and we could have died out here if it wasn't for your umbrella. I may not have magic. But now it's my turn to save you. We're getting out of this desert, and we're going to do it together. Then you're going to show me these machines you've been telling me about."

Marcus stared up at her, his jaw clenched and his muscles quivering with rage. He shook his head, biting his lower lip. "It's not because you're a . . . a girl. It's because I'm . . . a cripple. It's bad enough I can't help you. But I can't even help myself. Don't you see?" He glared at his useless arm and leg. "I'm broken. I'm no good."

Kyja knelt beside him, her eyes soft and silvery in the moonlight. "I'm broken, too. When you were in the jaws of the mimicker, I wanted more than anything to cast a spell that would free you. But I couldn't. And I couldn't do anything to protect us from the sun. Because when it comes to magic, I'm crippled as well. By ourselves maybe we aren't much. But together . . ." She let her words fade into the cool desert night air.

Marcus thought over what she'd said. As much as it hurt his pride to admit it, he did need her help. But maybe she was right. With his useless arm and leg, he'd always thought of himself as a burden to others. It wasn't until this very minute that he realized Kyja might need his help as much as he needed hers.

"Okay," he finally agreed, barely able to raise his arm. "It's a deal. We're in this together. You help me, and I help you."

She shook his hand. "Deal."

A little over an hour later—after too many rest stops to count, and one spill where Kyja accidentally rolled Marcus onto an angry Riph Raph—Kyja spotted something else. This time it wasn't an abandoned building, though. Kyja didn't know what the double red lights and row of smaller orange lights were, but to Marcus they were unmistakable. And now that he was listening for it, he could just make out the soft rumble of an idling diesel engine.

It was a truck—an eighteen-wheeler, parked on the side of the road while its driver caught a little sleep. The trailer was loaded with large rectangles that he thought might be bales of hay.

"What is it?" Kyja asked with a worried look on her face. "Is it another kind of creature?"

Marcus grinned. "Come on. I think we just found our way out of here."

CHAPTER 39

ON THE ROAD

KYJA WOKE TO AN EAR-SPLITTING WAIL that shook her entire body. Forgetting where she was and how she'd gotten there, she abruptly sat up and was nearly blown off her knees by a blast of cold wind.

"Careful," Marcus shouted, pulling her back into the nest they'd made by digging into several of the hay bales. "Keep your head down or someone will see you."

Rubbing her eyes, she remembered helping Marcus climb onto the back of what he'd called a *semi*—one of Ert's machines. When she'd gone to sleep, it had been night and the semi had been standing still. But now it was morning, and the semi was jittering and shaking in an alarming fashion. Lifting her head just above the top of the bale of sweet-smelling dry grass, she snuck a peek over the edge of the truck and gasped with shock.

The semi was not just moving; it was hurtling faster than she'd ever seen anything travel—faster even than the mist steed—along a great black road wide enough for three or four dozen people to walk side-by-side. And racing all around it were more machines of all different colors. Some were as big as the semi, and some were smaller, but all of them had people trapped inside—clinging to the machines for their very lives.

"What kind of magic is this?" she asked Marcus, her voice filled with terror. "We'd have been better off with the Thrathkin S'Bae."

Marcus rubbed at his arm and leg and groaned in pain. "I told you, it's not magic. It's just a truck. We've gone farther in one night than we could have in three days riding Galespinner."

Again, the earsplitting wail filled the air, and Kyja ducked, pressing her hands to the sides of her head.

Gently, Marcus took her hands from her ears and said, "Don't be afraid. That's just an air horn. Drivers use them to warn other drivers. Or sometimes just to be rude."

Kyja slowly lowered her hands, her heart thudding. "Drivers? Wizards drive these machines the way people drive . . . carts?" It seemed impossible that anyone, no matter how powerful their magic, could possibly control a beast this big and powerful. But Marcus nodded his head.

"That's right. Just like a cart. But you don't have to be a wizard. Anyone can drive a truck or a car after a few lessons."

Anyone? All at once an idea filled Kyja's head that was so big—so amazing—she could scarcely give it place in her mind. "This machine. It does not require magic?"

"No magic," Marcus said.

"Then *I* could control it? I could drive this machine?"

"Sure," Marcus said with a laugh. "As long as you could see over the steering wheel, that is."

"I will drive it then. As soon as we stop," Kyja said, dreaming of taking the reins of such a wonderful and powerful machine.

"Not so fast," Marcus said, shaking his head with a smile. "You can't just jump out and drive it."

Kyja gave him a confused glare. "But you just said I could."

"Driving a truck takes practice. And even if you did know how, it doesn't belong to you. We're not even supposed to be back here. If someone saw us, they'd probably call the police."

Riph Raph briefly blinked one eye open, before curling up and going back to sleep. Kyja had no idea what a *police* was and didn't care; she knew what she wanted. "How do I get a semi of my own?"

Marcus put his head in his hands. "You don't *get* a semi. You'd have to buy it, and even the smallest car costs more money than I have. Besides, we're not old enough to get a license. Let's just forget about driving right now and focus on what we're going to do next. Okay?"

"Fine," Kyja snapped. She folded her arms across her chest, refusing to meet Marcus's eyes. What was the point of having machines that didn't require magic if you couldn't use any of them? Lifting her head above the hay bales again, she saw the barren desert was long gone, replaced by boxy-looking buildings and more houses than she'd ever seen.

The temperature had changed too. Even though the position of the sun indicated it was late morning, the air had a cold bite to it. Walking across the desert, they had tied their cloaks around their waists. Now they untied them and put them back on.

"Let me help you with that," Marcus said. He leaned stiffly across Kyja and pulled her cloak over her head.

"Thanks," Kyja said. It wasn't Marcus's fault they were stuck in this predicament. She was just worried about Master Therapass. She hoped he had managed to escape. At least Galespinner would be all right. She was immune to the dark magic. "Do you have a plan?"

"Not a plan exactly," Marcus said, pulling a piece of straw from his hair. "More like an idea."

He shifted around in the hay, trying to stay out of the cold air blowing just above their heads. "When you sent me back to Earth, did you choose where I would go? I mean, did you specifically pick the spot where we landed?"

"No." Kyja couldn't help smiling at the idea of choosing to send Marcus to the middle of a desert and then being pulled along behind him. But the truth was, she barely understood how she'd sent him at all. She had no more idea how to send him to a specific spot than she did how to make a mist steed appear.

"That's what I thought." Marcus leaned forward, his eyes glowing. "What if we landed at that spot because that's where we were on Farworld?"

"What are you talking about?" she said. "We weren't in the middle of a desert when I pushed you."

Marcus pointed to a spot on the nearest bale of hay. "Let's say this is the Boys School in Cove Valley, Arizona. That's where I was when you brought me to Farworld."

Next he pointed to a spot farther up on the bale. "Now let's say this is somewhere north of Mesquite, Nevada. As far as I can tell, that's close to where we landed here on Earth. It's about four hundred miles north of Cove Valley. I think that's about five or six days by horse."

"How can you be sure?" Kyja asked.

Marcus ran his fingers through his hair with a self-conscious smile. "I like maps. I used to study them whenever I got a chance, imagining where I would go one day when I was on my own. It seemed crazy at the time—a kid like me ever going anywhere. But now look at us." He waved his hands in the air.

"What I was thinking, though," he continued, "was what if the reason we came back farther north on Earth is because we traveled north on Farworld? What if our movements there somehow carried over to here?"

Before Kyja could answer, the semi began to slow down with a gravelly, rumbling sound. Kyja lifted her head above the hay bales.

"Oh," she said, her mouth hanging open.

Marcus climbed up beside her, and the two of them looked out on a bustling city.

Marcus pointed to a big green sign. "Salt Lake City. That's in Utah," he said as the semi pulled off the road and parked beside a line of equally-imposing machines.

"Where you headed?" a man from one of the other semis called as the driver got out.

"Wendover," the driver called back, pulling his cap down tight on his head.

Marcus pointed at a building with a giant sign that read Burger Barn. "That's a restaurant," he whispered to Kyja. "Help me get down from here, and we can get some food and something to drink while the driver's taking care of his truck. I feel like I've been run over by a train, but I might be even hungrier than I am sore."

Kyja followed him, but even though she was hungry, it wasn't food she was thinking about. An idea had suddenly occurred to her—if she was from this world, then her parents lived here too.

CHAPTER 40

FRIES AND A SHAKE

"COME ON," MARCUS SAID, reaching up and pulling toward the double-glass doors of the Burger Barn. "I think Master Therapass was right—about only half of my body getting food. I feel like I could eat a whole cow."

Kyja hesitated for a moment, goggling at all the unfamiliar sights and sounds. She'd never seen this many buildings in one place, some of stone and others of glass—buildings with brick walls and buildings with hundreds of shiny windows. Several of them were even taller than the tower in Terra ne Staric. And the lines of machines that filled the street fascinated her. The large ones Marcus called *trucks* and the smaller ones he called *cars*, roared past with clouds of stinky, black smoke and loud honks that reminded her of a flock of angry geese.

Even on parade day when a new High Lord was chosen, Terra ne Staric never saw this much commotion. It made her feel both excited and frightened at the same time. She couldn't imagine living in a place like this, and she wondered if the Dark Circle had spies here, too. But she couldn't help thinking that one of the people in the big buildings or walking along the street might know who her parents were. One of them could even be her mother or father, buying clothes in a shop or driving a car.

Riph Raph cowered in her cloak pocket, peeking out for only seconds at a time.

As she watched the people come and go, a red-faced man leaned out of his car and shouted, "Get out of the way," to a man crossing the street. The man in the street shook his fist, and the first man made a loud honk with his car.

"Why are they so angry?" she asked Marcus. She couldn't imagine ever being angry if she had a machine of her own.

"Probably late for work," Marcus said, tugging at her.

He pulled open one of the glass doors, and a fascinating combination of smells came drifting out. Kyja's stomach growled, and she realized she hadn't eaten anything in over a day. Turning her back on the rumble of the cars and trucks, she followed Marcus through the doors.

Inside, the food shop was nothing like she'd expected. Back home, the inns and taverns which served food were filled with happy people, laughing and singing at big, wooden tables, while servers carried platters of food and drink from steaming kitchens.

Here, people waited in long lines, looking at pictures of food on the wall. When they reached the front of the line, they called out numbers, handed over money, and took away their food on trays or in sacks. And while the smells were intriguing, she couldn't see a single pot or pan in the kitchen. Where were the wood-burning ovens? Where were the spits of meat turning slowly around and around? And what were all the beeps and buzzes? She couldn't imagine Bella ever cooking in a kitchen like this.

"What's wrong?" Marcus asked as they took their place in line. Several of the people waiting in front of them gave Marcus and Kyja unusual looks before turning quickly away. Kyja didn't know if it was because of their clothes or because of Marcus. But he didn't seem to notice—or care about their stares.

"Why is everyone in such a hurry?" Kyja asked.

"It's called fast food. You know, for when you want to eat on the run. Or in my case, on the crawl."

"Eat on the run?" She'd never heard such an idea before. Why would people want to eat on the run? Then again, she'd never been in a city bigger than Terra ne Staric. Maybe that's just how things were done.

"This must be the biggest city on Ert," she said, watching a pair of little boys take toys out of their bags.

"This?" Marcus asked with a laugh. "Hardly. There are hundreds of cities bigger than this."

Hundreds? Hundreds of cities bigger than *this?* The idea boggled her mind. As they waited their turn to get food, she imagined what it would be like to live in such a fast-moving city where people drove machines everywhere they went, shouted at each other, and ate food on the run. It didn't sound very appealing. And how would she ever be able to find her parents among so many people?

Soon they reached the front of the line, where a man in a blue cap smiled at Kyja and asked, "What can I get'cha?"

Kyja looked from the man up to the pictures of food and back in a panic. None of the foods looked familiar.

Fortunately Marcus spoke up. "We'll have bacon cheeseburgers with large fries, and the biggest orange sodas you've got."

The man in the blue hat leaned over the counter and looked down at Marcus. "Sorry about that, buddy," he said. "I didn't see you down there. Can I get you anything else?"

Marcus began to shake his head, before changing his mind. "And two chocolate milkshakes."

"Okay. I've got two number fours with orange sodas and two chocolate shakes. That'll be nine dollars and twenty-seven cents."

Marcus reached into his leather bag to get his money, but as he pulled out a pair of crumpled bills, his eyes went wide, and his breath caught.

"What's wrong?" Kyja asked.

"Later," Marcus said with a quick shake of his head.

Once they were seated at a table—which was neither wood nor glass, but felt like a strange combination of both—Marcus reached into the bag and pulled out one of the red stones.

"Do you know what this is?" he asked holding it out to her.

Kyja shook her head. When Master Therapass had given the stones to Marcus back on Farworld, they had been shiny but unremarkable flat rocks. Now the stone glittered under the morning sun that shined through the window with a spectral radiance.

"Neither do I," Marcus said. "But I think it might be a ruby. And the green ones look like emeralds. If they are, this bag is worth money."

"How much money?" Kyja asked, fingering the red gem.

"A *lot.*" Marcus put the red stone back into the bag with a quick look around. "I think we'd better keep this out of sight."

"Here," he said, handing her a cup. "I'm so thirsty I feel like I could drink from a fire hose."

Kyja had never heard of a fire hose, but she *was* thirsty. She lifted the cup to her mouth, but the top was covered with some kind of clear lid.

"You have to use a straw," Marcus said. He pulled the paper off a small tube and slid it through the top of her cup.

As Kyja watched doubtfully, Marcus lifted his own cup and placed the straw in his mouth. When he sucked on the straw, orange liquid flowed up. "Try it," he said with a grin.

Kyja placed the straw into her mouth. Pursing her lips, she gave a hesitant suck. Instantly, a fruity-flavored, ice-cold liquid gushed over her tongue. Tiny bubbles filled her mouth and nose with a strange burning sensation, and she coughed the drink back out, spraying it across the table.

Marcus roared with laughter. At the next table, a large woman with curly, bright-red hair was talking animatedly into a tiny silver box. The woman put her hand over the silver thing by her ear and glared at Marcus and Kyja. A messy-faced child sitting across from the woman smeared a container of red sauce on the table and copied his mother's glare.

"What *was* that?" Kyja asked, touching her tongue with the tip of her finger.

"It's a soda," Marcus said, still laughing. "The bubbles are called carbonation. Try it again, more slowly."

Kyja took another small sip. This time she kept the drink in her mouth. It was wonderful—cold and sweet. And the bubbles were actually kind of fun once you got used to them. She gulped it down greedily.

Marcus handed Kyja a package wrapped in waxy paper. She sniffed it experimentally before opening the package. It looked like some kind of meat and sauce on bread.

"It's called a cheeseburger," Marcus said, talking around a mouthful of food.

Kyja lifted the cheeseburger and tried a bite. It was a little greasy, and the sauce was too sweet. But not bad. Next she took one of the hot, golden, stick-shaped things which Marcus called *fries*. She popped one into her mouth and moaned with pleasure. "These are delicious!" she said, taking several more. They were hot and salty—crunchy on the outside and soft and yummy on the inside.

Attracted by the smell of the food, Riph Raph climbed cautiously out of Kyja's cloak and onto the table. Kyja broke off a piece of meat from her burger and held it out to Riph Raph. The chameleon darted out his pink tongue and zapped the meat from Kyja's fingers.

"Almost as good as spider," Riph Raph said, chewing the meat.

"Look, Mommy. A lisser!" The boy at the next table leaned over the back of his seat and pointed a greasy finger at Riph Raph.

"Have some fries," his mother said, still talking into the silver package. The little boy shoved a handful of fries into his mouth—smearing red across his face—and continued to watch Riph Raph.

"When you were talking back in the truck," Kyja said, giving Riph Raph another piece of burger. "Were you saying the desert we landed in on Ert is the same distance from your school that we traveled back home?"

Marcus nodded. "It may not be an exact match, but it seems about right."

Kyja thought through his logic. She hadn't given it much consideration before. But it made a strange kind of sense.

"It sounds crazy to me," Riph Raph said.

"Mommy," the boy at the next table shouted, "the lisser talk."

"Hush, Timmykins," the woman said, pressing a couple of

brown lumps into his chubby hand. "Mommy's on the phone. Eat your nuggets."

"You want to hear something really crazy?" Marcus asked Kyja, holding out a fry like a pointer. "North of Cove Valley is a forest called Flagstaff, with lots of tall pine trees. There's a summer camp there where I used to go with some other boys in one of my old schools. I'm not sure, but I think it was a hundred miles or so from Cove Valley. I bet that's about the same distance we traveled in Farworld to get to the Westland Woods. As far as I remember, there's not a big river in Flagstaff, but there *is* a river to the north of it called the Colorado River. And northwest of Flagstaff is the desert where we landed."

He ran his fingers through his reddish-brown hair. "Does any of that sound familiar?"

It took Kyja a moment to understand what he was saying. "You think the forest in Flag-whatever is the same as the Westland Woods?"

"Yes and no. I mean, I don't think we'd find talking trees if we went to Flagstaff. And unless I missed something, we didn't cross the Grand Canyon on Farworld. So everything isn't exactly the same. But what if some things *are* the same? What if certain spots here match certain spots there?"

Kyja finished the last of her fries as she thought over Marcus's words.

"Are you going to eat that?" he asked, pointing to the rest of her burger. When she shook her head, he wolfed it down in two big bites.

"Try your milkshake," he said.

Copying what she'd seen Marcus do earlier, Kyja peeled the paper from her straw and pushed it into the cup. Prepared for more of the same bubbly liquid, she sipped cautiously. But what filled her mouth this time was so *incredible,* so absolutely *wonderful,* it took her breath away.

"Do you like it?" Marcus asked, watching her closely.

"It's delicious!" she said, only taking her lips off the straw long enough to speak before going back to drinking. When she finished the entire milkshake, she leaned back in her seat and sighed.

"So what do you think?" Marcus asked.

"If there are any more surprises like this on Ert, I might never go back."

"No, I mean about my idea."

"Oh, right." Kyja twirled her empty milkshake cup between her fingers. "Master Therapass talked about different worlds. Maybe he sent you here because there is a kind of link between our two worlds."

"A *link.*" Marcus's eyes glowed as he crumpled his empty wrapper. "Sure, that makes sense. Master Therapass wouldn't just send me to any old world. He'd want me to be somewhere close by. Maybe not close in distance. But close in another way."

As Kyja and Marcus talked, the little boy at the next table had been moving closer and closer. Without any warning, he reached out with a fat, greasy hand and tried to grab Riph Raph around the neck. Riph Raph jumped back with a hiss, then darted forward and snatched away the boy's last nugget. The food disappeared down the chameleon's throat in a single gulp.

"Mommy!" the boy howled. "The lisser eat my nugget."

For the first time during her entire meal, the red-haired woman seemed to actually hear what her child was saying. Snapping the silver package closed, she scooped her son up into her arms and gave Marcus and Kyja a look that could melt ice cubes.

"Come on," Kyja said, quickly shoving Riph Raph back into her cloak pocket. "I think it's time to leave."

CHAPTER 41

WHEELING AND DEALING

I GUESS WE'D BETTER GET BACK," Kyja said, sadly watching the cars that raced past. She'd never be able to find her parents in a world this big. She didn't know their names. She didn't even know *her* real name.

As she began walking toward the line of semis, Marcus tugged on the hem of her robe.

"Wait up," he said.

Kyja looked down at him with a curious glance.

"Master Therapass said Water Keep was east of the mountains, right?"

"Right." Kyja looked at the line of semis, wondering how long their's would wait before leaving.

"Well, Master Therapass said he was going north—around the mountains. What if we went *over* the mountains and met him on the other side?"

Kyja stared. "We can't. It's far too dangerous."

"Too dangerous on *your* world," Marcus said with the same mischievous look he'd gotten right before he jumped out of the tree in the Westland Woods. "But not in *this* world. If we go over the mountains here, then jump back to Farworld, we can save at least a week of travel. I'm sure Master Therapass travels faster on his own. He'll probably be waiting for us by the time we reach the city."

Kyja considered the idea. "Are you sure it's safe?" she asked.

"Of course," Marcus said, bouncing with excitement. "There's a highway that goes clear across. We can be over the mountains by this time tomorrow."

"Is our machine going that way?" Kyja asked, still feeling a little uncomfortable about the whole idea.

"No. But this time of year it's too cold to cross the mountains in the back of a truck anyway. I've got a better idea. We can take a bus."

"What's a *bus*?" Kyja asked.

"It's kind of like a car, only bigger. You can buy tickets to almost anywhere."

"I thought we were almost out of money."

"We are, but I've got an idea." Marcus waved to one of the drivers walking to his semi. "Excuse me, sir, but do you know where the closest bus station is?"

"'Bout three or four miles that way," the driver said, pointing past the restaurant. "Corner of Eighth West and Third South."

The man tilted his cap back, revealing a sunburned face and brown teeth. "Gonna catch a hound to Vegas to marry your sweetheart?"

Marcus and Kyja looked at each other and blushed.

"Can you make it that far?" Kyja asked, avoiding Marcus's eyes as the truck driver walked away with a chuckle. Marcus had crawled a long way in the desert, but the ground there had been softer, and the gloves Master Therapass had given him were already looking worn.

"Probably not," Marcus sighed, rubbing his leg.

Kyja glanced around the parking lot and saw something silver lying on its side by the wall of a building. It had wheels like the thing Marcus called a *wheelchair,* only smaller. "How about this one?" Kyja asked, walking toward it.

Marcus looked where she was pointing and instantly shook his head. "No. No way. I won't ride in that."

"Why not?" Kyja picked it up and tried it out. One of the wheels was a little shaky, but it worked fine. "Look," she said, "It's even got a seat."

Marcus folded his good arm across his chest and scowled. "I will *not* ride in a grocery cart."

———⟨◆⟩———

Half a block from the bus station, Marcus noticed a small building with an assortment of items displayed behind a dusty glass window—a laptop computer, a pair of used saxophones, a circular saw with a rusty blade, and an assortment of rings and necklaces laid out on a black velvet mat. "Over there," he said.

Kyja wheeled the grocery cart across the sidewalk and up to the door. Lined side by side along the outside of the shop were several old bicycles. Kyja ran her fingers across the seat of a mountain bike and curiously spun one of the pedals with the tip of her foot. She read the buzzing red sign above the door. "All-American Pawn Shop and Jewelry. What's a pawn shop?"

"It's a place where they buy and sell things. If we're lucky, we might be able to get enough money for the bus tickets and more."

Marcus leaned over the edge of the cart and pulled open the front door. Instantly a cracked speaker began playing a loud and fuzzy rendition of "The Star-Spangled Banner." It made Kyja jump.

Kyja pushed the cart into the shop, looking curiously around at the shelves of used items. Behind the counter, a bald man in a dingy, white shirt glared at the two of them as he rooted around in his ear with a long, dirty finger.

"Can't bring that in here." He pulled his finger out of his ear, checked its tip for wax, and pointed at the grocery cart. The man's fingernails looked like they hadn't been trimmed in months, and cleaned even less recently.

Marcus shifted uncomfortably in the wobbly metal cart and touched the leather pouch in his pants pocket. "We have something to sell," he said.

The man behind the counter took off his glasses—which were nearly as dirty as the shop windows—rubbed them on the untucked tail of his shirt, and hooked them back over his small, pink ears. As far as Marcus could tell, the rubbing had only managed to move the dirt around a little.

Pushing the glasses up on his nose, the man frowned. "Look here, kids, we don't buy comic books, action figures, or baseball cards so you might as well—"

While the man was talking, Marcus reached into his pocket, took one of the gems from the bag, and set the gleaming red stone on the counter.

For a second, the man's watery, blue eyes went wide. But a moment later, they narrowed. "What do you take me for? You kids expect me to fall for that cereal box toy?"

"No, it's a real—" Marcus began.

But Kyja stepped up to the counter and closed her fingers

around the ruby. "We'll take it somewhere else. It's clear you're too busy with all your other customers." She studied the obviously empty store, dropped the gem in the pocket of her robe, and began to turn the cart around.

"Hang on now," the man said as Kyja started toward the door.

Kyja glanced over her shoulder.

The man licked his lips. "You trying to tell me that thing's real? Where would a couple of kids like you get a stone worth—"

Marcus turned in the cart, anxious to hear exactly what a ruby of that size would be worth, but the man quickly caught himself.

"I guess I might be willing to take a look at it," he said, holding out his dirty hand.

As Kyja pulled the gem from her pocket, the man leaned over the counter. But just before giving it to him, she hesitated, looking around the store where nearly everything seemed to have a light coating of dust on it.

"I don't know," she said, glancing toward Marcus. "Maybe we should take this somewhere else. Someplace a little cleaner?"

Catching on to what she was up to, Marcus nodded. "You're right." He pointed to the large display of pistols and rifles beneath the glass countertop. "They seem to have plenty of guns and old power tools, but not so many gems. I bet a jewelry store would give us more for this."

"Now you wait just a minute," the man said, running his hand across his bald head. "If that thing *is* real, I'll pay top dollar. Those big jewelry stores are nothing but a bunch of con artists."

Kyja turned toward Marcus so the man couldn't see the grin playing at the edge of her lips. Marcus, who had no idea Kyja was so good at this kind of thing, nodded almost unnoticeably.

"All right," Kyja said, the doubt clear in her voice. "I *guess* we could at least let you look at it. But I'm not even sure I want to sell it anymore."

As soon as she let the stone fall into the man's hand, he closed his fingers around it with an audible sigh of relief. Turning it over in his fingers, he held it up to the store's sputtering florescent lights. "Didn't steal this, did you?" he asked with a sly grin.

"Of course not," Marcus said. "It was given to me by an old . . . family friend."

"Uh-huh," the man grunted, clearly not believing a word of it. "Because if this *is* stolen, the police are going to be looking for you two."

"We told you. It's not stolen," Kyja said with clear indignation. "If you don't believe us we can take it somewhere else."

"We'll see about that," the man said. From a drawer behind the counter, he took out a small, black jeweler's loupe. Setting his glasses aside, he tucked the lens up to his eye and studied the gem.

"Oh," the man whispered under his breath. The tip of his tongue slipped out from between his wet lips as he turned the gem first one way, then another.

The stone looks like a real ruby; but is it? Marcus wondered. On the way to the pawn shop, he'd considered the fact that some things stayed the same when they went from one world to another, while others clearly did not. His money, their clothes, the picture of Elder Ephraim, all appeared identical on both Farworld and Earth. But Riph Raph and the stones had changed dramatically. Was it because skytes and the stones didn't exist on Earth? Or was it because they were organic while the other items were man-made? Marcus didn't know, but if Riph Raph could turn into a chameleon, who was to say what the red stones really were?

"Well?" Marcus asked, unable to stop himself.

Laying the loupe on the countertop, the man pinched his lower lip and shook his head. "Sorry kids. Your old 'family friend' wasn't such a good friend after all. It's a fake. Nothing more than colored glass."

Marcus felt the air swoosh out of him like a blown bike tire. *A fake.* Now how were they going to buy bus tickets? Or food, for that matter? He only had a few dollars left of the money he'd taken from his suitcase—not even enough to buy them another full meal.

"You're lying," Kyja said.

Marcus looked at her in shock as she stomped up to the counter and leaned across it until she and the shop owner were only a few inches apart.

"You're lying. That gem's not a fake. You just want to steal it."

Clearly, the man was as surprised as Marcus. His eyes widened, and in that second, Marcus realized Kyja was right. What he saw in the brief moment of clarity was not anger or disbelief, but guilt.

"I . . . I don't know what you're talking about," the owner said, his face pale.

"Give us back our gem." Kyja said, holding out her hand. "We'll find someone honest. Someone who doesn't try to cheat little kids."

Brick-red spots rose in the center of each of the man's cheeks, spreading up toward his temples as he closed his fist around the stone. "How dare you accuse me of lying? It's you two who are the thieves. I don't know what you're up to, coming in here with those strange-looking costumes, riding around in a grocery cart, and trying to pass off fake gems. But I'll bet the police would like to talk to your parents."

Police? Marcus's stomach cramped at the thought of the police getting involved. They'd take him back to the boys school. And who knew what would happen to Kyja and Riph Raph? "Look, just give us the stone, and we'll go," he said. "If it really is a fake like you say, it shouldn't matter to you."

The man shook his head, a dark smile spreading across his face. "Don't want to get the police involved, do you? I'll tell you what. Why don't I just *keep* this, and maybe I'll give the two of you a five minute's head start before I call the cops."

At this point, that actually sounded pretty good to Marcus. It had been a bad plan from the beginning. He should have realized no one would ever seriously consider buying a valuable gem from a couple of kids.

But Kyja was staring at the man, her eyes drilling into him as if she could see right through his skin and into his soul.

"We're not the first people you've cheated, are we?" She looked slowly around from the man behind the counter to the items spread throughout his store. "How many of these things did you get by telling lies? And you don't even care if they're stolen. That just means you can make more money."

The man's eyes darted from Marcus to Kyja as if trying to understand what he was up against. His tongue inched out from between his lips again as he fingered the stone.

"Go ahead," Kyja said. "Call whomever you want. We'll wait. By the time we finish telling them how you tried to steal our gem, they'll close your shop down, like they should have a long time ago."

Now it was the man's turn to worry. "Look," he said, "maybe I was too quick. It is a pretty good fake. I could probably give you something for it." Stabbing a button on his cash register with one finger, he opened the drawer and took out two twenties. He laid them side by side on the counter, and, after another glance toward Kyja's stern gaze, added a third.

"There you go," he said, with an unnaturally large grin. "Sixty bucks. Just think how much candy you can buy with that."

Kyja looked to Marcus, clearly not understanding the currency of this world. Marcus shook his head. "That gem's probably worth thousands."

"Thousands?" The man choked back a cough. "Look, kids. I may not have been straight up with you before. But I'm being completely honest when I say I can't sell this for any more than a hundred." He added two more twenties from the cash register, peered toward Kyja—clearly unnerved by the way she seemed to be looking right through him—and added a crisp fifty-dollar bill. "Hundred and fifty, tops. And believe me. I'm losing money on this deal."

Marcus was reaching for the cash when Kyja placed her hand of top of his. "You stay here and keep on eye on him. I'm going outside to get the . . . *cops.*" She said it in a tone so serious Marcus could barely believe it was her.

If he hadn't been afraid of blowing Kyja's plan, Marcus would have burst into laughter at the way the pawn shop owner's face went instantly white. Every ounce of blood seemed to drain from his cheeks until he looked as if someone had given him a thorough dusting with flour.

"How . . . how much do you want?" he stammered.

Kyja checked with Marcus, who calculated inside his head. "Five hundred dollars," he blurted. He wasn't sure if it was too much or too little, but from the way the man behind the counter quickly counted out the bills, Marcus suspected he would still make a nice profit when he sold the stone.

As the man shoved the money across the counter, Kyja placed the tip of one finger on top of his hand—as though she couldn't stand the thought of actually having any closer contact with him.

"Don't think this gets you off the hook. If you ever cheat anyone again, I'll come back. And I'll bring the cops with me next time."

Just then, Riph Raph popped out from Kyja's pocket, where he'd been curled up napping after his big meal. Turning one eye toward Kyja and one toward Marcus, he shot out his tongue and grabbed a fly that had been walking slowly across the counter.

"Yum," he said. Then, looking toward the pawn shop owner, he asked, "Who's that?"

The man screamed.

CHAPTER 42

THE MAGIC BOX

I'M SORRY," SAID THE WOMAN behind the ticket counter, "but children must be accompanied by an adult."

She looked down suspiciously at Marcus, Kyja, and their grocery cart. "Where are your parents?"

"I'm, um, not sure," Marcus said. He wasn't lying, since he was pretty sure his parents were dead. But he thought it was better to leave before the woman asked any more questions.

"What are we going to do now?" Kyja asked as they crossed the crowded bus terminal.

"I don't know," he said with a frown. "But get me out of this thing."

As Kyja helped him from the cart, Marcus noticed a man in a dark suit watching them. When the man realized Marcus was looking at him, he quickly turned away.

"Marcus?" Kyja asked. "What's wrong?"

"Huh?" Marcus turned to Kyja, then back across the room. The man was gone. Marcus searched the terminal without seeing him anywhere. *At least it wasn't anyone I know,* he thought, wondering if Bonesplinter was still on Earth.

"Nothing," he said, climbing onto a plastic chair. "I'm just trying to think."

Kyja sat in the chair next to him. "What's this?" she asked, pointing to the small, blank television bolted to the side of the plastic seat.

Marcus fished a pair of quarters out of his pocket. He couldn't bring Kyja all the way to Earth without letting her see at least one TV show. He dropped the quarters into the slot on the side of the TV, and Kyja jerked back in her chair as a tiny, soap-opera man and woman appeared on the screen.

She put a hand forward and cautiously touched the front of the television, as though expecting to reach through the screen and pick up the people inside.

Marcus changed the channel and two cowboys rode across the TV on horseback.

"This *must* be magic," Kyja whispered, fascinated.

"Nope. Just another machine."

"Can I?" she asked, pointing to the buttons that changed the channel.

"Sure. Go ahead," Marcus said, wondering if Kyja had been as amused by his reaction to Farworld as he was by her surprise at such ordinary things as milkshakes and televisions.

Kyja changed the channel to a sports program that showed a pair of boxers punching each other inside a ring. Frowning, she changed the channel again, this time to a cartoon showing a crab and an octopus arguing over a pair of pants.

"That's *SpongeBob,*" said a little boy sitting in the next chair over.

He leaned across his seat and pointed to the figures on the screen. "Them are Mr. Crabs and Squidward."

"Would you like to watch too?" Kyja asked, turning the screen so the little boy could see it better.

"Yeah. It's my favorite show."

As the boy leaned across his seat to view the television, Marcus saw that the boy's right arm was in a sling, and there was a bump on his forehead. The boy's mother watched him closely. For a minute she seemed on the verge of pulling him back before deciding he was all right.

"What happened to you?" Marcus asked. "Fall off your bike?"

The boy glanced toward his mother, who gave him a sharp look. As she did, Marcus noticed the woman had a black eye and a puffy lip.

"Nah," the boy said, shaking his head. "I just got hurt. That's all."

The woman studied Marcus and Kyja for a moment before apparently deciding they were harmless and going back to her magazine. But Marcus noticed the way she kept looking up from her reading every few minutes and glancing nervously around the bus station.

"What happened to you?" the boy asked Marcus. "Why's your arm and leg like that?"

"I fell off my bike," Marcus said with mock seriousness.

"Really?" the boy asked, his bright blue eyes wide with amazement.

"No." Marcus laughed. "I'm just kidding. I got hurt when I was a baby."

The boy's eyes, which had glowed with wonder a moment before, now took on a knowing expression far too old for his young face.

Before Marcus could say anything else, Kyja leaned over to the little boy and placed one hand on top of his head. "Your father hurt you, didn't he?"

At once the woman looked up from her magazine and grabbed the boy's good arm as if to pull him away.

"It's okay," Kyja said, gently placing her hand over the woman's. "You're running away from your husband because he hurt you and your son. Don't worry—we won't tell anyone."

"How do you know that?" the woman asked. Marcus saw the fear clearly printed on the woman's face. She had the look of a rabbit, ready to flee at the first sign of danger. He was sure she would run, and yet something in Kyja's eyes seemed to hold her.

"We're running too," Kyja said. "From some very bad people. We're trying to reach someone who can help us."

For a moment the women said nothing, as though making up her mind about what to do. Then she nodded, her puffy lips pressed together. "Where are you going?"

"We need to get to the other side of the mountains," Kyja said. "We have the money to buy tickets, but we need an adult to buy them."

"Where are your parents?" the woman asked, still looking unsure of whether she could trust the two of them.

Marcus expected Kyja to make up a story. After all, who would believe the truth? But Kyja continued to stare into the woman's eyes and simply said. "I don't know. We don't even know who our parents are."

At last the woman seemed to relax. "My name's Kathleen, and this is Jerrick. He and I are going to Des Moines. You could go with us as far as that if you'd like."

Jerrick looked up into Kyja's face. "You gonna come with us?"

Kyja nodded. "I'd like that."

CHAPTER 43

DISCOVERED

KYJA LOOKED DOWN AT JERRICK as he lay sleeping on her lap, a green and red stone clutched in each of his fists. Marcus was sleeping in the next seat over. Peanut butter, cracker crumbs, and bits of cheese were smeared across his face from the snack the four of them had shared earlier.

He seemed to have recovered from the effects of Farworld, but Kyja was starting to feel the same queasy stomach Marcus had described, and her head pounded with a dull ache. She guessed Marcus was right about her being trapped between worlds and wondered where she could find some of the cures he'd told her about.

"He seems like a good boy," Kyja said, brushing Jerrick's dark hair.

Jerrick's mother nodded. "He is. I just wish I could do better for him. Nobody deserves to be treated like that. Especially not a child."

"You're taking him away from the person who hurt him," Kyja said. "That's a good start."

Kathleen's lips trembled as she brushed her eyes with the palm of her hand. She glanced out the darkened window of the bus at the miles of snow-covered ground. "I just wish I knew I was doing right by him. My sister's not exactly thrilled about us coming to live with her. She's got four kids of her own."

"You *are* doing the right thing," Kyja said without an ounce of hesitation. "It's all going to work out just fine with your sister."

"How could you possibly know that?" Kathleen asked.

Kyja shrugged. She had no idea how she knew. She just did. It was like how she'd known what was wrong with the Weather Guardians. "See if you can get him horseback riding lessons when you get there. I think he might have a way with animals."

Kathleen stared at her in disbelief, but she didn't argue.

Just then, the bus began to slow down. Marcus sat up and rubbed his eyes. "What's happening? Are we there yet?"

"No need to worry," the bus driver called out as he brought the bus to a shuddering stop with a high-pitched whine of the brakes. "Looks like there's been some kind of accident. We should be past it in a few minutes. Please stay in your seats."

"Mommy?" Jerrick jerked awake, confused by the unfamiliar surroundings.

"It's okay, baby." Kathleen reached across Kyja and took her son into her arms, careful of his injured arm.

"Where are we?" Jerrick asked, looking around. One of the colored stones fell out of his fist onto his mother's lap.

"This is beautiful," Kathleen said, admiring the large, red stone. "It can't be real but . . ."

She tried to hand it to Kyja, but Kyja pushed it back into her palm. "It's just a toy. Jerrick can keep it."

As Kyja closed Kathleen's fingers around the gem, Marcus pressed his face to the tinted window of the bus.

"I don't see any accident."

Kyja joined him and looked outside. A line of cars was stopped in front of them, and she could see men with flashlights making their way along the line of cars.

Marcus pulled sharply back from the window and looked around. "Something's wrong!"

"What is it?" Kyja followed his gaze but couldn't see anything out of the ordinary. "Is it the Dark Circle?"

"I don't know. I just . . ." He looked out at the highway, where the men with the flashlights were getting closer. All at once, he climbed out of his seat. "We need to get off the bus now."

Alarmed, Kathleen looked up from her son. "Is it the people you're running from?"

"Bad men?" Jerrick asked, clinging to his mother.

Marcus scooted to the front of the bus with Kyja close behind him.

"We need to get off," he told the driver.

"Now?" The bus driver, an older man with gray hair and a Middle-Eastern accent, gave Marcus and Kyja an incredulous look. "I can't let you children off the bus in the center of the highway. Where are your parents?"

By now, Kyja had caught Marcus's panic. She could see the men outside only a few cars away. They were showing something to the occupants of each car as they shined their lights inside. They appeared to be wearing some kind of uniform. "Please," she begged. "Open the door."

The driver looked from her panicked face to the uniformed men outside, and his lips tightened. "Are you in trouble with the police? Did you run away from home?"

Marcus reached for the big metal lever which opened the bus door, but the driver was too fast. "No," he said. "You will not get off my bus in the middle of the road."

Still gripping the door handle with his right hand, he waved his left hand at the men in front of the bus. "Over here!" he shouted.

One of the men outside looked up from the car he was inspecting. He grabbed the elbow of the man beside him and pointed to the bus.

"It's him!" Marcus cried.

"Who?" Kyja asked, feeling as trapped as she had in the net.

"The man in the bus station." Marcus turned and hurried toward the back of the bus.

"What can I do?" Kathleen asked as Marcus and Kyja reached her seat.

"Those men outside the bus aren't the police," Marcus hissed. "If they find Kyja and me, they'll kill us."

At the front of the bus, the door swung open with a whoosh of air. "Back there!" the driver shouted.

The man in the dark suit flashed some kind of badge as he stepped onto the bus. Marcus and Kyja dodged out of sight into a row of seats.

"This way," Kathleen whispered. She unlocked the emergency latch on her window and pushed it open. "I'll get their attention while you two go out the window."

She leaned over Jerrick. "Can you help me, baby? Can you help Kyja and Marcus?"

Jerrick had tears in his eyes, and his lips were trembling, but he nodded.

"Hide down here," Kathleen told her son. "Under the seat."

As Jerrick ducked under the seat in front of him, Kathleen jumped up. "My son!" she screamed. "Where is my son?"

The two men at the front of the bus both turned in her direction.

"Ma'am," said the first. "If you could just sit back—"

"Someone took my son!" Kathleen shrieked. "Everyone please help me find him."

Some of the people on the bus remained in their seats, but most of them got up and began to look around.

"Everyone return to your seats!" the second man shouted.

"Now," whispered Kathleen, giving a quick backward glance.

Blocked from view by the standing people, Marcus and Kyja scooted across the aisle and into the row of seats where Jerrick was hiding. "Bye-bye," Jerrick whispered, biting back his tears.

"Bye, sweetie," Kyja said. After a quick glance to make sure Marcus agreed, she emptied several of the gems into Kathleen's purse and gave Jerrick a quick squeeze. "Tell your mom to buy you a horse."

In the front of the bus, Kathleen was still shouting, but the men were pushing their way through the aisle—knocking people right and left.

"Go," Marcus said.

Keeping her head low, Kyja pushed her legs over the ledge of the window and slid out. She looked both ways, and although she could see more men with lights on the way, there was no one immediately beside the bus. Hanging from her fingertips, she released her grip on the window and dropped to the slushy street.

Although the drop was farther than she expected, she managed to land safely. "Come on," she whispered up to Marcus.

Marcus handed his staff to Kyja through the window and looked out. "I can't get my feet around," he said.

"Then go head first," Kyja said. "I'll catch you."

The sound of men shouting was close now. Inside the bus, Kathleen gave a loud squawk, and Marcus turned to look back.

"Come on," Kyja said.

Leaning over the edge of the window, Marcus somersaulted through. He nearly managed to hang on as his feet swung over his head, but at the last minute his grip failed, and his fingers slipped from the bus.

Kyja darted forward as Marcus started to fall. Holding up her hands, she grabbed for his body. He was much heavier than she expected, and they both collapsed to the street.

"Are you okay?" Marcus asked, pulling himself off her.

"I think so," she said. "Just lost my breath."

"That's good," a silky voice said. "I'd hate to have my two prizes injured before I kill them myself."

A tall, thin man stepped out of the shadows.

"Bonesplinter," Marcus growled. He turned to Kyja. "Jump to Farworld. Now!"

"I don't know how," Kyja said. She closed her eyes and tried to imagine the gray in-between world. If part of her was caught there, maybe she could push herself back and take Marcus with her the way he'd brought her.

"Not this time." The man closed his fingers around Kyja's arm. His grip was ice-cold, and suddenly Kyja couldn't think at all. The pain in her head flared, and her mind seemed frozen.

"Let her go!" Marcus shouted. He swung a fist at Bonesplinter, but the man knocked him aside like an insect.

"Your world-jumping days are over," he said, focusing his piercing gaze on Kyja.

She tried to pull from his grasp, but his fingers were like stone.

Lying on the wet asphalt, Marcus held out his hands toward Bonesplinter. "Air like bread dough thicken, please."

"What are you doing?" Bonesplinter said, his eyes narrowing.

One of the men in the bus shined his flashlight out the window. "Over here!" he shouted. Suddenly he cried out in pain and disappeared back inside the bus. "Ouch! The kid bit me."

"Bonesplinter fly off in the breeze," Marcus finished. At Marcus's words, a huge gust of wind lifted Bonesplinter from his feet and threw him across the highway.

As her arm broke free of the man's grip, Kyja's mind cleared. Men with lights came running from all directions. As Kyja watched, one of them changed into a snake, his suit ripping to shreds.

"Jump," Marcus shouted. "Jump!"

Kyja closed her eyes and grasped her amulet. Having done it twice before, she effortlessly found the in-between world. There she saw Riph Raph and herself floating in gray nothingness. As she took hold of her own shoulders and Riph Raph's wing and pushed, she felt herself slam back into her body. She was falling, but she wasn't going to fall alone. As she dropped, she reached out. For a moment, there was nothing. Then she found Marcus's rope and closed her fingers tightly around it.

CHAPTER 44

THE WINDLASH MOUNTAINS

THIS TIME MARCUS WAS READY for the inside-out feeling which twisted his stomach as he traveled from one world to another, and the burning feeling on his shoulder. What he wasn't prepared for was the thick snow which instantly numbed his cheeks and nose, or the howling wind that blasted every inch of exposed skin with tiny slivers of ice. He twisted around to find Kyja leaning into the storm and trying to pull the hood of her cloak over her head. The wind ripped it off again almost as soon as she got it up, and she had to grip it tightly with both hands to keep it on.

"Where are we?" Marcus shouted, the words ripped from his mouth by the ferocious wind. But the truth came to him with a thudding dread even before Kyja answered. The sharp spires of ice-covered rock rising hundreds of feet into the air and the snow which came up to Kyja's waist and Marcus's chest could only be one place, and it was his fault they were there.

"The Windlash Mountains!" Kyja cupped her hands to her

mouth to be heard above the storm. The gale blew down the hood of her cloak and whipped her hair to and fro across her face. The fear in her eyes was clear. "We have to go back."

"No!" Marcus shouted. "The Dark Circle will be waiting for us."

"We don't have any choice." She wiped snow from her face with quickly reddening fingers. "Where's Riph Raph?"

A blue head popped out of the pocket of her cloak, looked sharply around, and blinked. "What did Marcus do now?"

Marcus grimaced as he searched the exposed shelf of rock where they'd landed. The side of the mountain disappeared up into the clouds above them and dropped away at an alarming rate below. He didn't want to think about what would've happened if they'd landed even a hundred feet to their left.

"This way," he called. Using his staff, he tried to get to his feet, but the wind was too strong, and he had to crawl toward a small tree which slanted sharply away from the side of the mountain. Despite his gloves, he was quickly starting to lose all feeling in his hands.

"No!" Kyja pulled on the back of his cloak. "You don't understand. We can't stay here. There are stories about these mountains—about the terrible things that live here. No one comes into the Windlash Mountains. Especially not during the winter. It's death."

Marcus spun around. "What else can we do?" he asked. "If we go back now, the Dark Circle will take us."

"What if they follow us here?" Kyja's face faded in and out through the blowing snow like an ice-caked phantom.

"If they could follow us, they would have," Marcus said, his lungs aching from the cold. "I don't think their door works like that. If we can wait here even for a few hours before jumping back, maybe they'll be gone."

Kyja hesitated, clearly torn between the two impossible decisions.

"Come on," Marcus said, pounding his hand against his legs to stay warm.

"All right," she said at last, looking worriedly around. "But only for an hour. Then we go back no matter what. This is a very bad place."

—◆◇◆—

"I th-thought you were supposed to be good at this," Marcus groused to Riph Raph as the flame on the small stack of twigs and branches went out again.

"I'd like to see you make wet wood burn in a bank of snow," Riph Raph snipped back. He blew another fireball, and a meager tongue of flame flickered up from the damp pile of wood. "If you didn't keep getting us into these situations, you wouldn't need me to get you out."

"I don't see y-you k-keeping the wind and snow out," Marcus said. He held his shaking hands toward the fire, careful not to lose the fragile dome of protective air he had cast above them. "You're no more use than a cheap book of m-matches."

"If your magic is so good, why don't you melt the snow while you're at it?" Riph Raph said. "Or haven't you learned that spell yet?"

"Stop it, you two," Kyja said, glaring at both of them. "I really think we should go back now."

"C-c-can't," Marcus stammered, his teeth chattering. "It h-hasn't been an hour yet."

"And you can't keep this magic up much longer. Even *I* can see how it's draining your strength."

"I'm f-fine," Marcus said, gritting his teeth. He'd never done this much magic in one day before, and for some reason he didn't

understand, magic on Earth had taken much more energy than casting spells on Farworld. His body felt like it was one giant ice cube,
and it was all he could do to keep his protection spell from collaps-
ing. But he couldn't let Kyja know that, or she'd demand they go
back at once. "It's just taking me a while to g-get the hang of this spell
stuff. It's much harder than k-keeping a st-stick from hitting me."

"You're doing great," Kyja said from her spot against the trunk
of the bent tree. "But we can't stay here. There's something wrong
with this place. Don't you feel it?"

Marcus closed his eyes. He *did* feel it. Ever since they'd holed up
beneath the boughs of the little tree, the wind seemed to carry voices
on it—one minute howling like a wolf, the next crying like a child or
laughing like a lunatic. And it had only grown worse when he began
using magic.

It felt as if something out in the blinding white storm could
sense the spell he was casting. Shadows seemed to move out of the
corners of his eyes, but when he turned to look, there was nothing
there. Even the snow-covered ground appeared to somehow be
sneaking up on them. But going back to Earth now would be handing themselves over to the Dark Circle. He had to hold on as long as
he could and hope for the best.

"Did you see that?" Kyja cried.

"See what?" Marcus turned to look out into the storm. All he
could see were the constantly changing patterns of blowing snow.

"There." Kyja pointed her finger. "I saw something moving
again. Only now I can't quite . . ."

Marcus studied the shifting blanket of white. Surely nothing
could survive in that bitter cold. And even if it could, there was
nowhere to hide. Except for the spires of rock above them, everything was snow and ice.

"Are you sure the s-snow isn't just p-playing t-t-tricks on your eyes?" Marcus stammered. The fire had gone out again, but he was too exhausted to ask Riph Raph to relight it.

"No. I'm not." Kyja rubbed her reddened eyes with her palms. Master Therapass hadn't given her any gloves, and her fingertips were nearly blue. "Please," she said, blinking ice from her lashes, "can't we just go back? I'd almost rather face the Dark Circle than whatever is up here with us. Even if I can't see it, I can feel it. And I know you can too. It's not just evil, either. It feels completely unnatural."

Marcus nodded. He couldn't go on any longer anyway. His brain felt as frozen as his fingers and face. Just speaking was a monumental effort, and his grip on the protection spell was nearly gone. Something was sucking his strength away, and he didn't think it was just the cold. "A-all r-r-ight," he whispered. "G-go ah-head."

Speaking drained the last of his energy, and he felt the protection spell slip away like water through his fingers. Instantly, the snow slashed down at them with a furious intensity—as though angry they'd managed to hold out against it as long as they had.

"Hang on," Kyja said. "I'm going to—"

But her words were cut off by an explosion that shook the entire mountainside. All around them, the snow suddenly sprang to life. Icy limbs reached up from the ground and wrapped themselves around Marcus's arms and legs.

"Jump," he tried to scream, but as he opened his mouth, a drift of frigid, white snow slammed him to the ground, filling his mouth and throat with frozen fire. He struggled against it, but it was like trying to fight an avalanche. The last thing he saw before being covered completely was a ten-foot-high wall of ice and snow that rose up like a tidal wave, washing Kyja over the side of the mountain.

CHAPTER 45

CAVERNS AND CAGES

MARCUS WOKE TO THE STEADY dripping of water. His arms and legs ached, and his face burned. He tried to sit up and immediately regretted it, as a dizzying pain drove him back to the ground. He opened his eyes, and for a moment, nothing changed. Then slowly, his vision adjusted to the faint light of a distant, sputtering candle.

He was in some kind of cavern. The dripping he'd heard was coming from icicles whose tops disappeared in the darkness. He was lying on a damp floor of cold, rough stone.

"Kyja?" he whispered. The effort of speaking started a coughing fit that tore at the inside of his throat. He tried again—louder this time. "Kyja, where are you?"

There was no answer. Only the constant *tap, tap, tap,* of water on stone.

He tried to scoot toward the light, and his head banged against something hard. Reaching out with his fingers, he felt thick metal bars spaced three to four inches apart.

"Riph Raph?" he called. But if the skyte was nearby, he didn't answer.

He tried to sit up again—more slowly this time, resting his head against his shoulder. He rose inch by inch, until he was finally upright. He was in a small, stone cell—no more than three feet deep and five or six feet wide—with bars on three sides and jagged stone on the back. Turning his head to the right, he saw a pair of dark green eyes staring at him from the next cell over.

"Kyja?" he called, leaning against the bars. It was definitely her—he could just make out her pale face and the shape of her cloak. But she didn't answer him except with a wide, unblinking stare.

"Kyja, what's wrong with you?" he called. He reached out to her through the bars, but before he could touch her, his fingers stopped against something cold and hard. With a shock, he understood why she wasn't responding. She was encased in a block of solid ice.

Was she dead? He felt his mouth dry up as his heart leapt into his throat. She looked so alive, almost as if she was watching him. But how could she be? Tears burned his eyes and leaked down his cheeks as his fingers searched against the smooth, hard surface of the ice block.

"They're saving her," a raspy voice whispered from somewhere nearby. "For later."

"Who's there?" Marcus pressed his face against the bars at the front of his cell and found he could just manage to make out a shape in a cell on the other side of the stone corridor.

"You'll envy her before long." The man's voice was strangely flat and empty of all emotion.

"What are you talking about?" Marcus asked, pressing against the bars. "Come closer, where I can see you."

A skin-and-bones white face appeared at the bars, and Marcus gasped. It was like looking at a skeleton with a long, bushy beard. "Can you feel it yet?" the face asked.

"Feel what?"

"Feel yourself coming apart," the man said. His eyes glowed darkly from his gaunt face. "That's what they do, you know."

"What *who* does?" Marcus asked, wondering whether the man might be crazy. He certainly sounded crazy.

"The unmakers, of course. They start with whatever magic you've got. They feed on it the way a spider sucks the life out of a fly. Then your emotions. Once they've sucked you dry of all feelings of any kind, they start on your body." He held up an arm that was hardly more than a stick, and Marcus grimaced at the sight.

"When they first captured me, I had arms the size of your waist. Now I'm almost down to nothing. Soon they'll be done with my body, and they'll finish by siphoning away my will to live."

He fixed his blank eyes on Marcus. "It won't take long. I imagine that's why they went looking for you and the girl."

Marcus sat stunned, trying to understand what the man was telling him. Creatures that fed on emotions? "They're starving you, then?"

"No." The man slid a metal plate against his bars, and Marcus could just make out some kind of dark, lumpy shape on it. "They feed you. If you can call it food. But all it does is make the process of finishing you off last a little longer. Like fattening a holiday bird before serving it for dinner. Once they finish with me, they'll start on you. After that, they'll thaw out the girl and suck away her life as well."

"You mean she *is* alive?" Marcus turned to look at Kyja. Encased in her block of ice, she looked like she was sleeping, but . . . "How's that possible?"

"She's alive." The man lifted something from his plate and shoved it absently into his mouth. It made a squishy sound as he chewed it. "Don't know how it's possible. Don't really care."

"We have to escape," Marcus said. "You know all about this place, and I can do magic. Together we can unfreeze Kyja and find a way out."

"Don't want to escape," the man said, pushing another piece of the dark substance into his mouth. "And we couldn't even if we wanted to. You don't understand. Magic doesn't work in this place. The unmakers suck it away as soon as you try to use it. They gobble it up, like candy. The only one they let use magic is old Screech, and he won't help you. He serves them."

Ignoring the thumping in his head, Marcus got to his knees and slammed his fists on the unyielding bars. "Okay then, forget magic. We'll find a way to escape without it!" he shouted. "You can't tell me you really want to stay here?"

"Can't say I care much, one way or the other," the man said. He took a handful of goopy-looking gray stuff from his plate and offered it to Marcus.

"Yuck," Marcus said, wrinkling his nose. It smelled terrible, and looked like the stuff between the tiles of a bathroom floor.

"Suit yourself." The man shoved the glop into his mouth and licked his fingers. "Even if you could get past the bars, you'd never make it out. The unmakers are everywhere. You can't see 'em unless they want you to."

"You mean they're invisible?" That would explain how they'd

appeared out of nowhere. But how could he fight something he couldn't even see? Especially when he couldn't use magic?

"Not invisible," the man said, pushing his empty plate aside. "*Unmade.* They're the opposite of everything we are. You can't see 'em cause they aren't there in the way we think about it. Don't even know if they're alive. They're just nothing, and everything they touch eventually becomes part of that nothingness."

It was the closest Marcus had seen the man come to showing any kind of emotion, and the effort seemed to exhaust him. The man lay down on the cold stone floor, curled up into a ball, and began to hum softly to himself.

"You can't see them at all?" Marcus asked, picturing the black holes he'd learned about in school.

The man continued to hum in his cell, and Marcus didn't think he was going to answer. Then the humming stopped. "Not unless they want you to," the man said in the same dead voice. "I only met one man who did. And he spent every day drooling on himself."

Marcus didn't know if it was what the man had said, the cold, dreary cavern, or the force of the unmakers themselves, but he felt what little hope he'd been able to muster fading away. He was going to die in this dank, lifeless place. And after him, Kyja would die. What would happen to each of their worlds if they were gone? Would the Dark Circle take them both over, growing and growing until they destroyed everything that was good?

He couldn't give up. He had to find a way to hang on. But he was so tired, and it was so much easier to just lie down on the floor and rest.

Sometime later, Marcus heard the sound of rattling metal, and the light from the candle drew closer as a tall figure shuffled toward his cell.

"Rise and shine," said an eerily cheerful voice. "Time to go."

Marcus sat up, his back aching and stiff from the cold, hard floor, and stared at the figure before him. The man—if that's what he was—stood at least nine feet tall. Long, greasy hair hung from parts of his head in clumps and strings, while other areas of his gray scalp were completely bald. Scraps of tattered clothing—none of it seeming to have come from the same source—hung from long, bony arms and legs.

"Who are you?" Marcus asked, pressing against the back wall of his cell.

"Who am I?" the man cackled. He looked at the filthy figure in the cell across the tunnel from Marcus. "Didn't your friend tell you? I'm Screech." He pulled a ring of keys from his belt and unlocked the cell door. Marcus saw that each of the man's fingers ended in long, blackened claws that looked more like talons than nails.

As soon as the man swung back the bars, Marcus darted toward the opening. But Screech was much quicker than he looked. His clawed fingers closed around Marcus's neck and lifted him easily into the air.

"Eager are you, my sweet?" he said with a wet cackle.

With Screech's fingers wrapped around his throat, Marcus could only cough and gasp for air.

"That's good. Very good." The man grinned, revealing blackened gums and a few remaining teeth, sharpened to knife-like points. He picked up Marcus's staff from the cell floor, examined it briefly, and tossed it aside. "The unmakers are anxious to meet you too."

CHAPTER 46

THE UNMAKERS

SCREECH DROPPED MARCUS on the floor of the wide, circular cavern with a bone-jarring thump. Before Marcus could even think about moving, the long, cruel fingers snapped a rusty manacle around his wrist.

The creature, who had seemed absurdly cheerful before, glanced nervously about the empty room before whispering, "I'll be back," and lumbering away.

Marcus tugged on the chain. But although the enclosure was flaked with rust, it was plenty solid. All around the walls of the high-ceilinged chamber, torches spit and popped. The air had an odor that was both moldy and sweet—like apples gone bad. He glanced across the room, wondering how long he'd have to wait before the unmakers arrived.

Would whatever they did hurt? The man in the cell hadn't mentioned it, but maybe he was beyond pain the same way he was beyond emotions. Marcus tugged at the spike he was chained to, but the metal bar was embedded deep in the rock. He should have listened to Kyja and gone back to Earth instead of staying in these mountains. It seemed like every decision he made ended up getting them into trouble. He couldn't imagine how anyone could conceive of a failure like him even managing to save himself, let alone an entire world.

As he waited for the unmakers, a thought occurred to him. The man in the other cell had told him it was impossible to use magic here. But Marcus had never actually tried it. Maybe the man was wrong. Or maybe Marcus's magic was different. Just because it didn't work for one person didn't mean it might not work for another.

Gathering his strength, he focused on the spike and chain. He imagined a force of wind ripping the spike from the stone floor—shattering rock and metal. He could do it, now, before the unmakers arrived.

Concentrating all his will, he whispered, "Air like bread dough, thicken please. Shatter rock, pull metal free."

For a second he felt the air around him begin to gather force. Then it was as if someone had reached down his throat and ripped something vital from inside him. The pain was enormous. Unbearable. He felt his body slam to the floor, and colors blazed in front of his eyes.

"Stop!" he screamed, but the pain went on and on. It was like someone was sucking his insides out with a straw. All around the room he heard sloppy, wet sounds, like giant lips smacking against each other, and deep grunts of pleasure. The unmakers had been here all along.

"No!" he cried, his body rattling against the floor.

"So-o-o-o go-o-od," a thundering voice rumbled from one side of the room.

"Delicious-s-s-s," another voice sighed.

"Feed us," a voice whispered, and something wet brushed against Marcus's cheek. It burned like fire, and he jerked away.

He heard the sound of things slithering across the floor all around him, and the very walls of the cavern shook with their passing. They sounded enormous, and they had him surrounded.

On the floor, Marcus gagged and shook for what seemed like forever. It went on and on, until his breathing came in harsh, quick gasps and his head felt as if it were going to explode.

Finally the pain stopped, and he lay on the floor, trembling.

"This one is powerful," a thick voice boomed.

"He will last a long time," another said.

"No," Marcus moaned. "Please." He turned toward the sound of the voice and saw nothing. Then, for just a second, beneath the flickering light, the air appeared to twist and darken. It was as if the skin of reality had been ripped away for just a moment, and underneath was a vast, unending expanse of nothingness.

"Come along," a voice whispered. Screech was back. He gripped Marcus by the arm with his bony fingers, unlocked the manacle, and dragged him away.

Once they were outside the chamber, Screech's good humor returned. "Did you enjoy yourself, my sweet?" He chuckled.

Marcus could barely keep his head upright. His muscles ached, and his stomach felt like he'd swallowed a brick. He didn't know how he could take many more sessions with the unmakers. But he wouldn't give this foul creature the satisfaction of knowing it.

"It was nothing," he said with grim determination.

"*Nothing,* was it?" Screech said with a nasty grin. "You'll have lots more of that *nothing* to look forward to over the next few months."

Marcus couldn't stand the look of satisfaction on the big creature's face. He tried to think of something to wipe it off. "I wouldn't be so cheerful if I were you," Marcus said as Screech dragged him through one dank corridor after another.

"No?" Screech said, shaking the long, greasy hair out of his eyes with a look of amusement. "Why is that?"

Marcus thought furiously. "They were asking me questions," he blurted.

"They don't ask questions. They only feed."

"Fine," Marcus said, trying to hide the pain he was feeling. "Don't believe me. But some of the questions were about you."

"You're lying." Screech continued to grin, but Marcus thought he saw a hint of unease in his captor's big, dumb eyes. How confident was Screech that one day the unmakers wouldn't turn on *him?*

"They wanted to know about your magic," Marcus continued.

"My magic?" Screech paused for a moment before continuing to drag Marcus toward his cell. It was long enough for Marcus to see the worry on the creature's revolting face. It gave him a newfound strength.

He forced himself to smile. "They wanted to know if your magic was as strong as mine."

"Ridiculous," the creature screeched, and Marcus understood how he'd gotten his name. "Of course my magic is stronger than yours. You can't even do magic here. They won't let you."

Marcus shrugged. "That's not what they said. I got the feeling they were looking for someone to replace you."

"You're making that up!" Screech shook him like a doll. Marcus felt his arms and legs nearly rip from the sockets, but he gritted his teeth and grinned through the pain.

"Hey. I don't even want the job," Marcus replied. "But what could I say? My magic *is* stronger than yours. I couldn't lie to them, could I?"

By now they were back at Marcus's cell. Screech threw Marcus to the ground in a fit of rage. "I'll show you magic. I'll burn you to the ground." The towering creature pulled a crooked, black stick from the folds of his tattered clothes and pointed it at Marcus.

Marcus held out his hands, afraid he had carried his taunting too far. "Think for a minute. What would the unmakers do to you if anything happened to me?"

Screech continued to hold the wand wavering in front of him before finally lowering it. "You're lying."

Marcus had only been trying to unnerve the nasty creature, but all at once a hint of a plan came to mind. It wasn't much, but it was all he had. "There's an easy way to prove it."

"How?" Screech asked with a suspicious glare.

Marcus pointed to where Kyja was encased in her block of ice. "You try to cast a spell on her, and I'll try to stop it. Whoever wins has the strongest magic."

"The unmakers don't want her touched," Screech said. He gave a quick look over his shoulder. "They said she's special."

"What's the matter?" Marcus taunted. "Afraid they'll suck your magic away too?"

"No! They wouldn't. They promised." Swinging his greasy hair out of his eyes, he started to push Marcus into his cell.

"Wait," Marcus said, twisting away. "It doesn't have to be anything major. Just a little spell. Move her back a few inches. If I can't stop you from doing it, I'll tell the unmakers you have the most powerful magic."

"You won't," the creature said. But from behind his mat of long, dirty hair, he seemed to be considering Marcus's offer.

"Pinky promise," Marcus said. He reached up and hooked his pinky with Screech's disgustingly-dirty little finger.

"Pinky promise?"

Marcus nodded. "It's absolutely unbreakable."

"A *little* spell." Screech picked at the tip of his chin with his long, black claws as though trying to figure out what Marcus was up to.

"Tiny." Marcus held his thumb and index finger a fraction of an inch apart.

"All right," Screech said at last. "One little spell. Then you go straight into your cell. And you pinky promise to tell the unmakers I have the strongest magic."

"*If* your spell works. You can't expect me to lie if *my* magic is stronger."

"It isn't," Screech said. He pulled out his wand, pointed it at Kyja, and said something in a language Marcus didn't understand. It sounded sort of like "deep-fried mayonnaise."

Nothing happened.

Marcus folded his arms across his chest. "I was afraid of that. I guess your magic isn't quite as powerful as you thought it was. I have no choice but to tell the unmakers."

Screech glared at him. "Let me try again."

"What's the point?" Marcus asked. "It's not going to change anything. You tried a spell. I blocked it."

"That wasn't fair," Screech said, stomping his big, hairy foot. "You tricked me. You wanted me to cast a simple spell so it would be easier for you to block."

Marcus pretended to yawn, infuriating the imposing creature before him. "Let's face it. Your magic is weak. I'm surprised the unmakers even let you stick around."

"I'll show you," Screech said, holding his wand out before him with both hands. "I'll make her float up in the air, and you can't stop me." He shook his wand at Kyja and growled what sounded like "spinach-face librarian."

Again, nothing happened.

Marcus put up his hand in a what-did-I-tell-you gesture. "Better luck next time," he said, beginning to slide across the cold stone floor into his cell.

"Get back here," Screech said. He grabbed Marcus by the shoulder and pulled him out of his cell. "I can do it. I have stronger spells. Much stronger. Spells you can't even imagine."

"I'm sorry," Marcus said. "But we could be here all night trying new spells. It's clear my magic is stronger than yours. Besides, I'm really hungry for some of that gray, library-paste stuff. So if you'll just let me get back to my cell, I'll—"

"No," Screech howled. He brought his wand down from above his head in a great, slashing stroke. *"Srisket tromkin hasbrat kinstak!"*

Marcus rolled to the side as a huge ball of fire burst from the tip of Screech's wand. It flew straight toward Kyja. But her immunity to magic reflected the spell. It hit the block of ice, shattered it into a million tiny pieces and bounced straight back at Screech. Before he could utter a word, the fireball knocked him off his feet, threw him across the corridor, and slammed him against the bars of the far cell, where he slid, unconscious, to the floor.

CHAPTER 47

RHAIDNAN'S HOPE

YOU HAVE TO WAKE UP." Marcus rubbed Kyja's pale face. Her cheeks felt ice-cold, but at least she was breathing. Still, it had been almost ten minutes since Screech's spell had shattered her frozen prison, and Marcus had no idea how long the creature would stay unconscious or when the unmakers might discover what had happened. He'd tried to drag Screech into one of the cells, but the body was too heavy for him to move so he just took his keys.

"You're going to be in big trouble when he comes to," the man in the other cell said in the same tone of voice he might have commented on the temperature.

"I'm not going to be here when he comes to," Marcus said, turning back to Kyja.

"You'll never escape."

Marcus ignored him. "Come on, Kyja. You have to wake up." He shook her shoulders, worried by the way her head wobbled loosely back and forth. But at last she gave a tiny moan, and her eyelids fluttered ever so slightly.

"There are miles of caverns, and the unmakers are everywhere," the man said, resting casually back on his elbows.

Marcus shot an exasperated look over his shoulder. "If you're so worried about it, why don't you help me?"

"I'm not worried," the man said. "And I told you before—I don't want to escape. I don't want anything."

Marcus returned his attention to Kyja. The man was obviously beyond help. But even if what he said was true, Marcus wouldn't go down without a fight—and he wouldn't go anywhere without Kyja. "Can you hear me?" he said, leaning close to her face and rubbing his fingers over her cold hands.

"Unh," she groaned. Her eyes blinked, and Marcus thought he saw a spark of recognition.

"Kyja," he said, taking her face in his fingers. "It's Marcus. You have to wake up. We have to get out of here."

"Marcus?" she said thickly.

He tried to pull her up to a sitting position, but she flopped limply forward, banging her forehead against his.

"Ow," she said, rubbing her head. But the pain seemed to awaken her. She looked groggily around. "Where are we?"

Marcus sighed with relief as Kyja sat up. "I don't have time to tell you everything right now. But we're in danger, and if we don't get out of here soon, that *thing* over there is going to wake up, and we'll never escape."

Kyja looked where Marcus pointed, and her eyes widened. "A cave trulloch."

"Is that what it's called?" Marcus said. "Well, whatever it is, it's nothing compared to the unmakers it serves."

"Unmakers?" Kyja got wobbly to her feet, gripping the bars of her cell for support. "Those aren't real. They're just make-believe creatures from scary stories people tell to frighten little children."

"Believe me," Marcus said, "they're real."

"Where's Riph Raph?" Kyja asked.

Marcus shrugged, afraid of what Screech might have done with the skyte. "I don't know. But we have to get out of here."

Picking up his staff, he limped from Kyja's cell, and after a moment, she followed him. "Who's that man?" she said, peering into the cell across the corridor.

"He's a prisoner, too," Marcus said. "But he's too far gone to come with us." He glanced anxiously at the trulloch, who was beginning to make small, jerking motions.

"We can't just leave him here," she said, sounding completely awake for the first time.

"I offered to set him free," Marcus said. He showed her the key ring he'd taken. "But he won't leave."

Screech moaned, and Marcus jumped. "Come on. We have to go."

Kyja took the keys from Marcus and unlocked the man's cell door. He watched without much interest as she knelt before him. "Don't you want to escape with us?" she asked, looking over his disgusting quarters. "You can't want to stay here."

"Don't care either way," the man replied. He picked at his teeth with his fingernail.

"The unmakers have sucked all the emotions out of him," Marcus said, keeping an eye on the trulloch. "We have to leave him before it's too late."

While Kyja brushed the filthy hair from the man's eyes and

gazed into his face, Marcus looked anxiously down the corridor. Who knew how close the unmakers might be?

"Don't I know you?" Kyja suddenly asked.

"Don't know. Don't care," the man sighed.

"*Ky*-ja," Marcus pleaded.

"I *do* know you," Kyja said. "You're Rhaidnan Everwood. You disappeared months ago on a hunting trip."

The man blinked, but still showed no sign of moving. "If you say so."

Screech flopped an arm heavily against the stone floor. He could wake up at any minute.

"He's not going to come," Marcus said. "We have to leave, Kyja, or we'll end up just like him."

Kyja took the man's face in her hands and forced him to look into her eyes. "Your wife is Char. I tended your son and daughter, Rhaidnan Jr. and Paloi, while your wife looked for work."

All at once a spark of interest seemed to flicker in the man's eyes, and he sat up. "Char?"

"She was crushed when you didn't return," Kyja said, taking his hand. "You can't tell me you don't care about your own wife and children."

As if waking from a dream, Rhaidnan got slowly to his feet. "I . . . I *do* care about them," he said—seemingly amazed at the discovery. "I do."

Rhaidnan blinked, rubbing his eyes and looking around uncertainly, as though trying to remember where he was.

Screech babbled incoherently, and his eyes blinked.

"Quickly," Rhaidnan said, grabbing the cave trulloch's arms. "Help me get him into the cell."

Kyja and Rhaidnan took Screech by the arms, with Marcus

helping out the best he could. Together the three of them strained to drag the trulloch into Rhaidnan's cell.

"Wh-wh-" Screech muttered as Rhaidnan dropped him on the hard, stone floor.

Marcus swung the door closed and turned the key in the lock.

"See how *you* like it in there," Rhaidnan said. "And I don't think you'll be needing this anymore." He snapped the black stick he'd taken from Screech over his knee.

"Can he still cast magic without his wand?" Kyja asked.

"I'd rather not find out," Rhaidnan said.

"We need to go now," Marcus said. How long would it take before the unmakers realized something was wrong?

Rhaidnan flung the broken pieces of the wand into Marcus's old cell, and he and Kyja jogged down the corridor with Marcus hurrying to keep up.

They had just reached the first side passage when they heard the rattling of bars behind them, and an inhuman scream echoing through the cavern. Marcus glanced up at Kyja and Rhaidnan. "I think Screech just woke up."

CHAPTER 48

THE CAVE MAZE

WHICH WAY?" KYJA ASKED, checking left and right. Both of the damp tunnels looked equally forbidding.

"We went that way when Screech took me to the unmakers," Marcus said looking to the left. "Let's go right."

"What do the unmakers look like?" Kyja asked as they hurried along the uneven stone floor.

"They're sort of invisible," Marcus said, without stopping.

"Invisible?" Kyja paused as they reached another intersecting passage. "How can we avoid something we can't see?"

"We'll have to deal with that when we come to it," Marcus said. He checked the side corridors before finally pointing straight ahead. "Keep going."

But only a few seconds later, Rhaidnan skidded to a halt, gripping Marcus and Kyja by the shoulders. "We need to turn back," he said, raising his nose to the air. "Do you smell that?"

Kyja sniffed. "Spoiled fruit."

"I remember it," Marcus said. "From the big chamber."

Rhaidnan nodded. "It's the unmakers. The caverns all smell that way, but it gets stronger the closer they are."

They returned to the previous intersection. Rhaidnan shook his head. "I've never been this way."

In the distance they heard another howl echo through the cavern—this one closer. "Sounds like Screech got loose," Marcus said.

Making the decision for them, Kyja turned right. They hurried down a sloping passage. Marcus was breathing hard, his staff slipping on the wet floor as he tried to keep up. Kyja still felt dizzy and a little sick to her stomach from being trapped between worlds, but Rhaidnan finally looked alive.

At the next intersection, Rhaidnan sniffed the air in both directions. "Left," he said at once.

"Wait," Marcus called as they rounded a rock outcropping.

"What is it?" Kyja peered up and down the corridor, not knowing what to look for, but afraid of seeing it anyway.

"Why don't we just go back to Earth? I'm sure the Dark Circle has moved on by now."

"And leave Rhaidnan here alone?"

"No." Marcus slapped the stone wall in excitement. "We can take him with us."

"Earth?" Rhaidnan asked, clearly confused by their conversation.

Kyja considered Marcus's plan. It made sense. The unmakers could discover them any minute. And even if they managed to escape the unmakers' lair, they'd be stuck back on the side of the mountain.

But something about it didn't feel right.

"I . . ." She rubbed her temples, trying to clear her mind. "I don't think we can."

"Can *what?*"

Kyja shook her head. "I don't think we can take him to Ert with us. I know we took Riph Raph, but this feels different, somehow. It's like Riph Raph is a part of us and Rhaidnan's . . . not. If we jump, I think he'll be left behind."

"I'm not sure I understand what you're taking about," Rhaidnan said. The emaciated hunter rubbed his bony hand across the chest of his tattered shirt. "But if you two have some sort of magic that will let you escape this forsaken place, don't stop on my account. I'm probably going to die here anyway, but at least I'll die a free man because of you two. Don't worry about me. Just go."

Kyja and Marcus looked at each other.

"No," they said together.

"We're not going to leave you," Kyja said.

"We'll find a way to get us all out of this," Marcus added, shaking his hair out of his eyes.

All at once, the air filled with the smell of rotten fruit, accompanied by a wet, slithering sound, and Screech's voice sounded behind them. "This way!"

"Run," Marcus said, and the three of them hurried down to where the tunnel split into a fork. The sound of Screech's pounding feet was getting closer behind them, accompanied by the ominous squelching of one or more unmakers.

"Are you all right?" Kyja shouted, glancing back at Marcus, who was beginning to fall behind.

He nodded without stopping and gasped, "Keep going."

Rhaidnan pointed to a trail of brackish, black fluid on the floor to the right. "This way," he said, going to the left.

For the next few minutes, they followed Rhaidnan—taking rights and lefts almost at random until none of them had any idea where they were. The sound of Screech and the unmakers continued to draw ever closer, and Marcus was lagging behind. Seeing the way Marcus's arms and legs were trembling, Kyja wasn't sure how long he'd be able to keep going.

"Left," Rhaidnan said as they reached a three-way intersection. Kyja began to follow the hunter up a particularly steep passage before looking back and realizing Marcus wasn't coming. He was leaning against the wall at the bottom of the hill, gasping for breath.

"Keep . . . going," he wheezed when Kyja went back for him. Screech's howling echoed off the cavern walls, making it impossible to tell just how close he was, but the sound was deafening.

"No." Kyja leaned down and drew his arm around her shoulder, trying to help him up the hill.

"I can't do it!" he cried as they both nearly fell over. "I'm . . . too . . . weak. Go on, before they . . . catch . . . both . . . of us."

"Not without you," Kyja said, trying to ignore the wet snuffling sound of the unmakers. She strained against Marcus's weight, and without any warning, he was lifted from her grasp.

It was Rhaidnan. He had returned to take Marcus from the other side. Between him and Kyja, they drag-walked Marcus up the passage. Rounding the corner at the top, all three of them gasped.

It was a dead end. The passage stopped cold in a wall of collapsed rocks and debris.

"Back!" Rhaidnan shouted. He led them down the passage to the intersection.

"They're too close," Marcus said. "Leave me." Screech sounded like he was right on top of them.

Rhaidnan sniffed the air. He glanced left and right. "Their smell is every—" His words were cut off by a wavering of air to their left.

"Don't look!" Marcus shouted. But it was too late.

Kyja turned, and the world she knew collapsed before her like a house of cards crashing to the ground. Where once there had been a long, dank tunnel and the sound of voices around her, now there was nothing but blackness with a swirl of colors spinning into the middle of it.

Kyja's mouth dropped open in rapt wonder. Nothing was real. Everything up until this instant—Master Therapass, the Goodnuffs, Riph Raph, Marcus—had all been a dream. The only thing that mattered was darkness, because in the end, everything turned to darkness. Everything was unmade.

What she thought of as her life was all an illusion. No matter how much you fought against it, this was all you had to look forward to in the end. There was no point in even trying to struggle. Why not give in to it?

"Yes," she said, nodding her head. "I understand now. All a dream." The darkness gave a slow-beating thrum that seemed to match the beating of her heart. In the distance, she heard faint sounds. But they were far away and unimportant. All of her worries, all of her cares, slipped from her as she began to walk toward the swirling colors.

———◆———

For Marcus, everything seemed to happen at once. Rhaidnan was sniffing the air, looking uncertainly in all directions. The smell of rotten fruit was everywhere, and the strange configuration of the cavern walls made it impossible to know where the wet snuffling sounds were coming from.

Marcus heard Kyja suck in her breath, and he followed her gaze down the left passageway.

"Don't look!" he shouted, averting his eyes. But it was too late. Kyja stared dumbly down the tunnel toward the unmaker. Her mouth moved silently as if she were speaking to the repugnant creature, and her feet began to move toward it. Marcus grabbed onto her arm, but she dragged herself forward with a strength he'd never imagined she had.

At that moment, Screech rounded the corner, his eyes bright with fury. Behind him, the air thickened and swirled.

"Got you!" Screech howled. He stretched his black-clawed fingers toward Marcus, but before he could touch him, something blurred through the air and bounced off the trulloch's ridged forehead.

"Urrgh," Screech cried, stumbling backward. Rhaidnan reached to the ground, picked up a second rock, and hurled it. This one caught Screech directly in the front of his throat, and he fell to his knees. Instantly, Rhaidnan darted forward, clasped his fingers together and brought his fists down on the trulloch's head. Screech crumpled to the ground.

But right behind him were a swarm of unmakers. The air was heavy with their foul stench, and the sound of their wet movement filled the passage.

Keeping his gaze low, Marcus turned to the left where Kyja was almost halfway to the unmaker, and to the right which was the only option left to them.

"Take Kyja," he said to Rhaidnan.

The hunter motioned toward her. "It's too late."

"No!" Marcus screamed. Kyja had nearly reached the unmakers. He had to stop her. It was all his fault. If it weren't for his stupid, crippled body, Kyja and Rhaidnan would have escaped. He needed to divert the unmakers' attention if Rhaidnan and Kyja were to have any chance. And he knew only one way to do that.

Understanding the consequences all too well, he stretched back his head, clenched his fist, and let raw magic flow from him. Immediately, he felt the terrible ripping sensation he'd experienced in the chamber. A cold, wet hand seemed to ram itself down his throat, grabbing at his insides and ripping them out.

"Aaargh!" he screamed. The pain was unbearable. Maybe it was because there were more of them feeding, or maybe it was that he hadn't opened himself up this way last time, but his entire body lifted off the floor and slammed back down again and again. At least the unmakers had stopped coming toward Rhaidnan and Kyja.

He managed to turn his head to see Rhaidnan holding Kyja. She was struggling, but Rhaidnan held her tightly, the muscles on his thin arms straining.

Go, Marcus mouthed.

The hunter shook his head—his dark eyes filled with horror.

Marcus's head slammed against the stone floor, and the world went gray around him.

"Go!" he cried with the last of his strength.

Suddenly he felt a hand close around his wrist. He looked up to see Rhaidnan clutching the struggling Kyja in one arm and pulling Marcus with the other. He didn't know how the hunter still had the strength, but his face was set in grim determination. "For Char and the kids," Rhaidnan growled.

The unmakers cried out with rage, and although the pain still racked his body, Marcus felt it lessen slightly with distance.

"An opening!" Rhaidnan cried as they rounded a bend.

Marcus turned his head and saw a flash of clear blue sky.

Behind them, the sound of the unmakers drew closer. But now the smell of fresh air was strong.

The hunter gave a final lunge, and Marcus squinted at the bright light all around him.

"We made—" Rhaidnan began to shout, but all at once his words cut off, and Marcus felt the grip on his wrist relax.

Marcus turned to see what Rhaidnan was looking at, and his muscles went limp. They were outside the caverns, but the passageway they'd followed ended less than a dozen feet from the cave entrance in a sheer cliff that dropped thousands of feet.

Behind them, the sounds of the unmakers were unmistakable. In front of them was a drop that could only mean their deaths. As if that were not enough, he turned to the right and saw a creature that could only exist in nightmares.

Floating in the air less than a hundred feet from the edge of the cliff was a huge, fur-covered beast. Its silver head was easily as big as the cab of a semi and filled with sharp teeth. A ridge of bony horns taller than Rhaidnan crowned its enormous head, and its long neck stretched back to a body with six sets of legs ending in wicked talons. Wings that seemed to stretch forever beat the air in wide, ground-shaking strokes.

"No-o-o-o," the hunter moaned. His legs seemed to give out beneath him, and he dropped to the ground, still clutching Kyja in his arms.

The creature stretched its jaws wide, gave out an air-shattering roar, and sent a stream of icy-blue breath directly at the trio.

CHAPTER 49

THE FROST PINNOIS

THE CONE OF FRIGID BREATH passed close enough to Marcus's head to raise crystals of ice on the tips of his hair. But as it passed harmlessly over him, he heard a roar of pain come from the cavern behind, and his feeling of being drained disappeared at once.

"Down!" a voice shouted.

Marcus looked up in time to see a small, blue head rise into the air above the furry beast. It was dwarfed by the silver creature, but Marcus recognized it immediately. It was Riph Raph.

"Cover your heads," the skyte cried.

Without any further warning, the giant winged creature flew over them directly at the cave's opening. Marcus pressed his face to the ground—tucking his head under his arm as the air buffeted him from all sides. Beside him, Rhaidnan did the same, protecting Kyja with his body.

Marcus peeked through his fingers and watched the silver beast turn in midair. Its long tail—studded with sharp, blue spikes—

swung in a wide arc, slashing a deep gash into the side of the mountain. Dirt, rock, and snow cascaded downward in an enormous cloud of debris.

Dumbstruck, Marcus waved the dust away from his face. The cave opening was gone—as completely buried as if it had never existed. For a moment he thought he saw a bent figure climb from the pile of rocks and snow, and his stomach froze. But when he looked again, the rocky shelf was empty, and he realized nothing could have escaped.

"That should hold them," the creature said, landing on an outward-jutting spire of rock. It shook its long tail, sending a spray of dirt and snow out over the side of the cliff. "Foul creatures. Perhaps I'll come back later and dig them out. It would give me a great deal of pleasure to hunt them down one by one."

"Then you're not going to . . . kill us?" Marcus asked, a tremor in his voice.

As the creature cocked its head and scratched behind its ear with one of its six legs, Marcus realized that what he had taken for fur was actually a thick coat of fine, tiny ice crystals. The ice covered the creature from the tip of its tail all the way up to a narrow beard growing from the end of its chin. After a closer look, the spikes on its tail seemed to be deadly-sharp icicles.

The creature opened its enormous mouth in a wide grin, revealing all its teeth. "Kill you? Not today. I've already eaten my quota of humans for the week."

Marcus gasped, and Rhaidnan's face paled visibly.

"It's a joke," Riph Raph said, fluttering his wings as he landed beside Kyja. "Zhethar doesn't eat humans." He glanced up into the creature's gaping mouth, unsure. "You don't, do you?"

The silver beast only blinked its large, fathomless eyes.

Marcus sat up gingerly. He was covered in a layer of dirt and snow, and his muscles ached. But at least he was alive. Nearby, Kyja was rubbing her eyes and looking around in a daze, as if unsure of how she'd come to be there. Rhaidnan stood protectively at their sides, his right hand clasping and unclasping at his hip where he might have normally carried a sword.

"Are you a *dragon?*" Marcus asked, trying to hide his nervousness.

"A dragon?" The creature gouged its rocky perch with a set of glimmering claws and swished its tail disdainfully. "Silly little fire-breathing lizards who are entirely too full of themselves."

Marcus glanced at Riph Raph, who wisely kept his thoughts to himself for once.

"I am Zhethar, a pinnois—a frost pinnois, to be precise. Noblest of all flying creatures. Long before dragons took to the sky, the pinnois ruled the heavens." It shook its head, fluffing itself until Marcus thought it resembled nothing more than a giant, frozen pincushion.

Finally having regained her bearings, Kyja picked up Riph Raph and hugged him tightly to her chest. "How did you ever find us?" she asked the skyte.

Riph Raph raised his floppy ears and spread his wings. "It was really quite simple. As soon as I saw you were captured, I devised a plan to break you out from the unmakers. Of course, I knew you would—"

His story was interrupted by a pointed cough from the frost pinnois, and Riph Raph quickly glanced over his shoulder. "Well, I was *working* on coming up with a plan, when Zhethar arrived looking for you. And together . . ." he glanced up at the pinnois, who nodded, before continuing. "*Together,* we found the opening of the unmakers' lair."

Kyja scratched Riph Raph behind the ears, and he arched his back with pleasure. "I'm glad you did. " She looked up at Zhethar. "But how could you possibly have come looking for us? You don't even know who we are."

"On the contrary," the pinnois said, with an air of great formality, "I know exactly who you are, Kyja. I also know your friend Marcus and your companion Riph Raph. I was sent to find you by the Fontasians."

"The Fontasians?" Marcus asked. It sounded sort of like an all-girl rock band.

Zhethar nodded. "You may know them better as water elementals."

───◆──

For a moment no one said a word. Then Marcus and Kyja began babbling over the top of each other.

"Water elementals?"

"From Water Keep?"

"Can you take us there?"

"Have you seen Master Therapass?"

Zhethar waved a long-taloned foot. "Now, now. One question at a time, children."

"Go ahead," Marcus said to Kyja.

"How could the water elementals possibly know about *us?*" she asked.

"The Fontasians see everything," the pinnois said. "They have eyes in every river, stream, and lake. Every puddle is a messenger.

Even the drops of rain and morning dew whisper back to them what they see. They've known about you since you first started out on your quest. As a creature of frozen water, they sent me to find you."

"What about Master Therapass?" Marcus asked. "The wizard. Do you know where he is? If he's safe?"

Zhethar shook his bearded face. "The Fontasians said nothing about a wizard. I was sent to retrieve the two of you and your skyte. Now I suppose I'll have to bring your friend as well."

Rhaidnan stood up straight. "These water elementals. What do they want with us?"

"Nothing," Zhethar said, as if it should have been clear. "They want nothing to do with you."

Marcus scratched his head. "But if the water elem—I mean the *Fontasians* want nothing to do with us, why did they send you to bring us to Water Keep?"

The pinnois rolled its huge eyes. "Did I say anything about taking you to Water Keep? The Fontasians did not send me to bring you to them. They sent me to take you back to Terra ne Staric. They heard of your quest and refuse to meet with you."

CHAPTER 50

CITY WALLS

C OME ALONG." The frost pinnois climbed down from its perch and lowered its wing to the ground. "Get on my back. Wrap your cloaks tightly about you—and hurry. I'm afraid it's going to be a bit of a cold ride, but we've got to be moving if you want to reach home before sunset."

Rhaidnan began to crawl up onto the long, icy wing, but Marcus and Kyja met eyes quickly before turning as one toward Zhethar.

"We're not going anywhere with you," Kyja said, folding her arms across her chest.

"Pardon me?" Zhethar asked, tilting his silvery head.

"We're not turning back," Marcus said.

The pinnois rubbed the top of its head with one leg in a surprisingly human expression of confusion. "I'm afraid you don't understand. You have no choice in the matter. The Fontasians knew you had come all this way on a pointless errand. They sent me to take you back to your home."

"Then you've wasted your time," Marcus said. "Thanks for rescuing us. I'm sure Rhaidnan will appreciate a ride back to his wife and family. But we *are* going to Water Keep."

Rhaidnan stopped halfway up the pinnois's wing. Zhethar looked from Marcus and Kyja to the sheer drop-off. "This is foolish. You'll never find the Fontasians on your own. And even if you did, they *won't* meet with you."

Kyja turned her back on the pinnois, and Marcus did the same. "Good-bye," she said, waving over her shoulder. "Tell Char hi for me."

Rhaidnan shrugged his shoulders at Zhethar before climbing back down. "I'm with them."

The pinnois stomped two of its huge feet, rattling the ledge. "I'm taking you back to Terra ne Staric, whether you like it or not."

Marcus turned slowly, his blue eyes glittering, and set his staff in the snowy ground. "That might not be as easy as you think."

Kyja stood beside him, resting one hand on his shoulder. A moment later, Rhaidnan joined them, his calloused hands closed into fists. Riph Raph looked from the furious black eyes of the frost pinnois to Kyja and Marcus's determined faces, before gulping and flying across to land on Kyja's shoulder.

Zhethar bared his glittering teeth in a menacing-looking grin. "And how do you propose to get off this cliff on your own?"

Kyja and Marcus examined their surroundings. The cave entrance was now impassably buried beneath snow and rock. And even if it wasn't, the unmakers were still inside somewhere. Marcus edged toward the drop-off. His stomach turned somersaults as he looked out over the sheer cliff that fell straight down into empty space.

"Maybe we should reconsider," Riph Raph said, eyeing the

pinnois, as it lashed its long tail angrily back and forth, sending snow and rock over the edge of the cliff.

But Kyja—who had been exploring the side of the mountain close to where Marcus thought he'd seen movement earlier—pointed out a small crevice in the rock. "Over here," she called. "It's a trail."

"Trail" is too strong of a word, Marcus thought as he walked up beside her. No more than a foot and a half wide, the tiny lip of rock she pointed at was covered with a treacherous layer of snow and ice. It led out of sight around a ridge of bare rock. But who knew if it even went any farther.

Before he could voice his concerns, though, Kyja was stepping out onto the ledge. "Follow me," she said, as if they were heading out for a summer picnic—as if she didn't have a clue that the first big gust of wind could pluck her from the side of the mountain and send her plummeting to her death.

For the first time since he'd met her, Marcus seriously considered not following her lead. The ledge was bad enough for someone with two good legs. But with his staff, he'd be lucky to make it ten feet before his strength gave out. But when she turned back to look at him, and he saw the confidence in her dark-green eyes, he found himself edging along behind her. Before he had gone two steps, a strong hand clamped onto his left arm, helping him keep his balance, and he turned to see Rhaidnan standing beside him.

"Piece of cake," the hunter said.

Back on the cliff, Zhethar bared his teeth and gave an air-shattering growl. His claws ripped at the rock and ice. Marcus was sure they were goners. He knew he didn't have enough magic to stop a twig if the Pinnois attacked.

"Stop!" the pinnois blurted at last.

"You'll take us to Water Keep?" Kyja asked.

"No. I can't. But you'll never make it down the side of the mountain alive."

"What do you care?" Kyja asked, and Marcus thought he saw the same gleam in her eye that he'd seen when she was negotiating with the man in the pawn shop. "The only thing that matters to you is stopping us from reaching Water Keep. You should be glad if we fall. It would make your job that much easier."

"And have your deaths on my head?" Zethar scratched behind one ear, his cold eyes softening. "A frost pinnois is not a beast. We have feelings too. And we live much longer with those feelings than you humans."

"Well?" Kyja said, folding her arms. "If you won't take us to Water Keep, you leave us no choice but to go on our own." She turned as if to continue along the face of the cliff.

"Fine!" the creature snarled. "Come back. I'll take you to Water Keep. You can wait outside the gates until you all die of old age. It won't do you any good. You'll never get inside."

"Thank you," Kyja said, flashing her brightest smile. "We accept."

Lighting sizzled through the black clouds that had been growing thicker for the last half hour. Thunder rattled the air, making the pinnois's ice crystals chatter and jangle against one another like the prisms of a chandelier.

"The Fontasians are *not* happy," Zhethar growled as he tilted his wings, dropping lower in the sky.

Clutching his staff tightly, Marcus shifted and tried to get a peek over the side of pinnois's body. But all he could make out was an

occasional glimpse of flat bare ground through the silvery mist that
beaded against his cheeks and forehead. Quickly he pulled his head
back, tucking his face against his chest. All of their cloaks were damp
from the thick fog, and their clothing crackled with ice wherever the
material touched the pinnois's body. Even Riph Raph was curled
miserably into a teal-blue ball, his beak hidden beneath his tail and
his breath rising in small, white puffs.

"Are we close then?" Kyja asked through chattering teeth.

In answer, the pinnois dropped completely out of the clouds,
and for the first time Marcus could see the endless glimmering surface of Lake Aeternus. He'd never seen a body of water so large
before. Like pictures of the ocean he'd studied on the pages of maga-
zines, it seemed to stretch out endlessly. Waves rolled toward the
shore in long, white-tipped lines as though some giant, unseen hand
was running its fingers through the water.

"Oh, look!" Kyja called out, raising her hand. "Have you ever
seen anything so beautiful?"

Marcus followed her pointing finger, and his mouth dropped in
wonderment.

Ever since Olden had mentioned the water elementals, Marcus
had wondered what Water Keep might look like. He'd pictured
everything from a bunch of transparent domes to an actual underwater city like the Disney movie with all the merpeople. But what
he was looking at was so different from anything he'd ever imagined,
it was hard for his mind to grasp it.

All along, he'd assumed Water Keep would be *under* the water.
And part of the city *was* under the water. At least he thought it was.
Along the border of the lake—where land and water blurred
together—he could just make out shapes beneath the lake's choppy
surface.

But the city didn't stop there. He could only catch glimpses through the mist, but it looked like as the waves met land, they rose up into fantastical towers and spiraling staircases. Narrow walkways arched high into the air on carved pillars. A moment later, the walkways and towers washed away as if they'd never existed. But with the next wave, they were back again.

The buildings and arches glimmered in and out of focus as if they were made of nothing more substantial than soap bubbles. The only thing which remained solid was a thick, gray wall of mist which appeared to surround the city on all sides.

Kneeling on the pinnois's broad back between Marcus and Kyja, Rhaidnan swallowed. "I never would have thought such a place could exist."

"Look well," Zhethar said, annoyance clear in his rumbling voice. "It's the last time you'll see inside those walls."

Riph Raph studied the city with a mischievous glint in his eyes, but Zhethar glared back at him as though reading the skyte's mind. "Don't think about it, insect. Even *I* can not fly inside. You would be swatted out of the air the moment you tried."

Kyja tucked Riph Raph beneath her arm. "Thank you for bringing us here."

The pinnois shook its massive head as it circled toward the ground. "I do you no favors. It is a long journey back to Terra ne Staric—one filled with greater dangers every passing day. And the Fontasians care nothing for the doings of humans. They will let you die outside the walls of their city without blinking an eye."

"If they don't care about humans, why did they send you to get us in the first place?" Marcus asked.

"The Fontasians do not answer to me." Zhethar gave Marcus an irritated look before dropping to the ground in what seemed like an intentionally hard landing. Muddy water splashed high into the air as the pinnois's talons sunk into the marshy grass.

"This is your last chance," Zhethar said. "Ask, and I will take you back to Terra ne Staric. Stay, and you are on your own. I will not return no matter how great your need, and despite what you might think, the Fontasians will not open their walls to you."

Marcus glanced toward Kyja, who gave a tiny shake of her head. "Thanks for the warning," he said. "But this is where we need to be."

"Very well." The pinnois extended one great silver wing to the ground, and Marcus and Kyja began to climb off. When Rhaidnan tried to follow, however, Kyja held out her hand.

"You're not coming with us."

Rhaidnan stared at her—first in surprise, then in anger. "You saved my life. I'm not leaving two children here all alone."

Marcus thought he had never felt less like a child. He might still be thirteen, but the events of the past two weeks had changed him. He still didn't know what he was doing, still didn't feel up to the task Master Therapass had put on his shoulders, but the days when he'd been frightened by someone like Chet and his friends were long gone.

"Whatever we have to do here is for us alone," he said. "You need to return to your wife and children."

"You're sure?" Rhaidnan looked back and forth between the two of them.

Kyja nodded. "Char's spent enough time without you."

The thought of his wife finally seemed to make the decision for him. Rhaidnan swept the two of them into his arms—somehow managing to trap Riph Raph, who sputtered and squawked. "I won't forget you," he said, tears spilling down his gaunt cheeks. "If there's anything I can ever do for you . . . anything."

A minute later, Kyja helped Marcus to the ground, and the two-some watched as the pinnois prepared to take flight.

"You won't change your mind?" Zhethar asked. Marcus and Kyja shook their heads in unison.

"You won't get in," he said, blinking his big, dark eyes. "But if you somehow manage to, be careful. Elementals do not think the same way as other creatures. They view the world in a way we can't even comprehend."

With its warning given, the pinnois spread out its long, silver wings, launched itself into the air with all six legs, and rose into the sky.

Standing side by side, Kyja and Marcus waved to Rhaidnan until he and Zhethar were only a tiny black speck.

Then, once again, they were alone.

Marcus eyed the high wall of swirling, bluish-green mist which now blocked any view of the city. Kyja pressed her foot into the soft ground, watching as her footprint slowly filled with brownish water.

Riph Raph spied an insect scurrying up a blade of grass. With a chameleon-like dart of his head, he snatched the insect in his beak and swallowed. He cocked his head toward Kyja. "So. What now?"

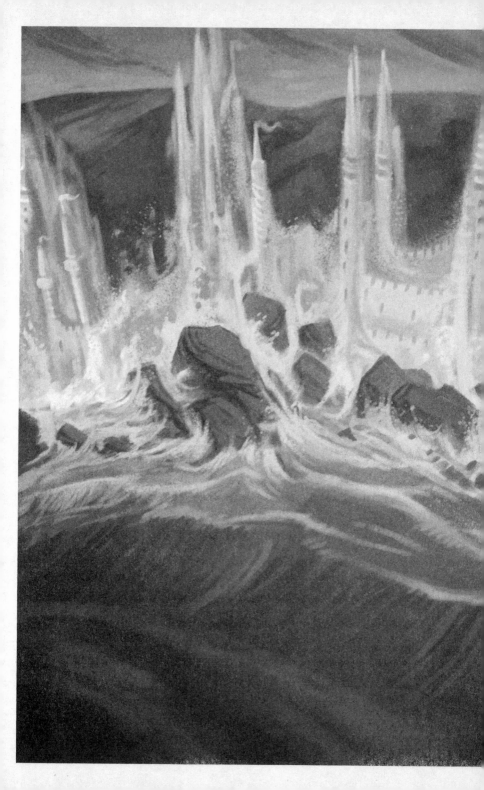

PART 4

Negotiation

CHAPTER 51

SOMETHING FISHY

ARE YOU SURE THIS IS SUCH A GOOD IDEA?" Kyja asked. She and Marcus stood at the edge of the mist. Staring into its depths, she could almost imagine things moving just beneath the fog's rippling surface.

"Of course it's not a good idea. *He* came up with it," Riph Raph said from his perch on Kyja's shoulder.

Kyja could tell Marcus had been making a special effort to be nicer to Riph Raph, since the skyte had been at least partially responsible for their rescue from the unmakers. She could see the effort it took him to keep from saying something rude back.

Marcus pressed his lips together and tightened his grip on his staff. "Do you have a better plan?"

"Wait for Master Therapass," Riph Raph said at once. "The wizard will know what to do."

"How long do you want to wait?" Marcus asked. "Hours? Days? Weeks? Maybe you hadn't noticed, but we can't eat bugs like you.

And I'm not all that excited about the idea of sleeping in this muddy field. Besides, even if Master Therapass *does* show up, what makes you think he'd know any more about this than we do?"

Riph Raph started to open his beak, but Kyja shushed him by placing a hand on the back of his ridged neck. "Marcus is right. We have to do something." She glanced in the direction they'd come from, where even the mountains were no longer visible, wishing she knew what had happened to the wizard.

Putting most of his weight on his left leg, Marcus poked the tip of his staff into the mist. "Zhethar said we couldn't get through the wall, but it doesn't seem to be solid. Maybe there's something else we don't know about."

"Maybe the Fontasians *want* you to go into the mist," Riph Raph said. "Maybe there's something inside waiting to—" He snapped his beak closed with a sharp clack, making his point all too clearly.

As if to confirm the skyte's suspicion, a splash came from a small river a few hundred yards to the east, which disappeared into the mist. Kyja turned quickly, and for a split second thought she saw something disappear into the fog.

"Just a fish," Marcus said. But his face was ashen.

"I guess," Kyja agreed. Still, she had the feeling something was watching her from inside the swirling, blue-green curtain. Out of the corner of her eye she could almost see a curious face, watching and waiting.

"Well, it's not like they're about to invite us in," she said. "If we're going to do this, I'd like to get it over with before dark."

"Right." Marcus wiped the sweat from his forehead with the back of his hand. "I can feel ahead with my staff. Kyja, you take my shoulder." He glared at Riph Raph. "You can wait out here if you're too scared."

The skyte flapped his ears. "Think I'd let her go in alone with *you?*"

Kyja took Marcus's arm. Beneath the damp of his cloak she could feel him shivering ever so slightly. In a way it was reassuring to know that he was just as scared as she was. She gave his shoulder a squeeze and followed him.

Watching Marcus disappear into the moving curtain of fog was like seeing him swallowed by some great beast. One minute he was there, and the next minute he was gone. Even though she was still holding his arm, she couldn't see any sign of him at all. As first her wrist and then her elbow disappeared along with him, it was all she could do to keep from letting go of his shoulder and pulling back.

Then she was inside as well. She quickly realized night wouldn't have made any difference. She couldn't see a thing. It was like wearing a strip of blue cloth wrapped over her eyes.

"It smells strange," Marcus remarked. "Sort of fishy."

His voice sounded oddly distant, and echoed as though it were coming from the bottom of a canyon. Kyja sniffed the air. It did smell like fish, but it also smelled dank, reminding her a little of the unmakers' caves.

Besides its smell, the mist also had an unpleasant feel to it: a cold, oily texture that made her grip on Marcus's shoulder seem slippery and uncertain. As she tightened her fingers, Marcus stopped moving.

"What . . . was . . . that?" he said. His words had a strange gargley sound to them. Kyja pictured someone trying to speak through a mouthful of water.

"What's wrong?" she asked, all at once wishing they'd waited outside after all.

" . . . thaw . . . heard . . . some—"

Heard what? Why was it so hard to understand him? Kyja strained to listen. There was nothing but the ragged sound of her own breathing, heavy and damp, as she inhaled the wet air.

Then, all at once, she *did* hear a sound—like the babbling of a stream. Outside the wall, she'd seen a slow-moving river which flowed into the lake, but it was nowhere near the place they'd entered into the mist. As she concentrated on the sound, it changed—no longer a brook, but a little girl's laughter. Not a happy laugh, but the teasing giggle of a child playing a practical joke.

"Who's there?" Kyja called.

The giggle floated through the mist coming first from in front, then from behind.

"I don't like this," Riph Raph said, pressing his beak against the side of Kyja's face.

"I don't, either." Kyja tried to pull Marcus toward her but couldn't get a tighter grip on the slippery cloth of his cloak.

"We need to go back!" Kyja shouted. She tried to close her hand around Marcus's arm, but suddenly he was jerked out of her grasp.

"Marcus!" she screamed, stumbling deeper into the mist, waving her arms before her.

For a moment she thought she could hear him calling her name. *"Kyja? Ky-ja!"*

But the heavy mist made it impossible to tell where the sound had come from or if it had been him at all. She started to her left, turned and went back to the right. Cupping her hands to her mouth, she cried, "Marcus! Where are you?"

There was no answer.

"Riph Raph, can you see anything?" She reached up to her

shoulder, where a moment before the skyte had been pressed against her, and realized with a sickening jolt that he was gone as well.

"Riph Raph!" How could he have disappeared without her noticing?

Something cold brushed against the back of her neck, and she spun around in time to see the mist part for just a moment, revealing the face of a girl no more than five or six. Kyja stumbled backward.

"You aren't allowed here." The voice came from behind her. Kyja turned to see a quick flash of long, green hair that looked almost like seaweed. Was it the same girl? How had she moved around so quickly?

"Who are you?" Kyja asked, her voice trembling. "What did you do with Marcus and Riph Raph?"

There was no answer. Instead, two flashes of brilliant purple appeared out of the blue-green fog. Kyja gasped, thinking they were eyes. A second later she realized they were two fish—small enough to fit in the palm of her hand, but with long, streamer-like fins and tails. How could fish be swimming in the middle of the air?

As one of the fish swam lazily to Kyja's right, she saw it was trailing an almost invisible thread behind it. The thread brushed coldly against the skin of her arm. She tried to swat it away, but the thread stuck to her skin like glue. The fish continued to swim around her, wrapping Kyja's arms tight against her sides.

She tugged at the thread. It was stronger than it looked. She couldn't break it. Panicking, she turned to run, lost her balance, and nearly fell. While the first fish had been wrapping her arms, the second had circled her legs.

"Stop it!" she screamed. "Let me go!"

"You shouldn't have come here," the child's voice called again.

"We'll go back," Kyja promised. "Just let us go."

The only answer was a fading giggle.

The small, purple fish continued to swim around and around her, wrapping her arms and legs tightly together. What if they didn't stop? What if they wrapped her in a tight cocoon like a slow worm before the hatch? Like a spider trapping its prey before eating?

But the fish didn't wrap her in a cocoon. Instead, once they had her securely tied, they began dragging her backward through the mist. She tried to struggle, but the strings held her fast. Where were they taking her? To someplace even more dangerous? She craned her head to look around, but couldn't see anything.

Without any warning, she felt herself falling. The blue-green clouds around her disappeared as she dropped into the knee-high grass outside the city walls with a muddy splash. Reaching out to catch herself, she realized the threads were gone from her arms and legs. As she pushed herself up onto her elbows, something flew out of the mist beside her.

With a stab of terror she recognized Marcus's staff. A second later a huge fish with glittering, reddish-brown scales flopped out from the wall of fog. Its gills opened and closed, gasping for oxygen as it curled and slapped its tail against the wet grass. Another fish landed right behind it. This one was small and blue with bulbous yellow eyes that looked almost familiar.

As Kyja stared at the fish, wondering what to make of them, the larger of the two fixed its wet blue eyes on her and cried out, "What happened to me?"

———◇———

Four hours later, the sun had long since set. The damp night air was cold, and there was no wood to start a fire and no food.

Resting his chin on his fist, Marcus stared grumpily at Kyja.

"What?" she finally said. "It's not like you stayed a fish for long."

He pressed his lips together until they nearly disappeared. "You thought it was funny."

"I didn't."

"You laughed." He scowled at her as she covered her mouth with her hands. "You know they would have changed you, too, if you weren't immune to magic."

"I wasn't laughing *at* you," she said from behind her fingers. "I was just surprised to see you as a . . . a . . ." She couldn't help herself from bursting into a fit of giggles all over again.

"Right." Marcus brooded. The wall of mist around Water Keep glowed, but outside, the patchy clouds had thickened, hiding the plains in a blanket of darkness. He was cold and wet, and his clothes smelled like . . . well, like *fish*.

Riph Raph seemed no worse for the experience. The skyte lay snoring softly, curled in Kyja's lap.

"What are we supposed to do now?" Marcus sighed.

Kyja took her hand from her mouth, her face serious again. "I'm not going back in there."

Marcus nodded. It *was* kind of humorous looking back on it now. But when he'd seen the flash of light and felt his body turn cold and slippery, it hadn't seemed funny at all. He'd been terrified. He wasn't about to see what would happen if he tried to go through the wall again. Maybe the next time, they'd leave him that way. He had no desire to spend the rest of his life as a big-mouth bass or whatever species of fish they had here.

"Do you think the girl you saw was one of them?" Marcus asked. "One of the Fontasians?" He hadn't seen anything but a flash of bright blue light before he found himself on the ground flipping and tossing.

"Maybe," Kyja said, her eyes locked on the glowing wall. "But she was just a child."

Marcus followed her gaze, glad they'd moved far away from the strange-smelling fog. None of it made any sense. Walls of mist. Cities made of water. Children that turned you into fish, seemingly just for the fun of it. "It's crazy, you know," he said softly.

"What is?" Kyja asked, pulling her cloak more tightly about her.

"You, me. This whole thing." Marcus rubbed his right leg. "Back in the caverns I nearly got us killed because I couldn't keep up. Who would choose a kid in a wheelchair to save their world?"

Kyja smiled softly. "Or the only person in the world who can't do a bit of magic?"

"Right," Marcus said. "We're just a couple of kids. Why not leave the world saving to people like Master Therapass?"

Kyja gazed out into the big, empty darkness and sighed. "Master Therapass isn't here."

"Do you think he's all right?" Marcus asked.

Kyja rubbed her eyes. "I'm sure he's just a few days behind us."

Marcus wondered if she really believed that. Master Therapass knew where they were headed. If he was okay, wouldn't he have found some way to get a message through to them? Marcus thought about the Summoner and the army of Fallen Ones. The thought brought goose bumps to his arms.

"Do you think the Dark Circle is out there somewhere?" Kyja asked.

Marcus ran his hands along his arms, trying to warm the tiny bumps away. "No," he said, remembering the warning he'd experienced just before the Fallen Ones attacked them outside the Westland Woods. "I think I'd feel it if they were. They might have learned where

336

we were headed on the bus. But as far as they know, we're still trapped in the mountains. If they're looking for us anywhere, it'll be there."

"Remember when I tried to send you back to Ert the first time?" Kyja asked. Marcus noticed she was rubbing her arms as well.

"The time something nearly trapped us?"

"Yes," Kyja said, petting the back of Riph Raph's head. "I've been thinking a lot about that. The second time, I braced myself against whatever was waiting for me. I thought that's why we got past. But what if they *let* us jump? What if instead of trying to stop us, the Dark Circle is watching where we're jumping to and from? Following us to learn what we're up to?"

Marcus nodded slowly. "That would explain how they knew where to search for us on Earth."

Kyja chewed on the tip of her thumb and looked out into the darkness. "Their door doesn't seem to work the way our jumping does. I think they might only be able to come and go from one spot. But once we jump, couldn't they follow us or send out spies?"

Marcus studied her face. "Sure. I guess. Why?"

"I might have an idea. But it's dangerous." Kyja turned to study the glowing wall of mist for a moment, then looked back at Marcus. "Remember how you said our movements on one world changed where we arrived on the other world?"

All at once Marcus understood her idea—and her concern.

"If we jump to Ert," she said, "we could walk a short distance and then jump back."

"And we'd be inside the city," Marcus added.

Kyja cupped her elbows in her palms. "But the Dark Circle would know where we are."

CHAPTER 52

BASSELBALL

RIPH RAPH UNLEASHED A BALL of blue fire and swung his tail angrily back and forth. "I do *not* want to be turned into a lizard again."

"It's the only way to get inside," Kyja said. "And besides, it will only be for a few minutes."

Marcus looked up at the glowing wall and away into the darkness. If Kyja's guess was right—and it felt right to him—the Dark Circle would know their location as soon as they jumped. And once they discovered where he and Kyja were, how long would it take the Dark Circle to realize what they were up to?

"If we're going to go," he said, rubbing his hands against his pants, "let's get it over with."

Kyja studied his face. "Are you sure you want to do this?"

"No. But I don't think we have any choice."

He didn't tell her he had another reason for worrying besides the Dark Circle. He didn't know for sure where they would arrive on

Earth. But the only big city located on the south shore of a really large lake in the middle of the plains that he knew of was Chicago. He'd never been to a city that big, and he had no idea what they'd have to face.

"All right then," Kyja said. "I'll hold Riph Raph and push you back to Ert. Don't forget to grab onto me when you jump."

Careful to face the wall so he'd know which direction to go when he reached Earth, Marcus held his staff tightly and closed his eyes. A cool sweat broke out on his forehead, and then he felt the familiar upside-down sensation in his stomach—he was falling. At once he reached out for Kyja and Riph Raph. It was easy to pull them along, like grabbing the strings of a pair of balloons, but this time he had the awful feeling something dark and dangerous was watching them.

When he opened his eyes, he found himself sitting on a cracked sidewalk, facing a tall, brick building. The crumbling wall was covered with layer upon layer of spray-painted graffiti. A faded yellow sign taped to the inside of a dirt-grimed window read "Building Condemned. No Trespassing."

Marcus turned his head to see a white ball of feathers bouncing toward him on the sidewalk.

"Something's wrong with me!" Riph Raph shouted. "Where's my tail? Where's my long tongue? What are these white things?"

As Marcus watched, the feather ball flapped its stubby wings, flew into the side of the building and landed on the sidewalk with a thump.

"You're a chicken," Marcus said, grinning from ear to ear. "Try laying an egg."

"A what?" Riph Raph tried to fly, but only managed to get a few feet in the air before performing an awkward somersault and dropping to the sidewalk with an explosion of feathers. "How can I be a chicken?" he wailed. "I'm supposed to turn into a . . . a . . . chameleon!"

Marcus shrugged. "I don't know. Maybe it's kind of random."

"That's one big chicken," said a bearded man sitting inside a cardboard box next to the building. He waved a filthy hand in Marcus's direction and gave a loud burp that smelled strongly of cheap wine. "You wanna share? I could help ya cook it."

"*Brawk!* Keep that monster away from me!" Riph Raph cried. He disappeared behind Marcus's back.

Inside his cardboard box, the man blinked, and his bloodshot eyes grew wide. "Your chicken *talks?*"

"I've gotta go," Marcus told the man. "Let's get out of here," he said to Riph Raph. Dragging his staff, he scooted along the sidewalk to where Kyja stood looking though a tall, chain-link fence, her fingers hooked around the squares of rusted wire. Riph Raph followed in nervous little hops, bobbing his head left and right as he made sure the man from the box wasn't following him.

"Well, at least he didn't turn into a lizard this time," Marcus said when he reached Kyja's side. But all of Kyja's attention was riveted to what was happening on the other side of the fence.

"Look," she said, pointing at a group of older boys playing basketball on a patched asphalt court. "Have you ever seen anything like that?"

Marcus glanced quickly at the boys, then up and down the street. "Sure," he said, looking around nervously. "It's just a game. Let's get out of here before anything bad happens." Loud music blasted out of the windows of the nearby apartment buildings, and a short distance away a group of swaying men took turns drinking from bottles wrapped in brown paper bags. All the kids on the basketball court were older than Kyja and him. And they looked tough, with bulging muscles and tattooed biceps.

He tugged at Kyja's robe, but she ignored him, her eyes locked on the basketball players. One of the boys took two long running steps, raised the ball over his head and slammed it through the rim. Marcus watched the move enviously. It was the kind of dunk he'd like to have tried—if he had two strong arms and legs.

"Oh! It looks fun," Kyja said, putting her hand to her mouth. She turned excitedly to Marcus. "Do you think they'd let me play?"

"Are you crazy?" Marcus hissed. "The Dark Circle could show up any minute." He reached for Riph Raph, who was still pacing nervously up and down the sidewalk, and the chicken pecked him on the leg.

"Ouch," Marcus said. He pushed Riph Raph away and frowned at Kyja. "Come on. Haven't you ever seen a basketball game before?"

"No." Kyja said. She watched a boy spin past his defender and shoot the ball through the sagging hoop. She bent her knees and took a pretend shot of her own. "All the games the kids play back home use magic."

Riph Raph strutted up to the fence and looked around with odd little jerking motions. *Probably checking to see if anyone else wants to cook him,* Marcus thought. *At least he has the good sense not to talk anymore.*

Noticing the way the men with the bottle were watching them, Marcus pulled Kyja's hand. "We have to go. We might not be safe here."

"Safe from what?" a voice asked.

Marcus turned to see a boy several years younger than him watching Kyja from the other side of the fence. At least two feet shorter than the boys on the court, he was dressed in a basketball jersey that came nearly to his knees and white high-top basketball shoes that looked too big for his feet.

"What *you* looking at?" the boy asked, resting a basketball on his hip.

"Basselball," Kyja said as Riph Raph quickly ducked behind her. She pointed to the orange ball in his hand. "Do you play too?"

"You kidding?" the boy said, puffing out his chest. The boy bounced the ball on the uneven pavement with a smooth, easy motion, shifting it from hand to hand, bouncing it between his legs and behind his back.

"That's great," Kyja said, clapping her hands. Marcus felt a wave of envy. "What's your name?"

"Ty," the boy said, shuffling his feet and pretending to make a fancy move around another player. "What's yours?"

"Kyja," she answered, ignoring Marcus as he tugged at her arm. "Why aren't you playing with the other boys?"

Ty glanced over his shoulder at the game, and his eyes flashed. "Them? They scared of me." He bounced the ball off the fence, spun around, and caught it with one hand. "You know Dwyane Wade and LeBron James?"

Kyja shook her head.

"No? Well, I'm better than both of them and Michael Jordan put together. I got moves so sweet, Ron Artest and Big Ben Wallace couldn't stop me. Only reason I'm not playing in the NBA right now is 'cause I'm too young. But one day I'll be making me some serious cash and driving a red Lamborghini. Maybe even a gold-plated Hummer."

Marcus rolled his eyes, but Kyja nodded excitedly. "I want to learn to drive too."

"Yeah?" The younger boy tried to spin the ball on his fingertip and had to grab it when it fell off. "Tell you what. When I get my Hummer, I'll let you drive it."

"That would be great," Kyja said, her eyes sparkling.

Fed up with all the nonsense, Marcus jerked Kyja's hand. "If you're done talking to Dwyane LeBron Jordan, we need to go. Or did you forget about you-know-who?"

For the first time, Ty looked past Kyja and noticed Marcus. "What's wrong with your friend? And what's he doing with that chicken?"

Before Kyja could answer, Marcus raised himself up as tall as he could while still sitting and said, "It's *her* chicken, and there's nothing wrong with me. If we didn't have to go, I'd school you out there on the court."

The boy grinned, which infuriated Marcus even further. "How you gonna do that with a messed up arm and leg?"

Realizing how upset Marcus was, Kyja stepped between him and Ty. "He's right," she said, picking up Riph Raph and Marcus's staff. "We really do have to go. Maybe I can drive your humbler some other time."

"Let's go." Marcus spun away and began scooting along the sidewalk, his face bright red. He didn't know why Kyja had to go around talking to strange people when the Dark Circle could be anywhere.

Before they had gone a dozen steps, Ty ran around the fence and joined them. "Hey," he said, putting a hand on Marcus's shoulder. "I didn't mean nothing. I was just mad 'cause my brother and his friends won't let me play ball with 'em."

Marcus jerked his shoulder out from under the boy's hand. "I thought you were too good."

The boy bounced the ball off the cracked sidewalk and held it against his hip. "I was just saying that. They think I'm too small."

"Look," Marcus said. "I don't mean to be rude or anything, but—"

Before he could finish his sentence, he glanced over his shoulder and saw one of the men who'd been drinking from the bottle. He was no longer swaying, but instead coming straight toward Marcus and Kyja.

CHAPTER 53

THE GOOD AND THE BAD

MARCUS GRABBED KYJA'S HAND. "That man behind us. I saw him back by the fence."

Ty glanced toward the man in the ragged, dark sweater and pulled-down hat. "Ain't nobody but one of them stew bums looking for a drink."

"There's no way they could have followed us here already," Kyja said, and yet as they increased their speed, the man picked up his pace.

"Kyja, look at that." Marcus nodded at a nearby telephone pole. Stapled to the pole was a picture of the two of them with the words, "Missing Children" above and "$10,000 Reward for Safe Return" below. "Somehow they knew we'd come here."

The man was less than fifty feet behind them. Kyja looked for a place to run, but other than a few broken-down cars, the street was empty.

Ty eyed the poster. "You two running away or something?"

"It's hard to explain," Marcus said. "Kyja's from somewhere else, and the people from where she lives are trying to kill us."

Ty's dark eyes widened. "You serious?" He glanced at Marcus with a newfound respect. "She from a different country or something?"

"More different than you'd ever believe," Marcus said.

"Thought you two was dressed kind of funny." Ty eyed the man, who had broken into a shuffling jog behind them. "Here's what you do," he whispered. "Soon as we get to the corner, run to the door on the left. It looks locked, but the chain's cut. Wait inside."

"What are you going to do?" Kyja asked.

Ty just grinned. When they reached the corner, he whispered, "Now."

At once Marcus and Kyja hurried down the sidewalk. Just like Ty had said, there was a rusty-looking door with a chain wrapped through the handle. When Kyja pushed on the handle, the chain slipped through the latch, and the door swung open. From around the corner behind them came the sound of a scuffle and a thud, followed by a loud cry of pain.

Seconds later, they heard footsteps outside the door, and a voice whispered, "It's me."

Kyja opened the door, and Ty slipped inside. Immediately he picked up a splintery board leaning against the wall and propped it under the handle of the door. He pointed to a sagging metal staircase that led into the darkness. "Can you make it up those?" he asked Marcus.

"Try to keep up with me," Marcus said, climbing the stairs like a monkey.

"Kid's fast," Ty said to Kyja as they hurried after him.

They had just reached the third landing when someone began pounding on the door below.

"Shhh," Ty said, placing his finger to his lips.

They stood silently on the stairs, listening as whoever was outside shook the knob and pounded on the door. Finally, the pounding stopped, and Ty nodded. "Use that all the time," he said.

Marcus found himself coming to like the boy after all. "What did you do to that man back there?"

Ty smirked and flipped his ball from one hand to the other behind his back. "My Dwayne Wade spin move."

Ty led them up the stairs to another door. This one was ripped off its top hinges, leaning crookedly against a dingy, water-stained wall. Pausing before the darkened doorway, Ty turned to Kyja and Marcus. "Stay close. Floor's falling apart up here."

Keeping her left hand on Ty's shoulder, Kyja followed him through the dim hall, wincing every time she heard movement around them. Marcus stuck close behind, and for once Riph Raph knew when to keep quiet.

At last, they rounded a corner and came out on the roof of another building. Ty led them across the tar-and-gravel surface and showed them how to climb some crates onto another building. They passed through a security door propped open with a brick and went down a second flight of stairs. Then they crossed the cracked linoleum floor of a small lobby in an ancient apartment building, where a man in a seedy, black suit gave them an angry glare.

"Don't worry 'bout him," Ty said, jerking a thumb in the man's direction. "He looks that way at everybody."

Outside it had started to rain, and the air was chilly. Marcus and Kyja glanced up and down the street. But the only people in sight were a couple of little girls playing some kind of game on the sidewalk in front of a brick apartment building, and a woman with a baby, sitting in a car with no tires.

"It's cool," Ty said. "Nobody knows that way but me."

"I think we'd better leave anyway," Marcus said. "No telling who else might be looking for us."

But Kyja's eyes were locked on the woman in the car. She didn't look much older than Kyja, and, despite the cold, she was wearing only a thin T-shirt. The windows of the car were down, letting in the rain, and the baby was fussing.

"Why doesn't she take her baby inside?" she asked Ty.

The boy shrugged and bounced his ball on the curb. "Her man left. She lives in the car 'til she gets some money."

"Kyja," Marcus said. "We really need to go."

"Why doesn't someone give her money?" Kyja asked.

Ty shrugged again. "Don't look at me." He turned his pockets inside out. "I ain't got no money. If she takes her baby to the shelter, maybe they'll take it away from her."

All at once something occurred to Kyja—something that seemed completely impossible. She grabbed Marcus by the shoulder of his cloak. "The man in the box. Was he *living* there?"

"I guess so." Marcus turned to Ty with a what's-the-big-deal look.

But Kyja felt her heart pounding. This was all wrong. What kind of world was it where amazing machines were everywhere, but a mother and her baby had to live in a broken car and an old man slept in a box?

Turning to Marcus she asked, "How much money do we have left?"

"A couple hundred dollars, I guess," Marcus said. "But—"

"Give it to me." As Marcus fumbled in his leather pouch, Kyja set Riph Raph down and pulled her cloak off over her head. "Give me your cloak, too."

"I don't think—" Marcus began, but Kyja took the money from his hand and yanked off his cloak before he could even get it untied.

"Everyone from her country crazy like that?" Ty asked.

Marcus shook his head with a rueful grin. "No. Only her."

Kyja hurried down the sidewalk, mindful of the rain that was falling harder and the baby who had gone from fussing to all-out crying. As Kyja reached the car, the woman looked up sharply, and her eyes narrowed.

"What do you want?" she asked, clutching the baby to her chest.

Kyja pushed the money and cloaks through the open window without saying a word. For a moment, the woman couldn't seem to comprehend what was happening. She stared at the cloaks and the wad of bills. Then she glanced warily past Kyja as if suspecting it was all some kind of trick.

Once the woman understood it was real, she ran her fingers over the fabric of the cloaks and closed her hand around the bills as her eyes began to well up. "Who are you?" she asked. "Why are you doing this?"

But Kyja couldn't speak. She was too choked up and confused. There were so many *good* things on Ert—things like chocolate shakes and TV, semi trucks and basselball. But most people seemed to take those things for granted and ignore the things that really mattered.

Instead of answering, she ran back to Marcus and squeezed his hand fiercely. "Good-bye, Ty," she said, biting her lip to keep from crying. "Thank you for your help. I hope you get your humbler."

With that, she picked up Riph Raph, found herself in the place between worlds, and pushed as hard she could. The last thing she saw was Ty watching her with wide eyes, his basketball bouncing, forgotten, down the street.

CHAPTER 54

WATER KEEP

THIS JUMP HAD BEEN WORSE than all the others combined. It felt like he'd been tossed over a waterfall. He would have thrown up for sure if his stomach hadn't been empty. Why had Kyja been so upset?

Before he could give it any more thought, Marcus realized three things. The first was that they were *inside* the city. All around them, the world glowed with a bluish-green light. And everything seemed to be in motion. Buildings, statues, and odd-looking trees floated alongside strange, blob-like shapes that looked liked huge piles of Jell-O constantly changing colors. It all bobbed and spun like leaves in a stream. Watching made Marcus's stomach feel even worse than it already did.

The second thing was that Kyja was upside down. Not standing on her head or hanging by her feet, but just sort of floating. Her hair, which should have dangled down—or up, depending on how you looked at it—lay across her shoulders.

But all of that was nothing compared to the last thing. He was standing without the use of his staff, which hung loosely in his hand, and there was no pain at all. He looked down at his leg, wondering if somehow he'd been magically healed. It didn't look any different, but it was almost as if he weighed nothing at all here.

"You're upside down," Kyja said with a shocked look on her upside down face.

"No, you are." He pointed to her feet, which were slightly above his head.

"Look around." She reached out and touched an umbrella-shaped object with a strange creature sticking out from the bottom of it. A stream of dark blue flowed down from the creature's mouth and spilled back up into the umbrella. At her touch, the object changed direction and floated off down the street.

Marcus realized it was an upside-down fountain. He looked down—or was it up?—at his feet and noticed they weren't touching anything. But then, neither were Kyja's. They were both sort of hovering in midair.

Riph Raph, changed back to his normal self, struggled out of Kyja's arms and tried to fly. But instead of soaring up into the sky, he spun awkwardly in a circle. "What's wrong with this place?" the skyte sputtered.

Kicking his leg and swinging his arm, Marcus managed to rotate himself until he and Kyja were facing the same direction. Once he got the hang of it, it was sort of fun. "Are we underwater?" he asked.

"If we are, how can we be breathing?" Kyja took a deep breath and let it out, demonstrating her point. There were no bubbles.

"He-l-l-l-p-p," Riph Raph cried, flapping his wings as he spun completely out of control.

Marcus reached out with one hand as the skyte floated past and managed to catch Riph Raph by the leg.

Riph Raph clutched tightly to Marcus's arm with his talons. "I don't like this place. Let's get out while we can."

"We can't leave," Kyja said. "We have to find the water elementals and get them to help us."

"Speaking of which, check that out." Marcus pointed to something moving slowly toward a nearby building that tilted like the leaning tower of Pisa. The creature was shaped sort of like a human, but with no discernable features and no fingers or toes—he looked more like a big gingerbread cookie. From inside its gray, semi-transparent body, occasional bursts of blue and yellow light flashed.

"Excuse me," Kyja called toward the gingerbread man. "We're looking for water elementals. Are you one? Or can you tell us where to find them?"

If the creature heard her, it gave no sign. Instead it continued its slow forward surge and disappeared into the doorway of the building.

"Let's catch up with it," Marcus said. Kicking his arms and legs in a swimming motion, he tried to go toward the building. But he quickly discovered that didn't work. All he accomplished with his paddling and kicking was a slow, graceless spin.

"Stop it," Riph Raph said from his shoulder. "I think I'm going to be sick."

Kyja seemed to be having better luck using a combination of jumping and walking motions while guiding herself with her arms.

Holding his hands out to balance himself, Marcus followed her example. It was sort of like the pictures he'd seen of astronauts walking across the moon. With no gravity pulling him down, he found he could leap ten to twelve feet with a single step.

His aim wasn't as good as Kyja's, though. While she stopped just in front of the door, Marcus found himself moving too quickly and ended up slamming against the wall three feet to the left.

"Look where you're going," Riph Raph muttered.

"Look at this, you two." Kyja stood peering into the building as she held onto the doorframe.

Marcus pulled himself hand-over-hand along the wall until he reached her. Staring into the building, he at first thought the large open room was full of paintings. Each of the walls was covered with what looked like large, round picture frames. Some of the frames were empty, but most of them held different pictures—grassy meadows, animals, a strange, pillar-like building with dark, gaping windows, even a family eating lunch on a patch of sandy beach. The frames that held pictures had glowing lights at the bottom.

But then he realized the things in the pictures were moving. Something that looked like a mix between a fox and a bear lumbered across the meadow and stopped to lap from a stream. Clouds blew past the unfamiliar-looking building. The children at the beach scampered in and out of their frame as though walking past the lens of a video camera.

But if there *were* cameras making the pictures, they were the best he'd ever seen. The pictures were so clear you almost expected the people to step right out. And he could swear he heard a child's distant laughter coming from one of them.

The pictures weren't just on the walls, either. Set among more of the color-changing blobs he'd seen outside the building were bowls that looked almost big enough to be small swimming pools. But instead of water, they held pictures too. Kyja moved to the nearest bowl and—placing her hands on the rim—leaned over it.

"I can actually smell them," she said, sniffing an image of

bright-red flowers. "It's like the TVs in your world, only much better." She reached toward the picture, but Marcus caught her arm.

"Look," he whispered, pointing to the gray creature they'd followed into the building. Across the room, it approached the family on the beach. For a moment it paused, then, pressing itself up against the image, it actually seemed to ooze right through.

In the picture, the sky above the beach had been a cloudless blue, but as soon as the creature disappeared into it, the horizon immediately began to darken. The family glanced nervously up at the clouds and began gathering their food. Lightning flashed from the thunderheads that rolled quickly in, and Marcus heard the peel of thunder and smelled the electrical aroma of hot ozone. Before the family had finished picking up their blankets, big drops of rain were falling on them.

"It's real, isn't it?" Kyja said. "Those people are real, and somehow that gray thing made it storm wherever they are."

"I think that gray thing *was* the storm," Marcus said.

Kyja's fingers had been hovering over the surface of the bowl in front of her. She snatched them back. "Do you think if you put your hand through one of the pictures, you'd go through too?"

"I don't know," Marcus said, "But I sure don't want to find out." Kneeling by the side of the bowl, he noticed a series of different-colored circles, glowing with a pulsing light like he'd seen on the frames around the wall.

As he reached tentatively toward a pink circle, it grew unexpectedly brighter for a moment.

"How did you do that?" Kyja gasped.

When Marcus looked back at the surface of the bowl, he saw the picture had zoomed out, so that now, instead of only a few of the red flowers, he could see an entire field of them. Cautiously, he touched a circle glowing a faint blue. Again the circle blazed brightly, and the picture zoomed in on a single flower.

"They're some kind of controls," he said. "Try one."

With a trembling hand, Kyja reached out to the gold circle. Instead of flashing as the pink and blue circles had, the gold only glowed a little more brightly. Flowers moved across the screen from right to left.

Marcus touched the pink again, and the picture zoomed back out. "Put your hand closer," he said.

The image began to move faster and faster. The field of flowers was gone, replaced by a long, rolling hill. Kyja put her hand even closer to the gold circle, and the picture raced across the bowl's surface. Grassy slopes and valleys flew past at a dizzying pace. Streams, trees, and a small crystal blue lake were only a blur. The grass began to be broken-up by clumps of rock as the hills grew into steep slopes and finally mountains.

Kyja took a deep breath, her cheeks glowing. "It's like flying," she said. "It's like we're on the back of a great big bird and—"

"What are you doing here?" a child's voice said from behind them.

Marcus and Kyja spun around to see a small girl in a pale aqua gown that came nearly to the tops of her bare feet. Her hair—which reached almost to her waist and looked like strands of seaweed—trailed out behind her as she kicked her small feet and glided through the door toward them.

"It's the girl from the wall," Kyja whispered, grabbing Marcus's hand. "The one who tied me up. The one who turned you and Riph Raph into fish."

CHAPTER 55

GAUGHT

HOW DID YOU GET INSIDE THE CITY?" the little girl asked with a curious smile. "No one ever gets past the walls."

"No thanks to you," Kyja said, glaring at the girl. "You didn't have to turn Marcus and Riph Raph into fish. And tying me up was rude, to say the least."

The girl raised her fingers to her mouth to cover a smile. "I didn't do that. It was the walls. I just wanted to see who you were. We don't get visitors very often."

"I can see why," Kyja shot back.

Marcus gave her a warning look. The last thing they needed was another argument. He tried putting on his friendliest smile. "Hi, there. What's your name?" He reached out toward her, thinking he might shake her hand, but with a flick of her wrists and feet she zipped out the door and vanished behind one of the shifting blobs.

"Come on," Marcus said. He and Kyja followed the little girl through the door, but when they reached the blob, she wasn't there. They searched all around, but she seemed to have disappeared.

"I'm not down there, silly," a voice called from behind them.

Marcus turned to see the girl looking out the second-story window of the building they had just left.

"How did you get up there?" Marcus asked.

The girl only giggled.

"Can you help us?" Kyja tried.

The child disappeared from the window.

"Help you what?" she asked. She was back in the room with the pictures again, sitting cross-legged on the floor, playing with a string of golden beads in her lap.

Kyja jump-kicked back to the door. "We need to talk to someone right away. A grown-up."

"*Grown-up?*" The girl took one of the beads from her string and let it float away. Arriving at Kyja's side, Marcus watched with fascination as the small, golden ball approached one of the empty frames on the wall and a picture began to appear in the dark center of the circle. Rays of sunlight peeked over the horizon of a still meadow, and the golden ball disappeared into the image. A moment later, tiny drops of water beaded on the flowers and blades of grass.

"Dew," Marcus breathed, and the little girl flashed a knowing smile in his direction.

Marcus approached her carefully, trying not to scare her off this time. "Could you please take us to someone older? Maybe your mom or dad?"

She plucked another bead from the string and held it up in front of her face—admiring its glittering surface before tossing it toward one of the bowls. "What's a *mom-or-dad?*"

Kyja put both hands on her hips. "This is very important. Isn't there someone in charge here?"

"In charge of what?" the girl asked, returning the beads to a pocket of her gown.

"Arghh," Kyja growled in frustration. "In charge of everything. You know, like a mayor or a king or something?"

The girl seemed to want to understand, so Marcus tried explaining. "There's a group called the Dark Circle trying to destroy Farworld. And there's something we might be able to do to stop them. Only we need the help of the water elementals to do that."

The girl had listened closely all through Marcus's explanation, but when he got to the part about needing the water elementals' help, she kicked her feet and burst into laughter as if that was the funniest joke she'd ever heard.

"Elementals don't help," she said with a giggle.

"You!" a gruff voice shouted from behind them.

Marcus turned to see two shapes racing in their direction. He stared at the figures in amazement. He'd thought the girl was strange. But she was nothing compared to these two.

At first glance, they looked sort of like fish. Each of them had gaping, big-lipped mouths and bulging eyes. And their skin was covered in glittering, rainbow-colored scales. But they also had arms and legs that looked almost human, except that instead of ending in hands and feet, they had broad, nearly-transparent fins. He wondered if they were some kind of guards.

"Stop where you are," the one on the left said.

"We aren't moving," Kyja answered.

That seemed to confuse the guard-fish for a minute, but the one on the right quickly took over. "Who are you?"

Before they could answer, the one on the left demanded, "What are you doing here?"

"We were just talking to . . ." Marcus turned to point to the girl, but she was gone.

CHAPTER 56

TRIAL AND ERROR

KYJA LOOKED AROUND the large chamber. Unlike the rest of Water Keep, the wide, bowl-shaped room was dark and clammy. There were none of the bright colors or unusual buildings. Only a big, empty, dreary space.

She wasn't exactly sure how they'd gotten there. The guard-fish—as she'd come to think of them—had led Marcus and her to one of the strange blob shapes. Suddenly, the shape opened up before them, and the next thing she knew, they were stepping out of another blob and into this room.

They'd been standing here for what felt like at least half an hour, doing absolutely nothing. But anytime she, Marcus, or Riph Raph tried to speak or move, the guard-fish made threatening gestures and told them to be still.

"If you'd just let me ex—" she tried again, but the guard-fish on the right tugged her arm.

"Ouch," she said, rubbing her shoulder.

"Leave her alone." Marcus yanked at the guard-fish holding him, but couldn't pull free.

Riph Raph tried to blow a fireball, but it sputtered out before it even left his mouth.

"Quiet!" Marcus's guard-fish said.

Kyja looked desperately around the room, a feeling of deep hopelessness settling over her. Was Zhethar right all along? Would they fail this close to the goal? She licked her lips and shivered. The guard-fish holding her continued to stare straight ahead as if watching something only he could see.

A low, vibrating hum filled the air, and the room began to grow brighter. Both of the guard-fish straightened. Kyja glanced nervously at Marcus and mouthed, *What is it?*

Marcus shook his head, looking as scared as Kyja felt.

"Is the council present?" A booming voice echoed through the room. Kyja turned to see that the room was no longer empty. A fat man with several chins stood before a golden throne shaped like a huge shell. On the wall above the shell, the symbol for water was emblazoned in shining gold. As he lowered himself into the chair, the man's chins shook and wobbled. He reached into a school of small fish circling his head and popped one into his mouth.

"Mist is present," said an airy voice. A fragile-looking woman with long, thin arms and legs materialized out of nowhere and reclined in a high-backed, nearly transparent chair. The woman and the chair were surrounded by a silvery cloud that sparkled as if it were made of tiny diamonds.

On the other side of the room, a squat woman with big, damp-looking eyes set in a fat but pleasant face dropped from the darkness to land softly on a puffy, white pillow. Each time she moved, her silky robe changed colors—flashing first red, then yellow, blue, red again, and finally a color Kyja didn't even recognize. "Raindrop is he-e-re," called the woman in a musical voice.

"Cascade is present." An athletic figure who didn't look to be much older than a boy strode gracefully into the room. He had a handsome face with spiky, white hair and a faintly-blue tinge to his skin. "Has anyone seen Morning Dew?" he asked, in a voice that soothed like a babbling brook.

There was a rustling as each of the others looked toward a large, empty, green leaf.

The fat man snapped his pudgy fingers, and another fish-guard appeared.

Cascade whispered something to the guard, and it zoomed away. "Morning Dew is *not* present, Tide," Cascade said before taking a seat on a sandstone bench.

"Very well. We will proceed without her," Tide said. "Bring the criminals forward."

Kyja turned to Marcus as the guards pulled them into the center of the room. Were they really *criminals?* Would they be thrown into some kind of underwater jail?

The guard-fish pushed them onto a large, blue circle with the water symbol at its center. The circle lifted up out of the floor, raising the three of them into the air.

When the platform stopped rising, Tide was just shoving another fish between his plump lips, but he quickly pushed himself out of his shell chair and swallowed. He fixed his eyes on Marcus, Kyja, and Riph Raph with a look that was almost recognition, as if he'd seen them before and was expecting them.

He tugged on his heavy robes and cleared his throat. "You three are charged with, *ahem,* unlawful ingress, desecration of effects, illegal interaction with—"

Marcus raised his hand. "I don't understand what any of that means."

"Silence!" Tide thundered.

Kyja held out her hands to the Fontasians. "Why do you have to use all those big words? If you think we did something wrong, just say what you mean."

Down below, the fish-guards scowled, but Raindrop nodded her head. "The humans are right. Get to the point, Tide. I have a storm to look after."

Tide coughed into his hand and looked around uncertainly. "Well," he said, his triple chins trembling. "That is . . ." Finally, he gestured to Cascade and returned to his shell.

Cascade turned to Kyja and Marcus. "We're not very good at this. You see, we . . ." He glanced at Mist, who gestured him to continue with her waif-like hand. "We don't do this very often. In fact, we've never done it before. You're the first outsiders to enter our city."

Cascade ran his hands down the sides of his deep blue robes, which rippled beneath his touch like a dancing brook. "We're not very good with your language. Dew is really the best, but she's not here at the moment. What we're trying to say is that you entered our city without . . ." He ran his fingers through his white hair in thought.

"Permission?" Marcus suggested.

Kyja gave him a dark look, and he mouthed, *Sorry.*

"That's right," Cascade said, brightening. "You entered our city without *permission*. And you touched things. Those are high crimes."

"We wouldn't have entered without permission if that little girl had let us in!" Kyja said.

"Little girl?" Cascade look at Raindrop, who shrugged her shoulders.

"You know." Kyja held out her hand. "About this tall. With long, green hair. She watched us inside the wall, but she wouldn't listen to us when we asked for help. Then we talked to her once we got inside. She was playing with gold beads."

"Dew drops?" Cascade asked, his eyes widening. "That could only have been Dew."

Tide growled. "How many times have I told her to stay away from the walls?"

Kyja blushed, remembering how she'd spoken to the girl. Who knew she was one of the city's leaders?

Marcus frowned at Kyja and quickly stepped forward. "Look, we didn't *want* to enter your city without permission. But we need your help with a problem. We're really sorry, and—"

His words were cut off by Tide's booming voice. "The penalty for entering Water Keep is death!"

———— ◆ ————

"Death?" Riph Raph squeaked, flapping his wings.

Kyja's face went white, and for a moment Marcus couldn't find his voice. Finally he swallowed hard. "Death just for coming into your city?"

"That's not fair!" Kyja said.

Raindrop nodded, blinking her big, damp eyes. "It does seem a little harsh."

Mist leaned forward, peering through the sparkling cloud that surrounded her. "Didn't the pinnois tell you that humans are not allowed to enter Water Keep?"

Kyja glanced guiltily toward Marcus. "Well, yes. But we needed your help."

"Help with what?" Mist asked.

Marcus turned to Kyja. She nodded. Slowly he raised the sleeve of his shirt, revealing the brand on his shoulder. He turned so that each of the Fontasians could get a look at it.

"Does this mean anything to you?" he asked.

Tide leaned forward in his throne, staring at the mark before leaning back and eating another fish. "You are the child spoken of in the story the humans tell," the Fontasian said carefully. "What does that have to do with us?"

Together Marcus and Kyja repeated the story Master Therapass had told them. They talked about the Dark Circle, told how the two of them had been switched as babies, and finally, what Master Therapass had told them about creating a drift.

When they finished, Tide rubbed his chins. "An interesting story. But I say again, what does that have to do with us?"

Marcus stared at the Fontasian, shocked by the big man's question. "We can't create a drift between our two worlds without all four of the elementals working together."

Tide snapped another fish from the air and popped it into his mouth like a kernel of popcorn. "Most unfortunate," he said.

Kyja stomped her foot, which would have launched her completely off the platform if Marcus hadn't grabbed her. "Aren't you listening?" she shouted. "We need a water elemental to come with us and join the other elementals so we can open a doorway between our worlds. The Scales of Balance have to be restored. That's why we're here—to ask one of you to come with us!"

For a moment there was stunned silence, then all of the Fontasians began shouting at once.

"Join you?"

"Help humans?"

"Outside!"

"Insane!"

Cascade waved his hands to calm of the room. "There must be some confusion," he said, when the others had quieted. "Clearly, you're not asking us to actually go with you, outside the city."

"If you don't join us, the Dark Circle will take over the world," Marcus said.

"That's a human problem," Cascade said with a confused look. "It has nothing to do with us."

"Don't you care what happens to anyone else but yourselves?" Kyja asked.

"Care?" Mist pressed a thin, white finger against her cheek. "We are water elementals. We bring rain to the forests and snow to the mountains. We fill oceans and carve out canyons. This is who we are. It is not in our nature to care."

Marcus recalled the words of Zhethar just before he flew away. *Elementals do not think the same way as other creatures. They view the world in a way we can't even comprehend.*

So this is what the pinnois had meant. Elementals had no feelings. It didn't matter to them whether the Dark Circle won or not. Olden had been right to laugh when Kyja suggested they ask the elementals for help. The quest had been hopeless all along.

"It's pointless," Marcus said to Kyja, his chin drooping to his chest.

Kyja turned to each of the Fontasians one by one until her gaze at last rested on Cascade. "You *know* what caring is," she said. "But you only care about yourselves. The whole world is in danger and you're afraid to go out of your city because then you might have to meet others. You might actually have to do something for someone else. You must live terrible lives. It must feel so sad to be that selfish."

Cascade looked away as a guard-fish hurried into the room. The guard whispered something to Cascade, and the Fontasian's eyes went wide.

He turned to Tide. "An army of the Dark Circle has gathered outside the city."

Tide's eyes glittered as he waved his fat hand in the air. "It's nothing to us. They cannot get through our walls."

Cascade ran a hand across his lips. "They have a Summoner with them."

Marcus turned to Kyja and a cold finger of fear ran down his back. Was this the same army that attacked Master Therapass?

"Even such a powerful creature of evil cannot pass our defenses," Tide said.

Cascade swallowed. He turned his eyes to Kyja and Marcus before looking quickly away. "They have captured Dew. They are holding her hostage until we give them the humans."

CHAPTER 57

THE VERDICT

TIDE BURST FROM HIS CHAIR with surprising speed for such a large man. "How is that possible?" he roared.

The rest of the Fontasians looked uncomfortably at one another.

"She's been exploring outside the city walls again, hasn't she?" Tide pounded his fist on top of his golden chair. The fish around his head scattered. "I told her not to go out. It isn't safe. But she didn't listen."

He pinched his sagging chins between his thumb and forefinger and studied Kyja and Marcus with cold, calculating eyes. "Very well then, the decision is made for us. Cascade, give the humans to the Summoner."

Kyja's mouth dried up. "You can't do this!" she shouted at Tide. "They'll kill us."

"My decision is final," Tide said. He rubbed his palms together in front of his fat belly. "You will be turned over to the Dark Circle. What they do with you is none of my concern."

The room grew dim again, and the platform lowered. One by one the Fontasians disappeared, until only Cascade and the guard-fish were left.

"We have to escape," Kyja whispered to Marcus as the guard-fish came for them. She expected Marcus to come up with a plan, but he looked completely defeated.

"What's the point? Without the water elementals' help, it's hopeless anyway."

The guard-fish took them by the arms and led them out of the room, down a long corridor. Marcus was right. It *was* hopeless. Even if they somehow managed to escape from the Dark Circle what could they do?

Even if they could convince the land, air, and fire elementals to join them, they needed all four to open a drift. And without the drift, they could never return to their own worlds. Besides, the other elementals were probably just as stubborn as these.

As the guard-fish led Kyja and Marcus down the hallway, Cascade hurried to walk beside Kyja. "What you said back there about being selfish? What did you mean?"

Kyja didn't bother looking at him. "You wouldn't understand."

"I'm trying to," the Fontasian persisted. "But it doesn't make any sense. Why would you expect us to risk our lives for something that doesn't benefit us?"

Kyja knew it was pointless to explain an emotion these creatures didn't seem to have, but she found herself trying anyway. "I was orphaned when I was a baby. But a family named the Goodnuffs let me live with them on their farm. They gave me food and clothing and a place to stay. Mrs. Goodnuff sang to me when I was afraid, and Mr. Goodnuff taught me to ride a horse and to hunt. Why do you think they did that?"

"They wanted someone else to help with chores around the farm?" Cascade suggested.

"No," Kyja scolded, tears filling her eyes as she remembered she would never see them again. "They did it out of the kindness of their hearts. Because it was the right thing to do."

"The right thing to do," Cascade repeated. "What makes it *right?*"

Kyja looked away, rubbing her face. Explaining anything to this creature was impossible. He didn't have the first clue what she was talking about. "Haven't you ever done something for someone else?"

"Of course," Cascade said. His sea-green eyes lit up. "I think I understand now. You humans do things for others so they will owe you a service in return. One day the Goodnuffs will grow old and come to live with *you* as repayment."

Kyja threw her hands up in despair. "That's not it at all. We don't help others just so they'll do things for us. We help them because they need it. Because we can. Because if we didn't, the world wouldn't be a very nice place to live."

The corridor sloped upward, and Kyja realized they were actually under the lake. Faintly through the ceiling, she could see fish swimming above them. But the water was not deep, and they would soon be back to the shore.

Cascade ran his fingers through his spiky hair. "So you didn't take Rhaidnan from the unmakers' cell because you thought he could help you escape?"

"How could you possibly know about that?" Kyja asked.

Now it was Cascade's turn to look surprised. "I'm a water elemental. I can see things anywhere there is water—rains, clouds, puddles, ice."

Kyja shrugged. "A lot of good it does you. We helped Rhaidnan because if we didn't, no one else would. The unmakers would have killed him. If you really *can* see everything, I'd think you'd understand that."

Cascade looked across at Marcus. "And the boy? You didn't bring him here because you thought he could help you get back to your world?"

They were out of the lake now. The wall wouldn't be far—and beyond it were the Summoner and the army of the Dark Circle.

"I brought Marcus here because he was about to be killed. He would have done the same for me." She turned to Cascade. "If we weren't here, wouldn't you find a way to go outside the city and save Morning Dew?"

"No," Cascade said at once. "It's far too dangerous to leave the city. Our powers are weaker outside, and we are more vulnerable. Dew should have known better."

Kyja shook her head sadly. "Then I wouldn't want your help even if you offered it."

The fish-guards pulled Marcus and Kyja to a halt in front of a large, blue blob. "We are here," the guard on the right said.

The guard on the left touched the blob, and its surface became transparent. Kyja and Marcus sucked in their breath. Standing in front of them was an army of Fallen Ones at least as big as the one that had attacked them with Master Therapass. In front of the ranks was a huge, blood-red Summoner. On the ground beside it—locked inside a cramped, iron cage—was Dew.

Marcus turned suddenly to Cascade. "You don't have to give them both of us, do you? Let Kyja go. They only care about me."

Before the Fontasian could answer, Kyja planted her fists on her hips. "I'm not going anywhere without you. We're in this together."

Cascade tilted his head and scratched his spiky, white hair. "You're right," he said. "I don't understand you at all."

He turned to the fish-guards. "You may leave now."

The guards looked at him questioningly, but he waved them away. "Go on," he said. "I'll turn them over to the Summoner."

As the fish-guards glided away, Kyja allowed herself the tiniest ray of hope. Was he going to set them free after all? Maybe something she'd said had gotten through to Cascade. Maybe he really had found a way to care about others.

"You're not going to give us to the—" she began, but before she could finish her sentence, Cascade put his hand on her back. Resting his other hand on the blob, he shoved her, and she went flying through.

CHAPTER 58

OUTSIDE THE WALLS

MARCUS WATCHED IN HORROR as Kyja tumbled into the blob.

"No!" he screamed.

A second later, Cascade pushed him through the blob as well, with Riph Raph close behind.

He was already gathering his magic as he collapsed to his knees on the wet ground outside the city. He might not be able to hold off the Dark Circle, but he was determined to fight as long as he still had breath.

Riph Raph flapped his wings, caught air, and wheeled protectively over Kyja with a cry of fury. Kyja had landed by the edge of a small stream. She jumped to her feet, raising her fists as though she intended to fight the Summoner with her bare hands.

Disoriented, Marcus was not sure from which direction the army would strike. Pushing himself to his feet with his staff, he looked right and left before realizing the Dark Circle must be gathered

373

behind him. He spun around, already beginning to cast a protection spell and saw . . . nothing.

Across from him, Kyja was looking around too. "Where are they?" she shouted, pivoting back and forth.

Riph Raph circled overhead, craned his neck, and pointed his beak. "There," he said in a shocked tone of voice.

Marcus looked in the direction Riph Raph had pointed. For a moment he saw nothing. Then, in the distance, he saw the shimmering wall of the city. Lined up in front of it—so far off it was little more than a blur—was the army of the Dark Circle. Cascade had sent Marcus, Kyja, and Riph Raph at least three miles past where the Summoner was waiting for them.

Slowly Kyja lowered her fists. "I don't understand."

Marcus brushed his hair out of his eyes. "Maybe he made a mistake."

"It was no mistake," came a voice from the direction of the stream. Marcus moved cautiously toward the running water, then stepped back as he saw a blurry face looking up at him.

"Cascade?" he asked, studying the reflection that rippled with the movement of the stream.

Kyja joined Marcus, leaning over the clear-running water. "Is that really you?" she asked.

"It's me," the face said. Marcus found himself looking up from the brook for the source of the reflection even though he knew Cascade wasn't there.

"You're letting us go?" Kyja said.

"I couldn't send you in Dew's place. You were wrong to enter the city, but she was just as wrong to leave. There is no reason you should be forced to pay for her crime."

"What will Tide say when he finds out what you've done?"

Marcus asked, still unable to believe they weren't in the hands of the Dark Circle.

"He will be angry," Cascade said, his voice burbling like the stream. "But he does not rule over the rest of us, even if he *does* control the seas."

"You *do* care then," Kyja said, beaming. But Cascade shook his head.

"I still do not understand what you call *caring*. I do not do this out of any affection for you. I do it because it is just."

Marcus rolled his eyes. At least they were free.

"Go now," Cascade said. "Before the Dark Circle realizes what I have done. The Summoner will come for you when it discovers you have escaped."

"What about Dew?" Kyja asked. "What will happen to her?"

"She will live with the consequences of her actions—or die. That, too, is just."

Marcus studied the land around them. To the north was Lake Aeternus and Water Keep, along with the Dark Circle. Somewhere out of sight to the west were the Windlash Mountains. To the east was vast open plain. The only cover was to the south where the distant rolling hills were peppered with small trees and brush. "Come on," Marcus said. "We should be able to make those hills before dark."

"You can't just leave Dew with the Dark Circle," Kyja shouted at the stream. But Cascade's face in the water was gone. She began to follow Marcus, then stopped and turned back toward Water Keep.

Seeing the look in her green eyes, it was easy enough for Marcus to guess what she was thinking. "I want to help her too," he said. "But she's surrounded by an entire army of Fallen Ones—not to mention a Summoner. We wouldn't stand a chance."

"They'll kill her," Kyja said.

Marcus shook his head in frustration. "They'd kill *us* before we could get anywhere near her. And they'd probably kill her anyway." It was only a matter of time before the Summoner realized it had been tricked. If that happened while they were still in sight of the Dark Circle, Dew wouldn't be the only one to die. Marcus tugged on Kyja's fingers. Even Riph Raph seemed anxious to be away from the Fallen Ones.

Kyja pulled her hand free. Her mouth set in a stubborn line. "Go if you want to. But I'm not leaving. Don't you see? If we leave her to the Dark Circle, we'd be just like the Fontasians. How could we live with ourselves if we didn't even try to help?"

Marcus was torn by two emotions. On the one hand, he knew they could never succeed if they tried to take on the Dark Circle. He remembered all too well the sight of Master Therapass falling to the ground as the Summoner struck him with its unimaginably powerful magic. The idea of voluntarily returning to face such a creature was crazy. Fear closed around his heart like an icy glove at the thought.

On the other hand, the look in Kyja's eyes did something strange to his insides. It was the same look she'd had when she took the money and the cloaks to the woman in the car. The look she'd worn when she'd sent Marcus back to Earth, even though she thought she would die at the hands of the Thrathkin S'Bae. It was a look that made absolutely no sense at a time like this. And yet, it was a look that made his chest swell with pride.

He took her hand again. But this time it wasn't to pull her away. When she looked at him, he smiled a crooked grin. "You might just be the craziest person I've ever known, but you're also the bravest."

She licked her lips and he noticed that even though her expression was firm, her chin was trembling. "Does that mean you'll come with me?"

It felt like the most foolhardy thing he'd ever done, and it would undoubtedly mean both their deaths. But he bobbed his head. "As long as you'll let me."

CHAPTER 59

RESCUE

DO YOU HAVE ANY IDEA how you intend to rescue her?" Marcus asked as the two of them walked toward Water Keep.

Kyja's smile lit up her entire face. "I was hoping *you'd* come up with something."

She burst into such infectious laughter that he couldn't help joining her. It was a wonderful sound. If he was going to die, he wouldn't mind if this was the last sound he ever heard.

"I guess a frontal assault is out," he said. And they started giggling all over again.

"You're both crazy," Riph Raph muttered under his breath.

Marcus cupped his hand over his eyes against the sun. They were close enough now to see the individual creatures of the Dark Circle's army, but not yet close enough to make out what they were.

"It would be nice if we could come up with some kind of diversion," he said, glancing in Riph Raph's direction.

Riph Raph scowled. "Don't even think about it."

"Maybe we could negotiate," Kyja said. "Give them something they want for something we want."

"The only thing they want is us."

"Good point."

"If we get any closer," the skyte said, "one of them is bound to see us."

"That's it!" Kyja said. "Marcus, your invisibility spell. If you make us invisible, we can walk right in and rescue her."

Marcus shook his head, his hair flopping back and forth. "I'm not sure it would work against something as powerful as the Summoner."

"I guess you're right," Kyja said.

"But . . ." Marcus ran his fingers through his hair as an idea occurred to him. It was crazy, and it almost surely wouldn't work. But what if it did?

He turned to Kyja and told her what he was thinking. Halfway through, Riph Raph began shaking his pointy blue head. "It has no chance," he said, wagging his ears. "You'll just get us caught."

But Kyja listened carefully. "Are you sure we can do that?" she asked.

"No," he replied. "But unless you can think of anything else, it's our only chance."

Riph Raph snapped his beak. "You'll get us all killed."

"If you have another idea, tell me now," Marcus said.

The skyte dug his talons into the ground, but he said nothing.

"Okay, then." Marcus looked at Kyja. "Are you in?"

"Yes," Kyja said at once. She turned to Riph Raph. "You don't have to come with us."

"I'm coming," the skyte said, then glared at Marcus. "But only because I have nothing better to do."

—◆—

Half an hour later, Marcus lay flat on his stomach beside Kyja and Riph Raph in the grass outside Water Keep. The skin on the back of his neck and head tightened against his skull—as if his scalp wanted to crawl away every bit as much as he did.

From this close, the Fallen Ones were no longer just shapes. They were a horde of nightmare creatures filling the horizon. It was as if a window had opened into every bad dream he'd ever had. Spiders taller than a horse rose on long, stilt-like legs, single eyes on wavering stalks rising out of each of their hairy bodies. Snakes boasted two heads and dozens of sharp fangs. Other creatures stood on two legs like men, but had the heads of wild animals or appeared as huge, furry balls with teeth and stingers jutting out all over. And standing among them, hundreds of the undead.

Their smell was clear too—dank and marshy, like something that had just climbed out of the grave. Under the smell of their corruption was something more threatening. It smelled wild and dangerous. Marcus thought it might be the smell of hunger.

Pressed to the ground, Kyja looked scared. "We *are* doing the right thing, aren't we?" she whispered.

"I think it's a little late to change our minds now," Marcus said. "I don't think we could make it out of here without being seen even if we wanted to." It was amazing they'd been able to get as close as they had. If the Dark Circle's attention hadn't been focused on the walls of Water Keep, they would have been spotted long before.

But now the army of horribly-mutated creatures was restless.

They paced back and forth, growling and snapping at each other. At the front of their ranks, the Summoner roared with displeasure. It shook Dew's cage with one gleaming talon, shouting, "Give me the children or she dies!"

Marcus took a deep breath and tried to keep his hands from trembling. "If we're going to do this, we'd better try now, before it's too late." He glanced at Kyja and Riph Raph, wondering if it was the last time he'd ever see his friends alive.

"Wait." Kyja grabbed him by the arm. "It wasn't fair of me to force you into this. If you want to leave, I'll understand. If you use your invisibility, there's a good chance you can get away."

"Finally she sees reason," Riph Raph muttered.

"What about you?" Marcus asked.

Kyja shook her head. "I have to stay."

Even though Marcus wanted nothing more than to put as much distance as possible between them and the Dark Circle, he shook his head. "You were right. You have been all along. I just didn't see it at first." He wiped the cold sweat from his forehead.

"I don't know if all this stuff about us saving our worlds is true or not. But if it is, we can't pick and choose who we save. The woman in that car with the baby and Kathleen and Jerrick on the bus—isn't saving them just as important as creating a drift?"

Kyja nodded, her clear eyes shining. "Morning Dew is part of *this* world."

"Right," Marcus said. "If we're going to save Farworld, we might as well start with her."

He slowly rose to his hands and knees and set his staff aside— knowing it would only slow him down for what he had in mind. Somehow this time, the idea of crawling didn't bother him as much as it had in the past. Then, because he knew he'd probably back out if he gave it anymore thought, he squeezed Kyja's hand, whispered, "Good luck," and burst up out of the grass, screaming as loudly as he could.

For a moment, the Fallen Ones seemed frozen by Marcus's unexpected appearance. They watched as he raced toward them with an awkward-yet-speedy lurching crawl, shouting at the top of his lungs.

The Summoner turned, still clutching Dew's cage in its long, black talons. For a moment Marcus locked eyes with the huge, winged serpent, and his blood froze. What was he doing here? The Dark Circle was invincible. The world darkened around him, and he felt his lungs constrict. Despair filled his heart, and he started to raise his hands in surrender. The Summoner's eyes gleamed with triumph.

"Don't give up," a voice whispered from behind him. Marcus tried to turn, but his eyes were locked on the Summoner's.

"You're stronger than them," the voice called again, and it was as if a warm summer breeze blew across the back of his neck, loosing the Summoner's grip on his mind. "Don't let it scare you."

All at once Marcus remembered where he was and what he was doing. He recalled Kyja's words to him in the desert. *By ourselves maybe we aren't much. But together . . .*

He could still feel the dark creature trying to steal away his will, but now he steeled himself against it. Slowly he clenched his raised hands into fists. Pumping them over his head, he gave his best war whoop. *"Whoo, whoo, whoo, whoo, whoo!"* and forced his gaze away.

"Get him," the Summoner bellowed. Flinging Dew's cage aside, the creature spread its long, bony wings and rose into the air.

Instantly Marcus cut to the right. The army of creatures—spurred to action by the call of their master—surged toward him.

Despite the fear that tried to suck the energy from his arms and legs, Marcus charged forward.

At the front of the pack, the blood-thirsty, eight-legged dogs bounded toward Marcus, barking and snapping, white foam dripping from their mouths. A pair of two-headed snakes rushed close behind. As they slithered toward him, Marcus could hear them hissing, "Marcus-s-s-s, Marcus-s-s-s."

From the corner of his eye, he saw a figure in a dark robe raise its forked staff. A flash of blue lightning barely sailed over his head. Marcus put on a burst of speed, scrambling for all he was worth, but suddenly a long-legged spider rose up out of the ground. Its oozing fangs gaped open as it reared in front of him.

Marcus tried to turn, but he slipped in the wet grass and tumbled head over heels. The dogs doubled their pace. As one, they launched themselves in the air. Marcus ducked away from their gnashing teeth, but it was too late. Behind him the spider reached out to spear him with one of its long, hairy legs.

Somewhere nearby, the Summoner howled in victory.

CHAPTER 60

THE PLAN

"NOW!" MARCUS SHOUTED.

Kyja popped out of the grass just in time to see the spider, dogs, and snakes launch themselves at Marcus. For a moment she was afraid she'd miscalculated. Why had he waited so long to shout? She closed her eyes, found Marcus in the between world, and pushed with all her might. Just as the dogs' teeth clamped viciously shut, Marcus disappeared from view.

Kyja burst from her hiding place. Ducking her head, she ran as hard as she could. Focused on the spot where Marcus had disappeared, none of the Fallen Ones noticed her as she raced silently through the knee-high grass, angling to the left away from the direction Marcus had gone.

Flying low and behind her, Riph Raph counted just loudly enough for her to hear. "One . . . two . . . three . . ."

In the distance, she could see Dew's cage lying abandoned on its side, partially imbedded in the dirt. She couldn't see whether Dew was moving or not.

To her right, a Thrathkin S'Bae wheeled around. "There!" it shrieked, pointing its staff in her direction.

Overhead, the Summoner's howl of victory turned to rage. It thrust its diamond-shaped head toward Kyja. All around her, rocks appeared, whistling out of the sky and punching deep craters into the wet ground.

"Turn!" Riph Raph called. Kyja cut to her right just as a rock bigger than she was tore a hole in the grass at her feet.

With a high-pitched whine, three bristly black creatures, almost all teeth, cut through the grass. Kyja accelerated, but the creatures were too fast. They closed in on her, tearing a ragged path in the ground.

"Fifteen!" Riph Raph counted. He flew toward the speeding creatures and launched a ball of blue flame.

"E-e-e-e," squealed the lead creature as Riph Raph's flame struck home. It buried its burning body in the wet dirt, forcing the two behind it to go wide.

"Eighteen," Riph Raph shouted.

Kyja dipped her head and ran for all she was worth as the two creatures raced toward her.

"Nineteen!"

She could hear the beasts right behind her. The ground shook beneath her feet, but she didn't dare look back. Something tugged at the hem of her robe, and she stumbled.

"Twenty!"

"Where is he?" screamed Riph Raph as the bristled creatures pulled Kyja down.

———◆———

"Nineteen," Marcus counted, gasping for breath. He scrambled across a rain-wet Chicago street up onto the sidewalk, narrowly missing glittering shards of a broken bottle. It was night, and for the moment, at least, the street was empty.

"Twenty."

He closed his eyes and looked for the golden ropes attached to Kyja and Riph Raph. For a terrible second he didn't think they were going to be there. It'd never taken this long before. But then they were there, hanging, just as they always did, in the gray between-place.

He tugged with all his strength, and Kyja and Riph Raph appeared at his side.

"That was too close!" Riph Raph shouted. He had come through as a chameleon again this time, and his bulging eyes searched two directions at once.

Marcus stared with horror at the shredded hem of Kyja's robe as she got up from the wet sidewalk.

"Are you—" he began, but Kyja cut him off with a wave of her hand.

"I'm fine," she puffed. "We have to go back before they catch on. Are you ready?"

"Yeah." Marcus's chest was burning from his efforts in Farworld and the distance he'd covered on Earth since Kyja sent him over. But Kyja was right. The only way the plan would work was by keeping the Summoner and his army off-guard.

Kyja closed her eyes, and instantly Marcus felt the stomach-churning sensation as she pushed herself back to Farworld, taking him and Riph Raph with her.

As soon as Marcus felt the damp ground of Farworld under his knees, he started scrambling again. He didn't look back, but he knew that behind him, Kyja and Riph Raph had hidden themselves below the top of the grass.

The plan worked perfectly. Glancing to his right, he saw the confused Fallen Ones still nosing around the spot where Kyja had disappeared. A few of them had gone back to where Marcus had disappeared. But none of them were looking in the direction where Marcus was now.

By hurrying as far up the street as he could after jumping to Earth, Marcus had changed the location he pulled Kyja and Riph Raph to by almost a hundred yards. So when Kyja sent them back to Farworld, they were also nearly a hundred yards away.

He checked the air for the Summoner, but the winged creature was nowhere in sight. There was a clear path between himself and Dew's cage. He made a beeline for it and skidded to a halt in front of her. Morning Dew looked up with big, scared eyes.

"Help me," she cried, clutching at the cold bars. Marcus examined the cage. Just as he expected, it was locked. If only he had the time, he might be able to figure out how to unlock it with magic. But already the Dark Circle's army was beginning to spread out. It wouldn't be long before they discovered what he was up to.

"You're going to be all right," Marcus said as Dew reached between the bars and touched his hand with her small, cold fingers. "As soon as I get you out of this cage," Marcus said, "return to the city. Don't stop, and don't look back."

Dew nodded. "Thank you," she said.

Marcus wrapped his hands around the thick bars of the cage. They felt nasty and frigid in his grip.

This was the last unsure part of the plan. Other than Marcus and

Riph Raph, Kyja didn't know how to send living things to Earth or back to Farworld. But objects *had* come across. The money, the trill stones, and the picture of Elder Ephraim had all made the jump. If he could manage to take the cage with him on the jump to Earth— and if Morning Dew stayed in Farworld—she would be free. They were big *ifs:* neither Marcus nor Kyja knew if he could take the cage across or how elementals might react to the jump. But it was too late to worry about that now.

As soon as he grabbed hold of the cage, he felt Kyja push. At first he didn't think he was going to be able to hang on. The cage twisted and bucked in his grip, resisting his efforts to take it with him. Marcus landed in the center of the street. Beside him, the oversized bird cage clanged to the asphalt, making a loud racket.

"Keep it down out there!" someone shouted.

Marcus checked the cage. It was empty.

"Yes," he said almost silently, pumping his fist in the air. Other than the taillights of a car in the distance, the street was empty. Closing his eyes, he reached out to take hold of the ropes to pull Kyja and Riph Raph to Earth.

But before he could pull them, something slammed against the back of his head, and he collapsed to the street, unconscious.

CHAPTER 61

STRANGE WEATHER

KYJA PEERED ABOVE THE TOP of the grass. As Marcus grabbed the bars of the cage, she held her breath. When he'd told her his idea, she'd known it was a good one. The plan could work, *had to* work. But what if the cage wouldn't jump? Worse, what if Marcus couldn't make the jump while he was holding it?

Would he be willing to let go? To give it all up?

Closing her eyes, Kyja saw Marcus's other half hanging limply in the gray nothingness between here and Ert. His lifeless body shook and trembled in the between world. *Please work,* she whispered in her mind as she pushed. Doubling her effort, she shoved with all her strength, and Marcus's body disappeared.

When she opened her eyes, the cage was gone, and Dew was free. Like a shot, the water elemental raced for the walls of Water Keep. She was inside before the Fallen Ones even knew she was gone.

A surge of joy welled up in Kyja's chest. They'd done it!

"She made it." Kyja breathed a sigh of relief. As she turned toward Riph Raph, sharp, black claws closed around her waist, and an icy voice growled, "The game is over."

The claws yanked Kyja around, and she found herself staring into the cold, dead eyes of the Summoner.

"Where is-s-s he?" the serpent hissed, lifting her off the ground. At its touch, Kyja felt her link to Marcus instantly vanish.

She tried to swallow, but her throat was locked. Even if she'd wanted to speak, she couldn't have. Her body went slack with fear. As the terrible creature pulled her close, she could smell the rotten-meat stink of its foul breath.

Riph Raph lay crumpled on the ground, unmoving, his eyes closed.

"Your lizard is dead," the Summoner said, squeezing her until she felt like she was going to explode. "Give me the boy, and I'll let you live."

Kyja found her voice. "No," she squeaked.

The talons bit into her sides like teeth, and the Summoner forced her to look into its eyes. Mind-numbing cold filled her body as the serpent's dark pupils swirled before her. She struggled to turn away, but couldn't move.

"We'll kill him anyway," the creature said. "Give him to us, and at least one of you will survive."

Kyja shook her head, but it was becoming harder and harder to think. The creature's huge eyes were like bottomless wells, pulling her down into darkness.

"I can teach you magic," the Summoner said. "I can even send you back to Earth permanently. Help you find your family."

"Magic?" Kyja moaned, slipping in and out of consciousness. "Family?" If she brought Marcus back, she could go to Ert—she could find her parents. The thought of her parents warmed her like a thick blanket.

"Yes-s-s-s," the Summoner hissed. "Just give me the boy."

"The boy." Kyja's hand moved without any conscious control, her fingers opening as though reaching for something. Behind her closed eyes she could see Marcus standing on a rain-drenched street. Somewhere in the back of her mind, a small part of her was screaming for her to stop. *What are you doing? You can't give Marcus to the Dark Circle. They will destroy him.* But that part of her was too small to overcome the huge power that was forcing her to reach out to Marcus—to close her fingers around the golden rope, to end her intense pain.

As she reached for the rope—the Summoner's foul, hot breath panting against her face—something smashed against the side of the Summoner's head. Kyja's eyes flew open, and she saw a bloody Riph Raph clinging to the top of the Summoner's long neck.

A blue ball of fire crashed into the side of the Summoner's face.

"Not . . . a . . . lizard," Riph Raph groaned.

The Summoner's talons tightened around Kyja's chest, sending spasms of pain through her body. It was enough to break the trance.

"No!" She spat in the Summoner's face. "I'll never give Marcus to you. Never!"

Snarling in anger, the Summoner flung her to the ground. Her ears rang with the impact. The creature flicked Riph Raph with the tip of its huge, red wing, and the skyte hit the dirt with a sickening thud.

Ripping scars into the ground, the Summoner leaned over her, opening its mouth to reveal the double rows of teeth inside. "I will make your death slow and painful," it growled.

Kyja tried to lift herself to her feet, but she had no strength left.

Instead, she dragged her body backwards. Pushing across the grass with trembling arms, she felt a cold mist settle over her. Strands of hair stuck to the side of her face.

"Hurry up, you three," a voice called.

"Who's there?" the Summoner barked, turning its massive head. Drops of water clung to its scaled body like tiny, shimmering rubies.

"Come on. Come on!" said a second voice Kyja thought she recognized.

"Don't rush me," a third voice answered. Overhead, the sky, which had been clear and blue a moment before, grew dark and menacing. A jagged bolt of lightning crashed down from the boiling clouds, striking the Summoner on the back of the head.

Roaring angrily, the Summoner whirled around as though chasing its own tail.

"That's better," a voice giggled.

"Dew?" Kyja said. As though in answer, a sparkling mist filled the air, and heavy drops of rain started to fall.

Something cold and wet touched Kyja's arms and legs, and she turned to see the stream she and Marcus had followed earlier over-flowing its banks. The water, which had meandered gently toward Water Keep before, was racing backward, away from the lake, in a torrent that quickly rose to the tops of the grass. Bits of debris and foam floated across the murky surface as the army of undead crea-tures looked about uneasily.

"What kind of trick is this?" the Summoner howled, turning back to Kyja. Its red eyes glared down at her as she struggled to stay afloat in the rising flow.

Before she could answer, something stirred nearby. A low groan-ing sound filled the air as a dark hump rose out of the fog for a moment before splashing back down.

The Summoner advanced on Kyja. "Your puny magic won't save you." As it raised a claw to spear her, a thick eel-like shape slithered out of the deep murk. It wrapped itself around the creature's leg, but the Summoner jerked its leg free, and the eel shattered into a million tiny drops of water.

But now, all around them, the dark water was roiling and bubbling. Deep moans and high-pitched squeals filled the air. The water was up to Kyja's chest, and she had to paddle her hands to keep from going under. Something brushed against the back of her leg, and she cried out. A hundred yards away, a row of wraith-like shapes seemed to rise up out of nowhere.

Kyja rubbed her eyes. The water-wraiths moved smoothly across the surface of the water, looking neither left nor right. Their faces were devoid of mouths, eyes, or noses, and Kyja swore she could see right through them as if they were made of the water itself.

As she watched, one of the giant spiders lunged toward the line of figures. Without hesitating, the wraith on the left wrapped itself around the spider's legs, and both of them disappeared beneath the dark water.

Nearby, one of the two-headed dogs—which had been paddling around looking for a place to escape the rising water—howled in pain, and Kyja saw something that looked like a giant turtle snap it down into the darkness. Roars and howls filled the air as water-creatures of all shapes and sizes rose from the water and attacked the Fallen Ones.

For the first time, the Summoner seemed unsure of itself. Watching its army disappear all around, it flapped its bony wings, looking right and left. Then, from far out in Lake Aeternus came a sound that seemed to make up the dark creature's mind. It started as a dull grinding—like an immense boulder being pried from the side of a mountain—but quickly rose in volume until it sounded like the roar of a hurricane.

A solid black wall of water rolled out from the lake, growing as it raced toward them. First ten feet, then twenty, finally fifty feet high.

"Riph Raph!" Kyja screamed as she was flung forward. Fighting to breathe, she turned her head to see the Summoner rise into the air, red wings beating at the stormy sky, eyes blazing.

Just as she was sure it was going to escape, something immense rose out of the water. At first it seemed to be a huge fish—its body so wide she had to turn her head from one side to the other to take it all in, like trying to see an entire mountain from close up. But no fish could be that big. Somehow it kept rising up and up. Meeting the Summoner in midair, it opened a broad, dark maw and swallowed the dark creature in one bite.

At that moment, Kyja slipped under and swallowed a mouthful of lake water. Coughing and gagging, she tried the fight her way to the surface, but the tide was too strong. She could swear she heard Marcus's voice screaming her name; then a pair of hands seemed to lift her until she could gulp the cold air into her burning lungs.

CHAPTER 62

FLIGHT OF THE BROKEN BIRD

MARCUS WOKE TO THE SOUND of shrieking brakes and honking horns. The floor shifted violently beneath him, and his head slammed against metal bars. He was in a dark, closed space. Had he somehow returned to his cell in the caverns of the unmakers? He opened his eyes and looked around.

He appeared to be in the back of some kind of janitorial van. Buckets, brooms, and various cleaning supplies rattled against one another on narrow metal shelves all about him. He was inside a cage that was either the same one Dew had been locked inside or one very much like it.

Street lights briefly illuminated the interior of the van and then disappeared again as the vehicle raced past them. Outside, horns blared as the van shifted again, tossing Marcus about like a stuffed doll. He threw his hands up to keep from being smashed against the bars again.

"Exciting, isn't it? Maneuvering through city traffic," came a voice from the front seat. Silver eyes stared out at him from the rearview mirror. Marcus's pulse raced.

"Bonesplinter," Marcus said, nearly gagging on the word. He wrapped his fingers around the bars of the cage and yanked at the door, but it was locked.

"I suppose you're looking for this," Bonesplinter laughed. He adjusted the mirror with a long-fingered hand and held up something black and rusty so Marcus could see it more clearly. Bonesplinter dropped the key into his pocket.

All at once, Marcus remembered Kyja and Riph Raph. Closing his eyes, he looked for the golden ropes, but they were gone.

As though reading his mind, Bonesplinter let out a dark chuckle. "I don't think you'll be doing any more world jumping. You see, the bars of that cage possess a few special properties."

Anger pulsed through Marcus's body as he thought of Kyja trapped in Farworld with the army of the Dark Circle. Tightening his fingers on the bars, Marcus imagined a gust of wind throwing Bonesplinter—who was not wearing a seatbelt—forward against the windshield. Under his breath, Marcus began muttering the words he'd used against the Thrathkin S'Bae outside the bus days before. But this time they seemed robbed of all force. They were just words.

Bonesplinter grinned into the mirror. "Did I mention one of the benefits of the cage is that it renders magic powerless?"

Marcus slumped against the bars. "Where are you taking me?"

"A very good question indeed, little bird." Bonesplinter jerked the steering wheel hard to the left, and outside the shrieking of tires accompanied a sudden glare of headlights. Marcus could only imagine how many accidents were taking place all around them as Bonesplinter maneuvered the van.

"Out of my way, you pitiful maggots!" the Thrathkin S'Bae

roared, rolling down his window and shaking his fist. Cold, wet air poured through the window, making Marcus shiver. "My only regret is that I won't be able to take any of these fascinating inventions with me when I return to the Master. But I guess you'll have to do."

"You're taking me back to Farworld?" Marcus asked, his throat tightening.

The Thrathkin S'Bae gave a feral grin. His teeth seemed to have grown larger over the last few minutes. "The Master would gladly accept the gift of your dead body. But how much better to deliver you alive—especially if you agreed to willingly serve him?"

"I'll never join the Dark Circle," Marcus growled.

Bonesplinter's eyes gleamed. "You won't have any choice once I take you through the drift."

"The drift?" Marcus remembered the words Master Therapass had spoken in the Westland Woods. *If the Dark Circle has created a drift, they did it by force. Before you could get halfway through it, you'd be as foul as they are.*

"You understand then? Once I take you through the drift, your soul will be as black as night, your magic confined to the dark arts. The only ones who *will* accept you are the Dark Circle. Who knows? Maybe you'll even learn to like it."

Marcus's skin went cold as the Thrathkin S'Bae chuckled. He had to find some way to escape and get back to Kyja. But what could he do? As long as he was trapped inside this cage, he was helpless.

His eyes returned to the front seat, where Bonesplinter's seatbelt hung unbuckled at his side. If only there was some way to cause the Thrathkin S'Bae to lose control of the van. But Marcus was too far away to reach the front of the van, and his magic wouldn't work.

The van tilted upward for a moment, and Marcus thought they might be pulling onto a freeway ramp. Bonesplinter shot him an amused glance. "It's a shame about your arms and legs. It must be a horrible inconvenience to slither about everywhere on your belly."

Marcus glared at him. "You would know, being a *snake.*"

The Thrathkin S'Bae remained composed. "The difference is that I *choose* to slither."

Marcus knew Bonesplinter's taunts were meant to unnerve him, to keep him off balance. Instead, he scanned the back of the van for something that might help him escape. With his eyes adjusted to the darkness, he took note of the bottles of chemicals and boxes of supplies around him. Some of the liquids might burn if he could manage to throw them in Bonesplinter's eyes. But Marcus knew he would never be able to get them through the bars of the cage, and even if he could, there was no way to throw them anywhere near Bonesplinter's face.

"Have you ever wondered who it was that mangled your arm and leg?" Bonesplinter asked.

Despite himself, Marcus felt his body stiffen.

In the mirror, the Thrathkin S'Bae watched Marcus's expression with an unpleasant smile. "Yes. I can see it in your eyes. I can see the hate. You *do* want to know who did this to you."

Ignore him, Marcus told himself. Biting the inside of his lip, he tried to shut out the Thrathkin S'Bae's words and focus on something he could use to escape. He scanned the bottles, buckets . . .

All at once his eyes landed on a mop. He remembered the day he'd fought off Chet and his friends. If he could manage to jam the head of the mop against the van's gas pedal, maybe . . .

"I'll give you a hint," Bonesplinter said. "The same person who turned you into a belly-crawling cripple also killed your parents— slowly and painfully."

Inside his cage, Marcus jerked, and his eyes found Bonesplinter's. "You're lying."

"You didn't know about your parents?" The Thrathkin S'Bae's smile extended from ear to ear. "Oh. I'm sorry. I just assumed the old man who called himself a *wizard* told you about your mother and father before he died."

Master Therapass dead? Marcus lunged for the mop—pressing his side against the far wall of the cage. But his arm wouldn't fit through. The bars were too close together, stopping his arm just above the wrist. The mop lay less than eight inches from his grasp, but it might as well have been a mile.

"It's probably better your parents died anyway," Bonesplinter continued cheerfully. "I'm sure they would have been so disappointed to see how you ended up. A nasty, broken bird in a nasty cage. A cripple who dreamed of flying."

Cripple. The word pounded over and over inside Marcus's head. It was true. He'd failed again, leaving Kyja alone with the Summoner. He was useless. It was crazy to think he would ever be anything else. If only he had two good arms and legs. If only . . .

Suddenly he stared down at his withered arm. He might be disabled, but maybe that wasn't such a bad thing. At least not this time. His left arm was much thinner than his right, and it fit between the bars easily. Crooked as it was, his arm was still long enough to tweeze his thumb and forefinger over the mop handle.

Giving a quick glance to the mirror to make sure Bonesplinter wasn't watching, Marcus edged the mop toward his cage until he could reach it with his right hand.

"It's only fair you should know." Bonesplinter was still talking in the front seat. "Since we're going to be friends for a long time, I might as well tell you. I'm the one. I'm the one who killed your parents. And left you the way you are."

Marcus felt fire burn in his cheeks. But it was no longer coming from Bonesplinter's words. The Thrathkin S'Bae was a liar. He always had been. Maybe he did kill Marcus's parents, or maybe he didn't, but what mattered now was that Marcus find a way to get back to Farworld and help Kyja.

He had to distract the Thrathkin S'Bae long enough to lift the mop and drive it forward. Looking at Bonesplinter's face in the mirror, the answer came to him in a flash.

"You failed though, didn't you?" Marcus said.

"What?" For once the Thrathkin S'Bae seemed to be taken off-guard. His broad smile faltered.

"You were supposed to kill me, weren't you? What would be the point of *nearly* finishing me off, while leaving everyone else dead? Your master sent you to kill me. And you thought you had."

"Be quiet." Bonesplinter's mouth curled into a sinister frown. "You don't know what you're talking about."

"How hard could it have been to kill a baby?" Marcus continued, knowing he'd hit the mark. "But you didn't. You failed. Your master must have been furious. That's why he gave you that scar, isn't it? Because you failed to kill me then, just like you're going to fail now."

"Shut up!" Bonesplinter screamed. Reaching up to touch the scar with one hand, he turned his head and glared furiously at Marcus.

That was all Marcus needed. Lifting the mop handle with his right hand and guiding it with the thumb and finger of his left, he jabbed the head of the mop at the gas pedal just like he'd jabbed the handle at Chet's friend Squint back at the boys school. His aim was every bit as good this time. As the mophead hit the accelerator, Marcus leaned on the end of the handle.

The van shot forward, and Bonesplinter spun back toward the wheel. "What are you doing?" he screamed, trying to kick the mop away. But Marcus had his whole weight on the handle, jamming the stringy mophead over the gas pedal and under the brake. It wouldn't budge.

Marcus couldn't see what was happening outside the van, but he could hear horns blaring as Bonesplinter cut the steering wheel left and right. Finally the Thrathkin S'Bae thought to step on the brake, but by then it was too late. "Look out!" Bonesplinter cried, throwing his arms up in front of his face as headlights flashed through the windows.

There was a stench of burning rubber followed by a jarring crunch, as Marcus, still in the cage, flew toward the front of the van. Burying his head in his arms, he lodged his body against the bars. A second crunch came from the back of the van, sending them spinning in a circle. Bonesplinter, who had locked his hands on the steering wheel, was thrown violently to the left. His head slammed against the side of the van, and his eyes rolled back.

With one final thud of bending metal and a tinkle of broken glass, the van finally came to a stop. Dizzy and disoriented, Marcus opened his eyes. His right arm was throbbing, and his head felt like someone had bowled a strike with it, but nothing seemed broken.

The cage had ended up jammed sideways between the two front seats, but not a bar was bent. The same couldn't be said for the Thrathkin S'Bae, who was bleeding from several cuts on his hands and face. His right arm was twisted at a strange angle, and his eyes were closed. He was breathing in slow, shallow breaths, as if asleep.

Realizing he might not have much time before Bonesplinter

came to, Marcus quickly slid his left arm through the bars of his cage. Ever so gently, Marcus dropped his hand into the Thrathkin S'Bae's pocket until his fingers found the long, metal key.

A moment later, he unlocked the door to his cage and climbed out. From all around the van he could hear the sound of angry voices and honking horns. Marcus looked at the unconscious Thrathkin S'Bae and realized he could kill him right now. If he couldn't do it with his bare hands, he could at least do it with magic.

But then he remembered Kyja. Where was she? Had the Dark Circle captured her? When he closed his eyes, the ropes were still gone. What did that mean?

"Kyja!" he screamed inside his head. "Kyja! Where are you?"

For a moment nothing happened. Then . . . he felt . . . *something*. Was it her? Had she heard him? There was the smallest tug at his stomach. It *was* her.

Pull me over! He silently shouted. The next second, he felt the inside-out feeling, and he was tumbling.

Before his feet even landed, he looked around. The entire plain was flattened, as though a giant hand had pressed every blade of grass to the ground. A strange mist was breaking up, and a layer of brown water flowed sluggishly across the grass toward the lake. A few feet away, Marcus saw Riph Raph blinking and shaking his head. Muddy sheets flew from his wings as he slowly flapped them.

"Where's Kyja?" Marcus shouted. "Is she all right?"

"I'm here," a voice called.

Marcus turned, and his heart leapt. It was Kyja. She was sopping wet, her hair plastered to her scalp in a soggy mess, and she was walking with a limp. But somehow she was alive.

Marcus clawed his way across the muddy ground until he and

Kyja were only inches apart. "Are you okay?" he asked, searching her for some sign of injury.

"I think so." She nodded, brushing a damp strand of hair from her cheek.

"The Summoner?" Marcus asked. "Where is it?"

Kyja shrugged. "Everything happened so fast."

Then they heard a familiar voice.

"It's all right," Cascade said. "You're safe."

CHAPTER 63

DAWN CHIMES

"TELL ME AGAIN ABOUT THE PART where you spit on the Summoner." Marcus was disappointed he'd missed all the excitement.

Kyja blushed. "I don't know if I really spat. It was more like some saliva flew out of my mouth."

"No. It was definitely spit," Riph Raph said. "A big, wet one right in the middle of the Summoner's face."

Marcus burst into laughter, and Kyja turned an even deeper shade of red. The three of them were sitting around a small, clear table inside Water Keep, ravenously eating their first good meal in what seemed like ages. Nearby, Raindrop, Mist, Morning Dew, and Cascade watched them with expressions ranging from amusement to complete confusion.

Lifting his half-full water glass, Marcus turned to Cascade. "Show me again how to do that spell." Ever since he'd learned the

Fontasians were masters of water magic, Marcus had been pestering them to teach him.

Cascade shook his white hair out of his eyes and smiled indulgently. "It's not a matter of *how* so much as *what* and *why*. Once you learn to communicate clearly to the element what you are trying to accomplish and why you want to do it, the rest is simple."

The Fontasian held out his right hand, and a slim rod that looked like cut glass but was actually made of water emerged from between his fingers. He pointed the rod at Marcus's glass. Slowly the water rose out of the glass and formed itself into the shape of a tiny figure.

"Look, Riph Raph, it's you!" Kyja said, clapping her hands. The little water skyte Cascade had created flapped its wings and flew gracefully through the air, circling Kyja's head and darting playfully toward the real Riph Raph before dropping back into Marcus's glass with a splash.

"Awesome! Let me try," Marcus said. He gave an envious glance toward Cascade's wand, but the Fontasian shook his head, and the clear rod disappeared from his fingers.

"A wand won't help you until you develop a better understanding of magic," Cascade said.

Marcus nodded. "I know, I know. Master Therapass told me. I was just hoping." At the mention of the wizard's name, the room grew silent for a moment. Marcus and Kyja had been surprised to learn that the water elementals had no clue what had become of Master Therapass. Although they'd searched for him, there was no sign from any of their sources.

Concentrating his will on the glass before him, Marcus reminded himself to think about *what* and *why*. Although he understood casting a spell didn't require him to say anything out loud, he still found it easier to focus his thoughts by creating little rhymes.

Shining water clear and bright, turn yourself into a skyte.

The water rose from his glass.

"You're doing it!" Kyja shouted.

He *was* doing it. His skyte wasn't quite as perfect as Cascade's—the wings looked more like blobs, and the head wobbled strangely to the left—but it rose into the air and stayed there.

"Is that supposed to be me?" Riph Raph snorted. "It looks more like a wilted pickle."

Grimacing, Marcus tried to fly the water skyte onto the real skyte's head. Instead, the water lost its shape and splashed on the tabletop, soaking the front of Marcus's shirt and pants.

"You got the what, but not the why," Cascade said with a chuckle. "Elements won't obey you on a whim. And revenge is one of the least effective *whys.*"

"Maybe you should change him into a fish again. He's already wet," Kyja joked.

Kyja turned to Morning Dew. "I never heard how the Summoner captured you in the first place. Did you go outside the walls?"

Dew shook her head. "We're not supposed to leave the city. It was the strangest thing. I was inside the walls looking out, when all at once, I found myself outside. And then the cage closed around me, and I couldn't escape."

Marcus wondered if she was telling the whole truth or just trying not to get in trouble. "If you can't leave the city, how did you rescue Kyja?" he asked, trying to mop his pants with a cloth napkin.

"Under . . . normal circumstances we . . . would not have—that is . . ." Cascade stammered.

"I told them if they didn't come outside with me, I'd tell

everyone they were a bunch of scared little fish," said Dew, with a mischievous grin.

Cascade's face tightened. "You freed one of us. We helped you. It seemed only . . . just."

"You might start to care about others if you don't watch out," Kyja teased.

"What will you do now?" Dew asked.

Though the Fontasians had offered to let them stay as long as they wanted, Marcus and Kyja could tell that having humans in their city made the water elementals very uncomfortable. And besides, they needed to leave soon before the Dark Circle could send another army to replace the one the Fontasians had defeated.

Marcus glanced at Kyja. "I guess we'll go looking for the other elementals."

"But how?" Kyja asked. "You can't stay here much longer. You're already starting to look sick again. And I can't stay on Ert for more than a few days at a time."

Marcus nodded. He *was* starting to get the dull pounding in his head again. "Then we'll just have to jump back and forth together. A few days on Earth for me. Then a few days here for you. One way or another, we'll find the others." The Fontasians still hadn't actually agreed to help create a drift, but hopefully Marcus could convince them if he and Kyja found the other three elementals and got them to join.

"You don't have any idea where we might find them, do you?" Kyja asked the Fontasians.

The water elementals shuffled about with surprising awkwardness for such graceful creatures. Finally Cascade spoke up. "This is a rather uncomfortable thing you ask of us. Elementals prefer to be left to themselves. Prying into another's affairs is highly discouraged. It could cause certain . . . unpleasantness . . . if they were to discover we told you of their whereabouts."

Kyja waited silently.

Cascade coughed into his hand. "Perhaps if you traveled west to the Noble River and followed it south until it meets the Sea of Eternal Sorrows . . ." He let his words drift away.

"Thank you," Kyja said. "If we find anything there, we won't mention you told us."

As Kyja leaned back in her chair, the sleeves of her robe pulled up enough to reveal the deep scratches on her arms from the Summoner's claws. All at once Marcus was struck by the realization of how close she had come to death and the memory of his inability to help her.

"When I woke up in the back of Bonesplinter's van and realized I couldn't pull you over, I thought . . ." His voice cracked, and he looked quickly away. He couldn't tell her how scared he'd felt, how alone.

"I'm fine," Kyja said, reaching out to squeeze his hand. Then she did something that surprised both of them. She leaned across the table and kissed him on the cheek.

Now it was Marcus's turn to blush. He could feel his face turning a bright shade of plum. Quickly he placed a hand over his mouth and gave an obvious yawn. "Well, we'd better get some sleep if we're going to leave in the morning."

"Right," Kyja said at once. Neither of them looked at each other, but Riph Raph watched them both with an amused look in his eyes.

Once Cascade had shown them to their beds, Marcus found himself unable to fall asleep. His body was bone weary—the last time he'd rested was briefly in the unmakers' cell. But his mind wouldn't seem to shut down. He tried to blame it on the pulsing blue and green walls, but the truth was, he couldn't stop thinking about Kyja.

He'd never had a girl kiss him before, and thinking about it made him feel both hot and cold at the same time. But even more than the kiss, the fact that he'd made his first true friend filled him with an excitement that burned like a flame in his chest.

He thought about Kyja's fear that she had no magic. Didn't she realize that without her, they never could have made it as far as they had? Cascade could say whatever he wanted, but the truth was, the water elementals would never have come to Kyja's aid if she hadn't decided to rescue Dew first. Did her ability to help people and to show them how to help each other have something to do with her magic?

What good was the ability to stop a stick from hitting you in the head compared to that?

With those thoughts, he drifted off to sleep.

———◇———

What felt like only an hour later, Cascade was pulling him awake.

"What time is it?" he asked, sitting up and rubbing his eyes.

"It's nearly dawn," the Fontasian said. "You need to leave early, before the Dark Circle sends another army."

"Right, right." Marcus scrambled from the bed and pulled on his shoes. Outside the room, Kyja and Riph Raph were already waiting.

"This way," Cascade said, leading them to a blob. When the Fontasian touched the blob, it showed an image of Lake Aeternus. Its gentle waves were still black this early in the morning.

Before entering the blob, Marcus paused. "I've been meaning to ask you," he said to the Fontasian. "I can float here in the city—almost like being underwater. But I can breathe, too." He gestured at the hallway and the surrounding space. "Is this water or air?"

"Yes," Cascade said, and without any further explanation, walked through the blob.

Marcus turned to Kyja, hoping she understood, but she only shrugged her shoulders and followed Cascade.

Marcus stood a moment longer before entering the blob, relishing the feeling of standing. How would it feel to be able to stand all the time? Even outside Water Keep? He'd give anything to find out. Well, *almost* anything.

With a sigh, he stepped through the blob and felt his weight return. It wasn't quite as bad as he'd expected, though. His leg seemed a little stronger. And his hand felt as if it was able to open a little farther. Maybe that meant Farworld was a little closer to healing. Still, it was a relief when Cascade handed him his walking staff.

"I found this outside the city," the Fontasian said.

At the edge of the Lake, Cascade stopped beside a small sailboat and ran his hand across the smooth hull. "If you're determined to keep looking for the rest of the elementals, the quickest way to get started is by water. And after what happened here, the Dark Circle may think twice before getting anywhere near Lake Aeternus."

"But I don't know how to sail," Marcus said. He turned to Kyja. "Do you?"

Kyja shook her head.

"That's all right," Cascade said. "I do."

"What?" Marcus asked, not sure he'd heard right.

"You're coming *with* us?" Kyja asked, not bothering to try and hide her delight.

"I believe you have set an impossible quest for yourselves. We elementals do not have the will or perhaps even the capacity to work together." The Fontasian tossed a rock into the water and watched as the ripples circled outward. "I can't promise to stay for long. But I'll join you for a time, if only to satisfy my curiosity."

"Does Tide know?" Marcus asked. It hadn't been lost on him that Tide was the only one of the city's leaders that hadn't joined him and Kyja for dinner.

"No," the Fontasian said. "I thought it was better not to tell him. He seemed quite upset that we rescued you at all."

"Won't he be even more upset when he finds out you've left?"

"Furious," Cascade agreed. "There's even a chance he won't let me back in when I return."

"Then you can't go," Kyja said. "This is your home."

Cascade looked back at Water Keep and then out at the endless expanse of lake. "I've been trapped inside these walls too long. It's time I experienced what is outside for myself, instead of seeing it only through streams and brooks. Besides," he said, turning to Kyja. "I want to learn more of what you humans mean by this *caring.*"

"Look." Kyja pointed to the horizon, where the first orange hue of the sun was painting the dawn sky purple.

"We need to go," Cascade said, beginning to climb into the boat.

"No," Marcus said. "Wait just a minute. I want to hear the dawn chimes. Do you have them here?"

"Of course." Cascade nodded. "Dew waters them every morning."

Side by side, Marcus, Kyja, Riph Raph, and Cascade watched the tiny purple flowers rise from their hiding places as dawn stole over the world on silent footsteps.

As sunlight hit them, first one and then another of the flowers opened their petals and broke into song. Watching them bob and weave like fairy princesses performing an unscripted ballet, he remembered the words of Master Therapass. *Perhaps if you focus hard enough you'll be able to understand some of it as well.* He wished the wizard could be with them now, listening to the song by his side.

Furrowing his brow, Marcus concentrated on the voices and attempted to understand their message. It was kind of like trying to unravel a single thread in an elaborate weave. But if he listened closely enough, he thought he could just make out—

All at once, he gasped and jerked forward as though pulled by a string.

"What's wrong?" Kyja asked.

"Shh," Marcus whispered. Turning back to the flowers, he tried to catch the thread again. But it was too late. The flowers were already beginning to bow their heads, their voices fading. The words—if they had been there at all—were impossible to make out.

"Let's go," he said and turned from the flowers toward the broad expanse of clear, blue water which lapped against the rocky shore. Leaning more heavily on his staff than he had a few minutes earlier, he limped to the boat where Cascade helped him climb up a short ramp onto the bobbing deck.

"What did you hear back there?" Kyja asked as she joined him on the boat.

"Nothing. Really," he said. "Just wishful thinking."

Cascade took hold of the tiller, and the boat sprang to life, pulling smoothly away from the shore, though there was barely enough wind to ruffle the tall, white sails. Purposefully ignoring Kyja's inquisitive glances, Marcus focused his eyes over the bow of the boat to the great blue emptiness beyond.

Whatever the future held for them was ahead, not behind. They couldn't afford to look back. Besides, there was no point in getting their hopes up. For all he knew, what he'd heard had been no more than insects humming in the grass, or the echo of the dawn chimes' voices bouncing off the water. It was only that for a moment—no more than a second or two at the most—he could have sworn he'd heard another voice calling out to him just below the flowers' song.

It was crazy. No doubt the result of what he'd been thinking before the singing began. But for that one brief instant, the voice he thought he'd heard belonged to Master Therapass.

FAR WORLD

DISCUSSION QUESTIONS

1. Marcus feels different from the other boys in his school because of his disabilities and because of the way he can grow dim and sense things before they happen. Kyja feels different because she can't do magic. Has there ever been a time when you felt different? Does being different have to be a bad thing? How can being different be good?

2. In chapter 8, Master Therapass tells Kyja, "The real power of magic lies *within* you. Who you are, what you do, and most importantly of all, what you may become." What do you think he means? Do you think Kyja found any of her magic by the end of the book?

3. In chapter 10, Kyja can't see anything in the aptura discerna until she sets aside feelings of hurt, disappointment, and jealousy from her past. How can holding onto angry feelings from the past keep us from seeing things clearly in the present? How can you get over bad feelings even when the memories still might hurt?

4. When Marcus guards the camp his first night in Farworld, Kyja

warns him to keep the fire burning at all times and to wake her if he sees anything. Because he doesn't take her warning seriously, they are nearly killed. Why do you think Marcus ignored Kyja's advice? What might he have been trying to prove?

5. Marcus and Kyja assume that Olden, the leader of the Weather Guardians, is one of the three largest trees in the Westland Woods. They are shocked to see that Olden is actually a scraggly little tree, barely larger than a bush. Why is it wrong to judge someone by what they look like? Have you ever assumed someone would look or talk a certain way, only to be surprised by the truth? Has anyone ever misjudged you because of how you look?

6. When Kyja and Marcus travel to each other's worlds, they are filled with conflicting emotions—excitement, fear, confusion, wonder, nervousness. They each make mistakes because of things they are unfamiliar with, but ultimately, with help from each other, they come to love the new place. Have you ever been to a new place? Had did you feel? If you were scared, how did you get over it? How could you help someone new to your town or school get over their fear?

7. In Water Keep, Cascade is confused about why humans would help each other without expecting something in return. Sometimes when we help others, we do get something in return; sometimes we don't. How many times can you remember where Kyja helped others? Why do you think she helped out each of them? What did she get back in each case?

8. Early in the book, Master Therapass tells Kyja and Marcus that their weaknesses may become their greatest strengths. Was he right? How did Marcus and Kyja benefit from their weaknesses? How can you turn one of your weaknesses into a strength?

Acknowledgments

O N YOUR FIRST DAY of kindergarten, when you head out to face the real world, there is usually someone making sure you're presentable to go out in public. The scrambled egg is washed off your chin. You're not wearing the shirt with the big jelly stain on the front. Your shoes are on the right feet. Your underwear isn't on backwards. That kind of thing. It might have seemed a little annoying to have your entire wardrobe checked before you walked out the door, but it saved you the embarrassment of having all the kids laugh at your brown and tan striped, bell bottom, corduroy pants that made you look like you were a clown. (Of course I'm not speaking from experience here.)

The person who gave you the final okay might have been your mom or dad. It might have been your dear Aunt Wilma or your grouchy Grandpa Wilbur. If you're really rich, it might have been Jeeves, the butler. For some of us, this continues until we're out of the house and married. It continues on with our wife or husband. "Honey, do you really want to wear *that* tie with *that* shirt?" For authors it continues pretty much as long as we are publishing novels. "Scott, do you *really* want to use seven –*ly* adverbs in one paragraph?"

So, if you don't mind, I'd like to take a minute to thank some of the people who kept me from going out into public with egg on my face. If there are any jelly stains, you can blame me completely.

Because this novel never would have happened without their belief, support, and incredible talent, I'd like to thank Lisa Mangum and Chris Schoebinger. An author could not ask for a more professional and knowledgeable pair of people into whose hands to place his work. They not only helped me make it what I wanted it to be, they made it much better. Thanks! Also to the other people at Shadow Mountain who turned this from a bunch of words into the book you are holding: Richard Erickson, Rachael Ward, Sheryl Dickert Smith, and Molly McGuire.

If you picked this book up because of the amazing cover, you have the incredibly talented Brandon Dorman to thank. He also did the wonderful inside illustrations. Brandon, thanks for giving image to the thoughts in my head.

Because I would never have written this novel at all if it hadn't been for their encouragement and the occasional kick in the pants, thanks to my family. Jen, who is my first and only true love as well as my first and last editor. Thanks for more than twenty great years. Erica, Scott, Jake, and Nick, who read all my books, make every day enjoyable, and regularly beat me at Wii Bowling. My Mom and Dad, Vicki and Dick—who embarrass me all the time by bragging about their son, the author. To Deanne, Kathy, Craig, and of course, Mark.

A special thanks to James Dashner, author extraordinaire of *The 13th Reality* series, for his insights, encouragement, and support over lunches too numerous to count. James is a man who truly loves interacting with kids, and if you are lucky enough to read his books or hear his school presentations, you are fortunate indeed. James, you are a great cheerleader, and I appreciate your support. Just one thing: the pom-poms are okay, but you really don't have the legs for the outfit. Then again, you don't have the arms, either, or the neck, or the face. Okay, just stop the whole cheering thing and get back to writing.

To the Women of Wednesday night: Annette Lyon, Heather Moore, Lu Ann Staheli, Michele Holmes, Lynda Keith, and Stephanni Myers. For more than six years you have been keeping my writing on track. I can never repay you. I mean that—really. Do you have any idea how much all of that editing would run on an hourly basis?

Thanks to all the people who read my manuscript in its early form and gave me such helpful feedback—Kathy Clement, Tyler Clement, Deanne Blackhurst, Julie Wright, Shirley Bahlmann, Kerry Blair, Alyssa Holmes, and my own little Jake.

As promised, a special shout-out to all my nieces and nephews who encouraged me so much: Abby-Kate, Abner, Amy, Anese, Anna, Antonio, Ashley, Benjamin, Caden, Caleb and Caleb, Cameron, Dallin, Daniel, Emma, Ethan, Jared, Jennie, Jeremy, Joshua, Madison, Matthew, Micah, Richard, Spencer, Steven, Tanner, Tiffany, Trenton, Trevor, Tyler and Tyler, and Victoria. (Yes, there really are that many. Whew!)

To Mr. Sheehy, the greatest creative writing teacher of all time. Thanks for lighting the torch.

And last of all, thanks to you, the readers. Ninety percent of what makes a story great is what you, the reader, create inside your head. All the author does is point you in the right direction.

And by the way, thanks for the school help, Mom. I'm sure I'll forgive you for the whole corduroy incident by the time I'm seventy or so.